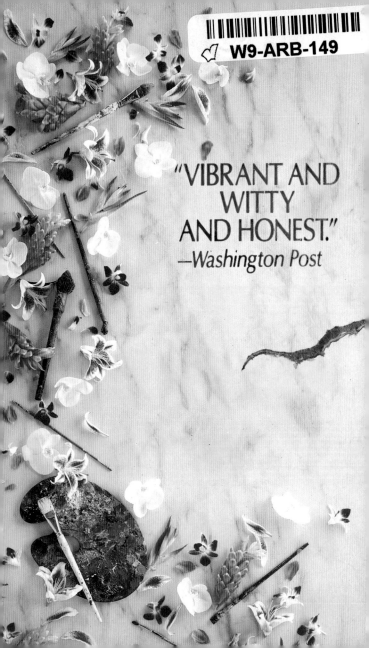

"VIBRANT AND
WITTY
AND HONEST."
—Washington Post

Most Boys Were Too Weak For Me.

I could manipulate them too easily. A young woman who knows her own sexual powers is a rarity indeed, but she is unbeatable. And if she happens also to be smart and talented and has the crazed bravado—I cannot call it self-confidence—that a mad mother and an alcoholic father inspire, then there's no stopping her. That is me precisely. Unsinkable, unbeatable, unstoppable.

ERICA JONG

ANY WOMAN'S BLUES

HarperPaperbacks

A Division of HarperCollinsPublishers

HarperPaperbacks *A Division of* HarperCollins*Publishers*
10 East 53rd Street, New York, N.Y. 10022

A hardcover edition of this book was published in 1990
by Harper & Row, Publishers, Inc.

Copyright acknowledgments follow page 362.

First HarperPaperbacks printing: February 1991

Cover photo by Herman Estevez

Printed in the United States of America

HarperPaperbacks and colophon are trademarks of
HarperCollins*Publishers*

10 9 8 7 6 5 4 3 2 1

For the impossible he
who lives inside me

And for M.N.B., with love

Special thanks to Ed Victor, Gladys Justin Carr, William Shinker, Margaret Kiley, Ken and Barbara Follett, Shirley Knight, Gerri Karetsky, and Georges Belmont for affectionate support above the call of duty or friendship. And a big hug to Molly Jong-Fast, the greatest daughter in the world, and to Ken Burrows, my darling husband, who appeared just at the moment I had stopped believing in darling husbands.

Throw your heart out in front of you
and run ahead to catch it.

—ARAB PROVERB

I intend to stake out my own
claim, a tiny one, but my own.
Lacking a name for it, I'll call
it—pro tem—The Land of Fuck.

—HENRY MILLER

Love has no words to spell
or lines to start and stop.

—ALCOHOLICS ANONYMOUS
  (The Big Book)

The blues ain't nothing
but the facts of life.

—WILLIE DIXON

CONTENTS

———————◆———————

CONTENTS

ANY
WOMAN'S
BLUES

FOREWORD

———◆———

How I came to edit this curious manuscript—and how indeed Isadora Wing came to write it—are two of the many bizarre stories the ensuing pages have to tell. I hesitate to label the book either "fiction" or "autobiography"—for it was Isadora Wing's unique genius to blur the boundaries between the two. But in editing Any Woman's Blues, *which was necessarily a partial and unpolished manuscript, there was another problem to contend with: namely that the author herself left, along with her unfinished book, her arguments with herself and her heroine in the margins of the working draft. These I have taken the liberty of inserting into the text—in italics—where I presume Isadora Wing wished them to go. Thus we have a unique record of an author arguing with, and indeed heckling, her creature—a cre-*

1

ative dialogue that must go on in the heads of all novelists, but that, in most cases, we are not privileged to see.

When did Isadora Wing write Any Woman's Blues?

Internal references in the manuscript make it probable that the novel was composed in the late eighties, at the tail end of the decade of greed and excess known as the Reagan years. This would in turn jibe with the known facts of Isadora Wing's life—that she nearly always wrote her "novels" in response to disastrous events in her personal life and that in the latter years of the eighties she was attempting to break an obsession with a much younger man, one Berkeley Sproul III, a handsome young WASP heir, who had an unfortunate dependence on drugs and alcohol.

The first chapter of the "novel" seems to me one of the most extraordinary pieces of writing I have ever read. It is raw and vulnerable to a degree that seems to push literary counter-phobia to the limit. Were Isadora Wing alive today, I wonder how she could tolerate the publication of this work—so exposed does it seem. She seems indeed to have known this, for a note to her research assistant and amanuensis, scrawled in the margins of the last page of Chapter One, reads:

> Pls. do a computer search and see how many times the word "cock" is used in this chapter. I feel like I'm drowning in pubic hair—if he prongs her once more I'll scream!

Perhaps a further word to the wise is necessary here before plunging willy-nilly, as it were, into the endometrial landscape of Any Woman's Blues.

This so-called novel is not for the prudish or the faint of heart. It is throbbing and raw to a degree that will shock the most hardened libertine. Nevertheless, I think there is merit in publishing it—if only to demonstrate what a dead end the so-called *sexual revolution had become, and how desperate so-called free women were in the last few years of our decadent epoch.*

Any Woman's Blues *is a fable for our times: a story of a woman lost in excess and extremism—a sexoholic, an alcoholic, and a food addict. It is the "novel" Isadora Wing was in the midst of writing when her rented plane—a de Havilland Beaver (whose name she must have chuckled over)—was reported missing over the South Pacific in the vicinity of the Trobriand Islands. (Her last desperate stab at serenity—conquering her fear of flying and going to the South Pacific in search of utopia—seems like a mad attempt to play Gauguin when playing Emma Goldman had failed.) At the date of this prefatory study, the wreckage has not been found.*

For several years, Ms. Wing had been taking flying lessons. She qualified as a pilot in 1987 and delighted in flying her own plane, a Bellanca, in the skies above her home state of Connecticut.

Her plane—a complex single-engine that "takes off fast and lands short," according to Ms. Wing—was called Amazon I, a name that I believe she used ironically. Like all poets, she had a penchant for giving names to inanimate objects, and at one time in her life drove a Mercedes whose license plate read QUIM.*

During Ms. Wing's final, tragic flight, she was accompanied by her fourth, and last, husband, the noted conductor and composer Sebastian Wanderlust, a friend of fifteen years whom she had just married. It is not known whether she or Sebastian was flying the plane, but internal evidence from her voluminous diaries suggests that it was she. She is survived by an eleven-year-

---

*Quim (queme, quimsby, quimbox, quin, quem, quente, or quivive) refers to the female pudendum, also called the divine monosyllable, the cunt, cock alley, the jampot, the Fanny, and a host of other fanciful names. Chaucer favored "quem" or "quente." Shakespeare had a menagerie of metaphors, including "dearest bodily part" and "eye that weeps most when best pleased."

old daughter, Amanda Ace, two stepsons, three sisters, her aged (but youthful though grief-stricken) parents, and eight nieces and nephews.

Ms. Wing's daughter being a minor, the executors of her estate quite properly sought a reputable feminist scholar to edit and prepare for the press Ms. Wing's last literary works, her "literary remains," so to speak. This sad but exhilarating task fell to me.

I had been very much taken with Ms. Wing's first book of poems, Vaginal Flowers, which I instantly recognized as something new in women's poetry, an antidote to the doom-ridden, deathward poetry of Sylvia Plath and Anne Sexton, a woman poet embracing and celebrating her own womanliness with verve and joie de vivre. Ms. Wing's first novel, Candida Confesses, the succès de scandale that made her a household name, had not yet been published, and Ms. Wing herself was then a part-time professor of English at CCNY in New York. We met as colleagues, as feminists, as contemporaries, both committed to the struggle for women's equality, both, if I may presume, Shakespeare's sisters. I remember a warm and engaging blonde in her late twenties, with a savagely self-mocking wit, a sort of gallows humor of the underdog, and a tendency to pepper her speech with Yiddishisms, four-letter words, and literary references. I was drawn to her immediately. But I also remember a great sadness in her eyes and a vulnerability that troubled and surprised me.

I never had met anyone that vulnerable except for the poet Anne Sexton (another reader in our series and, in fact, our stellar attraction that year), and I could not quite make sense of the bravado of Ms. Wing's writing and the vulnerability of her persona. It was as if the two halves of herself had not yet come together; and indeed it is still hard for me to associate the fragile young writer I met in 1973 with the woman of the world who piloted her own plane, had numerous lovers, and lived as hard as she wrote, taking the Hemingwayesque ideal of the novelist and appropriating it for the whole female sex.

Through the years, Ms. Wing and I met infrequently, but we continued to correspond sporadically. After Ms. Wing's tragic disappearance, I was invited by her stepson Charles Wanderlust, himself an eminent scholar of English literature (pre-Romantic poetry), and her sister Chloe, a psychotherapist in New York City, to make sense of the mass of papers on Ms. Wing's desk in Connecticut.

Ms. Wing's family seemed not to have tampered with her literary legacy, although one of her ex-husbands was threatening to sue if any part of the new book dealt with him. Fortunately that never became an issue, since his name hardly occurs even in her notebooks. When Isadora Wing moved on, she moved on, and if any ghosts from the past preoccupied her, they were the ghost of her grandfather, Samuel Stoloff, the painter, the ghost of Colette, with whom she felt a great kinship, and the ghost of Amelia Earhart, whose destiny she was soon to share.

Knowing this author's penchant for carrying all her manuscripts and notebooks with her on her endless travels, I feared to find nothing of value, feared in fact that the manuscripts and notebooks had gone down in the South Pacific with her. On the contrary, I found a rough and incomplete draft of her last "novel," Any Woman's Blues; a dozen or more marbled notebooks from Venice, going back to the late seventies, when she was writing Tintoretto's Daughter; a spring binder of new, unpublished poems, tentatively entitled Lullaby for a Dybbuk; a pile of unpublished essays (many of which I had never seen); another binder, in which was a fragment of a manuscript entitled The Amazon Handbook, by Isadora Wing and Emily Quinn; various folders of literary correspondence to various authors around the world; love letters from a surprising variety of men and women; piles of art and anthropology books; clippings about women artists; and the like. Of particular interest is the following excerpt from one of her notebooks, dated October 1987, which makes it contemporaneous with parts of the rough draft of Any Woman's Blues:

> For some time now I have wanted to write a novel that includes within it the materials of the creative hegira and that illustrates within its very form or formlessness the process of writing the book—particularly the arguments with one's self or one's heroine in the margins of the manuscript. What I want to convey is the creative flux itself, the feel of life battling art and art battling life—the chaos and clutter of dredging a novel up out of the self.
>
> I have always been struck by Proust's motto (which Colette appropriated): "Ce 'je' qui est moi et qui n'est peut-être pas moi" ("This 'I' which is myself and yet perhaps not myself"). Every novelist wrestles with this paradox, for we know that not only our protagonist but every character in every book is a part of that mysterious mosaic we call our "self."

It is in response to this declaration and other internal evidence in the diaries and letters (including scrawled notes to herself on the rough incomplete draft, indicating where she wished bits of marginal material to be inserted) that I have taken the liberty of reconstructing Ms. Wing's last manuscript as she doubtless wished it to appear.

Thus Any Woman's Blues, a conventional roman à clef about an artist called Leila Sand (who, at the outset of the book, is at once battling alcoholism and a sadomasochistic obsession with a much younger man), is punctuated passim with the interruptions of Isadora Wing arguing with Leila Sand (the author arguing with her protagonist—with herself, in short), which suggest the life that flowed alongside the novel.

Ms. Wing, like many contemporary women, apparently

believed that the secret of happiness was not to be found in the illusion of "the perfect man" but rather in finding strength within one's self. That strength once found, one could be happy with or without a partner. This search for inner happiness constitutes the fable of Any Woman's Blues. *It has as its theme a woman's search for a way out of addictive love and toward real self-love, which is not to be confused with narcissism. It should not surprise us that this is so, for inevitably in a writer's life, "one tends to subsume in a book one is writing all the conflicts one is trying to resolve at that particular time"* (Isadora Wing, Interview, 1987).

I trust that my foreword has made clear my deep interest in feminist literary history, my admiration for the late Ms. Wing, and my arduous preparation for the awesome task of editor, official biographer, and literary executor to so feminal—if I may use a Wingian locution—a writer of our time.

I have taken it upon myself to correct obvious solecisms, engage in minor copyediting, and change names and descriptions of characters to the satisfaction of both the publisher's lawyers and the lawyers for the Estate of Isadora Wing.

If, despite all my efforts to serve propriety without emasculating (effeminating?) literature, Ms. Wing's work still seems a bit too Rabelaisian for the faint of heart, I think we must understand that a total lustiness of body and mind was not only her chosen way of living but also her message to the world. She believed in the integration of body and mind, and it would probably be comforting to her to know that she lost both together. Fly on, Isadora Wing, wherever you are! Fly on!

CARYL FLEISHMANN-STANGER, Ph.D.
Chair, Department of English
Sophia College
Paugussett, Connecticut

1

SUGAR IN MY BOWL

◆

I need a little sugar in my bowl,
I need a little hot-dog between my roll.

—J. C. Johnson

I am a woman in the grip of an obsession. I sit here by the phone (which may in fact be out of order) and wait for his call. I listen for the sound of his motorcycle spraying pebbles on the curving driveway path. I imagine his body, his mocking mouth on mine, his curving cock, and I am a ruin of desire and the fight against desire. I don't know which is worse—the desire or the antidesire. Both undo me; both burn me and reduce me to ash. The Nazis could not have invented a more cunning crematorium. This is my auto-da-fé, my obsession, my addiction.

Friends come to me and urge me to give him up, fill me with reasons, all of which I agree with. They do no good. What I feel is something that does not respond to reason. Older than Pan and the dark gods and goddesses lurking in the shadows behind him, this burning I feel is in fact the primordial force of the universe. Who can explain that I have chosen to attach it to a blond boy-man who pours his lies in my ear as he pours his seed in that other place? Who would believe the addiction, the obsession, the degradation, or even the love? Only one who has felt its fire. Only one who has also been burned in that fire and whose skin has crackled like the skin of medieval martyrs.

But most women do not have the luxury to feel that fire. Nor, in fact, do I. In my waking life, I am a successful woman (does it matter for the moment what I do?), known as a tough deal-maker, an eagle-eyed reader of contracts, a good negotiator. All that I know of life from the other sphere does me no good whatsoever here. You might even say that it makes me more vulnerable. For the tougher I am in the lawyer's office, the more I desire to be tender here where the thought of his cock reduces me to ash.

Let me tell you about his cock. It is clawlike and demonic, a true prong. It has a curve where it should be straight, and in repose it lists to one side, the left. His politics, if he had any, would be the opposite. For he is the fascist, the boot in the face, the brute. All men worth having in bed are partly beasts. Every myth we have tells us this: Pan with his animal legs and human mouth; the beast that Beauty left her father for; the devil himself, with the wild witches—the bacchantes of Salem—cavorting about his puckered anus. And kissing it. Part of the lure is the degradation, the fact that we are creatures born between piss and shit, and in our darkest moments we obsessively recall that dilemma.

If twenty men were lined up before me with full

erections and sacks put over their heads and torsos, I could identify my love (may I call him that?) by the curve of his cock. Angry and red in erection, circumcised (not because of his religion but because of the age in which he was born), curving like a boomerang which always returns to its owner, is it beautiful only because it leaves me? Is it just because I can possess it merely for brief interludes that it holds me in such thrall? Would I love it less if it were there all the time?

No danger of that. For I love a runner. No sooner does he call me his witch, his bacchante, his lady, his love, than he has to flee.

Oh, I think there is some of this in all men—however they express it. The longing to return to the womb, to be engulfed, to be totally passive between the huge breasts of the mother goddess, is so strong that no sooner do they feel themselves yielding to our primordial power than they have to run. Hence the battle between the sexes: she wants him safe between her legs forever; he, being afraid he wants to stay there, flees.

Where he flees is immaterial. War. The office. Golf. The salt mines. Tennis. Outer space. Deep-sea diving. Basketball. Las Vegas. Another woman. It's all the same flight.

The man I love has constructed a museum to macho in my garage. Power saw. Punching bag. Motorcycle. Barbells. I love him in part because I cannot tame the wild creature that dwells inside him. For this is another paradox of the sexes: whatever we love in the other we seek to kill.

My love is a con man, a hustler, a cowboy, a cocksman, an addict, an artist, a fancy dancer, a dandy. He has no fixed address. Sometimes he'll give a P.O. box, sometimes an answering service, sometimes a number that no one answers, sometimes an address he's just made up. I once heard him tell his mother she could write him in Paris at the Charles de Gaulle Hotel.

"But you *know* there is no Charles de Gaulle Hotel," I said. "It's an *air*port. How can you do that to your own mother?"

"If you knew my mother as I do, you'd know it was only in self-defense. I had no choice."

If you knew my mother as I do and *self-defense.* These are the operative words. For he is sure (as only a very little boy can be sure) that wherever we are in the world, as we madly begin to fuck, his mother will find us and walk right through the wall of our boudoir like a vampire in a 1940s movie. So I know it is his mother he flees when he flees me—my vagabond, my warlock, my cocksman, my con man, my cowboy, my hustler, my lying love. Yet I also know that when he comes back he is as loyal, as faithful, as forthright, as sturdy and true, as that little boy scout who also dwells inside him. He'd lay down his life for me and my twins. He'd walk through fire and swim through ice. He'd hack the jungle with his bare hands, bite the heads off poisonous snakes, strip the skin from armadillos or porcupines. In short, he is my man, and I am addicted to the nectar he brews in his balls.

Since he cannot be good, it would be easier if he were entirely bad so at least I could hate him. But how can I hate him when the very badness in him makes him so very good where it counts—in bed?

He arrives, helmeted like Darth Vader, wearing black leather jeans and black leather jacket and black os-trich-leather boots with needle toes. Real spurs are on his heels. Silver spurs. They twinkle. He scoops me in his arms, holds me for a moment, my warm body against the wind-chilled smoothness of his black leather. From the moment

I hear the spray of pebbles on the driveway and the racing motor of his bike, my motor begins to race as well. The pounding begins in my heart, spreads through my body like a jungle tattoo, sets up a resounding echo in that other heart between my thighs, eventually moistening the red silk knickers I have worn for this occasion. (They really *are* knickers and not their meeker American cousin, "panties," for I have bought them in London, where the "dirty weekend" is still good and dirty, and the accoutrements produced for same are, accordingly, more risqué.)

Who can describe lust when it is this hot, this succulent, this compelling? Words cannot touch it. Perhaps only music can echo the swell and heft of it, the heat, the vibration. I once painted a picture of lust (all right: the secret is out: you know what I do). It was a round canvas with a burning center of orange and waves of red and lavender vibrating toward it. (That was in my so-called abstract period, which followed my so-called figurative period and preceded my so-called postmodernist film-still period.) These waves of red and lavender—a futurist contusion—are with me now, inside me, as he runs his hands down my buttocks, slides between my thighs, and finds the silky place where the red knickers part and I become pure liquid.

What happens next you know. I almost know it too, except that I am out of my mind with desire. We fall to the floor of the foyer (wide oaken planks, a hooked rug, a few dustballs chasing each other around as if they were tumbleweeds in the wake of our stampeding horses), and right there on the floorboards we make the beast with two backs in a tangle of black leather and silk, our clothes pulled away only enough to expose the parts that have the power to join.

Like this—dressed, helmeted, leathered by the goat under whose sign we couple—we come the first tumultuous time. It only seems to heat our blood for the next, and now we begin to strip off barriers of silk and skin and metal (my knickers, his black leather, his helmet), so that soon we are naked on the wide planks of the seventeenth-century floor, with a chaos of clothes flung about us everywhere—our witnesses.

"My witch," he whispers.

"My devil, my warlock, my love . . ."

He is inside me again, hard again, the curved shaft of his cock corresponding to the bent desire that drives me, the tip of his glans hitting the spot deep within me that squirts pure liquid, the witches' potion of the universe.

Shall I go on? How can two make love like this, then part? They should be joined forever, made one under the mocking moon that illuminates their bluish bodies, sky-clad. But it is one of the ironies of this sort of sex that it thrives on distance, and lovers who love like this either cannot live together, or when they do, then some magic goes out of their coupling; only that way can they live together long enough to make porridge, paint a house, plant a garden—or a baby.

We lived together once, Darth and I. (His real name is not far off: Darton—named for some distant family warlock of the past.) I never called him that. I called him Dart: it seemed so appropriate, since he lived in his cock and also was forever darting. Oh, when I was younger, I used to make fun of male hormones and what they make men do. I used to think that men ought to try to be more like women (who were more *rational,* I then supposed), but now that I am forty-four I know that the glory of the male sex lies in how different they are from us—though of course it infuriates us, as nature meant it to do, fury being an aspect of our drive to merge.

I met him at a dude ranch in Wyoming—the Lazy C Ranch, it was called (an upside-down C, not unlike his cock)—and I was a dude and he a cowboy. Not that he was *really* a cowboy. He was an aging prep school boy from the East, playing at cowboy for a summer, but I didn't know that. Under the Grand Tetons (or Big Tits, as the French so bluntly called them), on the wildflower-studded greensward made by the great Snake River, he looked as authentic as any cowboy, riding his nag. At least he looked authentic to this cowgirl from the canyons of New York, who wanted him to ride her.

I had come to this most beautiful part of the world (Moose, Wyoming) to shed an old love affair, there where the elk shed their antlers, and he was a passionate twenty-five and I an even more passionate thirty-nine, moseying through fields of Indian paintbrushes, blue lupine, and black-eyed Susans on my old cayuse. I looked at him—dirty-blond hair, battered cowboy hat, torn cowboy shirt, those touching purple lids like a baby's, and under them those penetrating (I use the adjective advisedly) blue, blue eyes—and I was hooked. Later he hooked me properly in bed. Only twenty-five, but he knew the power he had and made sure I knew it too. That he loved my work was the icing on the cock (as it were), for he aspired to an allied art himself and told me that he fashioned out of clay western sculptures à la Remington (when he wasn't fashioning female bodies with his extra rib).

After the summer we resumed in SoHo and Litchfield County. There was a girlfriend I had to dispose of (a little ninny of twenty-three, the first of many), but then we fell into living together—mainly because we could not bear to spend a night apart.

At first it was glorious: a mad drug-crazed affair, days of wine and roses, sinsemilla and chrysanthemums, cocaine and calla lilies. Nights of wild endless lovemaking in which one lost count of the number of acts of sex because they had neither beginnings nor endings. I could look up his nostril and see eternity. The nights might have been eons long, epochs measured in geologic time, or they might have been merely minutes. It was impossible to tell. As we coupled, mountain ranges rose and fell; rock was formed from molten lava; hot springs bubbled out of the earth; extinct volcanoes came to life. For a year I did no work, nor did he. We toured the world—from king-size triple-sheeted bed to king-size triple-sheeted bed.

All the travel was on someone else's tab. We went from Dokumenta to the Basel Art Fair, from the Whitney to Palazzo Grassi, from Düsseldorf to Munich, from Venice to Vienna, Nice to Paris, Madrid to Mallorca, London to Dublin, Stockholm to Oslo, Tokyo to Hong Kong to Beijing. Who cared where we were, as long as we were in bed? I remember a blur of other artists, art dealers, collectors, critics, like ghosts in a Shakespearean tragedy. Either they were as drunk and stoned as we were or we were drunk and stoned enough for both. From time to time, I (being the older and supposedly responsible party) would awaken and wonder if we were becoming drunks or drug addicts, but in that crowd, who could tell? All the artists drank and used that way. Or so I thought. The only time I really became upset was when Dart carried sinsemilla into the USSR—and without telling me.

We had arrived at our grand hotel in Москва, and

we were about to fall into bed and reassert our primal connection (it had, after all, been seven hours since we made love in Copenhagen, and we were both in a state of deprivation that prisoners of war may know), when Dart smiled at me with his shy "love me" smile (practiced from childhood on his mother, his nannies, his sisters, and any other females he might meet) and extracted from under the insole of his cowboy boots two flattened joints of purest Humboldt County sinsemilla. I remembered where we were, searched the ornate golden room for hidden TV cameras and mikes, looked at my child lover, and my blood literally ran cold. I had never said a cross word to him till now.

"Get rid of them," I said.

"You mean we're not going to smoke them?" said my incredulous little boy.

"Get rid of them, and *now.*"

"Just a puff?"

"Not even one." And then I watched as he flushed them down the Soviet john (shall we call it an ivan?), a tear in the corner of his bright blue eye for the dope, which he still did not realize might have been our passport to Siberia forever.

Furious as I was at his defection from my welfare, his incomprehension of the danger, I was powerless to yell at him, and this was not only because the room was bugged. My heart was bugged as well. I was so tied to him body and soul that yelling at him would have been like yelling at the little child in myself. What an odd combination of manly power and childlike credulity he was! He thought he could light up a joint and make the Gulag disappear!

We did not make love that afternoon. And for two who made love on arrival in *every* hotel room, that was a sort of sundering, the first of many. It had to do with drugs, which we thought joined us but which really sundered us—that being, of course, the paradox of drugs.

Dart's history was as deprived as any ghetto child's. He grew up rich, in Philadelphia, in a town house on Rittenhouse Square filled with Chippendale antiques, Chinese porcelain, seventeenth-century bedwarmers, threadbare Oriental rugs, rooms of unused shoes, piles of 1930s magazines, that sort of thing. His mother drank sherry and abused Seconal; his father drank bourbon and seduced debutantes. The nannies drank gin and seduced Dart. He was born with an erection, his mother always said (with her smoky, boozy laugh), and from then on no one who took care of him ever let him forget that they considered his cock the most important organ of his body. Once, I thought this was cute, but now I find it exceedingly sad that a young man should be valued above all for that appendage which he has in common with all other men—even if his *is* bigger and better shaped. Sometimes, when I think of this, I want to weep for Dart and change his name to something real—Daniel perhaps—and give him a real life, such as I would have wanted for my son.

But I have no son. I have twin daughters, Michaela and Edwina. Dart became my lover and my son, a dangerous (and perhaps impossible) combination.

This *Wanderjahr* continued after Москва. Tokyo, Taipei, Hong Kong, Canton, Shanghai, Beijing, Bangkok, Borobudur, Singapore, Bombay, New Delhi, Abu Dhabi, Baghdad, Jidda, Cairo, Athens, Tunis, Nice, Lisbon, Bahia, Rio—but life in bed at a deluxe hotel (whether the Okura, the Ritz, the Peninsula, the Oriental, the Shangri

La, the Goodwood Park, the Cipriani, the Bel Air, the Plaza Athénée or the Vier Jahreszeiten) is much the same everywhere.

My friend Emmie once remarked that a deluxe hotel is like a hospital, what with food being wheeled in and out and flowers being dutifully sent by business acquaintances (and never by the lovers you wish had sent them) and polite notes or mass-produced "greeting" cards appearing at irregular intervals. The help are usually dark-skinned and do not speak your language, and they have the same indifference to your condition whether you are lying in bed dying of some rare disease or lying in bed dying under your lover. It's all the same to them: more sheets to wash. Truly, you can go around the world with your lover and never see more than the pucker of his anus or the silhouette of his cock. Thus a year went by: one of the longest or shortest (depending on whether or not I was stoned at the time) years of my whole life.

But eventually all lovers must get out of bed—and that was how our problems started.

We set up house in Roxbury, my house, the core of which was built in the seventeenth century, with eighteenth- and nineteenth-century wings. There was also the loft in New York. He needed a car, of course, so I bought him one to bring him to me. I knew, of course, that it could also take him away, but at the beginning of a love affair one doesn't think that way. An ordinary car would not do for my Chéri, so I bought him a Mercedes. It was a beautiful old restored classic from 1969, when he was just thirteen: a thirteen-year-old's dream, and I gave it the license plate DART. (Oh, I had a sense of humor about my lover—even while he reduced me to ash.)

I used to love to buy him things: a white suede

cowboy suit with long fringes, and white-and-cream lizard-skin boots, with a ten-gallon white Stetson to crown the costume; monogrammed towels that said "DVD"; jewelry (which he usually lost); electronic equipment (which he usually broke); cashmere sweaters, crocodile loafers, costly artbooks, engraved stationery, silk pajamas, silk underwear, the lot. He was my shiksa, and I treated him accordingly, the way my rich English uncle Jakob from Odessa, East End furrier turned country squire in Surrey, treated his chorine. I had great style and recognized Dart at once as one of the great kept men.

But did *he* have great style? He never once refused a gift. In fact, despite his joy in receiving, there was always a little pout of the lower lip that seemed to indicate that the gift was a trifle *less* than he expected. If you gave him a car, it seemed he wanted a helicopter. If you gave him a white cowboy suit, it seemed he wanted a white horse to match. If you gave him a ring, it seemed he wanted a watch as well. This was never stated, and had you asked him he would have passionately denied it. But somehow you knew that the gift would only sate him for a little while, and then his hunger would require more fuel.

He was like a great hungry primitive god, ravenous for virgins, wreaths of flowers, plucked hearts, slaughtered oxen, chalices of blood, burnt offerings. . . . It was my joy to offer all these up. What was my success worth if I could not afford a man as beautiful and death-defying as Dart?

I had lived my life like a man, managed my career, my investments, even my pregnancy, exactly as a man would have done (Mike and Ed were born by caesarean on the day and at the hour I chose), so I thought I could manage Dart as well. Ah—there's the rub. Nature has not arranged men that way. And the more fun they are in bed, the more uncontrollable they are. For it is the wildness within that guarantees the wildness in bed.

Pan does not buy one life insurance nor come home for dinner at the same time each night. I could buy my own life insurance. But I did need a little more serenity than life with Dart provided.

But what about love? you ask. Where does love enter into the equation? I know he loved me passionately. He loved me as the knife loves the wound it makes, as the female tarantula loves the male whose head she gobbles, as the nursing baby boy loves the nipple he takes between his teeth and chews until it spurts blood mixed with milk.

He did not mean to be cruel. It was just his nature— like that of the scorpion who stings the horse who carries him across the stream (as in that ancient Aesopian joke about the nature of scorpions).

Somehow, when we were together, things had a tendency to get lost: wallets, credit cards, jewelry. Perhaps this was because we were often stoned or perhaps this was because together we entered a gyre in which whirl was king and all order and structure went out of our lives. I took this as a proof of love, for is not love, after all, self-forgetfulness? And who needs that self-forgetfulness more than one who has lived her whole life for discipline, for art, mimicking a man's hardness despite her woman's heart?

When I met Dart, I had spent thirty-nine years climbing the glass mountain of a woman artist's destiny—I wanted a treat, a reward for all that desperate climbing, and at first he seemed to give it to me, too. There was not only his generosity in bed, with its punitive kinkiness (which I felt I *deserved* somehow for challenging the gods by becoming so successful), but the way he cosseted me. He moved into my house and took over the care and protection of Leila Sand. He played bodyguard, cook, maître d'hotel, general factotum. He was good at keeping the world at bay, frightening off troublesome fans, ex-husbands, ex-lovers, would-be parasites. He installed himself, in short, as chief parasite, court jester, her majesty's pleasure barge, Robin Goodfellow—which, you may remember, was another name for the devil.

I had been, until the epoch of Dart, a very disciplined worker. No artist gets anywhere otherwise. I had a studio in Litchfield County—a silver silo with an observatory-like skylight, studding my country acreage—and in New York I had my loft. I preferred working in the country, where the birdsong did not invade but rather accompanied my work. But once I got going on a major project, I had to stay where I was, for my canvases at this point in my life were very large. Besides, there is something profoundly conservative about even the most avant-garde art: it likes to grow in one place.

Dart installed himself as my majordomo, made me dependent on his good offices (as I had never in my life allowed myself to be dependent on anyone), and then he began finding excuses to flee. Just when I was nursing the delusion of having found, at long last, my helpmeet, my live-in muse, the husband of my heart, Maurice Goudeket to my Colette, he began spending more and more time in New York, at the loft, and always with a good excuse: He had to meet a gallery owner who was interested in his work. He had to buy materials. He had to go to the foundry. I had given him every young artist's dream—a barn to work in, unlimited time, all his expenses paid—and that was when he started flying from me, or else he was flying from himself. I never knew.

Where did he go during all that time away—zooming

off in the car I bought him, refusing to be tied down to a specific time for dinner, refusing to tell me where he was going? My imagination immediately leapt to the worst conclusions: other women, hustling, drug smuggling, gambling, other men.

"I'll call you," he'd say, climbing into the blood-red Mercedes (bought with my blood), and sometimes he would and sometimes he wouldn't.

When I complained of this, he flew into a rage and said: "But I always come home to *you.*" Or else he would accuse: "You never *trust* me! You always question me!" *You always . . . you never*—the language of male bondage.

So I would pace my studio-silo, trying to work, my peace of mind destroyed: listening for the phone; listening for his/my car; wondering if he would or wouldn't be home for dinner; wondering whether to ask or (since asking only made him madder) whether to ignore it, and having another glass of wine. I began working drunk. *Never* had I done this before. For all my indulgence in pot, peyote, hash, coke, wine, I had never mixed it with my work. My work was sacred. But now my silo, my obvious phallic symbol, which had been my freedom, had become my prison. I paced and paced, tied to that silent phone as if it were a household god, afraid to go out lest he call, afraid to get in my car and drive to New York lest I find him with another woman in my loft, afraid to invite a friend over lest he suddenly come in and want me to himself, afraid to move, to paint, to pick up the phone and call for help.

I felt like that girl in *Story of O* chained by her labia to her lover, never allowed to forget her bondage and loving it even as she hated it, for the clanking of her chains made a woman of her. Did he deliberately plan this reduction, this destruction of me? Or was it something he did by instinct, learned at his father's knee, the fine art of reducing powerful women to ash?

And then he would come in, always when you had given up and stopped expecting him. And he would scoop me in his arms, never uttering a harsh word. "My love, my witch, my bacchante, my darling," he would murmur, the softness of the words cutting deeper than a dagger. And then he would turn me over and give it to me from behind with his hard, pronged, demonic cock. And I would whimper with the sheer relief of his being back, his being safe, his being deep inside me, and we would fuck the night away, no questions asked, until the next time.

2

DECIPHERING THE FIRE

———————— ◆ ————————

If you want to hear me rave,
Honey, give me what I crave.
It makes my love come down.

—Bessie Smith

Dart was sweet. Had Dart been sour or mean, it would have been much easier. I would have fled at once. But in the beginning he rarely said anything that wasn't loving, sweet, and dear. He spoke, in fact, like a Hallmark greeting card. It was just that his actions belied his words. He was like some actors or politicians—full of reassurances and good words, yet *doing* things that made you terribly mistrustful. "I'll always be there for you," he said. Yet the fact was that often you could not reach him.

I used to try to think up ways of keeping him with me. On trips it was relatively easy; he was always at my side (hence our compulsive traveling). But at home it was harder. If the studio I gave him did not suffice—that wonderful old barn, pierced with skylights, with the hayloft made into a sleeping balcony, and its own bathroom and little kitchen—then I would rack my brains to think up other things: joint projects we could work on (which I always wound up doing, because he was out God knows where—I realize now with a shock that I never actually *saw* him paint or sculpt), portraits and photographs I would do of him, brunches and dinners with important people who might help his career. All these things worked only for a little while. He was adamant that we should work together (which is hard for artists who have their own visions), and I would do anything to keep him near, so I attempted that folly.

I am looking now at one of the paintings I painted to his design (he had scribbled a rough sketch on a napkin; I, of course, had painted it), and there is no denying that it's an abortion. Not my style at all. I had painted (as if bewitched) a rather sappy rendition of our first meeting in the Tetons: cowboy and cowgirl riding beneath the sunset through fields of flowers, an image more suitable for one of those pseudo-hippie greeting cards than for a show of new works by Leila Sand. No danger of that, for when I look at how the painting is signed, I see no trace of my name but only "Darton Venable Donegal IV," in large vermilion letters.

In the name of our shared life, I even went so far as to buy a building on Greene Street and establish a gallery for new artists so that he could exhibit there (he'd had rotten luck, he said, in finding a gallery of his own). He worked devilishly hard renovating the building, setting up the first group show and launching the gallery—called, in honor of our liaison, the Grand Teton Gallery—but as soon as it began to show signs of actually succeeding, he lost interest, as he eventually lost interest in everything that promised him the success he claimed to want. Somehow he never got together the work for his projected one-man show, though he was always promising to. (He claimed *my* success blocked him.) Nor would he run the gallery, as he had said he would. Eventually I hired a pretty young thing to do this—and eventually he seduced her—but he never even *began* the work for his own show.

And yet he could be so tender with me at times and so *loving*. I remember his searching the city for a certain kind of gesso I wanted. I remember the time he waited a whole day at JFK because I had a shipment of supplies coming from Italy and he knew how worried I was about their safe arrival. I remember the way he nursed me when I was sick, bringing me tea, bringing me consommé, arguing with doctors about my possible allergy to this or that antibiotic. I don't want to think of these things now in my anger—but they happened, and I can't make them unhappen.

If only I could time-travel back to the beginning of our affair and relive the sweetness of it, I would mortgage my soul to the devil. It's easy enough to let the end poison the beginning when you are disaffected by all the betrayals. But in the beginning, when you hope you have found your One True Love, the world is full of sweetness, you walk with a winged step, and your heart seems a helium balloon that will never spring a leak.

"I'm only your mirror," Dart used to say in the mad, passionate beginning of our affair, when we would fuck the nights away all over the world—but I suppose I did not realize how true that was.

Dart was a moon who required a sun in order to gleam. He had a certain smile—head cocked to one side, blue eyes flashing, mouth turned up in a sort of antique crescent that could melt anyone's heart. On one of our very first trips, when we were sitting side by side in a haze of champagne and limerance in the first-class section of an airplane, I remember remarking to myself upon the way Dart was smiling at me: it seemed *rehearsed*. It seemed he had been told what charms lay in his smile and that he had practiced it in front of the mirror. I thought this in the early days and then, of course, promptly forgot it. Once I was gathered into his heart, beaten out of my common sense by the indefatigability of his cock, I did not look at him critically at all—and his smile became my smile, his causes my causes, his pains my pains.

If I had a lovers' time machine and I could drop myself back into the past at will and relive one of our trips, which trip would I pick? Hong Kong Harbor at sunset and our mad fucking in a king-size bed at the Mandarin? Vivaldi pouring out of the radio as we made passionate love in Hemingway's room at the Gritti in Venice? That tumbledown cabin (built of lodgepole pine) at the Lazy C Ranch in Wyoming, where we fucked the nights away in coltish wonder at having actually found our sexual mates? (Dart was the first man I'd ever met who was as mad for sex as I was, as unsqueamish about tastes and odors, as puppy-playful, as dark and kinky and wild.)

No—I would not pick any of the grand hotels we littered with our towels and sheets and slime and sperm and saliva. Nor would I go back to the first time in that Wyoming paradise of fly-tying and horseback riding and homemade honey muffins, broiled trout, and scrambled eggs. I would pick, oddly enough, a trip to Yugoslavia we once took to spend all the blocked dinars that had accumulated from sales of my paintings there.

I see him lying on a beach somewhere along the Dalmatian coast (between Dubrovnik and Split, I suppose). Above us is a corniche road cut into the limestone. It crumbles and falls away in places, like the odyssey of our lives. Below us, lapping, is the Adriatic. The beach is rocky, and we have spread blankets and towels, which are littered with snorkel gear and the remains of our peasant picnic of grapes, plums, cheese, bread, and homemade red wine in a wavy green glass bottle innocent of any label. The beach is deserted and we are both naked (not nude—that more polite cousin of nakedness) in the blinding sunlight. We are greasing each other's bodies in tandem: first he does my back with infinite tenderness; then I do his. Then he does my lips, my nipples, my thighs, my knees—and then he has plunged his sweet, tousled boyish head between my knees and he is slowly licking up one side of my clitoris and down the other, darting his tongue in and out of that cavity he would like to climb back into, making me come resoundingly again and again and again before he will deign to pull me to my knees and fuck me brutally, almost painfully, from behind, the heat of his cock corresponding to the heat of the sun that bakes us. When we are spent, we lie in each other's arms on that rocky beach, my head in his armpit, where I smell the odor that links my menstrual cycles to the moon, his sweet sweat clinging in trembling drops to the honey-blond ringlets in the curve of his armpit.

I can remember the curl of each hair in the sunlight, the tendency his armpit hair had to tangle in little knots—which later I would tenderly cut away with a nail scissors—the faint whorls of ashen-blond hair around his nipples, the curve of his warm belly (not as flat as he wished it, dammit—*his* dammit, not mine), and his battering ram of a cock deceptively sweet in repose, a little rosebud listing to the left and weeping one glistening dewdrop tear.

I remember the shape of his loins, the blue vein that pulsed where his leg joined his groin, the golden hair on his calves, the shape of those calves, the length of the tendons. And then I remember a slightly funny, moth-eaten odor his mouth had—not unpleasant but hinting faintly of corruption—"the moth-eaten odor of old money," he called it (for he could also be funny in a self-mocking sort of way). I noticed that odor in the beginning and then I stopped noticing it—only to notice it again right at the end.

We drove through Yugoslavia in a tiny cheap Yugoslavian car called a Zastava—the only car we could rent. The engine must have been made of plastic, and somewhere in the mountains of Macedonia it gave up the ghost. The car puttered to a halt on a mountain road in a region of infernal factories and mines, where leathery-faced peasants in sweaty bandannas seemed to be mining lead. Of course it wasn't lead, but it hung in the sky like a grayish haze, making one think of gnomes in the lands of Oz and Ev, underground factories, and regions of infernal gloom.

Not a soul spoke English in that infernal land, and there were no garages.

"Do you have a wire coat hanger, baby?" Dart asked, looking under the hood of the car, then strutting over to me as if he wanted to be awarded the Légion d'honneur.

I knew better than to ask why. In fact, I didn't really *want* to know why. From my expensive leather-trimmed tapestry suitcase I produced the hanger as if I were the nurse at one of those kitchen-table abortions of my youth. I was full of admiration for his WASP knack of fixing things . . . I who had grown up poor in Washington

Heights with Jewish men who thought that when something broke, you "called the guy"—inevitably a Polack, Irishman, or Latino, or some other member of that underclass that exists for the sole purpose of sparing Jewish men manual labor. Something about Dart's ability to fix things like throttle linkages got me hot. It seemed to have a sexual dimension.

And fix the Zastava he did. As we puttered off into the Yugoslavian sunset, I thought I had found my fixer at last: my mate, my addictive substance, my pusher, my love.

Love is the sweetest addiction. Who would not sell her soul for the dream of the two made one, for the sweetness of making love in the sunlight on an Adriatic beach with a young god whose armpits are lined with gold? I thought we were pals, partners, lovers, friends. I, who had always—even in my marriages—maintained my obsessive separateness, now let myself relax into the sweetness of coupling, the sweetness of partnership, the two who are united against a world of hostile strangers.

It must be admitted: famous women attract con men and carpetbaggers. The sweeter men, the normal men, are shyer and hesitate to come close. So one looks around and sees a world filled with Claus Von Bulows, Chéris, and Morris Townsends, in short, a world of heiress-hunters, gigolos, and grifters. The nice men, being nice, hesitate—and in love, as in war, he who hesitates is lost.

The real key to Dart was his father, though I resisted seeing that for nearly five years. Darton Venable Donegal III was a fortune-hunting scoundrel of the old school. Henry James could have done him justice—or Dickens. He was six feet six, white-haired, red-faced, and totally out of touch with human emotions. He spoke like a person, looked like a person, ate like a person—but the better you got to know him (which was a contradiction in terms, since he was basically unknowable), the more you realized that he was impersonating a human being in the way that certain malevolent life forms of stock science fiction impersonate human beings.

The first time I encountered Dart's father in the flesh was Thanksgiving of the first year Dart and I lived together. We were invited—nay, summoned—to the elder Donegals' manse in Philadelphia to partake of that *echt* American feast. I must admit that my Dyckman Street Jewish childhood had left me with a lifelong fascination for old WASP ways. I was not just fucking a man when I fucked Dart; I was fucking American history, the *Mayflower* myth, the colonial past. While my ancestors were tearing their pumpernickel apart in the Ukraine, Dart's were choosing amongst a plethora of silver forks and taking tea at the Colonial Dames of America. The table analogy was apt, for though Dart's family was downwardly mobile (as only Social Register WASPs can be), they still had enough sets of silver and bone china to serve presidents and kings—in the unlikely event that presidents and kings should come to call.

No presidents and kings came to call these days; only their twenty-five-year-old son and his thirty-nine-year-old inamorata. Dart was titillated by his father's jealousy over me (for Dart's father knew and admired my work). To be twenty-five and to bring home a mistress closer to one's parents' generation than to one's own is a sort of triumph, a flourish of oedipal one-upmanship that was not lost on me.

I could see Dart's delight when he brought me home

for dinner, and I could tell that his father was bested in the struggle, because he kept dropping things—cold silver, hot hors d'oeuvres, and lastly a Baccarat crystal wine goblet, whose glistening shards he was then obliged to sweep up with elaborate courtliness.

Dart's parents' house was cluttered and catworn. The Collyer brothers came to mind. Torn Naugahyde chairs stood beneath oval portraits of family progenitors. Chippendale antiques stood cheek by jowl with folding chairs from K mart. The fabric on the upholstered furniture hung in tatters from the ministrations of the four family cats—Catullus, Petronius, Brutus, and Julius Caesar (called respectively Cat, Pet, Brute, and Julie).

When we came into the living room, Dart's father was on his knees before the fire, poking it into flames (something the males in that family were good at).

He sprang to his feet, and one saw at once that the elder Darton was taller than his already rather tall son.

"Well, my lad," he said, shaking his son's hand briskly. "Introduce us."

"Leila Sand," said Dart, proud to be fucking a household name.

"Well, well, well," said the elder Darton. "What an honor."

I was seated near the fire in a red Naugahyde chair (whose stuffing seemed to want to view the light of day), and the two Dartons—father and son—went off to the kitchen to fetch the drinks and hors d'oeuvres. I sat and took in the scene, as exotic to me, given my background, as the twin palaces of the sultan of Brunei.

The formality between Darton III and Darton IV, the catworn furniture, the Chippendale antiques, the pervasive smell of mothballs and cat litter . . . all this spelled

WASPdom for me—and its essence was as aphrodisiac as, probably, my Jewishness was to Dart.

The sitting room of the town house looked out on a little garden with a fountain, atop which a smallish statue of Eros stood shivering in the cold. The light was wintry, but within the room it was warm. I missed Dart. Our physical connection was such that I felt cut off if he was out of the room for a moment. When we were together we were always holding hands, touching hipbones, stroking each other. When we touched each other we seemed to go into a primal place where nothing mattered but our touching. It was the most powerful feeling I had ever known, and it obliterated all discrimination, all judgment, all sense of time.

Dart's mother appeared.

Although Dart had told me she was obese, I was not quite prepared for the sight of her. She was a broad-shouldered woman who weighed perhaps three hundred pounds, and her small, pallid, little girl's face was lost in chins. She wore her fine silvery-blond hair as she must have when she was seven—held back on each side of her face by a tortoiseshell barrette—and there was about her the unmistakable look of a child who has got into the cookie jar. She wore a shapeless black crepe dress with a row of jets at the U-shaped neck, and on her feet she wore white sheepskin baby booties. When she sat down on the couch—which she promptly did—she was too fat either to cross her legs or to bring them together, so she sat with her knees wide apart, enabling me to see her old-fashioned bloomers and part of her fleshy thighs.

"Well, hello!" she said, in her dulcet, fat-choked voice. At sixty, she seemed more childlike than my own six-year-old daughters—as if something in her had been arrested and the body had aged while the mind blithely, indeed obstinately, remained in infancy. "I will *not* grow up," her blue eyes seemed to say. I immediately saw the resemblance between her and her son, the determination to cram oneself with goodies—to the point of nausea if necessary—simply to prove one could do as one pleased.

"Well, where is my drink?" Mrs. Donegal asked petulantly. "And where are my hors d'oeuvres?"

She looked at me. I felt I ought to apologize.

"Oh, Ven! Ven!" she called on a mellifluous ascending scale. "Oh, Ven!"—that being Dart's father's nickname. (Mrs. Donegal was called Muffie—for Martha—and Dart was, to his family, Trick, owing to some baby-talk etymology I hadn't quite got straight. Jewish families didn't have these problems of nomenclature. At the time, I found all this terrifically quaint. "Ven," "Muffie," "Trick": these were not names one often came across in Washington Heights.)

Mr. Donegal arrived with the hors d'oeuvres, which were arrayed on little aluminum tins apparently left over from TV dinners, and these in turn were set out on a very grand English silver tray in the rococo style. There were hot tidbits of various descriptions and also caviar, pâté de foie gras, and smoked salmon. The spread would easily have fed a dozen people.

Mrs. Donegal presided over the hors d'oeuvres. One was clearly not at liberty to help oneself.

"Would you like some caviar, dear?" Mrs. Donegal asked. And without waiting for a reply, she prepared me some, with the following commentary: "I've been eating caviar since I was three, which was when Mummy first gave it to me. Finished a whole pot of Beluga with a baby spoon. You can imagine how cross my nanny was. But Mummy said, 'Don't punish her, Nurse Frith'—she was my first nanny. 'It's never too soon for a girl to learn to love Beluga.' "

I laughed with some strain. The story seemed so manifestly canned—as if it had been told many times in these circumstances and for the same reason. It was a sort of code, and I had cracked it early. "I was born rich, eccentric, and spoiled," it said, "and I hope you find this charming, for it's my only gambit. I ate caviar as a baby, and I still eat caviar and am still a baby."

"Ha ha," I laughed. "Ha ha."

Mrs. Donegal did not appear to detect the hollowness of my laughter. Glad to have a new audience for old stories, she went on and on about Mummy's taste in caviar and her own debutante days at the Stork Club, her wedding trip to Europe with Ven (the Delahaye broke down in the Alps), and how darling Trick was as a baby. All the while she chain-smoked Pall Malls, downed martinis, and popped one hors d'oeuvre after another into her mouth.

Dart had told me that his mother slept till five each day, virtually never left the house, and was terrified of what she might find in the outside world, from which she had retreated shortly after his birth. I had expected to find her strange, but her strangeness surpassed even my expectations. It was not that she wasn't pleasant; she was. It was that she seemed to talk in set pieces, each of which seemed rehearsed.

"The cards!" said Mr. Donegal. "We have forgotten the cards!" Whereupon he retreated to the nearly impassable sun room (filled with newspapers, cartons, never-unpacked appliances, and clothes) to obtain a series of envelopes of assorted sizes and two waxy boxes from the florist's shop.

"Oh, Ven! How *sweet* of you," Mrs. Donegal said.

"One for you! And one for you!" Mr. Donegal said, giving each of the ladies a florist's box.

I opened mine with trepidation, for not only do I hate corsages, but I was wearing a very thin chamois dress, which would be ruined by a pin. In the box was a corsage of somewhat wilted Tropicana roses, festooned with orange and gold ribbons.

"Oh, thank you," I lied. Mrs. Donegal had an identical corsage, which seemed to delight her. She put it on immediately, pointing the tail crookedly at her jiggling bosom.

"Oh, goody!" she said. "Now let's see the cards."

I fiddled with my corsage, hoping no one would notice I wasn't wearing it. No such luck. Mr. Donegal came over and pinned it on my bosom, ruining my suede dress and copping a quick but unmistakable feel.

" 'Happy Thanksgiving to my beloved wife,' " Mrs. Donegal read aloud. " 'At this most special time of year, / My dearest wife, I bring you cheer. / For you make every holiday a cause for being bright and gay. / Without you life would be no fun, / so I salute you, dearest one. Happy Thanksgiving from your adoring Ven.' "

At his cue, Mr. Donegal bent down and kissed his immobilized wife.

"Oh, Ven," she said. "How sweet."

"Not as sweet as you, m'dear," said Ven, as if by rote.

"What a loving family we are!" said Mrs. Donegal.

You could tell from the expressions of the two men that this charade had been played many a time.

Mrs. Donegal proceeded to read out the other cards from her husband, all of them equally saccharine and self-serving. She seemed genuinely delighted with the sentiments expressed. Never before having met people who took greeting cards seriously, I was astonished. I had grown up in a world where such sentiments were occasions for wild hilarity. At my family dinner table—such as it was— wicked humor and satirical kvetching were the rule. I had always wondered who bought such greeting cards—and now I knew.

At some point before dinner, Dart disappeared into the upper reaches of the town house and was gone for some time.

I was left struggling for conversation with Muffie and Ven.

What was oddest about them both was that all their conversation seemed to be about things that had happened before 1947. She loved to talk about Miss Porter's School, her coming out party, and her honeymoon—a two-year spending spree in Europe—and *he* loved to talk about Princeton days, his eating club, and his classmates' merry pranks, and how he almost made *Review* at Harvard Law. This was the house where time stood still. Miss Havisham could have moved right in, not to mention Mr. Micawber. No wonder their only son had disappeared to the bathroom, seemingly never to return.

My heart went out to Dart, who had had to make a life out of such unpromising parental material. Really, he was an orphan, for nobody was home to raise him. Both his parents were trapped in the past.

"We have many artists in our family," Mr. Donegal said. "I'm not at *tall* surprised that you and Trick get on so well. Besides Trick, there was Uncle Wesley—wasn't there, Muffie?—who was a noted landscape painter in Vermont." Ven pointed to a tortured little study of a covered bridge that hung above the fireplace. "And then there was

Aunt Millicent, who did nudes."

"And that's not all," said Muffie, in eyeball-rolling disapproval. "She also did *other* things."

"Mrs. Donegal is referring to her lesbianic period, I presume, in which she depicted ladies in various, shall we say, compromising positions," Mr. Donegal informed me.

"I'll say," said Mrs. Donegal.

"Mrs. Donegal believes that oral sex is a passing fad," said Mr. Donegal, leering at me. "What do you think?"

I blushed. (For some reason, Mrs. Donegal made me think of Enid Bagnold's line: "In *my* day, only Negresses had orgasms.")

"Well, er, it *has* had its adherents throughout history. The ancient Greeks actually—"

"She's *perrrfect* for Trick," said Mrs. Donegal. "He's the only other person who would talk about ancient Greeks and oral sex in the same breath."

Just then Trick (or Dart) reappeared, looking as glazed as a Christmas ham. Whatever he had done in the bathroom, it wasn't purchased over the counter.

"Is dinner ready, Ven?" asked Mrs. Donegal.

"Not quite, m'dear," said Mr. Donegal. "The girls are still fussing about."

Conversation lagged. When in doubt, say nothing, I admonished myself. Normally ready with repartee, I could think of not a damn thing to say. Perhaps it was the pervasive odor of WASPdom, the cats, the conversation, or the straight vodka I had been consuming with the caviar, but all that came to mind were homilies like: "A stitch in time saves nine," or "A rolling stone gathers no moss," or "Penny wise, pound foolish." What was it about the Donegals that made me feel I was in *Poor Richard's Al-*

manack? (Even though I had been married to a WASP heir at one point during my hegira, that was in the sixties, when everyone was busy kicking over all traces of Heritage. Now, in the Reagan years, this stuff was *serious* again. Oddly enough, I responded.)

The maid appeared, to announce dinner. She was a sullen-looking brunette of about eighteen, wearing a white polyester minidress with a crooked hem. On her feet were white plastic cowboy boots, and there was a big white bow in her long, tangled hair. She looked as if she had been procured through the placement office of the local reform school.

"Dinner is served," she said between chews on her mouthful of gum.

Mr. Donegal stood up (he had been sitting on the sagging couch next to his wife), and when he did, a packet of condoms fell out of his green velvet smoking jacket. "Excita," they were called, in shocking-pink letters. I saw them. He saw that I saw them. And he looked me in the eye, challengingly, as he pocketed them. It was a moment, as they say in the theater. What aphorism in *Poor Richard's Almanack* applied to this?

And so to dinner. We repaired to the cluttered formal dining room, where the table was elaborately set with a forest of cut-crystal wine goblets, a dazzling variety of forks and spoons, twin silver candelabra festooned with little green and red Christmas balls.

"Let us say grace," said Mr. Donegal, taking my hand and his son's. My other hand clutched Muffie's, and she in turn held Dart's.

We bowed our heads.

"Heavenly Father, make us truly grateful for what we are about to receive and ever mindful of the needs of others. We thank Thee for all the blessings Thou hast bestowed upon us in the year past, and will bestow in the year to come. . . . Amen."

I thought of the condoms. Mr. Donegal looked up and blazed his malevolent blue eyes into mine. He was confident that I wouldn't say anything. This was not a house in which people bared their souls. An invisible gas pervaded the air, keeping one from communicating any disturbing truths. The conversation lurched forward over the melon balls, Christmas balls, bread and butter. Mr. Donegal returned to the subject of art, something in which he claimed to be knowledgeable. He asked me what I thought of Élisabeth Vigée-Lebrun, Mary Cassatt, Berthe Morisot, Rosa Bonheur. I allowed that I admired them greatly. He asked if women artists today were still discriminated against. And I said that the discrimination was still there but had taken new forms.

Dart looked at me with adoration and admiration. When I took on his father, his love knew no bounds. I had the feeling, as I often have in my life, that I was on stage, in some surrealistic play. Life often seems immensely strange to me, and the most ordinary of acts—Thanksgiving dinners, for example—can be stranger than space voyages. I am a visitor from another planet, observing human ritual with amazement and disbelief.

"I love you," Dart mouthed at me across the table.

"I love you," I silently mouthed back.

"Well, lad, what have you been doing?" Mr. Donegal asked his son. "Other than keeping Leila happy?" It was said rather as an accusation. Mr. Donegal was accusing his son of being a gigolo, the pot calling the kettle black. Dart looked as discomfited and defensive as he was meant to do.

"I've been trying to put Leila's business affairs in

order," he said. "We're thinking of building a gallery on Greene Street."

"What a splendid idea," said Mr. Donegal. "Excellent, excellent. For an artist to have her own gallery is really to be in control."

"I wasn't thinking of it for *my* work," I said. "I have a gallery that sells my work—the McCrae Gallery. But for Trick's, and other young artists'—to get them started."

"How splendid," said Mr. Donegal. "You sound like a real businesswoman, Leila—an admirable quality, especially in an artist." (Mr. Donegal often said things as if he were the final arbiter.) "What would you say if I told you I have a very interesting business proposition to make you?"

"Oh, no," said Mrs. Donegal. But Mr. Donegal went blithely on.

"If you would entrust me with a mere fifty thousand between now and January, I believe I could triple your money."

Dart groaned and looked at his mother. Mrs. Donegal now seemed even paler than usual.

"Another harebrained scheme to put us in the poorhouse," she said.

"Nonsense, m'dear. This is my way of preserving your capital. If you sincerely want to be rich, you have to take a chance every now and then. Mrs. Donegal believes that those stuffed shirts at the Morgan Bank know what to do with money. Why, they barely keep up with the rate of inflation." (I loved the way Mr. Donegal pronounced the word "shirts"; he gave it an extra syllable, so it became "shhh-ehrts." He had a voice full of money—the sort of voice Gatsby wanted and could never buy.)

"What would you do with the money?" I asked.

"Why, I could triple it in a mere three months by investing it in heating oil futures, as I am doing with my own money. . . ."

"Over my dead body," whispered Mrs. Donegal just audibly. "You've lost enough of my money already."

"Do we have to discuss money at Thanksgiving dinner?" Dart pleaded. "I, for one, think it's in execrable taste."

"Jews never got rich worrying about good taste," said Mr. Donegal. He looked at me. "I mean," he said, "Hebrews."

" 'Jews' is not a dirty word, Mr. Donegal," I said, my dinner suddenly sticking in my craw like vomit about to come up. I wanted to tell Mr. Donegal that his immediate association of Jews with bad taste and moneygrubbing was not only anti-Semitic but a cliché unworthy of his intellect, but I simply could not get the words out. I felt dizzy and faint. I wished I were elsewhere. It was a familiar dilemma: when people made anti-Semitic cracks, I felt pompous correcting them and sick to my stomach if I failed to. What was the answer? I ran my toe along Dart's leg under the table.

Mrs. Donegal picked up the crystal dinner bell and rang for Ms. Reform School. Thanksgiving dinner was off and running.

Following the melon balls, an enormous turkey was rolled out. The evening stretched before us like the vast Sahara. Mr. Donegal carved the turkey as if he were doing a live sex show. There was something pornographic about the way he manipulated the drumsticks, making them move at the joints and then severing them swiftly with a sharp knife.

Not happy with what was going on in the present tense, Mrs. Donegal dropped back in time to the forties, the last decade in which she had felt comfortable, and began telling us how she had been a poster girl for the USO during the war.

"Yes," said Mr. Donegal, "while I was risking my life for our country in the Pacific theater, Mrs. Donegal was posing nude for lascivious artists." The thought of Mrs. Donegal posing nude did not seem to accord with lasciviousness of any sort.

"He only *wanted* me to pose nude," Mrs. Donegal said. "I didn't actually *do* it."

"Yes, yes, dear," said Mr. Donegal, feigning the jealous mate—albeit rather unconvincingly.

Mrs. Donegal preened, tripled her chins, and smiled fetchingly. Mr. Donegal winked at her in a forties-movie parody of flirtation, and the previous discussion about heating oil futures was forgotten. The ritual dance of their marriage had been choreographed long before and was as unlikely to change as the routines in a tired but long-running musical. They were eating buddies, greeting card buddies, and partners in self-deception. Every good marriage is partly a folie à deux, but this one should have won a lifetime achievement award. It was as if Miss Havisham had mated with Mr. Micawber.

After dinner, Mr. Donegal insisted on taking me on a tour of the family heirlooms. While Dart communed with his mother, I trailed behind Mr. Donegal through rooms and rooms of packing boxes, cobwebby antiques, piled-up newspapers, sagging bookshelves crammed with dusty books, and armoires bursting with all sorts of unidentifiable stuff. Every object before which Mr. Donegal lingered was meant to reflect glory on the family. There was his father's World War I helmet, his smiling Irish mother's wedding portrait, the hood ornament from the famous Delahaye that gave up the ghost in the Alps, an aerial view of the family's former brickworks in Philadelphia (long since liquidated to pay off inheritance taxes). Finally we ascended to the attic, a musty top-floor emporium filled with dusty racks of clothes. It was virtually a costume museum, devoted to all the disembodied clothes of the Donegal ancestors: flapper dresses, World War I uniforms, bridal gowns, frock coats. If the clothes could have magically filled with the vanished forms of all the vanished Venables, Donegals, and Dartons—what a danse macabre they would have made!

Mr. Donegal held up a moonbeamy flapper dress, glimmering with bugle beads.

"My mother's," said Mr. Donegal. "Would you like to try it on?"

"Oh, no, thank you," I said.

"Please," said Mr. Donegal. "It would give me such pleasure to see someone wear it."

"I don't think it will fit," I said.

"Of course it will," said Mr. Donegal. "She was small like you—and also titian-haired. A Venetian blond, she called herself. It would be my honor to pass it on to you."

He was importunate, and I was afraid of seeming rude, so I took the dress, disappeared behind a rack of clothes, took off my chamois dress (corsage and all), and carefully raised the dusty, shimmering sheath above my head. So intent was I on not tearing the heirloom that I did not see (or hear) Mr. Donegal slither up beside me.

Before I knew it, one of his hands was on my breast and the other was fondling my crotch. He swiftly insinuated one index finger under the fastening of my cream-colored lace teddy and ran it teasingly along my clit. I let out a little shriek, but was immobilized both by my raised arms and by my care for the dress.

"Please!" I said through the fragile fabric, but Mr. Donegal ignored me. He was pressing himself against me now, and I could feel his erection, curiously crooked like his son's. I dropped the dress, a pile of dusty moonbeams, and darted behind another clothes rack, where I stood immobilized, waiting for Mr. Donegal to come claim me. Images of fox hunts came to mind, and I the terrified fox waiting for the dogs to scent my fear. Forty seconds went by, but Mr. Donegal did not come. My breath was jagged and rapid: a mixture of fear and—dare I say it?—sexual excitement. I waited shivering in my lace teddy until finally I realized that I was alone in the room.

Trembling, humiliated, I found my way back to my suede dress, put it on, collected myself, and went downstairs.

In the sitting room, I met with a Hogarthian tableau of the Donegal family chatting cozily around the fire as if nothing at all were the matter.

Mr. Donegal was fondling his mother's dress, which he held on his lap like a household pet. It occurred to me that this whole family was quite mad—dangerously so— and that I should escape at once. Alas, I did not heed my instinct.

As I descended into their midst, Mr. Donegal rose and handed me the glimmering dress.

"A little memento of our meeting," he said, meeting my gaze.

"I couldn't possibly . . . ," I said.

"Nonsense," said Mr. Donegal. "You must. It suits you perfectly."

I took the dress, feeling I was dangerously out of my depth.

On the long drive back to Roxbury from Philadelphia, Dart was desolate and not a little contrite.

"I am mortified that he asked you for money," Dart said.

"Not to worry," I said. "I see what you mean about him. He's quite an act to follow."

"You don't know the half of it," said Dart. "First of all, he never fought in the Pacific theater—that's a total fabrication. Furthermore, do you know he's been to jail?"

"It doesn't surprise me," I said. But after I heard Dart's story of his father's malfeasances (he embezzled money from a client and was disbarred), I did not have the heart to tell him what had happened in the attic. I almost wondered if it *had* happened—or if I had imagined it all, conjured it out of dust and moonbeams.

"I want to be a good man for you," said Dart/Trick, tears running down his cheeks. "I don't want to be like my father." And I believe that was true in every respect. But between men and their fathers, intention is the last thing that matters.

3

STRONG WOMAN'S BLUES

———— ◆ ————

No father to guide me,
no mother to care,
Must bear my troubles all alone.
Not even a brother to help me share,
This burden I must bear alone.

—Bessie Smith

I wasn't always the queen of SoHo and Litchfield County. I grew up poor, in Washington Heights, with a mother who had a habit of getting arrested in embarrassing places—the White House, the United Nations, the Russian consulate, demonstrations for the Rosenbergs—and a father who made silver jewelry on Eighth Street, was a beatnik and hippie before either of those terms was invented, and an alcoholic before anyone knew that drinking was more than good clean fun.

I came, in short, from a "dysfunctional family"—to use the lingo so in vogue nowadays. (Sometimes I wonder if there *is* any other kind of family. Certainly no one I know comes from a functional family, whatever that anomaly may be.)

My father had been a fixture in the Village and in Provincetown since the thirties: Dolph Zandberg, born 1900, died 1982—the year I met Dart. Dolph was a Marxist in the thirties, a war resister in the forties, a heavy user of weed, alcohol, mushrooms, in the fifties, and a Village legend in the psychedelic sixties. He knew everyone—from Edmund Wilson to Ken Kesey, from Henry Miller to Jackson Pollock. On the fringes of every fringe movement of the twentieth century, he could (like Mel Brooks's two-thousand-year-old man) say of any counterculture heroine from Louise Nevelson to Margaret Mead: "Honey—I went with her." He and my mother, Theda (named for Theda Bara, natch), had one of the first "open marriages." Theirs didn't work any better than the later ones did. It was patched together with the dubious glue of alcohol, Marxist theory, and me—the lonely only, born when my father was forty-four and my mother twenty-nine, almost an old maid for her generation.

Oh, I know that Dolph and Theda must have adored me, even as I adore my own twin girls, Edwina and Michaela, but that didn't make them automatically know how to love me into health. In fact, I'm sure they didn't even know what health was. Narcissists that they were, absorbed in the drama of their own stormy marriage, they alternately ignored me and treated me like the Wunderkind of the Western world.

From the time I was four, I was sketching, sketching, sketching; I almost don't remember a time when I *didn't* draw. I could always "get a likeness"—as my father called it. And from the start I picked up all his tricks: origami paper sculpture, bending silver wire as if it were saltwater taffy, making collages of cloth and paper, newsprint, plastic, and silk.

By the time I took the test for Music and Art, when I was twelve, I was a better artist than most of the teachers and they knew it. The oohing and aahing over my portfolio was fierce. I went to M&A in the mythic old days, when my schoolmates were legends-to-be like Charlie Gwathmey, Isadora Wing, and Tony Roberts. I wasn't particularly happy there—but who is happy at fifteen?

Isadora: Better get this right, kiddo, if you are going to do the unspeakable thing of introducing me into the book as a real character!

Leila: Who, then, is the potter and who the pot?

Isadora: When in doubt, quote Omar Khayyám! But the fact is you know damn well you have given Our Heroine an upside-down version of your own high school years. You were the good girl, so you made her bad. Any reader can spot these fictional reversals a mile away. You'll have to do better than that.

Leila: Just wait; it gets better.

M&A stood then at the top of a wino-studded hill at 135th Street and Convent Avenue, and I took the exhibitionist-studded subway down from Dyckman Street to get there. The school was enveloped in a gemütlich haze of marijuana and black jazz.

At M&A I learned four things: that Bessie Smith knew all there was to know about womanhood; that blacks had the secret key to America's heart of darkness; that The Land of Fuck was expensive but worth the price; and that an artist was always an outcast and a rebel in bourgeois America—no matter what anyone said.

At M&A I dressed all in black (stockings to stocking cap), smoked Gauloises, and had a tall boyfriend from Harlem called Snack—a saxophone player who taught me all about jazz and weed and sex. I changed my name from Louise Zandberg to Leila Sand (to my father's horror and my mother's delight—George Sand was one of her heroines), and I learned how to ring my eyes with kohl, rouge my nipples (not that my pink fifteen-year-old nipples *needed* rouging), and cut my hair in a shiny helmet à la Louise Brooks (one of my early idols). The hair was Pre-Raphaelite red (Venetian, as Mr. Donegal would have it), but the style was pure 1920s. I was the Greenwich Village kid—a regular at the Peacock, the White Horse, the Lion's Head—as I shuttled between Dyckman Street, where my mom lived (in increasing chaos and squalor), and Eighth Street, where my dad lived over the store.

By the time I was a teenager, Theda's craziness had long since driven Dolph away. He had a mistress named Maxine, who sometimes stayed with him above the store and who tried in vain to woo me with pseudomaternal affection. But I was intransigent and must have given her a terrible time—almost as terrible as the time I gave my mother. Much as I hated my mother, I was fiercely loyal to her around Dolph and Maxine.

Sullen, silent, dressed all in black, squired by a black boyfriend—I was every parent's nightmare of a teenager. I walked down Eighth Street in a cloud of Gauloise smoke, clutching a copy of *Being and Nothingness* under the arm that wasn't twined around Snack, while he, in turn, carried his saxophone and a switchblade. Snack was six feet three inches (I have always liked tall men), and I was then, as now, a mere five feet four (like Elizabeth Taylor, another heroine of mine). My tits were big, my hips big, and my waist almost as tiny as Scarlett O'Hara's. Considered sexy in a gamine sort of way, I never really thought I was pretty, but boys flocked to me because apparently I had "It." The scent of sex is a powerful aphrodisiac, and some girls have it, while others—even very pretty ones—most emphatically do not. It has less to do with looks than with smell, for human beings are closer to the insect and invertebrate worlds than their hubris lets them know. With all that sex appeal from my teen years on, I was usually more concerned with protecting myself against the opposite sex than with attracting it. (Oh, nature is cruelly unfair when it comes to love.)

I fought the white boys off with my wicked sarcasm and my prodigious talent—which I flaunted like a cock—and turned instead to the rebels, outcasts, and blacks. I had no penis envy; I really thought I had a penis. I graduated from M&A in '61, went to Yale School of Fine Arts, and the summer of '64 (the summer of my junior year) found me in Mississippi with Goodman, Schwerner, and Chaney. That I didn't get killed is a tribute not to prudence but to providence or sheer dumb luck—the same luck that mysteriously preserved me during my drinking, drugging, and driving days. The gods must have spared me for some awesome task, for certainly I was careless enough with my own life. What that awesome task was I did not yet know, but whatever it was, I would fashion it with my own two capable hands.

From my father I inherited immense skill in making things: craftsman's hands, an eye that could immediately see the right juxtaposition of shapes and colors. All this I believe is inborn. We are not taught it but merely grow into our real selves if our real selves are not blocked. From my mother I inherited a gift for theatrics that bordered on madness. I was a bad girl in high school and an even badder girl in college. I had a gift for publicity even then. Once, long before Charlotte Moorman wrapped herself in Saran Wrap to play the cello, I wrapped myself in tinfoil to attend the Halloween party of an M&A classmate. At Yale, *years* before the advent of the Guerrilla Girls, I railed against the male-dominated art world (this was in the early sixties, before feminism was chic, let alone tolerated), yet I was not at all against wooing art critics with my sex appeal if it would help my career. I felt even then—perhaps the spectacle of my mother's victimization by my father inspired this—that women were so discriminated against as a class that all was fair in love and war. I continued to think so until Dart.

Because I was so strong in my integrity against the opposite sex, skinlessness was what I sought. Most boys were too weak for me. I could manipulate them too easily. A young woman who knows her own sexual powers is a rarity indeed, but she is unbeatable. And if she happens also to be smart and talented and has the crazed bravado—I cannot call it self-confidence—that a mad mother and an alcoholic father inspire, then there's no stopping her. That was me precisely. Unsinkable, unbeatable, unstoppable.

After breaking the requisite number of hearts in high school and college, I did in graduate school what no one expected me to do: I married an heir. Thomas Winslow was the scion of a family just as alcoholic as mine but a lot richer. He was studying English lit at Yale, with a special interest in Romantic poetry, and I don't know whether I married him because he was the tallest guy I'd ever dated (six feet six) or because he was blond and blue-eyed (with eyes the color of faded denim) or because he declared his intentions to leave the whole of his legacy to SNCC— there's an acronym out of the past—or because he could recite "Ode to a Nightingale" on cue. ("My heart aches, and a drowsy numbness pains / My sense, as though of hemlock I had drunk, / Or emptied some dull opiate to the drains"—how's that for a premonition?) It could have been any of these reasons. Or perhaps I was just tired of fighting off men, and getting married seemed like the answer. At least it would allow me to concentrate on my work.

Thom and I were set up by his parents in a mansion in Southport, which we proceeded to fill with radicals, black militants, and war resisters. We painted the windows black, filled the rooms with pop art, and set about drinking and drugging our way out of the good graces of a community that had sheltered Thom's family for nearly a century. We took a glorious Greek Revival mansion and turned it into a slum—all in the name of art and social revolution. For these were the days of the Beatles, the Vietnam war, happenings, peace marches, and Summers of Love. Thom, like every man I ever loved, was too weak for me, but he adored my work and would do anything to further it. At that time my style was eclectic, to say the least. I produced happenings with Yoko Ono (when she was still with Tony Cox, before she snagged her Beatle)—dubious performances at which the bourgeois participants were forced to strip naked and crawl through canvas tubes or drop their drawers to be photographed mooning at old-fashioned cameras. (Even then I was interested in film stills—which later figured so prominently in my relationship with Dart, as you will presently hear.)

Thom Winslow aided and abetted me in all these ventures: buying the art, supporting the radicals and their movements, renting the lofts, financing all my brash, hare-brained schemes. Because he was so complaisant, I was fairly contemptuous of him. I knew he was hopelessly in love with me—and it made me careless. But then the sixties were careless days. Everyone knew the pricelessness of everything and the value of nothing. Unlike our younger siblings the yuppies, we claimed contempt for money—but what we really had contempt for was struggle and pain. We expected the world to be handed to us on a silver (albeit graffiti-covered) platter—and for a while it was.

Thom Winslow was a good, nice, stoned guy. I was his anger—the rebellion he didn't have the nerve to act out himself. Once, before we split, I overheard him telling a famous art dealer at a dinner party: "All my life, I went to the right schools, the right clubs, the right debutante cotillions, and then I married Leila Sand, née Louise Zandberg!" Thom said this with considerable pride—it was in fact the great achievement of his life at that point—but I was pissed off because he gave away my original name. (Maybe I also heard the undertone of anger that was soon to sunder us.)

What a difference twenty years can make! Thom is now married to a lockjawed debutante of his own faith (godless Protestantism) and social class (trust fund radicalism), who might even have gone to dancing school with him in Southport. They live in Vermont and produce environmentally sound toilets that turn your shit into compost for roses. Heartbroken as he was when I bolted with Elmore Dworkin, the abstract expressionist, he was able to turn it into compost. It takes *merde* to grow roses, as the French say.

Which brings us back to skinlessness—which I was seeking when I fell in love with Elmore, who was older, far more established, and knew everything there was to know about cunnilingus (tongue tricks he had learned during his salad days, to mix a metaphor, in Paris). I met Elmore, fell in love with his paintings and his tongue (though perhaps not in that order). It was 1974; I had received enough recognition as a painter to be earning a good living from my work, be written up in *The New Yorker* and *Vogue* (*People* and *Architectural Digest* would come later). It was not the household-word sort of fame but a classier, more discreet variety—fame in the art world before the art world became a total media circus.

I met Elmore at a dinner party in New York that Thom had not come to because he had a terrible case of the flu. What a wife I was! At seven o'clock I left my husband alone on Park Avenue coughing his guts out, and at eleven I left a dinner party with a hirsute artist twenty years my senior. By midnight I was having my pussy licked into purring ecstasy in a loft on John Street. By 3:30 A.M. I was home in bed on Park Avenue again, embracing my soon-to-be ex-husband, without even the good grace to feel guilty. In the meantime I had admired, from the windows of Elmore's loft, that pink-as-a-baby's-bottom look the sky gets during a snowstorm, and I had equally admired Elmore's cock and paintings. In one evening I was introduced to the New York School's most promising younger artist, multiple orgasms, and Humboldt County sinsemilla.

"Have a good time, honey?" Thom asked, rolling over and coughing convulsively.

"Mmmmm," I said, and he drew my hand to his

penis. We fucked like mad then, our coupling made more passionate by the unmistakable—if ghostly—presence of a third person in our bed. Never had I enjoyed Thom more. But still I had not come to skinlessness.

My marriage to Elmore, the birth of the twins, our inevitable parting, cannot be given short shrift. I always feel that when the parents-to-be of extraordinary children meet—whether at a dinner party, at a health spa, at AA, or wherever it is fashionable for the young and nubile to meet nowadays—angels, fates, and sibyls (painted by Michelangelo, or at least by Tiepolo or Veronese) are hovering on clouds above them and nudging them toward the most convenient counterpane. All of nature is in a fury to reproduce. Why should human beings think themselves exempt? Elmore's loft, Elmore's tongue, and Elmore's drugs (not to mention Thom's flu) were merely snares to get the twins out of the ether and onto the planet as soon as possible.

At the moment one's children are conceived, one ceases to be an ego and becomes merely a cosmic tube, a funnel into timelessness. That, I suspect, is why having children is such a critical stage in one's development. With parenthood comes our first taste of egolessness, our joining of the cosmic dance. From the moment I opened my thighs to Elmore Dworkin in that loft on John Street, my marriage to Thom Winslow was doomed. Perhaps it was doomed anyway—for the twins were dying to be born—and it was the twins as much as I who picked their father.

Looking back now that the twins are ten (they were my bicentennial babes, born in the bicentennial year), I realize that they had to be fathered by a hirsute Jew of my blood and bone—another dark-eyed anarchist whose ancestors hailed from the Ukraine. I could no more have brought WASP babies into the world than I could have stopped drawing and painting. I remember once when I was pregnant with Mike and Ed (Elmore and I lived that year in Tuscany, in a farmhouse in Strada in Chianti), watching an RAI documentary on Auschwitz, which showed the destruction of Jewish babies like the two I was carrying, and weeping with joy and pain to be replenishing the Jewish race. This amazed no one more than it did the weeper in question—for I had never been religious in the least (it was, in fact, an article of my sort of Jewish faith to be faithless). But where having babies is concerned, all our conservatism seems to burgeon. Pregnant, I became hyper-Jewish, hyperartistic, hypersensitive. Pregnancy, in short, brought out my true Buddha nature. I only became more myself.

Was my marriage to Elmore good? At the beginning, it was heavenly. At the end, it was purgatorial—if not quite hellish (hell would come later, with Dart). What could be more joyful than two artists living together, doing their work, nurturing their babies, cooking, loving, walking through the churches and art galleries of Italy?

We lived in a friend's farmhouse in Chianti, looked out on fields of silvery olive trees and vines that danced crookedly across the hillsides. We slept every night in each other's arms—until my pregnancy made that impossible—and then we slept spoonlike, Elmore's chest to my back and his cock to my buttocks, nudging me from the rear and often waking up inside me.

Oh, how sweet love is when it is sweet! Two salty, sweaty lovers waking up in a shared bed that is rutted with love. And how rare it is! At the times in our lives when we have it, we scarcely appreciate it. It is appreciated more in the loss than in the having—like so many things we reckless humans have, including our lives.

I remember us as we were then: Elmore was fifty-two to my thirty-four and as besotted with me as I with him. He wore his dark hair long, his graying beard long, and his red lips poked out of it like a cunt. (Bearded men often have cuntlike mouths; perhaps that is why they so love to eat pussy: it is like kissing themselves in a mirror.)

We lived that year in a tangle of thighs, art history, and extra-virgin olive oil. We drank the wine of our own campagna; we slathered olive oil on our own tomatoes. We puttered down to Florence in our old Fiat to stroll arm in arm through the Uffizi, the Accademia, the Pitti; we ate bistecca alla fiorentina (for the sake of the babies) and huge grilled porcini (for the sake of ourselves); and we painted our hearts out in the same drafty studio, Vivaldi and Monteverdi blaring out of the radio.

We lived for love, for art, for bed, for babies. It is easy to do that in Italy, a country whose priorities are in order—in *that* order, in fact. I can still remember the rapture in Elmore's dark eyes as he lay listening to my belly as if to the sound of the sea in a nautilus shell. Our work prospered, our babies grew, our love grew. Our song was "Our Love Is Here to Stay"—and we never doubted for a moment that it was. Ah, the Rockies might crumble, Gibraltar might tumble ("They're only made of clay . . ."), but our love was here to stay. Or so we thought at the time. Actually, it was our *babies* who were here to stay.

I remember the day in July when we loaded up the Fiat with food, clothes, radio, and dog to begin our drive to Switzerland and to the clinic in Lausanne where we had decided the twins should be born. We were both singing (we were often both singing). Life, we thought, held nothing sweeter—and we were right.

It took us three days to get to Switzerland. We were not racing the clock, because it had long since been decided that when I was eight months pregnant we would drive to Switzerland and stay in a hotel near the clinic— twins are often born prematurely (I might live and paint in Italy, but I would, like Sophia Loren, have my babies born in Switzerland). As it happened, a week or so after we arrived, I started leaking amniotic fluid, and it proved prudent to put me to bed at the clinic to preserve the pregnancy. Elmore and Boner (our German shepherd) just about moved into the clinic with me (the rules being bent, as usual, for the famous), and Elmore read to me while we waited to see whether I should have a caesarean or wait to go into "natural" labor.

It was the most glorious time of my life! I lay in bed like a queen, waiting to bear my princesses (amniocentesis had informed me of their health and sex), while Elmore read *Songs of Innocence* and *Songs of Experience.* We both kept notebooks. And we both drew. I kept a pregnancy notebook in which there are many sketches of Elmore reading to me, listening to my belly, painting in his studio, and he kept a pregnancy notebook in which there are many sketches of me in differing degrees of pregnancy. (I have both notebooks back to back—or belly to belly—on a shelf in my studio in Connecticut, and I still cannot look at them without a twinge. What a blessed, blissed time that was! How could it have ended?)

It began to end on August 1, when, the pregnancy having been endangered by the rupturing of the amniotic sac, it was decided by us and by our surrealistic doctor —Dr. Breton, believe it or not!—to bring the little sweet-ies into the world by caesarean.

I went into the OR an artist and a lover and came out an artist and a mother. From the moment those little pink twins were delivered to me in their little pink blankets, the universe of love began to shift—irrevocably.

Or perhaps it was not only parenthood that began to erode the marriage. Perhaps it was the fact that my star was in the ascendancy while Elmore's was in eclipse. On the crest of the interest in women's art generated by the women's movement, my paintings (which at that time were erotic canvases of ordinary objects—shells, flowers, stones, bones, made into monumental icons in a manner reminiscent of Georgia O'Keeffe's) began to generate a great amount of interest, at a time when Elmore's Hans Hofmann–like abstractions were beginning to seem passé. Or perhaps it was alcoholism, for Elmore was drinking more and more heavily. Or else he was drinking the same as always, yet had crossed that invisible line. It is hard to say just which of these three factors delivered the coup de grace.

We moved back to New York, set up house, studio, and nursery in the loft Dart now uses for his liaisons, and began the challenge of raising twins, managing twin careers, and battling the New York art world.

Suddenly I was the token woman artist of the moment, the exception that proved the rule, the flavor of the month. Vaginal art was in, and my forms—shells or bones, flowers or stones—seemed to be what everyone required. The fact that I had two beautiful twin daughters didn't hurt, either. Photographed like a double madonna in my studio before a fuchsia lily's painted lips, I represented the perfect image of the artist for that vaginal age. I blossomed and Elmore sulked. Less and less was his tongue felt on my clit or his cock on my buttocks.

Less and less did we sing "Our Love Is Here to Stay." More and more did we find excuses to go to dinner parties alone, to complain of each other to our friends, to snap at each other in the kitchen, in the bathroom, in the nursery.

Who can say why a marriage breaks down? The reasons for it are as ineffable as the reasons a couple is created in the first place. We live in a world in which all the rules of love and marriage have changed drastically and continue to change in ever-shortening cycles. Marriage used to be for the having and growing of children; now there are few marriages that can withstand the pressures of those events. Children are pesky interruptions to addiction and narcissism, the twin obsessions of our age. If one child is an interruption—imagine two! For the fact is that nature has made human beings too complex and too intelligent for their own good. We are creatures desperately in need of priorities in order to thrive, even survive, and in the modern age, our priorities have grown too murky. Love is too mutable a thing to live for. And art is too lonely. Love and art are sufficient. But when one artist is a woman and the other is a man, whose work shall come first? The male ego, the rush of testosterone, and most of society's rules dictate that the man must be central, or he will sulk. But what if, for the moment, the woman's work is in the ascendancy? And what if it is she who puts the food on the table as well as the tits into the babies' mouths? Can she also pretend, for his ego's sake, that she is *not* doing these things even as she continues to do them? Reader, I *tried.* But I could not maintain the illusion. When the babies were two, I had my most successful show ever, in the same year that Elmore had a fight with his dealer and left his gallery, and it was those twin events that delivered the coup de grace to the marriage.

Elmore moved out, leaving me with my success, the terrible twos times two (for Mike and Ed were not easy babies), the big brown standard poodle Boner (named for both Michelangelo Buonarroti and Rosa Bonheur), and the easy anodynes of gin, vodka, wine, and dope. For it was then that I began to get into trouble with drink and drugs.

I was alone with my babies and my work, and my sense of abandonment was fierce. I felt I had been punished for my success (and, in fact, I *had*). For the first time in my life, I found it hard to cope. In other words, for the first time in my life, I (who had thought myself exempt) submitted to the fate of most women: I began to feel like a victim.

How I hated that feeling! All my life, I had despised women who whined, women who cursed woman's lot, women who claimed to be through with love. I had never *called* myself a feminist. I abhorred the label. But motherhood had radicalized me in a strange new way. And abandonment with two female babies had opened up feelings so terrifying I did not know what to do with them. So I drank.

On the surface, life went on. My life was hardly destitute. I had a glorious loft, a house in the country, an assistant, a nanny. If I felt abandoned with this support system in place, imagine what other women must feel! A deep blow had been struck to the heart of my humanity. I had fulfilled my destiny as an artist and a woman, and to punish me for it, Elmore had left.

Let's be fair. Elmore had problems of his own. It should be a plank in the NOW platform that men turning fifty ought to be given special dispensation, and Elmore was already turning fifty-five. He worried a lot. His heart, his penis, his career, all were failing—and there was I, at thirty-six, on the top of the world (or so it seemed). He couldn't bear it, and neither, it seemed, could I.

So to make it all that much worse, we split. And we both drank more and more. And we both fucked around. And none of these things made us feel anything but worse (though this is all hindsight), and the little babies suffered from our selfishness, as little babies are wont.

I went through a number of lovers—younger, older, the same age—but nothing really stuck. I was seeking ecstasy, skinlessness. When the truth was that marriage to another artist is the greatest ecstasy of all, and I had lost it. I was mourning a death—the death of my sweet little family—and nothing could replace that. I bumped along for a few years, trying to do my work, trying to raise my little ones, with the increasing obstacle of alcohol (which I denied was an obstacle at all)—and I then met Dart.

Dart was not just a great lay; he was a knight on a white charger. He found me when my confidence was at its lowest, and he bucked me up. Fucked me up—or bucked me up: it's all the same, really, for what he gave me was nothing less than an infusion of life force, and he squirted it both out of his penis and out of his pores.

I loved him. How I loved him! The film stills were born of my love for him—and so were the cowboy canvases. For out of my adoration of this beautiful man I did what Rembrandt did for Saskia, what Wyeth did for Helga, what da Vinci did for Mona Lisa: I painted him (or photographed him) and made him famous as my muse.

The film stills were born of my love *and* my desire

to keep him near. When he was posing, at least he was *there*. His narcissism demanded it; my art demanded it—and they had found a place where they could fit together, every bit as well as our bodies did.

From the moment I met Dart, I was sketching him. He beguiled me so. I was fascinated with him, in the archaic sense of the word—enchantment—bound to him with magic, with rapture, with invisible ropes of allure.

From the sketches of him, I evolved the cowboy canvases—enormous mixed-media close-ups of Dart as the Lone Ranger, Dart as Roy Rogers, Dart as Gary Cooper in *High Noon*. I took these cultural icons of my childhood and superimposed this beautiful young man upon them. I hybridized this man born in the fifties with these images from my fifties childhood, and the passion with which I did this was lost on no one.

Of course not everyone loved these paintings. Some people hated them—a proof that they were *alive*. But the passion was undeniable—and passion is the key to art as it is the key to everything in life. Without it, people, paintings, plants, books, babies, die.

Dart had given me back the gift of life, and so I returned the favor. After the cowboy canvases were exhibited—and sold out almost instantly—I sought other ways to memorialize my lover, which is how I hit upon the film stills.

I had always been fascinated by photography, had not thought of it as a lesser art but as a manipulation of light upon the retina, containing every bit as much of its own integrity as oil painting or the carving of marble.

In art school, I had studied with a disciple of Moholy-Nagy, who had opened my eyes to the possibilities of photographs—silver bromide prints, gold-toned platinum prints, and the entire arsenal of photographic effects available to the artist who would see photography as art. I had tucked these lessons away in my brain for future reference—and now I remembered them in my passion to memorialize Dart.

Providing myself with an old-fashioned camera ca. 1910 (not unlike the one I had experimented with in my Yoko Ono days), I began photographing Dart in various costumes, which were metaphors for his multiple personalities: Arlecchino in motley; the Lone Ranger (again); rock star as heartthrob (with Elvis Presley pelvis thrust at the camera); fifties truckdriver in T-shirt, with beer can in hand; young WASP in black tie; St. Sebastian pierced by arrows; Hell's Angel in black leather; Jesus in a loincloth on the cross. I photographed him in my studio (where I could perfectly control the light and the background), and I printed in either platinum or silver, depending on the look I sought. The best prints were then blown up to the overlifesize C prints, like movie posters. This series, called simply "Film Stills of Dart/Trick Donegal," was even more successful than the cowboy canvases and made Dart, by my hand, a star.

The Pygmalion story has been told and retold many times—but never with the woman as artist and the man as Galatea! Eliza Doolittle becomes a lie-dy, but she is still, after all, a good girl ("I'm a good girl, I am"), and whether in Shaw's version (where she rebels against Higgins) or in Lerner and Loewe's, where she abandons Freddy Eynsford-Hill for the Rex Harrison daddy figure, she still winds up loyal to one man at the end—in short, toeing the mark for any female in society.

But what happens to Pygmalion when our creator is a woman and her creation is a man? Simple: the creation betrays the creator with as many nubile young groupies as possible.

It was not that Trick/Dart *wanted* to betray me. It was just that, having become a star through my loving re-creations of him, he was now besieged by young cuties. The sexuality I had found in him exuded from those C prints, from those cowboy canvases, and every spectator could feel it. Dart had become the property of the world, and everyone wanted to fuck him. It was my own damn fault. As an aficionado of Bessie Smith, I should have known enough to heed the advice she proffers in "Empty-Bed Blues."

> When you git good lovin'
> Never go and spread the news—
> Gals will double-cross you
> And leave you with them empty-bed blues. . . .

But I was hoist on my own petard: the artist in me was stronger than the woman. A fierce lover would have kept her beautiful man under wraps. A fierce artist instead made a star of him—and chaos ensued.

Art reshapes life even more than life shapes art. Imagine if Helga had walked off the covers of *Time* and *Newsweek* and into the arms of every young man who lusted for her? What would Wyeth have done? Gone mad? Taken to drink and drugs? But he was tended by women—both wived and modeled, cushioned, cosseted. And time, that great softener, had intervened. He had Helga (in whatever sense he had her), and he also had Mrs. Wyeth. Not so the fate of the woman artist. I had my twins, I had Dart, and now I had all these bimbos calling up and asking for Dart. It struck me as a wee bit unfair.

Well, I was strong, I thought. I would ride out the crises. Sexual infidelity was not the worst thing in the world. Let Dart fuck bimbos, as long as he always comes home to me. Or so I thought. This proved to be easier to say than to do.

Which brings us to the summer in question, in which Leila (I talk about myself in the third person only in jest— or in extreme crisis) is waiting by the phone for Dart to appear on his motorcycle. The twins are in California with their father (who is teaching at UCLA). And I am in Connecticut, trying to get together some paintings for a new show. But my concentration is utterly blasted—my muse has flown the coop. I tell myself the muse is within me and I should be able to work, but in reality all I do is listen for the sound of Dart's motorcycle on the gravel pathway, for the sound of the telephone announcing his arrival.

Connecticut is greenly beautiful, as only Connecticut can be—and I am utterly wretched. Alone with my dog in my studio-silo, without even Mike and Ed to distract me, all I can do is listen for the crushed gravel under Dart's motorcycle wheels, which seem to ride right over my heart.

4

PLAYING PENELOPE

———— ◆ ————

The meanest things he could say would thrill you through and through,
The meanest things he could say would thrill you through and through,
And there wasn't nothing too dirty for that man to do.

—Bessie Smith

Penelope knew this, loving Ulysses: years of waiting for a man to come home makes a woman mad.

I wait. I wait. And as I wait, I try to paint. Unable to paint, I drink. And having drunk, I plunge into despair. It is midnight on a Friday night when he comes back. He has been in the city one, two, or three days—I have lost track. I have gotten through the time talking to Emmie on the phone, which is where I am right now.

"He's back," I say, scratching Boner's belly with one bare toe. (The dog, mirroring my mood as dogs do, seems as depressed as I am.) "What do I do? And what do I do about the *guns*?"

"He has *guns*?" Emmie asks.

"Emmie," I say, "goyim have guns."

"Well, *I* don't," says Emmie.

"I never think of you as goyim," I say.

"Thanks," says Emmie, understanding the compliment. "Just promise me you'll tell him to take the guns out of the house. Okay?"

Strange, isn't it, the way all relationships unroll backward? When I met Dart nearly five years ago, he rode a motorcycle, which he abandoned for the blood-red Mercedes I bought him. Now, for some reason, he is using the motorcycle again and leaving the Mercedes (DART—his alter ego) in the garage. He is terribly guilty about something—even he who feels so little guilt, compared to real people.

The motorcycle stops with a roar and a put-put-putter, and I hear his boots on the gravel path.

I spray myself with Lumière, fluff my hair, and run to the door. I don't want him to see I've been on the phone with Emmie, whom he resents because he knows (all men know this instinctively) that we talk about him. That this talk is a matter of survival is something no man understands (or perhaps they do—and that's why they resent it: how dare we survive them?). All they know is that we have something they can't touch or enter: a sisterhood of shared affection, a safety net to catch us when they drop us and we fall.

"Baby," says Dart, taking off the Darth Vader helmet and grabbing my ass.

"Hello, darling," I say, looking up at him to be kissed. No "Where the hell have you been?" or "Why didn't you call me?" If a woman wants an animal like Dart, she has to be disciplined and clever, never betray jealousy, never show possessiveness.

Alas, this is impossible. Even women are only human.

No kiss is forthcoming. "Have you been working?" he asks, almost as though he knows he has blasted my concentration and is glad of it.

"Yes," I lie. "A new series of paintings."

"Of me?" he asks, greedy to be my muse even though he is no longer keeping his part of the bargain.

"Of course, darling."

"Are you lying?" he asks. "I feel you are lying. You know what happens when you lie, bad girl, don't you?"

"Yes," I say, very gamine, very excited.

"Come into the studio. I want to see what you've done."

And he strides out the back door, across the grass, and into my studio-silo, giving off a goatish whiff of black leather and dust of the road.

In my studio, all is chaos. Blank canvases stacked against the walls, rejected C prints from the film-stills show (on some of these I have doodled in acrylic, covering the photographic images with Warholesque scrawls), rejected canvases from the Cowboy show, one canvas of the twins for a double portrait entitled *Doppelgänger Daughters*, which I have abandoned as not good enough, and the usual self-portraits I begin when no other model comes to hand.

The chaos in my studio mirrors the chaos in my mind—a million things begun and nothing finished—a wild casting about to find inspiration in the past, in my children, in myself.

"So—you are lying," he says. "You know the punishment."

"I know," I say, growing very excited.

"Bend over the easel," he says, "and take down your jeans."

Isadora: I can't really believe that Leila would do this. After all, she's an artist, a heroine, a feminist. Why would she let this putz abuse her?

Leila: Love. Surely you remember love?

Isadora: What's love got to do with it?

Leila: Everything. This is a story about the fine line between love and self-annihilation. We're talking skinlessness here. Surely you yourself have sometimes sought it—or am I dreaming?

Isadora: I've read The Story of O, *but I'm not French enough to buy it.*

Leila: Wait.

He starts to unzip me, and I, anticipating this moment, have worn black lace bikini pants under my jeans. He tears the denims away from my behind but leaves the lace drawers in place. Then, extracting a black riding crop from one high black leather boot, he begins to sting my bottom teasingly, taking special pleasure from the fact that I am leaning over my own easel, on which is perched an unfinished portrait of myself.

The rain of leather hailstones on my buttocks excites me beyond my power to resist him. The humiliation is more mental than physical, since it is not so much the crop that is hurting me as it is my knowledge that he has been with another woman for however many days he has been gone. I urge him on with cries and apologies as he stings my rear. (I am apologizing to him for *his* fault—as women in love are wont.) As he whips me—first lightly, then harder and harder—my cunt begins to ache for him, heat for him, swell for him. Not a moment too soon does he pull me to the floor and cover me, black leather against black lace, cold metal zipper against warm white belly, and at last his hard pronged cock probing inside me, finding my center, finding his home.

"Witch," he hisses.

"My man, my fit, my mate," I moan.

I bite his ear, draw blood, bite his lip, growl, claw his back beneath the lipstick-stained white turtleneck he wears under his motorcycle jacket.

When he is deep within me, he stops, holds me very tight, bites my neck, draws blood, then starts moving in me again.

"My witch, my mate," he mutters, plunging into me again and again and again. And I see that contorted look his face gets just before he comes.

"Give me all of it, baby, all of it," I moan, and he comes inside me in a convulsion so strong it shakes the canvas above us.

"I love you, Leila."

"I know." I cup his head, like a baby's. And I do. I know I will always be his lady, his love, his Guinevere. But whether I can bear the pain of that, I do not know.

And a small part of me—the part that is still Louise Zandberg, perhaps, the part my analyst would call my sane mind—is standing off at a distance, saying, This must stop or I will not survive.

He stays with me all weekend. And it is a weekend as devilishly sweet as weekends were at the very start of our idyll. We spend hours in bed listening alternately to Mozart and Tom Waits, with the dog—now not so depressed—nestled at our feet. We cook together, take long walks—only to stop by a stream and fuck in the woods. We swim in a beautiful lake near my property. We picnic. We talk. We commune.

I am starting to unwind, to feel loved again, to feel that life is not so bad, that I can work again, feel again. The clenched fist of my mind begins to relax.

And just as that begins to happen, Dart picks it up with his warlocky sixth sense. He feels me opening to him, loving him, loving myself—and so he looks at the gold Rolex I bought him (we have just made tender love on the couch in the living room before an open fire, and it is ten o'clock on a Saturday night) and says, "Baby—I have to go."

Wrenched out of myself, whipped and whiplashed, I get up with him—my face as contorted with pain as his was at the moment of coming—and walk with him to the bathroom, where I watch him shave (admiring his own face through my eyes as I watch him), splash on Vetiver (a scent I introduced him to—which suits him), and gird his loins in black leather to leave me again.

I offer no protest. I am determined to open my hand to let him go, because I know that only if I do not hold him may he be drawn back of his own free will.

He is waiting for me to beg and plead with him, but I will not give him the satisfaction. He is waiting for me to ask him where he's going, but I will not. My jaw clenched, my brow knotted, I merely attend him in his toilette, helping him dress, knowing he will in all probability be undressed by somebody else.

All my considerable will and discipline is focused on letting him go, on not showing my pain (though how he could fail to see it, knowing me as he does, is a mystery to me). Boner howls in pain, as if on my behalf. "Shh, puppy," says Dart, nuzzling him as I wish he would nuzzle me.

I watch Dart dress in black leather jeans with no underwear. ("I hate underwear—the restriction of it," he once told me. Oh, beware of men who wear no underwear—your mother warned you about men like that!) I watch him pull on a black silk turtleneck (he has left the lipstick-stained white one for me to wash). And I focus on my own courage in not restraining him. Sometimes the hardest thing in the world is to let somebody go.

At the last possible moment, when he is kissing me goodbye and donning the helmet, some imp inside me, some creature not of my own making, some dybbuk possessing me, blurts out: "But if I need you, where can I find you?" The words are no sooner out than I regret them, than I long to take them back, than I despair like one of the wretched in Dante's *Inferno,* endlessly replaying the fatal act.

And he turns to me and nearly spits out these words: "You didn't expect that after you threw me out you'd be able to find me!" And he is off, revving up the motorcycle and taking off for New York—or wherever—again.

I pour myself another glass of wine and call Emmie. I have forgotten even to *mention* the guns.

My best friend, Emily Quinn, has been saving my life for more years than I like to remember. The product of convent schools and an upper-class childhood in Manhattan and Virginia, she now earns her living as a writer of nonfiction books on trendy subjects. *Joy of Woman* made her rich in the seventies. A meticulously researched biography of Victoria Woodhull made her respected in the eighties; and now she is writing the first no-holds-barred book on menopause for the nineties.

"Did you ever think we'd live to see *menopausal chic?*" she asked me a couple of days—it now seems a couple of years—ago.

"We're going to live long enough to see *everything*," I told her. Now I'm not so sure. Dart's departure has devastated me in a new way. I thought I was a survivor—to use that much overused word. Tonight I wonder.

Emmie is tough but soothing; she is walking me through this parting from Dart with infinite tenderness. As I ring her phone, I imagine Emmie with her shoulder-length auburn hair crowned with a black velvet bow, her astounding cheekbones, her slender waist and lovely high bosom. She looks the way everyone should look at fifty. Serene, wise, willowy, clear-eyed, just crinkly enough to be womanly—and infinitely kind. Emmie has a will of iron. She is also funny. We often say we are laughing our way toward the apocalypse. At seventy, we both expect to be working, giggling, and getting laid.

But Emmie is not home tonight, writing, as she so often is on Saturday nights. (Emmie has a married lover in Paris, a Greek shipping tycoon who sails into New York Harbor just often enough to keep her happy and goes away just often enough to let her write—a new arrangement not entirely unpleasing to the working woman of the fin de siècle.)

The phone rings and rings. At last it clicks, and Emmie's answering machine picks up.

A blast of Bach and then: "You have reached 798-2727. Please leave a message after the dumb little beep."

"Help!" I scream into the phone, and then, as an afterthought: "I'm in Connecticut!" I hang up the phone.

The exquisite cruelty of Dart's leaving on a Saturday night is not lost on me. Nor is the cruelty of his fucking me, cosseting me, and then disappearing. I think of all the crises we have endured in the last six months—and it is clear to me that I will have to break with Dart and break completely if I am to survive. The pain is too great. Every time I accept some behavior of his—last week I received credit card bills for a hotel he stayed in with another girl; the week before, pictures of some trashy little blonde who looked like a waitress in a B-movie diner; the week before that, love letters from a redhead who used to work at the gallery—he ups the ante. I know it is his own sense of inadequacy—always the model, never the artist—that leads him to these excesses. I know that in his own way he loves me. But that isn't any longer enough. I have to love myself. The good ship Leila must sail on, and how can it sail, with this pirate down in the hold punching holes in the hull? Between forgiveness and self-protection, where does one draw the line? I wish I had a penny for every woman in love who has ever asked that question.

Alone with the silent telephone, my bottle, my dog, and my chaos of a studio, I collapse. I seem to lose control of the rest of my life. All my success is worth nothing beside this devastation. Children pull you out of it—and my children are not even here.

I think of Dart: he is his own finest creation. If he cannot paint and sculpt, it is because all his artistic ability has gone into the creation of his own persona, a not inconsiderable feat. He is always inventing him*self*—how can he invent mere paintings? An artist must be a funnel from the muse into matter. Dart is both muse himself and self-creation. I merely photographed what I saw. Protean, changing—now the Lone Ranger, now Harlequin, now

Elvis Presley—Dart was infinitely inspiring, infinitely bewitching, infinitely alluring. It was not just his cock—it was his fantasy. And the way it locked into my fantasy. The best lovers know how to use their fantasies as well as their cocks. The former being rarer than the latter.

I collapse in my bed with all the lights on—the bed so lately anointed by Dart. I think of all the cruel things he has done lately, the lies—useless lies about small things and big lies about big things. I think of seeing his motorcycle parked at the railroad station on a day he said he was going to a neighbor's to help paint her house. I think of all the time I answered the phone, only to hear the caller listen to my voice, then hang up. I think of the photos of other women left around, the bills, the love letters, the credit card charges. Dart turns thirty next weekend. Will all this stop—or has it only just begun? Shall I wait it out or shall I change the locks and give him the boot? Who can advise me—who but the voice within myself?

This is the voice that Sybille, my shrink, calls the voice of my sane mind. "But in your sane mind, what do you think?" she always asks. And I know precisely what she means. She means the voice of that fierce advocate within myself, the sane, centered part of me that is on my *own* side, that shining nugget of self-love surrounded by fathomless darkness. I listen in vain for the voice of my sane mind—but I can hear it only intermittently, through the static of obsession.

I crawl into my big disheveled bed and pull up the covers. Boner settles in at my feet and heaves a big, doggy sigh. My bed is my sanctuary. A monument to passion and celibacy both. It's a white-lacquered antique iron bedstead with curlicues of steel and brass, covered with a brilliant Amish quilt emblazoned with a kaleidoscopic star, festooned with pillows of all sizes covered in antique cream and white lace.

I feel *safe* in this bed. Climbing into it, I often think, She took to her bed, and I understand perfectly the sense of refuge in that phrase. Outside the big picture window (punched into this seventeenth-century wall) is dreamy green Connecticut, now shrouded in darkness. In my mind's eye I see its mammary humps of hills, its red barns, its silver silos, nestled below the golden gibbous moon half-veiled by scudding clouds.

I love this state. I feel safe and mothered in these hills. I love to work here: far enough from Monster Gotham not to hear its mental static, near enough to catch its lightning charge. But then I am a sucker for gentle mammary hills—whether in Tuscany or Litchfield County, Umbria or the Veneto. The only thing I like better is the sea. The Mediterranean, the Pacific, the Atlantic, the Aegean, the Caribbean—any sea will do.

The sea, the sea. Dart and I used to dream of sailing in the "sugar isles," as the eighteenth-century pirates called them. We loved the Caribbean, and at the height of our idyll would often run away to Barbados, Jamaica, Tortola, Saint Kitts, or Saint Barts. Dart taught me to swim in Jamaica, off a white sandy beach near Port Antonio. In Tortola he taught me to sail and snorkel. When I think of him I still see him swimming like a blond merman—a big tall blond WASP (raised on tennis and swimming and shooting) teaching a little flame-haired Jewish girl (raised on physical cowardice) how not to wince at hammerhead sharks, how to be physically brave, how to treat nature as your friend and the sea as your natural element; how to expand in the water rather than contract in fear.

He taught me a lot. He gave me a lot. It was not an

uneven exchange. I gave him gifts, made him a star, but he also gave me gifts—chief among them bringing me back from the dead. Lovers give each other life. That is what makes love so irresistible—no matter what the killjoys say. Who can resist the one who makes you feel alive? Who can resist salt and sperm and sea and shakti? For love is nothing less than the gift of life. (Though sometimes you have to pay for it with your death.) And if artists love so often and so hard, it is because they have a rage to live.

I drink my wine and weep. The loss of Dart seems deep, abysmal, fatal. If I had the number of the little waitress, I would call, humiliate myself, offer him anything to come back. Thank God, I don't have her number.

I get up and put on Bessie Smith. As she belts out blues after blues, I cry myself to sleep with all the lights on.

> Yes I'm mad
> and have a right to be
> after what my Daddy did to me.
> I lavished all my love on him.
> But I swear I'll never love again.
> All you women understand
> what it is to be
> in love with a two-time man.
> The next time he calls me sweet mama in
> his lovin' way
> This is what I'm going to say:
> I used to be your sweet mama, sweet papa—
> but now I'm just as sour as can be. . . .

5

THE LAND OF FUCK
(OR, ANY WOMAN'S BLUES)

◆

Good morning blues, blues how do you do?
Well I just come here to have a few words with you.

—Bessie Smith and Clarence Williams

I am back at Yale—or somehow it is a cross between Yale and Music and Art. High above the park at Convent Avenue someone has built a cage that stands upon crossed steel girders like the old Third Avenue el, which thundered past Bloomingdale's when I was a child. There, up in the sky, is a special cagelike room where lovers meet when they wish to enter The Land of Fuck.

I have gone there—cutting all sorts of classes, risking losing my credits for the year—and when I arrive, the first thing I do is pull the blinds—venetian blinds they are: what other kind of blinds would The Land of Fuck have?

In a state of high excitement, I wait for my lover—Dart—to arrive.

In the dream, I am wet, throbbing, terribly excited. I know somehow that my whole life depends upon this meeting.

He arrives, dressed not in black leather but in white silk. He really *is* Elvis Presley and not Dart—dark hair, a pudgy, bloated face, a pair of Kewpie doll's lips, which open and shut mechanically like plastic Dr. Dentons. Maybe he really *is* a giant Kewpie doll and not a person. And yet I want him—how I want him! I am unzipping the white silk jeans, unbuttoning the white silk cowboy shirt, holding him, stroking him, murmuring words of encouragement and love. And then, as I open the fly of his satin jeans, I see that in place of a penis he has a deep gash, which is crawling with earthworms, slugs, snails. Disgusted—yet also oddly aroused—I try to rezip his fly, but I cannot. The worms and slugs are wriggling out. One snail is making its slow, slime-trailed way down a shiny white trouser leg. Earthworms are beheaded by the zipper I tug. I look up at Dart's face and see that the Kewpie doll face has peeled away. Beneath it is blankness—white blankness. Featureless eyes, nose, mouth, like a wooden doll's head washed clean by the sea.

Bitterly disappointed, I push the doll-man aside and look for the way out of The Land of Fuck. There is no door. Just this cage high above the city—New York? New Haven?—where I am trapped forever. I hear my mother's voice saying: "Louise, you always think the rules that apply to other people don't apply to you!" And my sane mind is nowhere in sight.

I wake up in greenly docile and benign Connecticut, with all the shades up and the lights and the stereo on.

Outside my picture window, poplars and hemlocks sway. Below my hilltop are the red barns and silver silos of halcyon Litchfield County. I am in my white iron bed, sailing through the cosmos as in an iron ship, but the aftertaste of the dream will not go away.

I stretch out in the middle of the bed and let the dream take me again. Now the images are starting to unravel, like the woolen sleeves of a sweater let slip from the circular knitting needles. I try to crawl back inside the dream, if only to understand it—but the dream is gone. I am alone in my bed in the green hills of Connecticut, and where Dart is, God alone knows.

I imagine my bed as an intergalactic starship. In this white iron bed, in this white clapboard house, I am sailing through the universe. Below me, stars are twinkling in black space. All around me, on asteroids, are the people who have touched my life: my twins, waving like two little princesses drawn by Saint-Exupéry; my mother, Theda, waving from her intergalactic funny farm; my father, making origami birds to sail off across space to the twins (the twins he never saw, yet of course *sees*). Snack, Thom, Elmore, Dart—each waving from his own asteroid. Emily planting a rose garden on her asteroid and praising the astounding energy of postmenopausal women.

The earth, I see, is a tiny spore hurtling through deep space. From my vantage point in the intergalactic bed—which has now left the earth and is sailing effortlessly through the cosmos alone, with me in it—I see not only the smallness of the earth but its astonishing vulnerability. Earth, moon, and stars all can be snuffed in a second by a whiff of cosmic breath. And I in my bed hurtling through space-time, with only a dog to comfort me. Solitude is the final abode, some wise old roshi said. And yet it is a populous solitude, a solitude peopled by both ghosts and flesh. From my bed I wave to everyone I've ever loved. This vision soothes me. I stagger up and out of bed, let out Boner, and rub my eyes.

Off to the kitchen—with a pit stop at the stereo system to put on another Bessie Smith record, *Any Woman's Blues*. As Bessie sings "My Sweetie Went Away," I clatter my pots and pans, making coffee, starting a pot of oatmeal for myself that I don't really feel like eating.

> My sweetie went away,
> but he didn't say where,
> he didn't say when,
> he didn't say why,
> or bid me goodbye—
> I'm blue as I can be. . . .
> I know he loves another one
> but he didn't say who. . . .
> I know I'll die.
> Why don't he hurry home?

Listening to Bessie Smith makes it all seem so simple. The voice of female pain predicting male unpredictability, declaring in song that nothing between men and women is new under the sun. You think your heart is breaking, you think no one has ever felt this way before? Well, here's Bessie to remind you that millions of women—black, white, yellow, and brown—have cried this way before you, have turned these griefs into rich, resonant song. Does it comfort me? Not much.

In the kitchen, on the counter, is an array of empty bottles that strike terror into my heart. Did I drink all these bottles of Pomerol, Meursault, Pinot Grigio? It hardly seems possible. Surely Dart and I drank them together. But the pounding in my head and the dryness in my mouth convince me I must have had a little something to do with these empty bottles. My head throbs, my coordination is none too good. I drink my coffee as if it were the elixir of life, then stumble into the bathroom to brush my teeth. On the way, I slosh the coffee over the oak floorboards, almost slip on it, kneel down to mop it up with my bathrobe, and carry on.

I confront my face in the bathroom mirror. I don't like what I see. My face is full of pain, rings under my eyes, mouth pouty and sad, cheeks puffy and white. My face is the mirror of my life; more even than most faces, it conceals nothing. This is the face of a woman in deep trouble.

Always, I have looked ten years younger than my chronological age—but now I wonder. I seem to look ten years older. Whatever this man is doing to me, it is not making me more beautiful.

My face is like my palette. I know every inch of it—every enlarged pore, every birthmark, every sag of skin, every discoloration. My once hazel-green eyes have dulled to mud. My titian curls are nondescript wisps on my once rosy cheeks. I open my bathrobe and check my body. Even my breasts are defeated and seem to sag. The big pink nipples loved and praised by all my men, from Snack to Dart, appear to have shrunk in defeat. And my caesarean scar, now faded to a pale zipper of flesh above my reddish bush, is angry and inflamed again. I turn around to see red welts on my buttocks. My heart lurches in my chest. How did I get these? I have no recollection.

A burning smell reaches my nostrils. I run to the kitchen and find the oatmeal pot smoking and burning on the stove. An acrid odor of burnt cereal fills my nose. I turn off the stove and clatter the oatmeal pot into the sink. It hisses evilly. I run cold water into the pot and a cloud of oatmeal smoke assaults my nose. Who wanted oatmeal anyway?

The phone rings.

"Hey, what's up?" It's Emmie (who, for the moment, is as close as I can come to the voice of my sane mind).

"I burned the fucking oatmeal," I say.

"What happened with Dart last night?"

"He left. First he got me all relaxed and gooey and warm and open to him, and then he left—the bastard. I'd like to cut his cock off and stuff it in his mouth. I'd like to kill him—kill all of them. They're Martians. They can't just fuck us. They have to open us up, make us love them, fuck us, and *then* they leave. I'm ready to join the Lesbian Commune. C'mon, Emmie—want to be my girl?" (The Lesbian Commune is an old joke with us. It's where we're heading when we finally give up on men. Soon, in short.)

"Wait a minute. Back up. Tell me what really happened."

And I try, I patiently try to explain all that happened with me and Dart between his arrival and his departure. I tell her everything, leaving out only the red welts on the buttocks and the parade of empty bottles. Leaving out everything, in short.

"So how did you feel when you got up this morning?" she asks.

"Why?"

"Just tell me."

"I woke up in a panic, after having these terrible dreams. The first thing I felt was despair—my whole life seemed mad, crazed, out of control. I felt suicidal. Then I began to pull myself together, and I had visions of myself floating through the cosmos in my bed. . . ." I start to cry. "Emmie, I can't live like this anymore. I can't stand it. Everything is *pain, pain, pain.*"

"Why, do you suppose?"

"Because life is pain, pain, pain."

"And wonderful. A gift. A blessing."

"Don't feed me that simple Pollyanna shit—"

"It's simple, but it isn't shit. You can *choose* how you see your life. Whether you live in Eeyore's gloomy place or in sunshine. Whose choice is it if not yours? What other reason for this passage than joy?"

"Crap."

"Do you know why people love your work? Because of the joy, the life force that comes through—"

"What work? I can't work, I don't work. All I do is sit here and think about Dart. And drink."

"Leila, do you want to stop? Is that what this is about? Do you really want to stop and get your life back?"

"Yes."

"Think about it. There's no law that says you have to get your life back. You can go on the way you're going. You can kill yourself if you want to. I'd miss you—but you have that right. You can leave your twins the legacy of another suicidal woman artist, or you can do something different."

"How?"

"Will you let me show you how? Will you trust me?"

"What choice do I have? I can't stay *here.*"

"Then wait for me. I'm driving right up."

Waiting for Emmie, I drink a whole bottle of Pinot Grigio. At first it relaxes me and makes me feel calm and spacey while I listen to Bessie Smith, but then, when the blurry feeling gives way to a pounding headache, I begin to think of ways to do myself in. I could open my veins in the bathtub—all that red blood marbleizing the clear water. I could do a film-still self-portrait as my life ebbs away. Set the camera on time exposure, get in the tub, and . . . When they came for me, they'd find not only my dead body but a photographic record of the very act that had killed me. Talk about postmodernist images! Or I could puncture my veins and smear the fresh blood all over a canvas. *Dart Gone,* I'd call it. Or I could open the oven, turn on the gas, and do a Sylvia Plath. (But I have an electric oven!) Or wrap myself in Theda's old mink coat (the one I've kept in the coat closet since my mother died), climb into the oxblood Mercedes called DART, and inhale the carbon monoxide fumes à la Anne Sexton (but the Mercedes is a convertible, so the carbon monoxide might escape!).

As the wine wears off, I dose myself with Valium and aspirin. Then I scrounge around under the bed for the bag of dope I saw Dart rolling cigarettes from last night before he left. Goddamn it—he's even taken the dope.

"The bastard even took the dope!" I scream.

Sighting a barely smokable roach under the bed, I flatten myself on the oaken floorboards to reach it, but it just eludes the tips of my raggedy fingernails. Finally I skewer it with my index finger and pull myself up. I begin searching for a match, ransacking the house from living room fireplace to kitchen wood stove. There's no incendiary gear but me! I stomp about the house, cursing, unable to find a match, a lighter, anything—and the phone rings.

Dart! Dart wants to come back. He loves me. He's sorry. He's been with some little bimbo, and he misses me terribly. He realizes my true worth. I race to the phone. Perhaps it's the voice of my sane mind.

"Ms. Sand?" An unfamiliar voice.

"Yes?"

"Ms. Sand, my name is Wesley Hunnicutt, and I represent the Paugussett Memorial Gardens of Paugussett, Connecticut—"

"The *what?*"

"The Paugussett Memorial Gardens. We are contacting all the home owners in this county because we have a unique opportunity for the purchase of burial plots we'd like to make you aware of—"

"The purchase of *what?*"

"Of burial plots for you and your nearest and dearest."

"Where did you get my name?"

"As a home owner in the town of Roxbury, your name is available at the town hall. If you'll give me a moment of your—"

"A burial plot!"

"Well, we like to think of it as an investment in your peace of mind, a slice of serenity."

I slam down the phone.

And fall on the floor sobbing, my cheek to the warm wood of the floorboards where Dart and I have so often made love. Boner comes up and licks my face. I think of the hooded man in *Amadeus* who came to Mozart to commission his Requiem, predicting his death. That is what has just happened to *me*. Death has made an appointment. (And he didn't say when he'd be back.)

I bang my forehead on the floor like an autistic child. I bang until it's bloody, feeling no pain. Finally the pain begins and with it some new twinge of consciousness.

"God," I say aloud, "I don't want to die. I want my life back. Please, God, give me my life back."

I am still kneeling on the foyer floor, with my forehead caked with blood and the dog lying beside me, when, two hours later, Emmie opens the front door and walks in.

Isadora: You certainly have made Leila a hopeless case. Everyone will think she's me. Everyone will say I beat my head on the floor and did S&M and abased myself for some twerp. I was never that bad. Why are you making her so pathetic?

Leila: Every woman has that potential.

Isadora: Not me. Not you.

Leila: Your memory is very selective. Haven't you beat your head on the floor?

Isadora: Never.

Leila: And drunk yourself into oblivion?

Isadora: Well—once or twice.

Leila: And succumbed to drink, drugs, cock?

Isadora: That word again. I never want you to use that word again.

Leila: Prick? Shall I go on with my pricksongs?

Isadora: Does what I say really matter? You are my creature, but like my child, you seem to have taken on a life of your own.

Leila: And wasn't that what you wanted?

Isadora (sighing): We little know the things for which we pray.

6

EXPERIENCE, STRENGTH, HOPE

———————— ◆ ————————

Gimme a reefer and a gang o' gin.
Slay me, 'cause I'm in my sin.
Slay me, 'cause I'm full of gin.

—*Wesley Wilson*

And that was how I got to my first AA meeting.

Imagine a little white Greek Revival church in rural Connecticut with no one going in the front door and all these people going in the back. (Ah, the return to church through the back door!) My plumber, Mr. Raffella, is one of them; a wizened, gray-bearded artist from New Milford whom I met once at a dinner party (and whose name I don't remember); the local lady librarian; some raggedy teenagers and some scrubbed and shining ones; an old black man with five or six teeth; a number of solid-looking burghers, housewives, and other Connecticut swamp Yankees in their Top-Siders, corduroys, and madras shirts. *Why am I shaking?*

Emmie leads me into the church-basement rec room as if I were a two-year-old being taken to my first day at play group. The room is intensely smoky and intensely friendly. People sit on folding chairs or stand near the lone table, drinking coffee, chain-smoking, eating cookies, hugging each other, talking among themselves. My first impulse is to bolt. *What the hell am I doing here?*

My plumber nods his head and says, "Welcome." I'm too flustered to respond. Neither Miss Manners nor her opposite, my mother, taught me what to say when your plumber greets you at a meeting of Alcoholics Anonymous. Emmie takes me to the coffee urn, makes me coffee with lots of milk and sugar, leads me to a chair near the front of the room.

"How did you know this meeting was here? You're not even *from* Connecticut."

"There's a meeting book."

"You're so fucking efficient," I say.

She looks at me and smiles. Gently. "I was absolutely terrified the first time I came. We all are."

"What do I have to do?"

"Nothing."

"You know that's the hardest thing in the world for me to do."

"That's why I brought you here. If you hate it, you don't have to come back."

"Ever?"

Emmie laughs.

On the walls of the rec room are signs lettered on little oak-tag panels. "EGO=Easing God Out." "First Things First." "Think." (That one is upside down.) "Easy Does It." Platitudes. Don't these people speak English? There are also two enormous scrolls. One is headed "The

Twelve Steps." The other is headed "The Twelve Traditions." The first line of the twelve steps reads: "We admitted we were powerless over alcohol—that our lives had become unmanageable." I read no further.

"What are the steps *to?*" I ask Emmie.

"Your own mountain," she says. "Whatever you call it."

"Mount Leila," I say.

"Is that a noun or a verb?"

"A verb," I say flippantly, to cover my terror.

I hate the jargon. I want desperately to leave.

"I don't belong here," I say to Emmie.

"Try editing the first step: 'I discovered that I was powerless over Dart, that my life had become unmanageable.' Then listen and see if you like what you hear."

I look up at the first step, substituting "Dart" for "alcohol." My life is nothing if not unmanageable. My life is . . . I begin to cry. Nobody seems to notice, except for one woman who comes over and hugs me. "You're in the right place," she says, and gives me her phone number on a little slip of yellow paper. Having entered a world in which kindness seems the rule, not the exception, I want to leave.

The meeting begins.

After someone makes announcements and reads a preamble full of words like "strength," "hope," "fellowship," and "sobriety," a woman, introduced as Fleur from Boston, gets up and begins to speak.

I decide that Fleur-from-Boston, a small, frightened-looking soul in her mid-forties, would be perfectly cast as Blanche DuBois in an amateur production of *Streetcar*. She has wispy brownish hair, a faraway gaze in her greenish eyes, and a birdlike scrawniness that seems almost brittle.

Her wrists are so frail, you feel that a mere touch could snap them.

"It is said," she begins, in a strong Back Bay accent, "that alcoholics deform the lives of the people around them. I never fell in love with a man who wasn't an alcoholic, and I seldom drank except in connection with the men in my life. They drank, so I drank. I drank not to drink, you see, but for love."

The last thing I want to hear is the story of a woman who gets free from love. I am terrified—not that the program will fail me but that it might possibly succeed. I hate all the mellowness and security in this room. I want the roaring back: the roaring inside.

"I woke up in a lot of beds without knowing how I got there, and I looked over at a lot of snoring men whose names I didn't know," says Fleur. "At first they were men I went to school with, men whose families I knew, men whose parents went to my church, but eventually they were men who hadn't gone to school at all, who no longer had families or mothers, and had never even *been* to church."

Is this where *my* life will take me—to a church basement, listening to platitudes? I'm an artist. My life has *never* been like other people's. Even now I am in Dubrovnik with Dart, skidding down a cobbled street in the Zastava. It's midnight. July. We can't find a hotel. We have been drinking local wine by the bottleful all day—and when the car spins out of control on a nearly vertical street, we narrowly miss the massive wall of a fortress. I scream. "A miss is as good as a mile, baby," says Dart.

"When the police came and found my little girl," Fleur says, "I was passed out in the bedroom. . . ."

A child has died while I was in Dubrovnik with Dart.

A little girl. I have *two* little girls. I *try* to listen but cannot actually focus on Fleur's words.

Instead I look at the scroll entitled "The Twelve Steps."

1. We admitted we were powerless over alcohol—that our lives had become unmanageable.
2. Came to believe that a Power greater than ourselves could restore us to sanity.
3. Made a decision to turn our will and our lives over to the care of God *as we understood Him.*

Perhaps "God" is really the sane mind, I think.

"My other child was taken from me and put in a foster home," says Fleur. "I was sent to jail, where I tried three times to take my own life and was confined in a psychiatric prison hospital before I finally got sober and began to change my life."

Give me a break, I think, the tears running down my face.

"Why me? I would cry out to God—and why my daughter? For years I could find no satisfactory answer. Drunk, I took strangers into my home. I could just as easily have killed my children and myself in an automobile accident or a fire or shot them by mistake with the gun I kept to repel intruders—intruders I invited into my own home with love as the excuse."

I want to tune out Fleur's story as much as I want to hear it. I am restless, raging—and oddly riveted. Between snatches of Fleur's story and dreams of Dart, I'm trembling and fidgeting. I get up and grab a fistful of cookies, then go back to my folding chair.

4. Made a searching and fearless moral inventory of ourselves.

5. Admitted to God, to ourselves, and to another human being the exact nature of our wrongs.

6. Were entirely ready to have God remove all these defects of character.

There follows a long, tedious account of the steps in Fleur's recovery, a recovery that includes her fight to recover her remaining child—a son named, believe it or not, Donegal. Fleur has been "sober" for a decade now. The daughter she lost would now be nineteen. She works in a children's hospital for minimum wage and takes "special pleasure" in caring for teenage girls. She reports having given up sex for at least seven of the ten years she has been sober—give me a break!—but recently she has "met a man who loves me for what I have endured and the peace I have found." He has brought another daughter to her, in whom she sees a chance to "unwork her karma."

Jesus, I hate Pollyannas. And the worst is yet to come.

"Because of the Program," Fleur says, "I am glad to be alive. I begin every day asking God for guidance and go to sleep every night thanking Him. My special work at the hospital is to counsel adolescent girls. I try to help them see that love includes the power to love yourself, and that each of them has a garden inside her, that they do not have to have men in order to validate their existence. I feel that even in these supposedly feminist times, girls do not know this. They think they are nothing without a man, and they sacrifice themselves on the altar of romantic love, sexual love—forgetting God, forgetting divine love, forgetting everything but the blind need to be validated by the attention of a man. They look everywhere for a love object, in short, when the worthiest object of love is right there—in themselves."

"Let's get the fuck out of here," I say to Emmie.

"Soon," says Emmie.

"After all my suicide attempts," says Fleur, "I discovered that I could make my little girl's death mean something only by staying on after her and giving my life to the service of other girls. And I have found in this work an enduring joy—and pain—that has transformed everything I thought I knew before. I don't know why God chose to send me such a bitter lesson, but perhaps I drew it to myself with my extreme stubbornness. For I believe that we ourselves fashion our lessons according to our own needs."

Stunned silence greets her speech. Then, slowly, the room begins to come to life. One by one, people stand up and applaud and hug Fleur.

There is a five-minute recess for coffee before the sharing begins.

"Are all the meetings like this?" I whisper.

Emmie laughs. "None are. This one was sent especially for you. The Program is like Mary Poppins's elixir: it becomes the specific medicine for whatever ails you. You asked for a cure for sex addiction? You got it."

"The last thing I want is to be cured," I say.

"I know," says Emmie. "Fighting being cured is the first step in being cured."

"Do I have to talk?"

"Only if you want to feel better."

During most of the sharing, I sniffle and study the steps.

7. Humbly asked Him to remove our shortcomings.

8. Made a list of all persons we had harmed, and became willing to make amends to them all.

9. Made direct amends to such people wherever possible, except when to do so would injure them or others.

10. Continued to take personal inventory and when we were wrong promptly admitted it.

11. Sought through prayer and meditation to improve our conscious contact with God *as we understood Him*, praying only for knowledge of His will for us and the power to carry that out.

12. Having had a spiritual awakening as the result of these steps, we tried to carry this message to alcoholics, and to practice these principles in all our affairs.

At the end, after a basket is passed and just before the meeting is adjourned, Fleur calls on me.

"The lady with the red hair," she says, pointing at me.

I look at Emmie for guidance. Perhaps the speaker is really calling on her.

She shrugs.

"I'm Leila," I say. "I haven't had a drink in an hour."

"Welcome," says Fleur. "It works if you work it."

Nearly everyone in the room turns and begins to clap for me, as if I were a heroine.

After the meeting, people linger over coffee and cookies. Several women come up to me, proffering phone numbers. I take all the little slips of paper and tuck them into my Filofax, planning to throw them away when I get home. If I take them, at least I can get out of here.

Driving me back to my house in her old silver Volvo station wagon, Emmie says, "Do you know I didn't speak at all at meetings for the first year? I just sat in the back and *lurked*."

"I *had* to say something. I don't even know why. Most of the time, I wasn't listening. I was staring at 'The Twelve Steps' and thinking how much they resemble 'The Rules of Love.' "

"What are 'The Rules of Love'?"

" 'The Rules of Love' of the Provençal poets are nothing less than a complete codification of love. They were written *centuries* ago. And nothing whatsoever has changed."

"So what did you think of the meeting?" asks Emmie.

"Boring," I say. "There should be a stronger word: *boringissimo*."

"I know what you mean. Some meetings seem so boring you think you could die. And the smoke gets to you. And the platitudes—an attitude of platitude, I call it. And yet it *works*. As they say, it works if you work it. I don't even know *why* it works. Grace, I guess."

"How long have you been doing this, Emmie? And why didn't you ever tell me?"

"You never asked."

"But you could have *told* me."

"Why? If drinking and drugging were still fun for you, why would you *want* to know? You didn't want to know, in fact, or *you* would have asked."

"How long have you been a member?"

"About a decade. I got into it in Paris, when I lived on the Boulevard Raspail. You remember, my orgy period in Paris? Ah, the sixties turning seventies . . . before the drugs turned on us."

Emmie had lived in Paris from 1969 to 1979, a good time to live in Paris. She had written her first book there—a book about sexual liberation for women, which was, in fact, about her own liberation. In Paris she had belonged to an orgy set that included everyone who was anyone in the intellectual and film worlds, doing drugs and sex and rock and roll to a fare-thee-well. The perfect way for a convent girl to spend the seventies. Since I was living another life at the time—first with Thom, then with Elmore, then with Elmore and the twins—I saw her only on my infrequent trips to Paris. I never knew she'd been addicted to anything but sex and chocolate. (Her emergency supply ran to ten-inch Toblerones.) She certainly did not fit my—or anyone else's—description of an alcoholic.

"So you got sober without telling me. Did you know I had a problem?"

"I knew you thought you could control everything in your life. Which, in itself, is a problem, since we can't."

"Do you think I'm an alcoholic?"

"What *I* think doesn't matter. Do *you* think you are? This is one of the few great diseases that's self-diagnosed— like love. It doesn't matter what I—or anyone else—think. Maybe you're just a garden-variety love addict and you just drink with men. *I* don't know. I do know the Program saved *my* life."

"Oh, come on, Emmie, that's a cop-out."

"No it's not. The truth is that I never have *seen* you falling-down drunk, and the truth is that you stumble through your life reasonably enough, taking care of everyone—including me—but you seem not to be having much fun. Here you are with those beautiful twins, the meteoric career, all that intelligence and wit and vitality—and you're ready to throw in the towel because of a very damaged young man."

"A what?"

"A Dart."

"But I *love* Dart. I've never felt—"

"I know how much you love Dart. How much do you love *Leila*?"

Stung by the question, I answer it.

"Not much."

"Then something is drastically wrong. Because Leila is lovable."

"*Is* she?" I ask, leaking tears. "Is she *really*?"

"Oh, darling, why on earth do you think I've been here all this time—because you're not lovable? Even with all your craziness, what you call your *mishegoss*, you're the best person I know. You give and give and give. To everyone. Except Leila. Now it's her turn."

"But am I an *alcoholic*?"

"I don't know," says Emmie. "Ask yourself, don't ask me."

We ramble through green Connecticut, buying things. Bunches of flowers. Tomatoes. Garlic. Pasta. Then we go back to my house and start cooking.

We make fresh tomato sauce for the pasta, and grill swordfish steaks and ears of corn. Puttering in the kitchen and at the outdoor grill, we are absurdly happy.

"At five o'clock," Emmie says, "we'll have muffins and tea with honey."

"I'm going to get fat as a pig."

"I doubt it," says Emmie.

For an hour or so, sitting with Emmie and the dog in the early summer green of sweet Connecticut, I am at peace. After lunch, we lie on my hillside and watch the clouds go by, naming them according to the animals and birds they resemble. Something seems drastically wrong, missing.

"Dart—I wonder when I'll hear from Dart."

"Never, I hope. But I doubt he can stay away."

"How can you say that?"

"Leila, you need Dart like a fish needs a bicycle. Dart needs you far more than you need him."

"If he needs me so much, where *is* he?"

"Off provoking you. If you stopped being provoked, *he'd* be the one going crazy. It's a dance you're doing. You need to be on the hook, and he needs to hook you."

"What about sex?"

"What *about* it?"

"I never had sex that good with anyone. The truth is, if I start feeling this good about myself, I won't let Dart knock me around anymore, and if I don't let Dart knock me around, he won't fuck me. . . ."

"You said it—I didn't."

"I don't think it's *possible* to have great sex without domination and abuse—it's built *in* somehow. When we adore them, we give it all away. All my intellect rebels against this notion, but my *kishkes* know it's true. When Dart fucks me I feel *alive*. When he doesn't, I wither."

"Did it ever occur to you that feelings are not facts?"

"I've never lived without a man. I need sex to power my creativity. I need that skinlessness to get in touch with the muse."

"You need *you* to power your creativity. Dart takes you away from you. From the twins. From your work. If you make yourself the center of your life, if you stop giving away your power, other kinds of men will be drawn to you—equals, not dominators or wimps."

"Like who? Thom was a wimp. Elmore, for all his bravado about equality, was both a dominator *and* a wimp. Even the twins know it. Ed said to me when I took them to the airport, 'Why do we have to go to Daddy's, Mom? Daddy's a big baby. You support us. You take care of us. He just bosses us around.' I said, 'He's your dad, and you love him,' and Mike said, 'Are you *sure* he's our dad?' 'Absolutely sure,' I said. 'Okay, Mom,' said Ed, 'we take your word for it.'

"*They* know he's a wimp and a weakling. They know who they can depend upon and who they can't. I try to tell them how great Elmore is, and they laugh at me. Ten years old, and they know everything. They even asked me once if I'd ever done it on a plane. 'Yes,' I said. 'Wet or dry?' I thought for a minute and then said, 'Dry.' 'Oh,' said Ed, 'that doesn't count, Mom. We were wondering about the Mile High Club.' 'How do you little *pishers* know about the Mile High Club?' I asked. 'We read,' said Mike. 'And watch those videos you have,' said Ed. This was a shock, but I pretended to be cool. 'Well,' I said, 'if there's ever anything you want to know about sex, please ask your mom. Don't go to strangers, okay?' 'Okay, Mom,' said Ed, 'but we know about *every*thing.' 'Even pantric sex,' said Mike. 'You mean tantric,' I said, glad for some little corner of expertise. 'I told you it wasn't pantric,' said Ed to Mike. And off they ran, to play with their Barbies."

Emmie laughs and laughs. "What do they play?"

"They play Barbie joins the Mile High Club, I guess. With twins you never know—they have a whole secret life."

During the evening, Fleur's story drifts back to me. Some of it is even starting to make sense.

"I keep thinking of Fleur," I say, "of women not loving their daughters into health unless they can love themselves into health—you know what I mean?"

"I do," says Emmie.

"And that makes me think of Theda, who certainly didn't love herself—and yet she gave me this crazed bravado, this notion that I can do *anything*. And Dolph too. I am so much my father's daughter. My mother's madness fired my ambition in a strange way too. I want to redeem her life and make her pain worthwhile. If only she could have stopped drinking."

"Tell me about 'The Rules of Love,'" says Emmie.

"Let me find the book."

I run up to the attic and look among the shelves where I keep the books from my Yale days. There it is, a dusty greenish volume called *Italian Social Customs of the Sixteenth Century* which I have saved all these years because of its account of the tradition of courtly love and its survival into the Renaissance. I pull the book out as carefully as I would an ancient scroll, sealed in a tomb, preserved from ordinary air. As if by magic, it falls open to a page headed "The Rules of Love." I stand alone in the attic and read in the dusty sunlight from the dormers:

I.	Marriage is not a just excuse for not loving.
II.	He who is not jealous cannot love.
III.	No one can be bound by a double love.
IV.	Love always increases or diminishes.
V.	What the lover takes from his beloved against her will has no relish.

VI. A man can love only when he has reached full manhood.

VII. A dead lover must be mourned by the survivor for two years.

VIII. No one should be deprived of love without abundant reason.

IX. No one can love unless he is compelled to do so by the persuasion of love.

X. Love is always wont to shun the abode of avarice.

XI. It is unseemly to love those whom one would be ashamed to marry.

XII. A true lover does not wish to enjoy the love of another than his beloved.

XIII. Love seldom lasts after it is divulged.

XIV. Love easily won becomes contemptible; love won with difficulty is held dear.

XV. Every lover is wont to turn pale at the sight of his beloved.

XVI. A lover's heart trembles at the sudden sight of his beloved.

XVII. A new love drives away the old.

XVIII. Probity alone makes one worthy of love.

XIX. If love diminishes, it soon ends and rarely revives.

XX. A lover is always timid.

XXI. A lover's affection is always increased by true jealousy.

XXII. A lover's zeal and affection are increased by suspicion of the beloved.

XXIII. He eats and sleeps less whom the thought of love distresses.

XXIV.   Every act of the lover is bounded by the thought of the beloved.

XXV.   A true lover believes nothing good but what he thinks will please the beloved.

XXVI.   Love can refuse nothing to love.

XXVII.   A lover cannot tire of the favors of his beloved.

XXVIII.   A slight presumption forces the lover to suspect his beloved.

XXIX.   He is not wont to love who is tormented by lewdness.

XXX.   A true lover dwells in the uninterrupted contemplation of the beloved.

XXXI.   Nothing forbids a woman to be loved by two men, and a man by two women.

"Love always increases or diminishes," I say aloud. "A dead lover must be mourned for two years." I hold on to those thoughts as if they are the very pillars of my sane mind.

I run downstairs to read "The Rules of Love" to Emmie, who listens intently.

"Why do they remind you of 'The Twelve Steps'?" she asks.

"Because human beings have this need to codify everything, even heartbreak, even despair. 'The Rules of Love' and 'The Twelve Steps' are parallel universes. They're like floating spars to a drowning person. It's comforting to know that others have passed that way before."

"You mean you're not the only stumbling human being, the only stumbling lover?" Emmie asks, not without irony. "You mean you're *allowed* to be imperfect?"

"Precisely," I say, pretending to be in my sane mind. This is one of the first principles of the Program, I have learned from Emmie: "Act as if." Perhaps even if I cannot find my sane mind, I can *pretend* to have found it. And perhaps by pretending enough, I will eventually cease having to pretend.

Emmie stays with me that night and the next and the next. The first three days without booze are hard. Every day at five, I crave wine so badly I think I can't live without it—and instead we go to a meeting and then come home and gorge on ice cream. Something seems missing in my life. The days seem three times as long as before. The house is empty without Dart, without the twins, without the ritual of drinking.

Emmie and I cart all the wine down to a storage closet in the cellar and lock it up, then bury the key somewhere in the ground near my silo.

"If you ever want to drink, you'll have to call a locksmith," Emmie says. "Ideally, we should throw it away—but you might have a party and need the stuff."

"How long will it be before I stop wanting wine every day at five?"

"I think you're like a lot of women—you drink with men."

"And since there's no sex in my life, I won't need to drink, right?"

"I didn't say there'd *never* be—"

"Oh, Emmie, why did I ever let you drag me to that goddamned meeting?"

"Drag you? You dragged *me*. You think I'd come all the way up here just for a *meeting*?"

*   *   *

On the fourth day I go to my silo and start a still life. Emmie is in the guest room, sprawled out on the water bed, reading a half-dozen books about osteoporosis while keeping a nostril and an ear out for the gallons of tomato sauce she's making in the kitchen. The whole house smells like an Italian restaurant. The cooking smells give me comfort—as does Emmie's presence.

Out in my silo, I set up my still life. I choose the elements carefully: a dozen white jumbo eggs in a Lalique crystal bowl with maenads dancing around its borders, a clear crystal egg, a white china milk pitcher in the shape of a cow, a cylindrical clear-glass vase filled with white roses and calla lilies, and under it all an antique white lace tablecloth, which I gather into folds so that it looks like snowy alps.

I erect my little traveling easel near the still life, stand a freshly stretched square canvas upon it, squeeze out my oil paints in umber, ocher, blue, green, and every shade of white, and begin losing myself in the challenge of finding the kaleidoscope of colors within the word "white."

Wholly happy, wholly content, I feel that I am ten again and have regained that true self I knew before the dance of sex, the tidal waves of hormones, overtook my life. I am happy—happier than I have been in years.

Five o'clock comes and goes without my needing a drink *or* a meeting. I paint as if in a trance, entirely absorbed in the drama of the white tablecloth, the angles of changing light on the crystal, the maenads dancing as they have danced for centuries, the womanly eggs, the cow full of milk, the clouds full of rain in the darkening sky.

For once I don't mind the setting of the sun, since I am painting this still life not in real light but in the light of the mind. I switch on the powerful strobes I use for my photographs and go on painting. The valleys of the table-cloth glimmer as if with alpine snow. The eggs show little calcified bumps, like ovaries about to burst their follicles. The crystal egg seems to hold the future in its depths. The roses and lilies open before my eyes.

In a trance, I paint and paint. My head clear, my heart singing in my chest, I am in ecstasy.

At about eleven, Emmie comes in with a dish of pasta, a glass of iced chamomile tea with honey, and a heaping bowl of sliced peaches.

We sit at my drafting table, and she watches me eat.

"Four days sober," she says. "Mazel tov. And the White Goddess sent you a gift to celebrate."

We both turn and look at the still life, which seems actually finished. It has a clarity my work has never possessed before. I know that I am onto something new—something beyond cowboys or self-portraits, something pure, clear, complex, and glittering as snow.

"*L'chaim!*" says Emmie, toasting me with her glass of chamomile tea. We clink glasses, then laugh and laugh.

Dart calls late that night. It is one o'clock or so, and Emmie is asleep.

When I hear his voice on the phone, my heart does a funny little dance. I think I have been longing for him to call, but now I am a bit thrown. I want to keep the clarity I have.

"Baby—what are you up to?" he asks.

"Oh, just painting," I say. "The usual."

"Do you miss me?"

"Of course I do."

"I miss you terribly, baby," he says, his voice cracking. "There's no one like you—no one as sweet and wild and sexy. Baby, I'm coming home."

In four days, I have become a queen; now I go back to pawn. When Dart appears, Leila disappears.

I toss and turn in my bed, waiting for him, unable to sleep. I get up and do my makeup, put on perfume and a silk nightgown, put in my diaphragm, and go back to bed. I wish I were strong enough to tell him never to darken my door again, but I am not. Emmie sleeps in the guest room; my wet canvas glistens in the studio. I wait in bed as if for a dybbuk to claim me. Outside my window, a full moon with a ring around it floats over the hills. I drift off to sleep, awaken to find that it is now three o'clock. I get up, wash my face, brush my teeth, put a sweater on over the nightgown, and wander out onto my hillside.

The moon has almost completed her arc. Her ring is gone now, and she lies low on the other side of the horizon. I gaze at her, then bend my head nine times, trying to think of my supreme wish. Always before, that wish has been for Dart. Now it is for me: I wish for the power to keep the clarity these four days have brought.

No sooner have I made the wish than I hear the putter of Dart's motorcycle and the spray of pebbles in the driveway. The dog barks. I kneel down on my hillside and raise my hands to the moon.

What am I praying for? I think I'm praying for the return of my sane mind.

I am on my knees, immobilized in the moonlight, as he enters the house, using his key, storms into the bedroom, looking for me, and then storms out again, heading for my silo.

I am seized with panic—somehow convinced that if he sees the crystalline still life he will destroy it (so clear will it be to him that he has been replaced as my muse). I run after him, calling, "Dart, Dart," catching up with him just before he enters my studio.

I embrace him, drag him out to the grassy slope again. There, under the mocking moon, we couple like witch and warlock, screaming and crying in the dewy grass, rolling over and over laughing like maniacs and even rolling down the hill to the border of my ha-ha. There we stop by the side of the ditch and fuck again, powered by the blue fullness of the moon.

"Baby, you're wild—wild," says Dart, who does not know that all my wildness was to keep him from my still life, or that in my screaming and coming, I hold back a little piece of my heart—a small sane sober corner that can never give itself away again.

I lead Dart to bed, where he collapses, spent, reaching his arms around me and sleeping on my breast like a baby. Immobilized by his need, I lie awake watching the pink light of dawn begin to rise behind my trees. On one side of my bedroom the moon sets: on the other side the sun rises. I lie in the middle—Isis with Horus in her arms, Astarte with Adonis, Rhea with the Zeus who is destined to dethrone her.

But can we ever dethrone the earth? The earth is there, whatever we do. We have but to take off our shoes and reassert the contact of our soles with the soil.

Dart groans and turns, letting go his hold, and suddenly I am free to breathe. I stretch out on my back, my mind racing. I know he will sleep for hours, know he has a small boy's need for sleep, especially after sex.

I slip out of bed, pull on a sweat suit and slippers, and

pad back out to the studio. Can my still life possibly be as good as I remember it?

The studio smells of turpentine, the piny, woodsy smell of earth. I switch on the light—and there, on the easel, is my glimmering testament to a new life.

"Thank you, Moon," I say.

In a rage of excitement I wash my brushes, clean my palette, put a new canvas on the easel, and set the first painting aside to dry. I rearrange the crystalline elements of my still life and begin a second version of this albino study—this one much more fantastical and abstract, with the moon setting behind the dancing maenads and the eggs transformed into little whirling planets and the cow spraying milk through the starry universe.

I paint and paint—rapt, happy, imagining a whole series of paintings based on this crystalline theme, with each of these objects—moon, maenads, eggs, cow, milk— becoming an emblem of a new life for women, for children, for the planet. I will call it *Albino Lives* I, II, III, and so on to infinity, and I will even do large canvases of eggs, of maenads, of white roses—taking these same several elements and considering them from every vantage point, in all sizes.

I see a new show, a new period, a new way of mirroring my life. At 8:00 A.M. I am still painting like this—my mind galloping, my heart full—when Dart staggers in with a cup of coffee and says:

"What's the matter, baby, don't you like to sleep in my arms anymore?"

I turn and look at him, at the purplish lids, that tousled blond hair, that six feet two inches of macho masculinity—and I am slightly annoyed to be interrupted. I am also slightly scared.

"What do you think?" I say, pointing to my new canvas.

Dart staggers backward (is he somewhat stoned?).

"Do you really want to know, baby?"

"Yes," I say, lying.

"Well," he says. "You know I think you're the greatest painter since Michelangelo, but I still remember the time when you slept all night in my arms and nothing could tear you away." He pouts prettily, knowing I am stung with guilt—as if this chaos of broken connections were all my doing. And he turns and strides out of the room, letting me admire the shape of his beautiful calves.

7

THE PAINTER
AND THE PIMP

───────◆───────

Lawd, I really don't think no man's love can last;
They'll love you to death, then treat you like a thing of the past.

—*Bessie Smith*

Emmie and Dart and I have an uneasy breakfast. Emmie makes it—toasted bagels, jam, eggs, fresh coffee, peaches. Though she doesn't impose her presence between me and Dart, I feel it, and so does he. Emmie is on my side. She says nothing, does nothing (but feed us a delicious breakfast), and yet Dart, especially, resents her because he senses that she loosens his hold on me. He would like to tell her to go, but of course he cannot. If I am alone in the house, waiting for him to come and go at will, I am wholly at his mercy. With Emmie there, I am not.

This is the paradox of weak men and strong women: they drain us of our strength in the hopes of equalizing the struggle. But since they cannot absorb our strength, they accomplish only the negative goal of draining us. In a society that gives the *official* power to men, the line between mental and physical abuse is a very fine one. Who can discover where one ends and the other begins? Dart never beat me (except in sexual play) nor put a gun to my head, but the weapons he kept in the house, and his wholly unpredictable comings and goings, accomplished the same end.

Emmie: "So how's New York, Dart?"

Dart (sullen): "The same."

Emmie: "What have you been up to?"

Dart (resentful): "Oh, this and that."

Leila: "Tell Emmie about your new project, Dart."

Dart (looking up): "The show of new artists? The building we're buying?" (Dart always has a dozen projects, none of which reach fruition and all of which require infusions of capital—my capital.)

Leila: "Whichever."

Dart: "Well—the building is a giant pain in the ass. None of the workmen show up on time, the building inspectors expect bigger and bigger bribes, and the city harasses us with summonses. I'd only do this for you, baby." (A soulful look.)

Leila: "I know—and don't think I don't appreciate it." (This absurd statement should have remained stuck in my throat, because I know the whole project for the sham it is: a futile attempt to buck up Dart's self-esteem.)

Emmie: "But isn't it exciting that you're renovating the building?"

Dart: "Exciting to you, exciting to *her*—since neither of you has to be there."

Emmie: "I thought you enjoyed construction."

Dart: "Sure. I love thankless work. . . ." (A reproachful look—to which I actually react with guilt. Dart wanted me to buy the building he now complains of so bitterly. I end up responsible for both his idleness and his labor, his stardom and his obscurity, his success and his failure.)

Leila: "But, darling, you're so *good* at what you do."

Dart: "I want to be the best man for you, but you're never satisfied. Whatever I do, it's not enough—I can't win for losing!"

Leila: "That's *not* true."

Dart: "Yes it is—you're so critical of me. You don't say it, but I feel it. It's always there."

Emmie: "Think I'll go back to osteoporosis." (Slipping away to the guest room.)

Leila: "What on earth are you talking about?"

Dart: "I try to do everything I can for you—pose for you, renovate your property—and it's never enough. Never. You don't take me seriously. For years I've been begging you to marry me, and you won't do it. How can I take myself seriously if you won't marry me? You treat me like your gigolo, not your man. No wonder I feel like a pimp, like a stud, like a fucking consort. You deball me—and then you waltz off and paint another still life."

I get up and put my arms around him. "The Rules of Love" are thundering in my head: "It is unseemly to love those whom one would be ashamed to marry." As if he could hear this, Dart pushes me away.

Dart: "Do you know what happened to me yesterday? I was walking through Harlem, on my way to get some building supplies"—read: drugs—"and a big black man yells out at me: 'You a pimp, boy, and you don' even know it. Hey, white boy—you a born pimp!'"

Dart says this with a mixture of pride and disgust—a

unique combination he has mastered in emulation of his father.

Leila: "You're not a pimp, darling—you're my *lover*."

Dart (tears rolling down his cheeks): "Yes, I am, I am, I am. Unless you marry me, I'm just your pimp, your gigolo. Everybody knows that—I wish *you* did!"

By now I am almost in tears myself. I know that "pimp" is how Dart sees himself, but what can I do? I can't remake this man's self-image, make him healthy, whole, sound. He has to do that for himself.

He takes me by the hand and drags me back to the bedroom. He locks the door. In the white iron bed, with the sun flooding the coverlet, he begins to make love to me, licking and teasing me and making me come and come. My orgasms are strangely cold and unfeeling. Pure reflex. Robotics, not passion. "Love always increases or diminishes," I hear my sane mind saying. I try to reciprocate, but Dart won't let me touch his cock. "No, baby—I have *my* hand on the joystick." Whereupon he makes me come again and again—until coming is almost painful and I beg him to stop.

Isadora: Stop!
Leila: *You used to like this sort of thing.*
Isadora: *I like it tender and sweet, not merely massage!*
Leila: *You must have changed since the last book!*

Then he pulls me to my knees, asks me to clutch a pile of pillows, and fucks me maniacally from behind.

Suddenly he stops, feeling my diaphragm with his hard hooked cock, reaches inside me, and pulls it out— sailing it across the room like a Frisbee. I let out a scream and try to run to retrieve it, but he holds me fast, fucking and fucking me until he comes in a mad convulsion, filling me with his seed.

"Baby, baby, baby," he moans, pulling me down with him on the bed, covering me with his body, wet with sweat and come. I lie there with him, mastered, taken, spent—at once hoping I won't conceive and that I will, for my ambivalence is now total. With my newfound clarity, I see that sex is a weapon for him, but some vestigial part of me accepts this as the fate of womanhood.

Dart falls into a deep sleep, and so do I. In my dream I am giving suck to a newborn baby, who looks up at me, turning suddenly into a little porcelain cow. The elements of my still life dance through the dream—eggs, roses, lilies, maenads, crystal bowl, and cow—and I am immobilized beneath the weight of Dart, unable to get up and paint. This will be my version of hell, I think: immobilized beneath some man—unable to get up and paint—for all eternity.

I drift into a quirky dream about Professor Max Doerner, whose book *The Materials of the Artist* was much touted by a professor of mine at Yale—the same professor who introduced me to "The Rules of Love." In the dream it is not this professor but Max Doerner himself who lectures me:

"Your paintinks are disintegratink," Professor Doerner is saying. "You haff abandoned za teknik off za Old Masters." He struts about the studio. "Pigments! Gesso! Old linen!" he shouts. "Old fat slaked lime aged in za pit! Benozzo Gozzoli! Benozzo Gozzoli! Benozzo Gozzoli!"

Professor Doerner is a dwarf. He opens his fly and waves his cock at the class. "Old fat lime!" he shouts.

At some point in this tirade (the bright sunlight tells me it must be almost noon) I awaken beside the sleeping

Dart, hoping the result of last night's mad sexual power struggle will not be pregnancy. The twins are enough to handle. Any notion that I could juggle Dart, twins, another baby, and my art is a delusion. Every canvas I have seized from chaos has been done at the expense of the chthonic deities who cry out for blood, blood, female blood, and childbirth at any price. Any woman producing *any* painting should get combat pay—for that battle waged in the sky between Rhea and Zeus. I would never have had an abortion, because, despite my political beliefs, I see every egg as an incipient human life, and I could no more destroy one than I could rip apart my own canvas. But in a way I have been lucky, because I am not a terribly fertile woman, so I haven't been plagued with pregnancy like some. One pregnancy produced two beautiful daughters, who have given me, thus far, mostly joy and laughter—pain no doubt to come, which I hope I will be ready for.

I know that the struggle between art and life is a never-ending one. Difficult enough for a man, who is not indentured to the species' very survival. But for a woman, a true dilemma and conundrum, never to be resolved—until, perhaps, the freedom of menopause that Emmie talks about. Do I believe her? Emmie, after all, has never been a mother and does not know how motherhood reshapes the heart. But am I Dart's mother—or the twins'? Or somebody else's that I have never met? If I had a son, Dart would never have been in my life this long. The notion starts to turn in the gyres of my brain. *Stop it,* I tell myself, and doze off for a while, hoping that sleep will knit this particular raveled sleeve of care.

By the time Dart awakens, it's lunchtime. Terrified of what new stunt he will pull today, I awake suddenly, with a lurch of terror, wanting a drink, a meeting, *any*thing but Dart.

Dart rolls over and smiles his bogus blue-eyed smile. "Baby, you look beautiful."

"Do I?"

"Yes." He nuzzles my hair, my breasts, my navel. "God—I have a headache, cottonmouth, got to brush my teeth."

And he lurches up and into the bathroom to make his ablutions.

Torn between waiting for him to come back and fuck me and bouncing up out of bed, I lie there, totally lost to myself, admitting that the last few days without him have been easier than most days with him.

Suddenly I have this terrible thought: What if women all admitted to themselves that men are more trouble than they're worth? Think of how free we could be! But that admission opens such abysses of terror! If a self-supporting woman with as many children as she wants is *still* dependent on men, then the need must be deep and unfathomable. Nor is it only a sexual need. Can it be the need for validation in a world in which being a woman is not in itself enough validation? And when will we learn to validate *ourselves*?

Dart comes back to bed. He dives into the covers as I have so often watched him dive into the Caribbean.

He kisses my neck, my ears, my breasts. He seems about to make love to me again, but both of us hold back, as if a decision has been made. I am remembering Dart once saying to me, "You've got it on tap, baby." There was considerable resentment in his tone, as if his "I can't give you anything but love, baby" stance troubled even him. He has always used sex as a weapon, all the while resenting the fact that it's the only weapon he has.

When the only place a relationship wholly works is in bed, both people eventually get nervous. They get nervous because they never want to get out of bed. They get nervous because they *have* to get out of bed. They get nervous because The Land of Fuck is a place where you lose all your boundaries. Skinlessness is what you seek, yet skinlessness terrifies.

Dart and I seem to have come to the end of a long and winding road. The sex is starting to pall. ("A lover cannot tire of the favors of his beloved.")

"Baby," says Dart, playing his final trump card, "we *have* to stop drinking and drugging. I'm ready to try AA—are you?"

Now, this is a subject Dart and I have talked about from time to time but not lately. It's as if Dart has intuited my conversations with Emmie and is ready to try anything to keep our danse macabre going. Only I am not quite so cynical in my response.

"Oh, darling," I say like a robot, "how wonderful!" And the sad fact is, I mean it.

Which is how Dart and Emmie and I end up at the same meeting in the same Greek Revival church.

Dart is uncomfortable, sits stiffly on his chair, looking desperately around.

I am uncomfortable, feeling responsible somehow for his reaction to the Program. What if he doesn't like the meeting? What if he quits the Program? Will I then be tempted to quit? Emmie is right. I think I can control everything.

Somewhere deep in this anxiety lies the key to the

mess I have made of my life. If only I could just *be* and stop worrying the same old sad bone of my responsibility for everyone's feelings. Surrender is what I seek. I thought I was seeking skinlessness; what I was really seeking was surrender. Acceptance of the universe. Acceptance of the fact that God, not Leila, is in charge.

The meeting begins with the preamble and the introduction of the speaker, a white-haired man of about fifty, who smokes compulsively and whose right eye twitches. I wonder if Dart has noticed the man's disturbing resemblance to his father.

Dart paws the ground like a colt. He seems terribly anxious. Well, why *shouldn't* he be? Wasn't *I* at my first meeting?

The speaker, who introduces himself as Lyle from New York, begins his monologue.

"If you really wanna know how I was drunk versus how I am sober, all I have to tell you is that I used to live on an island off the coast of Maine with my first wife and my seven kids. There was no way to get to the mainland but a little speedboat. My idea of fun was to take the speedboat and take off for weeks, leaving the family stranded. Whenever my first wife complained of this treatment, I would deck her. I'm not proud of it, but I'd come home, punch everybody out, and take off again. They were my prisoners—see?—and I figured they *had* to take it, because I paid the bills. I'm not proud of the fact that I treated them all like my property."

Dart listens intently, but I can't figure out what his response is.

Emmie whispers, "Stop trying to figure out what

Dart is feeling—what are *you* feeling?"

"Angry," I say. "Disgusted."

Lyle goes on with his saga of wife abuse, child abuse, psychological abuse, mental abuse. The world is so full of abuse of all kinds. If I were God, I'd wipe 'em all out and start again. I am furious, listening to this drunkalogue. I can identify with nothing in it. The men in the Program are such *thugs,* I think. The women are victims and the men thugs. And what am I? A little of both?

Lyle's story concludes with his sobering up at an expensive funny farm, his leaving his first family and starting a second, his ten years in the Program and how they made him into if not a better person then at least a rotten person who no longer gets drunk and hits women and children.

At the sharing, I am dumbfounded by the number of men who claim to identify with Lyle. I hate him, hate his violence, his self-righteousness. This hatred is an excruciating emotion in the nonjudgmental atmosphere of the meeting. But does confessing to rotten behavior make it all okay?

Dart raises his hand. "I'm Dart, a drug addict and an alcoholic," he says, "and this is my first meeting. Your story made me think of the way my father once held my face under water and tried to drown me because I talked back to him. I'm full of conflicted feelings, but I'm glad to be here. I want to get sober with all my heart." People look at Dart as if his confession has triggered something powerful in them. How many drunks in this room have struggled through drownings and beatings just to arrive here, at this church basement in rural Connecticut? I think of the odds against all of us, and my eyes fill with tears.

I hug Dart. "Darling, I'm *so* proud of you," I say,

suddenly revising my opinion of Lyle's story. If it can bring out this response in Dart, it must be worthwhile. I even decide to reserve judgment on the human race and not kill them all off. Yet.

Apparently, I still think I'm God. And my sane mind, far off and barely audible, whispers: "Leila, you're lovable, you really are. You don't have to put up with this shit."

Isadora: I don't really like the chapters where you get into AA. AA is basically impossible to write about. What happens there sounds banal but really isn't. Group process cannot be captured on paper.

Leila: Then what do you suggest we do? Leave our heroine drunk, despairing, hopeless? AA helped me.

Isadora: I know. After all, I sent you there. It's only one of many roads to self-knowledge. As long as one learns that the answer is within . . . as long as one stops blaming other people . . .

Leila: Hush. I have this story.

8

WHITE NIGHTS
AND AFTER

◆

Gypsy, don't hurt him,
fix him for me one more time.
Oh, don't hurt him, gypsy,
fix him for me one more time.
Just make him love me,
but please, ma'am, take him off my mind.

—*Bessie Smith*

Dart got sober with a vengeance—at least for a little while. The Program became his raison d'être. He stayed in the country with me all week, going to at least two meetings a day, talking Program, Program, Program—like a convert to some new religion—and neither drinking nor drugging.

He also milked it for all it was worth. In the name of his new "conversion," he got me to put him on the payroll of my company for a thousand dollars a week and to get him an American Express platinum card in his own name. It was not that he actually asked me for these things openly—it was that in my new delirium about his actually *being there,* I *offered* them, and he, at first reluctantly, accepted.

I was thrilled about our new life. We were going to meetings together, working together, reading AA books together. We were not, however, sleeping together. Or rather, we were sleeping together, but we were not fucking. In sobriety, Dart's indefatigable cock went limp. In sobriety, Dart, who never was listless (or lustless), became both. In sobriety, Dart wept and raged and screamed and soul-searched, but he did not screw.

Dart impotent was not a pretty sight. He was convinced his life was over. All men perhaps identify themselves with their cocks, but in Dart's case the identification was total. He lay on the bed as limp as his organ. He cried real tears. He blamed me.

I tried everything. Black garter belts with bikini underwear; black garter belts with no underwear. Tongue tricks, finger grips, baby oil. Erotic videos, erotic books, magazines from *Hustler* to *Puritan*—there really is such a magazine!—from *Penthouse* to *Screw.* Nothing availed. In my mouth, Dart's cock felt limper than my tongue. I held my baby boy in my arms and rocked him.

"It happens to everyone from time to time," I said, starting to feel bored with my role.

"Never to me," said Dart, "not even when I was a baby."

"I promise you, darling, it will get better."

"How do *you* know?" Dart asked petulantly.

And in my heart I was more on his side than on my own. If I could have "cured" him by bringing home a bimbo, I would have.

He hung in with me—so to speak—for a week, and by the end of it he was off on the motorcycle again, taking the platinum card, the paycheck, and his limp cock with him.

That was when I really crashed. That was when I wanted to drink, to throw myself under the wheels of a train, to incinerate the cowboy canvases and the film stills. Emmie reappeared to prevent me.

"I don't want to live anymore," I told her. "Sobriety has taken everything from me that I care about—sex, my work, Dart. . . ."

"That simply isn't true," she says. "You only feel that way now. Feelings are not facts."

"Emmie, I hate my life. My life sucks. I am totally fucked. Or not fucked. I hate the dumb meetings. I hate the crummy smoke-filled basements and the stale Oreos and the Styrofoam coffee. The best thing about the Program was giving me Dart back, and now it has even taken Dart away. I can't bear it. I am in such pain."

"I know you are," says Emmie. "Nothing can eradicate that pain, but if I tell you that a year from now your whole life will look different, will you believe me?"

"No."

"Well—it will. I can only ask you to go to meetings and wait. Try to live one day at a time. Try not to anticipate. All of this will change you in ways that are so amazing you won't believe them. Remember your maenads and crystal? It will be maenads and crystal from now on."

But it wasn't. It was horniness and emptiness and tears. I felt like an orphan. I missed Dart in my gut. He was a part of me—the crazy, irresponsible part maybe—the part that wanted to run, to bolt, to drink, to drug, to be Donna Giovanna, Donna Quixota, the madcap picara with no fixed address and a million aliases. Dart was precious to me because he *was* me. Or at least—a part of myself I couldn't freely express—the bad boy roaring inside me.

I would get all dressed up and go to AA meetings and sit there, crossing my legs in a miniskirt for my plumber, the old lady who sold antiques on Route 7, the former actress who ran a gourmet shop in town. I would look longingly at the spacey thirty-year-old equine veterinarian who made barn visits all over the county (I was hoping he would visit *my* stall) and at the balding guy who sold nails in the hardware store and at the raspberry-nosed limo driver who now called me Leila rather than Ms. Sand because we were both in the Program. I would be thinking about fucking all these guys, but instead we would go out for coffee and talk Program.

I became a regular in the coffee shop in town where everyone went after meetings, and I even got to *like* the feeling of sitting and talking with a man without sizing him up as a sex object. I started to listen to men, hear what they had to say about their lives, their wives and ex-wives, their fathers, their frustrations, their cocks. I learned that if you stopped looking at a man as someone to give you an orgasm or a baby or save your life, you could really be friends with him and find him quite as human as yourself. I realized that my whole life I had regarded men as both enemy and prey—entirely without being aware of it—so therefore they must have regarded me the same way. I also realized that life without sex was not the worst thing in the world. It was like fasting. The first three days were wretched, but after a while you got high and even came to like it. As I gave up expectations from men, I found myself learning things I never could have anticipated.

The highs were high—and the lows were lower than low. Sometimes I would drive through the countryside in

DART, singing at the top of my lungs, and other times I would collapse in my bed feeling like holy shit, looking desperately for my sane mind and not being able to find it. I would look at myself in the mirror, pinch the skin under my chin, and decide that I was going through menopause and was drying up for want of a good fuck. I am not the sort of woman who goes without sex without a protest. I will not go gentle into that good night. I have always regarded a stiff cock as a health and beauty aid—and here I was living without my main beauty treatment, health food, and sleeping potion. I considered suicide in various forms—self-immolation with my paintings, carbon monoxide poisoning, driving off a cliff in Dart's car. (I couldn't do sleeping pills or tranquilizers because I was in the Program!) But then I would see in my mind's eye the distraught expressions on the faces of my sweet little twins—their horror, their betrayal, their lostness—and I would change my mind. There was no way I would do that to my girls. I was beginning to understand that all my actions had consequences.

Understanding the consequences of one's actions is not the same thing as guilt. Guilt is useless. So is self-flagellation. But understanding that your acts have consequences and that you have choices is another matter altogether. This was the main thing the Program was starting to teach me. I began to realize that I was an energy field, whose motions left reverberations through the universe. And I began to take the responsibility—and the credit—for those reverberations, to realize that I was not a victim of "fate." Yes, God, Goddess, the Higher Power, the Holy Ghost, worked *through* me; I was a human vessel for a divine energy force. But to be a vessel was not the same as to be a victim or a pawn. Life flowed through me, and therefore my body and mind had to be respected. They were temples of spirit. They could not lightly be thrown away.

Isadora: I must admit I get very itchy when you fall into all this Shirley Malarkey stuff about Higher Powers, Temples of Spirit, healing crystals, und so weiter. *The sex slop is bad enough, but all that* spiritual shit *adds insult to injury! Do you think it's what the age demands?*

Leila: Millions of women are seeking spiritual solutions to our crazed addictive society. . . .

Isadora: In other words, "It's what's happenin', baby"?

Leila: For one who started the whole thing, you really are closed-minded.

Isadora: I'm sorry I started it, really I am. I think we'd all be better off in crinolines and chastity belts.

Leila: You don't really. . . .

Isadora: No comment.

Leila: Then may I continue?

Isadora: Your spiritual search for newer and better skinlessness? Be my guest.

I began to meditate—my own form of meditation, in which I sat alone on my hillside (the grass blades tickling my knees and ass, the little ants crawling harmlessly over my immobilized legs) and focused on the middle distance (a humpbacked cloud, a silver silo glinting in the sun) and blessed God for my life.

I began to notice things I had never noticed before: the red raspberry brambles growing alongside my driveway, the water lilies in my clogged pond, the golden lichen covering the stones at the perimeter. I began to thank God for the lichen, for the raspberries, for the clouds. I began to praise.

One day, sitting in the grass, gazing into the middle distance, I began to repeat like a mantra: thank you, and with each phrase I felt more and more grateful, more and more alive.

I knew that the praising breath was both within me and without me and that God had put me here for a purpose, which didn't have to be clear to me at every moment. I had merely to honor the breath within me and to carry it forward into the universe. To destroy it would be as great a heresy as destroying my paintings or strangling my twins. Life had been given to me. I had only to say yes to the gift.

And then Dart came home. He came home stoned, bearing gifts bought with my money and credit cards. There is nothing more unsettling than that. W. H. Auden says that it is more morally confusing to be goosed by a bishop than by a traveling salesman. But receiving gifts that you will soon get bills for is more confusing even than that.

Dart hands me a Tiffany box in which there is a large sapphire engagement ring, surrounded by diamond baguettes.

"Marry me," he says, "or I'll leave again."

Now, this is not the sort of proposal one dreams of. Much as I think I love Dart, much as I cannot imagine my life without him, I know that to marry him is to wed my life to the kind of wretchedness and upheaval I am experiencing now: it is a kind of sentence. Things will be this way always—abrupt arrivals and painful departures, serenity smashed, tranquillity taxed to the breaking point, and no hope of anything else in the future.

"Dart, darling," I say, "let's get married when we've been in the Program a year, okay?"

Dart scowls at me. "You're putting me off," he says.

And maybe I am. The phone in the kitchen rings. We both run for it. I get there first.

"Hello?" I say. Someone breathes and hangs up. I imagine the blond girl whose pictures I found, and the redhead whose letters I found, and the brunette whose makeup I found in DART.

"Who is it?" Dart asks.

"You tell *me*. I don't have friends who call and hang up when I answer. Do you?"

"You don't trust me!" Dart shouts, stomping off into the bedroom.

"How can I trust you when you leave for days and come back smelling of someone else's perfume, with someone else's lipstick on your shirt? How can I trust you when you buy me presents with my own money and expect me to thank you, when you rage and stomp about the house because I won't be grateful for that sort of behavior? How can I trust you when you're not trustworthy!"

"That's it!" screams Dart. "The last straw! I can't stay with a woman who can't trust me—it's too demeaning! I'm leaving!" and he throws the ring at me and leaves (taking my credit card with him). As if in the grip of some habit, I fall to the floor and weep, feeling my life utterly over. I listen as the motorcycle putters up the driveway and out of my life again.

Isadora: Couldn't she weep in a chair for once?
Leila: Could you?

As I lie there on the floor, with my tears falling to the oaken floorboards, some glimmer of light begins to dawn, my sane mind is returning. I don't have to live like this. I don't have to have my self-esteem shattered every other day just to get skinless sex. Even the sex has become not what it once was. As I begin to *see* what Dart is doing with sex, it becomes less and less alluring. I see the game of it. And with vision comes freedom. I get up from the floor, dry my tears, and call Emmie—who is, mercifully, home.

"Dart's gone, again."

"Thank God," says Emmie.

"And I'm almost glad."

"Thank God for that too," says Emmie.

"I almost feel exhilarated. I'm almost wishing he'll never come back."

"I'm going to remind you of that," says Emmie, "when you least expect it."

"I know."

"Look—why don't you drive into the city and be with me? The fact is, you're not going to work. We could go to a meeting in New York or go see the tarot reader or just have dinner in the city. . . ."

"But what if Dart calls and I'm not here?"

"So let him call. . . . It will be good for him," says Emmie. "Anyway, instead of worrying about Dart, you could be doing what's best for Leila. Make *yourself* your first priority—you don't have to be at the affect of someone else. *Seize* your life. Dart's incidental—and *boring. You* give him all the power he has."

Panic grips me at the thought of going into the city and leaving the telephone, that household god, unattended. I could go to my own loft in the city, but somehow I am afraid of what I'll find there.

"Come on," says Emmie. "If you drive into the city, I'll treat you to supper."

"You're on," I say, feeling I am making the most courageous decision of my life.

I put on the engagement ring Dart bought me and say to myself: "Marry me!" It's the one solution to my marital dilemma I've never tried.

It's glorious midsummer in Connecticut, and I have taken possession of the car I bought for Dart. With its oxblood exterior, its white leather seats, its new sound system, and its rebuilt engine, it drives like a wet dream. But Dart has made a mess of the interior, as he makes a mess of everything. Broken tools on the floor, crushed Kleenex boxes, banana peels, peach pits. He treats the car the way his father treats the house on Rittenhouse Square: as a sort of elegant Dumpster. A rebuke to his woman's money, because he didn't earn it. His mess infuriates me, and the fury gives me the power to drive to New York. The gas is incidental.

I zoom down to the city with the Bessie Smith blaring. (I have two sets of the complete Bessie Smith—records for home, cassettes for the car.) I am singing along with "Kitchen Man," one of her most evocative songs:

> Mad about his turnip tops,
> Love the way he warms my chops,
> I cain't live without my kitchen man. . . .

Driving, my head clears, and I start to think about my situation—honestly, I hope. I wanted the freedom to do my work, and it led me to this lonely pass. I left Thom to have babies with Elmore, and I left Elmore because eventually he sulked every time I put brush to canvas. I let Dart peel off because I wouldn't do drugs with him anymore. He found others to do drugs with. Can it possibly be that simple?

Nobody prepared my generation of women—we baby boomers, we pregnant bulge in the population curve—for the changes that have overtaken us as women. We wanted to have it all—work and love, paintings and babies—and we have had it, but we have paid a price: the price of loneliness and isolation. Nobody prepared us for all this because nobody knew *how* to prepare us. We were caught in a strange historical moment. The lives of our mothers and grandmothers simply did not apply. If it were 1920 or 1945, I would never have left Thom Winslow to pursue twins and twin careers in Chianti. And if it were 1930 or 1955, I would never have left Elmore and wound up with Dart. My generation of women was experimenting with a new life pattern, one never tried by women before in all of history. No wonder we felt so lost, alternatively like pariahs or like pioneers. We were breaking every female taboo—putting our creative lives, our self-expression, ahead of the demands of the species.

Isadora: Where is Margaret Mead, now that we need her?
Leila: Why don't you go to the Trobriands and leave me alone?
Isadora: Because you'll never get out of this mess without me!

No wonder we felt like traitors to our mothers and grandmothers and, often, to our children and to our men. There were no rituals for us. We had smashed the old and not built the new. There were no patterns. We had unraveled the past and not woven the future. How to do that? Ah—the question of the century.

And the men? The men were just as lost and lonely as we. They expected nurturance and got a kick in the balls. They expected us to be warm bodies in bed, cups and cup bearers, baby bearers—and then they had to listen to us kvetch about our blasted creativity. They wanted what they had always *had*: a warm tush in bed. How could a still life of maenads and crystal *ever* replace a warm tush in bed?

The Warm Tush Theory: All of history could be traced to the longing for the warm tush in bed. I thought this and laughed and laughed aloud to myself.

Good, Leila, good, I thought. At least you're laughing—that's an improvement.

It was comforting to see my life as part of a historical process—comforting and possibly even true. I was partly the victim of my own addiction, partly the victim of my own talent and fame, but I was partly also a casualty of history: too many women born and not enough men, no life patterns for any of us to live by, the family breaking down and being replaced by—what? Nothing.

We tried to recreate it with group love: AA, OA, Al-Anon, therapy. We were all group groping desperately toward the apocalypse. We were searching for a new way to be communal animals. We needed new tribal identities, because the old ones could not hold us. We were trying to reinvent the human species in church basements, with coffee instead of sacramental wine, Oreos instead of holy wafers. The blood and the body: instant coffee and chocolate cream cookies. A caffeine-and-sugar rush to lift us toward God.

I drive down to SoHo, park in my garage, toy with going to my loft, and then decide that I am not going to do that until after supper. Perhaps I'm postponing being brave, but procrastination is not the worst sin in the world—as long as I recognize it. Then I walk through lower Manhattan to meet Emmie at our appointed place: Da Silvano.

The city has that gloriously dirty reek it has in midsummer—the opposite of verdant Connecticut. Overflowing garbage cans, water bugs leisurely crossing the streets as if they owned them, blaring radios, honking traffic, bums, beggars, handsome gay hunks in shorts, and gorgeous young women in T-shirts and minis flashing their bosoms and knees in vain, in vain. I am exuberant with the energy of New York. This is the Imperial City—Rome at the end of the empire, Paris at the fin de siècle, Hogarth's London. This is the red-hot center of the action, and for once the live current of New York is feeding me, charging me, giving me power rather than draining it away.

I walk past a particularly odoriferous heap of garbage, and in my newfound state I find it beautiful—quite as beautiful as my Connecticut hillside. This must be Zen wisdom, I think, to find the garbage as beautiful as the raspberry bramble. This must be joy—to see the world in a garbage heap as well as in a silver silo.

The whole city seems to be melting! It has that special liquescent feeling it gets on certain ninety-eight-degree days. The air itself an animal—gamy, full of life. I love the feel of the humidity on my skin, the way my sweat is making my gauzy shirt stick to my back. I am delighting in the day rather than being irritated by it—another gift of AA.

Every day is a good day, I think, even bad days. Every day is a gift. The smell may be bad, but we should rejoice in having noses at all. Nobody promised us a nose. Nobody promised us a nose garden.

I am staring at the garbage heap and thinking of a garden. The garbage heap is beautiful in its way—cans overflowing with all the wretched refuse of our lives: orange halves glowing like split suns, aluminum cans gleaming like Christmas tree ornaments, crushed bags in all the colors of the rainbow, beer bottles in every shade of grass green and earth brown.

I am seeing this garden in the garbage heap because,

suddenly, I am feeling a garden inside me. Always before, I would imagine my chest as a tangle of chopped veins and severed arteries. Always before, there was the howling emptiness inside, the emptiness that needed a cock to make it feel whole, the emptiness that demanded another glass of wine, another joint, another mad departure to Hong Kong on the next flight. But now I am starting to experience a taste of serenity, a soupçon of serenity—and it is utterly transforming. Where did it come from?

Grace, I guess.

I envision the inside of my chest, and suddenly I see a garden filled with sunflowers bending their heads, heavy with seeds. And zinnias in brilliant pinks and oranges and reds. And baskets of fuchsias hanging their reddish-purplish bells, and rambling red roses, and pruned trees of white roses, and musky marigolds blazing out of the earth. This is *my* garden, and *no*body can take it away, no matter what betrayals are practiced on my flesh. This garden is totally mine; this garden sustains me; it grows because I grow. Suddenly I want to paint it. I want to drive right home and paint it now.

Instead I meet Emmie for supper at Da Silvano. Walking in, I recognize and nod to half a dozen people from my business—artists, dealers, designers of catalogs, hangers of shows, and people hoping to be mistaken for same.

There's an elegant blonde in her fifties whose husband is a mafioso, who founded her gallery on West Broadway as a money-laundering scheme—none of which stops her from being the toast of New York. The stories I wish I didn't know about art dealing in New York. Dart and his devastations seem suddenly very far away.

Emmie is sitting at a front table drinking a Tab with lime and looking radiant.

"You look great," I say. (As the joke goes, there are two stages of life: youth and "you look great.")

"You too," says Emmie. "Losing Dart has made you lose all the stress lines in your face."

"I feel wonderful," I say. "It suddenly seems as if my life is beginning, not ending."

"Odd, isn't it?" says Emmie, laughing her twinkly laugh. "Remember how in *The Golden Notebook* the two women keep saying, 'Odd, isn't it'?"

"I haven't read that in *years*," I say. "When I was a teenager I forced myself to, but it seemed very heavy to me."

"Well, read it now. It's the story of our lives. 'Free Women'—in inverted commas, of course."

"Funny you should say that, because, driving down, I've been thinking that we represent an entirely new form of woman."

"In the Middle Ages, they burned us as witches," Emmie says.

We order the Italian supper that now passes as *echt* New York fare—figs and prosciutto, pasta, veal, arugula salad. I am amused by the way the cute young waiter—with the ponytail and the emerald earring in his left ear—reels off the specials as if he were auditioning for a Broadway musical. Only in New York, I think, where every waiter is an actor. In Italy, waiters are waiters.

"Maybe we should take a trip together," I say, "to Europe."

"What? And leave Dart here?"

"Fuck Dart," I say, with a bravado I really, for the moment, feel.

"What's that ring?" Emmie asks. "It's gorgeous."

"I'm engaged," I say.

"You're *what?*"

"I'm engaged to Louise Zandberg. Leila Sand is engaged to marry Louise Zandberg."

"*Mazel tov,*" says Emmie, with a convent school accent.

We drink our Tabs and happily eat our food, looking around the restaurant to nod and wave to various amiable presences from my thoroughly corrupt world. Just getting into the city has cheered me and made me happy. I belong somewhere other than on the floor of my foyer, weeping. My sane mind is back, and welcome to it!

"I don't know why I don't do this more often," I say.

"Because you're alone in Connecticut, drinking and waiting for Dart to fuck you," says Emmie.

We gossip about friends, about Emmie's menopause book, about the imminent return of my twins, about my new paintings. Life seems good again—even without Dart. At some point, I get up and go to pee.

Walking toward the ladies' room, I see, at a bad table, in the Siberia reserved for the unknown or nonfamous, the face of the trashy little blonde whose pictures I found among Dart's things. She is sitting there, smiling smugly and reading the *New York Times*. On the chair next to her is a white linen jacket I remember buying for Dart.

My heart skips at least ten beats. I break out in a sweat. I can hardly breathe.

The girl looks up, focuses on me for a moment, seems not to recognize me at first, and then goes back to reading the paper.

Seeing the face from those photographs come alive fills me with panic. Where is Dart? He must be in the men's room.

I go to the ladies' room, try to pee and can't, knowing he is right across the wall. I sit on the can with my head in my hands. At once despairing and utterly confused, I finally force myself to pee, get up, fix my makeup, and open the door. Outside is the trashy blonde, leaning against the men's room door, whispering something into its wood. Then she looks at me, this time with recognition, and turns and goes back to the table.

I rap on the men's room door loudly.

"I know you're in there, you coward—come on out!"

No answer. Just the sound of a toilet flushing.

"You bastard!" I yell. "Stop hiding from me! Come on out!"

The lock turns, and a very sheepish-looking Dart emerges from the men's room.

"The trouble with lying," I blurt out, "is that it leaves you terribly lonely. You lie to the one person who really loves you, and then you have no one to trust and no one who really trusts you!"

Isadora: Speech! Speech!

He's edging back toward the men's room, this big macho guy who always made such a big deal of protecting me and protecting the twins.

He looks at me pleadingly, as if to say: "Mommy, I'm sorry." He shrugs. "I *tried*," he says. The trouble is, I know it's true. The girl comes up behind us.

"I hope you can afford him. He's *very* expensive," I say.

"There's more to life than money," she answers, snippily, in a way that tells me he has complained to her of me, of my not spending enough on him. Ha! What I spent on that man would buy a nice medium-size villa in the south of France!

"You're getting more like your father every day," I say.

"That's a low blow," the girl counters.

"Low, but true."

Dart says nothing. Let the women fight it out, his silence screams.

"I feel *sorry* for you," she says, with all the contempt a woman of twenty-five can have for a woman of forty-four—a contempt born of blissful ignorance. "Come on, darlin'," she says.

And she takes him by the hand to the table where the Amex slip awaits—along with the platinum card whose bills come to me.

"Oh, no you don't," I say. "I've paid for your last meal!" And I snatch the card and tear up the Amex slip, fluttering it over my head like confetti.

"How *petty*," the girl spits contemptuously, producing, out of her shabby wallet, a MasterCard drawn on a bank in Ohio.

"Here," she says to the maître d'hotel (who by now has appeared to see whether a fight's in the offing). "I'll pay for this one."

"You certainly will," I say, before stomping off and rejoining Emmie at our table. "You'll pay and pay."

"What on earth *happened* to you?" says Emmie.

"Didn't you hear?"

"There was some commotion in the other room, but I couldn't tell what it was."

I am sweating and out of breath.

"I just played my last scene with Dart," I say. "Next thing I do is cut this in half and change the locks." And I give Emmie the credit card that reads: Darton Venable Donegal IV.

"It's all yours," I say. "Why don't we have a witches' sabbath and burn it? We could sprinkle the ashes into our caldron. . . ."

"What *happened*?" asks Emmie.

"See that couple?" I ask. "That's Dart and my replacement. I hope her credit's good—she's going to need it."

9

BRAVADO AND AFTER

———— ◆ ————

When I woke up my pillow was wet with tears,
Just one day from that man o' mine seems like a thousand years. . . .
I need a whole lot of lovin' 'cause I'm down in the dumps.

—Leola P. Wilson and Wesley Wilson

It doesn't really matter who breaks up a relationship. Whether it's you or him, the pain is the same.

You sleep with a man for almost five years, smelling his sweat, feeling his hairy legs brush you in the night, and you are bonded to him. His leaving has to feel like an amputation. And you go out looking for a wooden stump, knowing it will do no good at all.

It doesn't matter whether or not you know the man is bad for you. It doesn't matter whether or not you know the man is bad. At the end of a love affair, you subscribe to the Stella Kowalski school of logic: there are things that happen in the dark between two people that make everything that happens in the light seem all right.

149

The first night was the worst. I forced myself to sleep alone at the loft, which was littered with Dart's things—and with the little bimbo's. She was some piece of work. Her tatty wired bras and stained bikini panties were hanging insolently over my sink; her half-used birth control pills were on my dresser; her perfume (Charlie!) was on the night table.

I went through her things with rage and curiosity. Her dirty makeup bag, filled with broken bits of cheap cosmetics I would never use, her curled snake of a rubber douche tucked in a nylon pouch in her club bag. Her polyester dressing gown, festooned with pink and aqua flowers. Her scuffed bedroom slippers, in filthy aqua terry cloth.

I contemplated making a collage of all these found objects (and the photos from before) and entitling it *Dart's Bimbo*—but the pain was too great, so I let anger triumph over art and tossed them all out the window. The big window of the loft had to be cranked open and turned around sideways. (It had been made in Germany at great cost and shipped here.) When you opened it, you figured you might as well jump down all six stories—but I resisted the temptation. From the loft I could feel the heat of the street, the singing of the car tires on the wet pavement (it had started to rain), the lure of the open window.

I threw all the nameless bimbo's shit out into the street: birth control pills, douche bag, makeup kit—all. The makeups cracked and scattered on the street below, a million bits of broken mirror bringing bad luck (to her, I hoped, and not to me—though who could tell?). The douche bag seemed to bounce a little, and then it burst its pouch and lay in the street like a boa constrictor that had swallowed a football. (I hate girls who are always deodorizing their pussies; I thought Dart knew better than to hook up with one of those; I thought he understood the value of natural smells.) I threw all the rest of the stuff out, and then I cranked shut the window and collapsed on the bed, too desolate even to cry.

There is no worse betrayal than having a lover bring another woman to your bed; the very mattress vibrates with their sex, interrupting your sleep: your dreams are infected with their treacherous lovemaking. You know how central you were to their love, how much a participant you were, and the thought curdles your blood. No use telling yourself that their love is now diluted and weakened by no longer being secret. No use telling yourself that they, too, are experiencing a sort of loss. You lie in bed unable to find any position that invites sleep. Your back, your side, your stomach, your other side—all are itchy with their sex, crawly with it, as if bedbugs had infested the bed.

The city boils around you. The great, steaming Rome-at-the-end-of-the-empire city. Police cars screaming, ambulances tearing through the streets, garbage pail lids bouncing noisily on pavement, bottles breaking, ghetto blasters blaring endless songs about the flood of hormones, the crescendo of testosterone seeking estrogen and estrogen seeking testosterone—the pulse of the universe.

Everyone has someone, and you are alone. Everyone is grinding pelvis to pelvis, hip to hip, and you are all alone.

Suddenly the love comes to attack you. You want to summon bad memories, but all the good ones come flooding back. You want to hate him, but the love is still there, pulsing like a severed heart. You want to forget, but you can do nothing but remember.

The Dalmatian coast in summer, and Dart lying in the sun like a young god. The tender purple veins in his lids. The gold of his chest. The trace of a crack in his forehead where the windshield stopped him once on his way to a coke-propelled car crash in Bucks County. Dart killing a copperhead by blasting its head off with a shotgun. Dart fucking you on the floor of the Connecticut house. Dart darting. Dart gone. Dart back. Surely Dart is coming back.

This time I doubt it. The con man needs the mark to feel real. The drunk needs the drink. The addict the needle. The prick the pussy. Where have all my gratitude and grace gone now?

I get up, snap on the light, and go to the bar. There, in a mirrored cabinet designed by Ettore Sottsass himself especially for this loft, I admire the parade of bottles: Chivas Regal, Jack Daniel's, Stolichnaya, Beefeater, Canadian Club, Pernod, Lillet, Cinzano, Noilly Prat. . . . The bottles confront me with their amber and crystal lights. The bottles goad me and tease me.

What's the difference? I think. Why not?

I uncork the Chivas (though Scotch was never my drink) and dare myself to take a slug. I do. And another. And another. As soon as my head starts to get fuzzy, I know I'm in trouble. I pour the liquor down the sink and smash the bottle on the floor.

The meetings have ruined my drinking. I used to drink, waiting for the click in my head (as Brick says in *Cat on a Hot Tin Roof*), and now I *hate* it when my head gets fuzzy. The minute the fuzziness starts, I know I'm doomed: doomed to a week of depression and sadness and self-hate. Doomed to the long and winding fall to the bottom of the rabbit hole.

I toss and turn on my bed, waiting for the booze to work its way out of my system. Dart's sheepish look haunts me. I remember how the bimbo did all the talking for him, and I am desolate. I want to comfort Dart, not blame him. Somehow I know that Dart is the victim of his own weakness and despair—and far more lost than I am. He hates his dependency even more than I hate it, and yet he doesn't know any other way to be.

The hell of my condition is that I understand Dart so bloody well. He is my baby, my darling, my man, and I want to nurture and protect him even as he is slaughtering me. If Dart were to write his side of the story, what would he say? That big, bad Leila emasculated him and made him feel weak? That big bad Leila took all his marbles away? I appreciate the problem of being the model, not the artist.

Once, when I was in art school, I was the model for a friend of mine—a figurative painter named Mikhailovich, who painted me for a month (out of love, I believe) but who made me look a way that was not at all to my liking. I remember the sense of being under another's spell, of bad magic, and I remember, too, the feeling of being out of control. Dart feels this way all the time. Dart is trying to control me by bringing the bimbo to my loft, by darting, by fucking her in my bed.

Impossible. I switch on the light, get dressed, flip through my AA booklet, and go out in search of an all-night meeting. My loins girded in denim, I venture out, searching for a refuge from my pain. As I walk, indifferent to danger, I seem to see the book of my life riffling before my eyes. How many years do I have left to paint? I could die tonight on these streets, or I could have one, two, ten, twenty, thirty years. My life is more than half over. Already the small print swims on the page when I try to read. Already my periods are either too long or too short. Already my knees ache and my elbow joints pain me in the rain. I have no time to suffer over Dart. I have work to do.

I find the meeting (in a shabby church a few blocks from the loft) and meet my people—the bums, the street people, the homeless.

The all-night meeting is as much a shelter as it is a place of prayer and guidance. Old men and women who have nothing to eat but these sugary cookies, nothing to drink but this tepid coffee or tea.

What a shabby, ragtag bunch they are! Some of the men have no teeth, and one talks to himself in the back row of the battered little wooden chairs. The women could be hookers, homeless maniacs, the sick, the half dead. New York has increasingly become a city of poverty and great wealth. Here in Hogarth's London, the great lady in her designer dress disdains the beggar who importunes her from the street. But in the Program we are all leveled.

The meeting has not yet started, and people mill about, drinking coffee and greeting each other. All strangers, but bound together by kindness and an agreement to try to be honest. I love AA's reprieve from the standards that hold sway in the rest of our society. Elsewhere greed and falsehood and egotism are the rule. Here, generosity, truth, humility. I am nervous because I drank tonight and I will have to say so, but there is something healing about just being here in this room. The love in the room is palpable. Somewhere, here, my sane mind is waiting.

Someone comes up to me and taps me on the shoulder.

At first I recoil. It seems to be a bag lady, face swimming in fat, eyes buried in wrinkles. On her head she wears a red knitted cap with dangling sequins, on her body a tent of red polyester.

"Louise?" she says tentatively. "Louise?"

"Yes."

"I'm Rivka Landesman, remember? Music and Art?"

I look at her in disbelief. This huge wallowing-in-fat bag lady is a classmate of mine from high school—a talented painter, someone who had a gallery before I did, someone I was once envious of because she seemed to have it made, when I was still struggling for my first recognition as a painter. Rivka was a prodigy even in high school. She used to hang out with Andy Warhol, did movies with him, sold her work to important collectors, was written up everywhere—then vanished. I hadn't heard of her in years.

"How *are* you?" I asked. The question was ridiculous. I could see how she was. Worse off than I.

My kindness released something in her: a flood of self-pity.

"Well," she said, "when my fourth marriage—to the Italian—broke up and he absconded with my entire life savings, I really hit bottom. You won't believe this, but in the last year I've lost everything. My daughter's left for college, my boyfriend vanished to Italy with a million dollars of mine and three of Andy's paintings, I've had a partial hysterectomy, my hormones are all fucked up, I've gained eighty pounds, my mother died. . . . I'm hoping AA can help me. I don't know where else to go. I'm as close to suicide as I've ever been."

Something in me recoils at the self-pity. I feel that Rivka is about to get her hooks into me and not let go. I feel trapped, claustrophobic. But when somebody reaches out for help, you have to help.

"Louise," she says, "what gallery are you with now?

Do you think they'd look at my work?"

"I don't know," I say, suddenly feeling my pocket being picked. "I'm not here to be your agent. I'm here because I'm a drunk."

"Of course," says Rivka, "but you're so fortunate. You've always had more success than me. Always been in the right place at the right time. Always on the crest of the wave of the moment."

I look at her in disbelief. She's insulting me and guilt-tripping me at the same time. "Networking" at a meeting! Is there any *lower* a person can sink!

"You're so pretty. You always have men. You always have the critics in the palm of your hand. You've no idea how hard it's been for me. . . ."

Now she's really pushing my buttons. I want to scream at her, to denounce her for her kvetching and self-absorption, tell her that she's probably driven away everyone who's ever tried to help her, but then I realize that this reaction is exactly why I was meant to come to this meeting: to see myself reflected in this woman—to see what I could become if I don't pull myself together and get tough with myself, to see an example of a woman squandering her life by playing the victim.

"Rivka," I say gently, "if you want me to help you get sober, I'll try. I'm not having an easy time myself. Perhaps I can help you in some way—but please don't insult me by trying to guilt-trip me into selling your work. That's not what the Program's about, and all you're doing is driving me away."

She looks at me, uncomprehending.

"Don't you want to help me?"

"I do, I want to help you, but I don't want you to insult me and manipulate me. I'm struggling too. I drank tonight after not drinking for a month and feeling better than I've ever felt in my life. I am still trying to take things one step at a time. I am still trying to learn how to lead my life. All my success led me to pressures of a *different* sort from the ones you've had—but they are pressures just the same. There's no competition between us. We're all stumbling human beings. The Program led me to see my life in spiritual terms, and I blew it—maybe because I couldn't *take* my life actually getting better. I wanted the pain back. I made a little bargain with God that I would get sober if I could have my lover back, and I got him back for a while, and that misled me. But God doesn't play by our rules. And we can't be like petulant little kids and say, 'Well, if God doesn't play by my rules, I'm not playing, I'll destroy myself—so *there!*' We really haven't *got* that option. We can choose to live or choose to die—but we can't straddle the fence. And if we want to live we have no choice but to *submit*—not to our own will, to God's.''

"Oh, Her," said Rivka.

"Right," I said. "Her. Or Him. It doesn't even matter; it's a sort of vanity even to argue about the sex of God. We're talking about spirit here, the gift of life—and whether you choose to affirm it or deny it. That's all this is about."

Was I trying to convince Rivka—or myself?

Rivka's eyes blinked. A flicker of intuition.

"I almost see," she said.

"Of course you do; you're a painter." I hugged her. I couldn't even get my arms around her, but I hugged her.

Isadora: My skin gets crawly when our heroine launches into sermons about drink and drugs. She's barely sober, after all.

Leila: It's those of us who are barely sober who preach the hardest. When you're really beyond addiction, you don't need to preach.

    Isadora: And I don't know where you're going with this chapter. I sniff an epiphany at hand. Epiphany on the Bowery. God—I hate epiphanies.

    Leila: You've gotten so cynical in your old age. What became of the old Isadora, who was afraid but flew anyway?

    Isadora: Don't ask. It would take another book to tell you.

    The meeting was called to order by the secretary, who looked like a street hooker in her black leather micro-mini, red halter top, huge red hair bow, and red spike-heeled sandals. It was difficult to tell how old she was. Anywhere between eighteen and thirty, I guessed. But she had a hard look, the look that a life on the streets leaves you with. I knew that compared to mine, her life was tough. Just seeing her spirited, cocky little body and hearing her jaunty reading of the preamble made me cry. I was so glad to be back here, in the meeting, so glad to have a meeting to go to.

    The speaker was introduced as Lenore B. Much rowdy applause. She was known to the members.

    Lenore B. was a wiry little black woman in her fifties or sixties who told a story that could have made anyone's hair stand on end: a battering husband, a son shot on the streets of Harlem, a daughter with breast cancer, a mother with lung cancer, a brother with AIDS. Some people have more than their share of afflictions, and Lenore was one of these. In AA, I'd finally come to understand the story of Job and why God reserves the right to strip us in order to punish us for our hubris and self-absorption. It was a good lesson, a lesson I could often grasp during meetings but that would float right out of my head when I wasn't at meetings. Now, hearing Lenore, I was reminded of it again. I wondered what Rivka thought. Never mind. I wondered what *I* thought.

Lenore spoke about her life, and my mind wandered. I looked at the scroll listing the Twelve Steps and realized you could spend your whole life on any one of them. I could do a conceptual piece on AA scrolls—but wouldn't risk it for fear of tampering with the magic.

Allowing the steps to drift through my mind, I focused on the sixth—something about being "entirely ready" to have God remove one's "defects of character"— which was the subject of tonight's meeting. What did "entirely ready" mean? It meant you were ready to open your heart to God. It meant you really wanted to get better. It meant you were through with self-pity. It meant you were *entirely ready* to listen to your own sane mind.

Was I? Absolutely not. I was too attached to my pain and self-pity, too attached to Dart, too attached to the me that was just *like* Dart, too attached to my own willfulness.

As so often happens at meetings, the speaker and I collided thought waves.

Lenore B. said: "Watchin' my brother die of AIDS, I axed myself: Does you really believe in spirit, or is you only pretendin' to? Because he lost his faith in his final sickness, an' I almos' did myseff. He was a *terrble* sight: tumors comin' out of his tongue, a sickenin' smell, a wasted body. I nursed him, an' many's the time I wanted to drink, but even more often I wanted to curse God for his afflictions. And for mine. It was the sixth step that save me. Specially two words of the sixth step. The words 'entirely ready.' Was I entirely ready to give up the flesh? I wasn't— not till I saw my brother's flesh rottin' and fallin' off. We don' like death. We don' like disease. We think we be too big for death and disease. We think we be *beyond* the flesh. But flesh is mostly there as a lesson. Once we learn it, we pass on.

"I *bless* the day God took my brother Harold. I bless the day I saw him lyin' there, a heap of bones and stinkin' flesh. Till that day, I didn't *believe* I was mortal. But now I believes it. I am *entirely ready.* And whenever I become unready, God sends me another reminder. . . ."

There is a strange wheezing sound in the back of the room. Several of us turn and look back, to see an old bum in the back row grab his chest and double over.

Propelled by a force I don't understand, I rush to his side.

The man's face turns stony blue, then he falls forward, hitting his head on the chair in front of him with a *thunk.* He crumples on the floor, reeking of sweat, piss, dung—the smell of destitution. His head turned to one side, his eyelids flutter, and I can see that what's left of his one visible eye is cloudy blue. His mouth moves—toothlessly. A thin rivulet of saliva slimes out of one corner of his mouth onto the floor. I think of Dart, who always loved the bums, identified with them, wanted, in fact, to go around the city putting blankets on all of them like some crazed catcher in the rye. And I try to pretend that this heavy lump of decaying flesh is my beautiful Dart. For it is.

The red hole of a mouth speaks: "I tole 'im it was no good goin' to the center of the lake . . . but would he lissen? No, siree. Never. I told 'im the raft wouldn't hole 'im, but would he lissen? No, siree. Gone . . . all gone . . . summer gone . . . and winter . . . and the good booze. . . . I told 'im, I tried to tell 'im. . . ."

His slate-colored face takes on an utterly peaceful expression, and he is gone into some forgotten summer on some forgotten lake, with some never to be forgotten companion. Perhaps they are together now. Then all the muscles in his face relax. He is entirely ready. And then his bladder lets go, and I am kneeling in a pool of piss that spreads from his reeking trousers.

The calm in his bluish face as the urine spreads around him, wetting even my knees and calves, makes me think I am watching a tiny baby returning to Mama. Life is so hard for some people. They never can get the hang of taking care of themselves. Death must be such a relief. No more pretense. No more holding on. The warm pool of pee in the bed turning cool and sticky on the legs. Back to Mommy, back to the big breast.

The members of the meeting are standing around us now.

In astonishment at the rapidity with which life passes to death, I can only say: "God, God."

"Amen," says Lenore, coming up behind me.

Several members of the meeting are crying. Someone has gone to call the ambulance (although it is clear that our friend is beyond ambulances now). And Rivka has fled. She is not entirely ready. Perhaps someday she will be.

10

BLUE BLUES

———◆———

> When I get home
> I gonna change
> my lock and key.
>
> —J. C. Johnson

So I changed the locks. I had no choice, really. I didn't do it gleefully. When the locksmith came, I cried. But there was no way I was letting the bimbo into my bed again. It was insupportable. I had lost Leila somewhere between New York and Connecticut, and I had to get her back. Changing the locks was the first step.

It wasn't easy. I would think about Dart all the time. His cock. His sweet half-crooked smile. His beautiful calf muscles. His tight buns. His cock.

I would lie in bed at night missing him viscerally, missing him in my gut, my heart, my fingertips. When I loved Dart, I loved him so hard that often my fingertips ached, and now my fingertips missed him. They could still feel the texture of his skin. And my nostrils. My nostrils could still smell him.

It's no easy thing to give up booze and a lover at the same time. One addiction is hard enough. But what choice did I have? There was nothing left in the bottle for me. Nothing but depression and sadness and pain. I couldn't kid myself that drinking would make anything better. It always made everything worse.

So I turned to Pop Lit. Femme 101. *Women Who Love Too Much; Men Who Hate Women and the Women Who Love Them; Smart Women, Foolish Choices* . . . all the books that promise relief from man addiction. I drew the line at man-addiction groups, as I drew the line at Sexoholics Anonymous. For one mad moment, I thought of going to Sexoholics Anonymous to *meet* men, but I couldn't quite bring myself to. The very notion made my sane mind giggle.

The books were *something.* They told you everything that was wrong with your relationship (heavily implying that it was all your fault), but they didn't tell you how to find a *good* relationship. Were you masochistic? A doormat? A sexoholic? Did you use sweets to assuage your loneliness? Wine? Dope? Coke? Well, just follow these simple twelve steps, and it would all get better. You had to focus on your own recovery. You had to be entirely ready.

Nobody seemed to be writing these books for *men*. It was women who had to be entirely ready to give up their addictions. It was women who were hooked on heartless bastards. (Could that be because of the percentages: seven million more women than men, so why *should* men behave?) At times, I thought these books were part of a conspiracy of female authors to get other women's men. Because if every female reader followed the hard-nosed suggestions in these books, a lot of men would come loose and be on the open market again. That was my theory for a while—until I realized that it didn't account for the fact that some of these books were written by men! Were they homosexuals, hoping to spring loose a few more men who were now disaffected with the whole female sex?

And who could blame men for being disaffected with the whole female sex? Men are so vulnerable—all their vulnerability hanging so nakedly between their legs. Frightened of their mommies, of shrieking women—all they ask is a little softness and tenderness from us. No wonder armies of screaming women on the march terrify them. Wouldn't *I* react with terror and with rage if I were a man? In my sane mind, I know I would.

I tried to take care of business. During the death throes of my affair with Dart, when things were crashing and burning, not a lot of work had got done, as you can imagine.

After the success of the film stills of Dart/Trick, which launched Dart/Trick into a sort of SoHo stardom—complete with all the appurtenances thereto pertaining, particularly toot and tootsies—*my* work went to the dogs. How can you paint when you never know when or if your lover is coming home? Better to be Georgia O'Keeffe, alone on her mesa beneath the scudding clouds (with a pretty young wrangler to carry your easel and a pretty young potter to catalog your work—no fool Georgia). Better to live in splendid isolation than to look for love in all the wrong places with a tricky Dart or a darting Trick.

So now that he was gone, and I was left on the rock of my half-assed sobriety, I tried to get back to business. Invited by my dealer, one André McCrae (the McCrae Gallery), to a shindig at his Fifth Avenue digs, I accepted—

though of late I had made myself scarcer than scarce.

André was a symptom of everything wrong with the art biz. He knew nothing about art and had no idea what he liked. He liked what sold, and the more it sold for, the more he liked it. If it stopped selling, he stopped liking it. If it sold a lot and the artist died, he liked it best of all. His idea of a perfect artist was a dead artist—preferably one who had died at the height of his fame. Once, before I signed with André, he told me at a dinner party in Cornwall Bridge that he really preferred to deal with dead artists. "They don't puke all over you," he said. I should have taken this as a warning, but I didn't. I thought I could manage André—which only goes to show how wrong I can be.

On a hot Wednesday night in July, I drive down from Connecticut in DART and park in the Carlyle garage, then walk over to André's duplex at Seventy-fourth and Fifth. It's that rare thing—a summer party in New York, which can only be held on Tuesday or Wednesday night; all the other nights, the city is likely to be left to the poor. The rich are in the Hamptons, the Vineyard, Newport, Nantucket, Maine, the Cape, Tuscany, Greece, Venice, the south of France.

André and his wife, Sally, have devised a unique scheme for saving their marriage: separate co-ops in adjacent Fifth Avenue buildings. This party is being held in André's, the grander of the two.

Going to parties stone cold sober is new for me—new and scary. I see too much, feel too much, am too aware of all the lying.

I go up in the paneled elevator and am let out on the fourteenth floor—really the thirteenth, but this building skips from twelve to fourteen for good luck. The apartment is actually on the thirteenth and fourteenth floors. Knowing André, he probably negotiated a discount because of that.

André was not born André, and his father was not named McCrae any more than mine was named Sand. André McCrae is a self-created character. Born Arbit Malamud in Lithuania in the twenties or thirties, he started life as a furrier but soon discovered that there was more pelf in canvases than in pelts.

His first painting, as he likes to tell everyone who will listen (and with André you often have no *choice* but to listen), was given to him as part of a divorce settlement by his first wife. Apocryphal stories about André's first marriage abound: it is said he was married to a Rothschild, a Churchill, a Vanderbilt, a Rockefeller—perhaps all four at once. She was rich, in any case, defied caste and class to marry this pushy little redheaded Jew (five feet two inches, even in his elevator shoes), and lived to regret it. She bought him off with a Van Gogh (which still hangs in the grand co-op foyer—along with other, more recent acquisitions). The Van Gogh (whose companion piece hangs in the Phillips Gallery in Washington) depicts the public gardens at Arles in 1888, with a man and a woman walking through its verdant summer foliage.

Van Gogh is the perfect artist for André to own, because Van Gogh is André's polar opposite. This tormented artist who never sold a painting—except, as a sort of mercy fuck, to his brother—but was driven by an inner frenzy to produce them represents everything André will never be and therefore hopes he can either buy or destroy: inner fire, inner certainty, the driving force of genius.

"How are you, Tsatskeleh?" says André, opening the

door himself and characteristically not waiting for any answer. (André affects *Yiddishkeit* to shock the goyim. He piles it on with a trowel, particularly in the presence of Gettys, Du Ponts, and Mellons, who find him *cute.* Sort of the pet Jew.)

Sally rushes up to admire my dress.

"Don't tell me. Let me guess. Zoran? Karan? Koos?"

"No. Guess again."

"Krizia?"

"No."

"You made it yourself? So clever of you."

"It's an ancient Zandra Rhodes."

"I should have known." Sally is thin enough to have flunked selection at Auschwitz. She and André have one of those marriage-is-a-business marriages so dear to the hearts of New York's New Money Elite. They own things together rather than fuck. This is their form of sex.

Sally wears a size two dress, and going to bed with her would be like going to bed with a bicycle. Her hair is raving red—though expensively done, at Monsieur Marc, no doubt—and her art deco jewelry is always dazzling. It covers her breastbones, which otherwise would show. She wears a Scaasi pouf over her pick-up-sticks legs, and she is the mistress of the touch-me-not kiss. She turns her smile on and off like a bare light bulb in a cheap hotel. You will never know what she's thinking. André is more transparent.

Even at his own party, André's eyes scan the room to see if there's a more important person to talk to than the one he's with. When André is with you, you always have the sense he's just about to dart away. Dart. Everything reminds you of Dart.

"How's Dart?" says André.

"Gone," I say.

"It was only a matter of time," says André. "What are you drinking?"

"Tab, Perrier . . ."

"Roberto will get it," he says, waving a hand at the South American butler, and he sprints off across the room to talk to someone who looks like Princess Di but isn't. André has the chutzpah of an elephant, and the attention span of a gnat.

The room seems to swim. All these people laughing mirthlessly, all these darting eyes working the room.

André's parties always have a smattering of royalty, a hint of Hollywood, a major media celebrity who mouths the news, a press lord or two, a Wall Street tycoon or two, a real estate baron or two—all appropriately wived in women who come (like certain designer dresses) only in sizes two to eight. Double digits are out. The artists are there, of course, André's artists, but they are sort of like zoo animals on their best behavior. At André's parties, they always have the sense that their endeavors are vaguely peripheral to the main event: buying and selling. They often get quietly drunk or stoned, pass out in the guest room or discreetly throw up in the powder room, perhaps nauseated by so much proximity to the beau monde to which their success has entitled them.

Sally takes me by the hand and leads me over to a little nest of ninnies: six size-six women who look just like her—except for the hair color (they are all straw-into-gold blond) and the skinny legs perched upon spikes.

I recognize the names from Liz Smith's column and the faces from the central hatchery: some plastic surgeon is turning out that chin this year. They all have the razor-sharp jawline not even nature bestows on a twenty-two-year-old. Each one of them looks delighted to meet me. It isn't long before I am recruited to do my bit for various chic diseases—AIDS, heart disease, cancer: the fashionable plagues of the moment. One blonde wants a drawing to auction, another my company at an "exclusive little dinner," whose seats on either side of me will be auctioned, another for me to teach a class at her daughter's school. I am expected to be honored by their requests to have my pocket genteelly picked, though if I asked one of these women for her diamond necklace, she would be horrified and call the police. But an artist's time and an artist's work is of no worth—unless of course it is bartered by André.

I am polite. I make vague promises. Then, spotting someone I know, I cross the room.

It's Wayne Riboud—the Nevada biker who has become the flavor of the month by meticulously reproducing dollar bills, yen, francs, and lire, and trading them for necessaries like food and clothing. It has become quite fashionable in New York to hang money on the walls. None of your arcane symbolism here. Pass the buck: that is all ye know on earth and all ye need to know.

"How are you, kid?" says Wayne, peering down my cleavage.

"Still living."

"That bad, huh?"

"Worse."

"Kid split?"

"Mmm."

"Who with?"

"Does it matter?"

"No," says Wayne. "Endings are all the same: the bimbo, the bills, the blues. God, people bore me. Why can't they love one another for a change?"

"Can you?"

"No. Can you?"

I laugh. "I honestly don't know, Wayne."

"You wanna split?"

"Where?"

"We could dance. Nell's—if it isn't over yet. Somewhere. We could take a garbage scow around Manhattan, hear Bobby Short at the Carlyle."

"Not the way you're dressed."

"We could split to the country. Your place or mine?"

Wayne does a sort of Groucho Marx imitation of lust.

"I gotta circulate first."

Wayne nods and makes for the loo. I wander over to talk to André's best friend, Lionel Schaeffer, who is such a *gruber yung* that he makes André seem like Percy Bysshe Shelley.

"Leila, pussycat," says Lionel. "Long time no see. What's up?"

"What's up with you?"

I shouldn't have asked. Lionel begins a recitation of everything he's *bought* in the last two months. Two companies. One old master. A villa in Beaulieu. An apartment in Beijing. ("Beijing is the next place," says Lionel.) Jon Bannenberg is redesigning his schooner, *Lion's Share*. (Most men name their boats after their daughters or wives; Lionel named his after himself: a key to his character.) "I'm only in New York for one day. Tomorrow I leave for Paris to go ballooning with you-know-who, then I'm off to London to meet with Jon about the tub"—(his mock-deprecatory title for his boat)—"then to Venice for some cockamamy charity ball at some cockamamy palazzo rented by some cockamamy friends of Lindsay's." Lionel has won the shiksa sweepstakes with this marriage. He indicates his third wife, Lindsay, a thirty-five-year-old who is fast turning into a replica of his second wife, Lizbeth, and his first wife, Shirley: emaciated charity ballers both. (Is photography the reason that anorexia has become equated with beauty? These women photograph well, though they look terrifyingly like death's-heads in the flesh. Has the image become so much more important than the thing itself?)

    Isadora: Yes! *And you'll never be thin enough.*
    Leila: Or *rich enough.*

"Leila!" sings Lindsay.
"Lindsay!" sings Leila, embracing Ms. Bones.
Lindsay is dressed in a short Lacroix with a bell-shaped cerise skirt over black petticoats and gold upholstery braid all over the black velvet bolero jacket. She looks as if she was dressed by Scarlett O'Hara out of the window drapes at Tara. She is about two heads taller than Lionel, who, with his bulgy blue eyes, his implanted hair, and his perfectly tailored suit, could be in any business at all—from crack to art, from publishing to movies to finance.
The truth is, he made his fortune in the news business, inherited chains of newsstands from his father, Izzy Schaeffer, who traveled everywhere with a little man called Lefty Lifshitz, who packed a rod. Izzy and Lefty were not unknown to Meyer Lansky, though to hear Lionel talk today you'd think his father had been a concert violinist—a myth he likes to perpetuate, because Izzy did, in fact, play the fiddle. Lionel gives lots of money to the New York Philharmonic and the Metropolitan Opera, and every time he comes up with another million-dollar check, Rogers & Cowan gets him plenty of media coverage for it.

Last year he was hailed as "Philanthropist of the Year" in *Manhattan, inc.,* got the Légion d'honneur in France and an O.B.E. in England. These things are not exactly bought, but it is astonishing how gullible people who should know better are about the motives for philanthropy. Lionel and Lindsay move in social circles in which giving million-dollar checks to arts organizations has become as de rigueur as the Lacroix pouf and the Turnbull and Asser tie.

Lionel opens his jacket to show me something. Inside, on the paisley silk, I see his initials, "LS," and below that a little label that says, in silk script, "Turnbull and Chung." Lionel laughs.

"Whaddya think? I had thirty-seven cashmere suits made in Hong Kong, and I got 'em to make up these labels—Turnbull and Chung. Jeezus, they fought me on it—but I prevailed." He makes the universal money gesture by rubbing thumb and forefinger together.

I laugh and hug Lionel. He sees the game of it all, and for that I like him.

"If you *dare* do that at the Principessa Tavola-Calda's in Venice, I'll *kill* you," says Lindsay, a former stewardess from K.C., who doesn't see the game of it and never will.

"Leila, baby," says Lionel, "if you ever get rid of that stud, don't go to strangers—okay, babe?" He looks down my dress and raises his eyebrows. "*Mamma mia,* what a *poitrine.*" He does this in front of Lindsay to keep her in line. She pretends not to care, but she glares at me briefly before wandering off.

"She hates doing it," Lionel says. "And you know me—can't get enough, pussycat. Where are you gonna be this summer?"

"In Connecticut. Painting."

"In your famed phallic silo?"

"The same."

"Where's the stud?"

"He went out."

"Lissen—I'll call you when I get back from Europe, okay? Maybe I'll take the chopper up to your neck of the woods."

"Call me," I say. And I go off to find Wayne. Maybe what I need is a vulgar billionaire in Turnbull and Chung suits. Could it possibly be worse than Dart?

Where is Wayne? I haven't seen him since he took off for the loo.

I make my way through the sprawling apartment, which has recently been redone by some hot new decorator much addicted to Concordeing back and forth to London. All the latest trends are represented: one room in Biedermeier fruitwood and Impressionist paintings; another room full of Important Pieces in seventeenth-century japanning and gilt, with seventeenth-century Dutch still lives of dead birds and fruit on the walls; another room full of Victoriana—chairs with leopard legs, chandeliers and tables made out of antlers and that sort of thing, Pre-Raphaelite paintings. The place is a hodgepodge. Sally often jokes that she moved next door because she and André couldn't agree on decor. She is into Bauhaus-minimalist-modern, he into excess with a vengeance.

His bed, for example, which I come upon in the master bedroom overlooking leafy Central Park, once belonged to Henry VIII. A taller tycoon than André would never fit. But this hideous regal Tudor four-poster has been outfitted with an inner mirrored canopy, a sound system built into the four posts, and a television that rises ominously from a steel-banded antique sea trunk at its foot.

(This media *boîte* once belonged to a sailor in the Armada.)

When I come into the bedroom, Wayne is stretched out half naked in André's bed, moving the television up and down and giggling maniacally. The sweet smell of sinsemilla fills the room.

"Join me?"

"You're crazy, Wayne. I'm going to call André."

"Call him. He *expects* us to act like maniacs. That's why we're here. 'Round up the usual suspects,' he tells his secretary. 'See if the tsatskeleh will drive down from Connecticut and the biker will bike up from SoHo. We're the sideshow to his Barnum. You know what Barnum said?"

"No. What did Barnum say?"

"Nobody ever went broke underestimating the taste of the American public. That's why I sell them money. I *used* to do sensitive nudes and still lives, Turneresque luminescent skies, mad Pollockian abstractions. Now I give 'em what they already know the value of—money. Fuck 'em. The whole business makes me sick. Come to bed."

"No, Wayne."

"What the fuck are you standing there for? Come to bed."

"Get your clothes on, and let's blow this dump."

"Where to?"

"Anywhere. Nell's. The garbage scow. Connecticut."

"Will you fuck me if I wear a rubber?"

"No."

"If I don't?"

"Maybe."

Wayne laughs and bounces out of bed. I check out his shlong, but who can tell under those circumstances?

"I see you're checking out my shlong," Wayne says.

"Yep."

"And . . . ?"

"Frankly, I'm underwhelmed."

"You cunt," says Wayne, laughing again.

We head for Connecticut, out of the city and into the hills of the Nutmeg State. Leaving the city, one feels the head clear, the heart leap.

Wayne, Mr. Macho Man, drives like a drunk. Actually, he *is* drunk, but he won't let me drive, denying it. I keep telling him I want to drive, and he keeps telling me no. Every time he turns to tell me no, I get a blast of booze breath. His whole body reeks of alcohol and dope—something I never smelled before I got sober, but now it is overwhelming. *Sickening.*

"Let me drive, Wayne," I say. "It's my fucking car."

"Baby, I'm fine," he says, nearly careening into a side barrier as he takes the curving ramp up to the Triborough Bridge.

"Let me drive the car. . . . You're drunk."

"I am *not* drunk," he says drunkenly, turning to me and nearly hitting the toll booth. Wayne has those funny little teeth that are three-quarters gums. They look like Chiclets. His hair is sandy, his green eyes squinty, and he has the flattened, turned-up-tip nose of an Irishman. A drunken leprechaun. I think of all the times I used to get drunk and stoned with Dart so that we could do mad sex together, and I realize that I am outside that world now, isolated from men and sex by sobriety. Possibly I will never get laid again. I can't stand the way this man smells. His pores reek of alcohol and dope. Why have I never smelled this before?

I never much liked coke; sinsemilla and wine were my drugs of choice. Actually, it was not sinsemilla and wine so much as sex—sex was my drug of choice. Sex was what blotted out the world for me. Sex was my opium, my anodyne, my laudanum, my love. Sex was what I used to kill the pain of life—the pot and the wine were just my avenues to bed. Open your mouth and close your eyes. Open your legs and close your eyes. Open your heart and close your eyes.

A line comes back to me from a poem I read in college: "Wax to receive and marble to retain." Don Juan's heart. Byron's *Don Juan.* Dart's heart. Wax to receive and marble to retain. I don't want to fall in love with Don Juan again.

I imagine a piece based on this insight, using the materials of marble—faux marble—and real wax. It would be called *Don Juan,* and it would deal with all the many possibilities of this theme. The marble heart. The wax heart. The heartless heart.

But I myself am Donna Giovanna, I think, and Dart was a sort of karmic revenge—the revenge of my own philandering. I lived for sex, for falling in love with love, for breaking (or at least collecting) hearts—and Dart was the gods' revenge. What goes around comes around, they say in the Program. Dart was the visible manifestation of my own addiction.

Jesus. Wayne has nearly careened into another lamp-post. The open car, the drunken driver . . . I could be killed! Worse still, I could be creamed and crippled. I have twins to raise, work to do.

"Stop the car this instant." (Ah, my sane mind has not deserted me utterly.)

"Oh, baby—don't be a drag," Wayne says, nearly hitting the side barrier again. "I'm perfectly okay."

I clutch the seat in terror. We are careening from side

to side, making lazy snakes around the white line in the middle of the road.

I am paralyzed. Here is the voice of male authority telling me "don't be a drag."

Don't be a drag, Leila. This used to be fun. Drunk, I got in a lot of careening cars and thought it was fun. This is not fun.

"Stop the car, Wayne."

"I know a place," Wayne says. "Just let me take you to the place I know."

He careens on. I try to take the wheel, but he jerks it away. The car veers from side to side as we struggle.

I'm not sure whether it's more dangerous to resist or not to resist.

"Take me to your place," I say.

Wayne drives like a maniac to Westchester, where he burns rubber along back roads until he finds a little roadhouse buried in the foliage of the summer night.

He parks the car at a rakish angle, pockets the keys, puts his arm around me, and steers me inside.

Blaring jukebox. People drinking. Girls at the bar looking us over as we enter.

"Hi, girls!" says Wayne sloppily. "Wanna fuck a real artist?"

They don't seem impressed.

Wayne finds a barstool amid the pulchritude—three young women whose combined ages, I think with a stab of pain, don't even total mine. (It's not true, of course, but sober, I feel like the Ancient Mariness.)

I head for the ladies' room, leaving Wayne with the pulchritude. There, I pee, wash up, fix my makeup. I take a good look at myself in the mirror. My chin is starting to get a bit loose, and the circles under my eyes are deepening.

I feel *old*. My bravado has carried me through a lot, but now I'm beginning to wonder if bravado is enough. I *long* for someone to nurture me. I seem to have been bouncing around alone for *years*. Ah, for a nurturing man, a daddy to tell my troubles to—wouldn't that be sweet for a change? Someone to buy *me* a gold Rolex, or a cowboy suit, or a car.

My daddy was never like that, even when I had him. The tenderest memory I have of Dolph is of him making me origami birds or pulling silver like taffy to make me jewelry.

When my mother died, I found one of his brooches gathering dust in her jewelry box. My initials in silver script interlaced in a silver heart. Louise Zandberg aka Leila Sand. Wax to receive and marble to retain. Like the memory of my daddy. Oh, how our daddies hook us on all our addictions, pressing the packet of junkie love into our little-girl hands. Daddy! He comes and goes. He runs. He leaves Mommy and baby girl, and she longs ever after for the man who darts.

Out of the bathroom, back to the bar. Wayne surrounded by cuties, flirting. Arm around an eighteen-year-old curly redhead, who laughs and laughs and clinks glasses with him, not caring that he smells of booze and drives like the red menace.

I saunter over, sit at the bar, to hear Wayne telling the girl to call him in the city, then scribbling his phone number on a damp napkin for her. Another girl, next to her, looks at me avidly, then says: "Hey, I saw you on TV! Didn't you do those big pictures of your boyfriend or somethin'?"

"You must be mistaking me for someone else."

"Nah. I never forget a face. You had that cute boyfriend, and you photographed him. There was this show about you on TV! Hey—that's really neat. Hey, Liza—hey, Jennifer." She turns to her two friends. "This chick is really neat. She photographed this dude in *costumes*. Where is he? He was *cute*."

"Gone the way of cute men."

"Then it *was* you. Jeez. You're neat. I wish I was an artist."

Wayne seems discomforted by no longer being the center of attention.

"Don't you love me anymore, girls?" He sulks.

"Can I ask you somethin'?" The girl called Jennifer, with long black hair down her back and a gauze minidress, is speaking.

"Sure," I say.

"Why do we always fall in love with the bastards? I mean is there somethin' about their bein' nasty that turns us on?"

I laugh. "The first woman who figures out the answer to *that* is gonna be *sainted*."

"Do *you* fall in love with the bastards?" asks her friend Liza, with the flaxen blond hair and the face of a Scandinavian angel.

"She just *said* so," Jennifer interrupts. "She's just *like* us."

"It's what one of my English friends calls 'The Great Nasty Man Question,' " I say in my mock-English accent. 'The *nahst*ier they are, the hotter we get,' she says."

The young women look up at me, waiting for an answer.

"Don't you *ever* get smart?" asks Jennifer.

"That depends," I say.

"On what?" asks Liza.

"On whether or not you finally realize that Big Daddy is *not* coming home and you have to be your own Big Daddy."

The girls look at me, wide-eyed and full of reverence.

"How do you get to *that* point?" asks Jennifer.

"When I get to it, I'll tell you," I say, slipping my hand in Wayne's pocket and retrieving my car keys.

He thinks I'm feeling him up, so he gets a sort of Lucky Pierre expression on his face. Then it dawns on him that I'm just retrieving my keys.

"I want to get something out of the glove compartment," I say. "Or the *love* compartment, as I'd prefer to call it."

"Okay, babe," says Wayne, thinking something sexual is in the offing.

I take the keys, leave the roadhouse, get into DART, start up the motor, and take off for Connecticut alone. Wayne can find his way home with the cuties or not. It's up to him.

Maybe I'll never get laid again as long as I live, but at least I'll live—and for the moment, that seems like enough.

11

SOBRIETY BLUES

———— ◆ ————

I've got the world in a jug,
The stopper's in my hand.

—"*Down Hearted Blues*"

Listening to Bessie Smith and painting stone cold sober. The locks are changed. Dart's gone. I don't expect to hear from him, and the twins aren't coming back for another week.

I'm in the silo alone, looking out over the hills of Connecticut and painting. Good old Boner would bark to alert me if Dart's motorcycle drove up. I am working on another version of the maenads and crystal. Sometimes in bliss, sometimes in despair. The loneliness of being an artist is something you cannot communicate to another living soul. Me, at my easel, overlooking the hills, smelling the primal turpentine smell, stoned on my own solitude and the woodsy aroma of the solvent, the hydrocarbon high of painting alone and the low of knowing I may be alone for the rest of my life.

If I've decided (and I seem to have decided) not to fall in bed with the Waynes of this world (who pick up other girls in bars when they're with you), not to grovel to Dart and pay for his bimbo's dinners, then what is there left for me but this endless solitude before the easel?

I love it and I hate it. I thank God for giving me a livelihood out of this solitary bliss, and I curse God for the gut-wrenching loneliness of it.

Elsewhere in the world people are making phone calls, faxing documents, circulating at cocktail parties. Whenever I think I'm missing something, I have only to drive into New York and see how little, in fact, I am missing.

At parties, I miss this blissful solitude. When I'm in my solitude, I think I'm missing "Life" by not going to the parties.

What is "Life" anyway?

My life, at its truest and purest, seems to consist of standing before an easel, smelling the turpentine smell and arranging the hues of white on a white canvas before green hills. I could stand here for all eternity. I seem, in fact, to have been standing here for all eternity. This is your life, Leila Sand, I think, the youness of you. How lucky to have found it, or to have come back to it before it was too late.

I call up the ghosts of female artists of the past— Marietta Robusti, "La Tintoretta," Lavinia Fontana, Rosalba Carriera, Élisabeth Vigée-Lebrun, Adelaide Labille-Guiard, Angelika Kauffman, Anna Peale, Rosa Bonheur, Berthe Morisot, Mary Cassatt, Käthe Kollwitz, Paula Modersohn-Becker, Vanessa Bell, Georgia O'Keeffe—to protect me like ranks of guardian angels, painted in wet lime on some Venetian ceiling. All the technique, the love, the infinite capacity for taking pains, the courage, the guts, the *heart* of these women who drew and painted *against all odds*, comes into my aching fingers. Oh, the longing to make the difficult look easy! I want to be like those old fresco painters who had such talent, such craft, such knowledge of chemistry, even, that they could put down the color before the lime had time to dry, leaving the illusion of *sprezzatura*—that wonderful Italian ideal of making the difficult look easy—for all eternity, or at least five hundred years.

I think of the scene last night in the bar. All the young pulchritude gathered around Wayne. The difference between forty-four and twenty-two in a woman's life is not just a question of looks. I don't *look* worse than a twenty-two-year-old—to some men I look better—but I *know* too much. I am less easily conned. I don't beam up at them with those eager eyes. I don't smell the bullshit and call it roses.

Is it all a matter of hormones? *Estrogen über alles?* Nature gives us thirty years of blindness to male bullshit so we can make the maximum number of babies. And then the estrogen begins to wane, and we come back to ourselves again. We return to the bliss we knew as nine-year-olds, coloring in our coloring books. We get our lives back, our autonomy back, our power back. And is that the moment when we become witches to be stoned in the marketplace? Not because we are ugly but because we *know* too much. We are onto their game, and they don't like it.

"I love my man better than I love myself," sings Bessie, "and if he don't have me, he won't have nobody else. . . ." Ah, the estrogen talking. The wail of female fertility. "I love my man better than I love myself." Do we *have* to feel that way to take them into our bodies and make babies, putting the future of the species above our own ease, our own rest, our own peace of mind?

Yes, apparently.

I break down and cry. Fall at the foot of the easel and cry salty tears, which slide into the corners of my mouth. The dog comes up and licks my face. "I shall get myself a mastiff bitch," said Enid Bagnold. Ladies of a certain age always wind up with animals and gardening as their consolations. Is that where I'm headed? Is that what my sane mind wants for me?

I get up and pace. Think of going to a meeting and reject that. Think of going for a walk with the dog but postpone that. Think of a drink but tell myself I won't drink today—one day at a time.

The telephone. That's what I need to do—call people. The last addiction I'm allowed.

So I start phoning. My friend Maria in Paris, where it is almost midnight and raining. My friend Lorelei in Venice, where it is almost midnight and also raining. My ex-boyfriend Stan in New York, where it is the same time and weather as here. My old friend Julian in Los Angeles, where it is midafternoon and sunny with yellow smog.

Julian is locked in his house in the Hollywood hills, playing with his synthesizer. Through his Kurzweil, Julian communes with the music of the spheres.

"What do people eat?" Julian asks across the continental divide.

"What do people *what?*"

"Eat," says Julian. "What do they eat?"

I think of Julian, who is slender and small, with shoulder-length white hair. Julian has the most astonishing eyes—the eyes of an alien from another planet, where everyone's IQ is 503.

"I don't know what people eat," he says. "Since Christina left, I've only eaten pizza—but now I want *real* groceries. But for the life of me I don't know what people eat. Give me a list of stuff to stock the house."

"Okay—got a pen? Raisin bran, milk, bananas, coffee, apples, sliced turkey, rye bread, mayonnaise, mustard, a barbecued chicken, tuna fish, butter cookies, chocolate ice cream, aspirin, Valium, yogurt. That should hold you for a while."

"Thank you, thank you," Julian says, really sounding grateful. "I'll never know how to thank you."

"Don't worry—I'll think of something," I say. On Julian's planet, they have astral observatories but no supermarkets.

"So what else is new?" I ask Julian.

"*Listen,*" he says. "It's the mating song of the quarks."

Unearthly sounds fill my ear. The sound of Julian's Kurzweil mating the quarks.

"What's that for?" I ask.

"A major motion picture called *Thrust,*" says Julian.

"You're making that up," I say.

"I wish," says Julian.

In my present mood, the strangeness of this web of friendships strikes me. How close yet how alienated we all are—alone in our houses painting or writing or composing and phoning each other all over the world. Each of us living alone and calling out through the cosmos to a network of loving friends we seldom see. Sometimes when I meet my good friends, their physical presence assaults me. I am shocked to see them in the flesh. I am used to their voices, but their faces seem too intense, troublingly intense. Are we all preparing for life in space capsules? Is that why we lead these podlike existences, in which social life is conducted digitally? Lovers we touch and smell. But friends we increasingly "visit with" only electronically—even when we live a few blocks away. What is the meaning of this? The human race preparing itself for space?

The dog barks. An actual person is arriving.

For a few minutes, there is hushed anticipation. Then, the sound of boots on gravel. Then, a knock at the door. (The studio-silo has neither bell nor lock.) I run downstairs to open the door, and in walks Darth Vader, holding a rose.

He might as well be a Martian arriving from outer space, or some other species of Spielbergian alien heralded by bright light and bad television reception.

"Leila," says Dart, "I had to kiss my lucky person before I left for L.A."

I look at him—the bullshit smile, the sheepish expression, the sheer chutzpah of his coming back after the scene in the restaurant—and I am in a rage.

"I'm not the Blarney Stone," I scream. "I'm a woman!"

"Leila, baby," says Dart. "I've been asked to go to L.A. to audition for a movie about a young artist, and I had to kiss you before I left."

Now, this could be true or not be true. This could be the sheerest invention on Dart's part or it could have some little grain of truth—like the bead the Japanese pearl fisherman slips into an oyster to con the mollusk into secreting its precious bodily radiance. With Dart you never know how much is pearl and how much is plastic.

"How nice for you," I say. "Stardom."

"Baby, I'm sorry," says Dart. "Maybe someday I'll be fit to live with." And he turns on his sheepish love-me smile.

"Get out of here," I yell. "I'm not some amulet you touch for luck! I'm not your mother! I'm not your banker! Get out!"

He looks at me like a petulant child. (It's at this point that my twins would stamp their ten-year-old feet and snarl, "Not fair.")

"Baby, I tried," says Dart. "I was a seed, and you were a whole forest. I couldn't grow in your shadow."

"Oh—it's my fault, is it? My shadow was too big? I love being fucked over and then blamed for it too." But the trouble is, I know there's truth in what he says. His truth.

"You were always my artist," says Dart, falling to his knees and throwing his arms around my thighs. He is crying real tears. They wet my jeans.

Torn between rage and despair, I struggle for a moment, wanting him and wanting to kill him. (It's not unlike the feeling one often has with one's kids—to kill or to cuddle, that is the question.)

I crumple to the floor, crying copious salty tears, and we hold each other, both weeping.

Time seems suspended as we rock in each other's arms. I never knew there were so many tears! The whole sea seems to be feeding our tears. They are endless—a tidal wave of brine taking us back to some prenatal existence in which we hold each other like twins embracing in the amniotic sac.

He is me and I am him, the bond so deep and unbreakable it astounds me even now. The con man in me, the heartbreaker, the faker, the phony—all of these aspects of Leila/Louise Dart embodied, and I loved him as I loved my baby self, the little girl who never got enough love and would lie and cheat and charm for it, break hearts for it, die for it, cry for it. We hold each other for what seems like eons, geologic time, light-years. We cry together the way we used to fuck.

Then, wordlessly, we get up, separate, and Dart goes down the silo stairs again. I pick up my brush and paint a highlight on one maenad's cheek. A tear. But only one. And Dart is gone.

Later I discover he's taken some of his things. The white cowboy shirt, boots, hat, some jewelry. I don't care. What interests me is that the house was locked and that he entered it, leaving no trace: no broken locks, no finger-prints, no trail. The perfect second-story man. Born to it. Or maybe he never really existed. Emerged from under an earth barrow like one of the little people. The green man. Robin Goodfellow. Peter Pan. The horned god of the witches. And, like all devils, our own creation.

Dart gone. I won't go into detail about the week between his final departure and the arrival of the twins. The utter amputation of it. The way I attempted to follow every helmeted man on a motorcycle and very nearly creamed myself on various ancient deciduous trees; the hopeless suitors who called—old boyfriends, friends from the fellowship, those first bedraggled ones who stagger in during Week I, postamputation: the walking wounded, raging over their divorces, their teen-addict children, their business collapses, their chapter elevens . . . belly-upping to your bar to partake of your nonalcoholic warmth. Mostly they come to mope and talk, sensing another lost soul who hates to be alone at sundown, and they eye you and you eye them, thinking sexual thoughts but deciding that it is just too much trouble—this being after all the second summer of heterosexual-AIDS hysteria—and not knowing whether to hand them a Kinsey questionnaire or a condom, or both, you finally do nothing, escort them to the door, and offer a chaste cheek for them to kiss, and so to bed.

You have your trusty old white plastic vibrator—capped with an Excita condom to make it trendy—and you have your life-size marble cock, that ten-inch circumcised specimen sent by a famous Japanese sculptor when your film stills of Dart opened in Tokyo.

The marble cock is of white Carrara marble as pure as Michelangelo's early Pietà—the one in the Vatican, which was not long ago defaced by some thug. Its cold white purity—half Brancusi bird, half Marini horse cock—takes forever to get warm within your cold abandoned cunt. You warm it and warm it, feeling the marble heat on the surface but stay cold inside, like your heart. Wax to receive and marble to retain. This is the pleasure of it—making these connections. Sex, even self-sex, is a question of completing some circle, making some synapses snap, some cosmic synapses that link your nerve ends to the stars.

How hard it is, and how hard it is to connect with another person, or with one's self, or, finally, with God. To crash through that wall of flesh into spirit, to open yourself to the cosmos in the neon flashings of the orgasm.

My God, my God. Dart, Dart, Dart, Dart. I convulse around the Michelangelo-Brancusi-Marini marble, shouting Dart's name and God's name as if they were one. Tears run down my cheeks. I am all liquid. And the marble? The marble at last is warm.

Thank God the twins came home and I could lose myself in motherhood. The whole household drifted back in to greet them—my raw-boned dykey assistant, Natasha, with her black punk crew cut, her safety pin earrings, her big shoulders, her horsey face, her glittering green eyes. The "executive housekeeper," Lily, once upon a time the nanny, now chief Amazon in our Amazon commune— soft-spoken, Scottish, and serene. Even my shrink came home from Europe and was suddenly available for coun-sel—from her little thatched cottage in Cornwall Bridge— my shrink, the incredibly brilliant Dr. Sybille Panoff, who gave Freudian-Jungian-Reichian analysis as well as tarot card readings, medical referrals, and healing crystals. Dr. Panoff had studied with Melanie Klein in London, Wil-helm Reich in New York, and Henry Miller in Big Sur. She was eclectic, to say the least.

I had for some time believed that her healing powers would have been as strong in the Middle Ages as in the twentieth century. Sybille was ferociously psychic, almost to the point of being telepathic. A poet in her soul, she dispensed a form of analysis that was two parts chicken soup, one part metempsychosis, and the rest wise-woman-of-the-woods. Sybille, as her name indicated, was a witch. Her black eyes and long black hair said so. Her saffron robes said so. And her little cottage, perched at one edge of a waterfall and filled with cats and crystals, said so. She lived about fifteen minutes away from me, under the mock-Tudor thatching of what had once been a mock mill house on a mock millionaire's estate. The mill wheel still spun beneath our sessions. The cats leapt from chair to chair. On one chair there was a pillow that said, in needlepoint:

> Life can only be understood backward,
> but it must be lived forward. . . .
> Kierkegaard

That was the sort of shrink Sybille was.

I drive to the airport with Lily and Natasha to get Mike and Ed. We are all in a state of high excitement about seeing the girls.

Divorced mommies learn, eventually, to put mother love in the icebox for weeks at a time—when the babies are with their daddies—or go mad. And I had learned my lesson well by now. When Mike and Ed were away, I put them out of my mind—if not out of my dreams. I learned to keep them near yet far. I learned to suspend feelings. This trick will be necessary in the afterlife, if there is one. For, of course, we are already *in* the afterlife: it intersects with our world, threading in and out of our days like a candy ribbon. Some days we are serene and all-knowing, other days frantic and caught up in the mortal coil. I seem always to have been obsessed by the myth of Persephone, as if somehow I knew that I would live a life in which I needed her wisdom to cope with the chronic departures of my daughters. They come and go—to Hades and back again—and when they return, it is always spring.

We wait at the airport in the crush of people—relatives roiling in familial frenzy, bored limo drivers smoking and loitering with the glazed, indifferent eyes of those who are going to meet strangers. They carry big paper lollipops with these strangers' names. But the family members carry their passion and expectation: flashing eyes, auras of anticipation and anger—whole family histories read in their pacing feet, their troubled brows.

Airports have always affected me deeply, made me want to cry. All these arrivals and departures, losses and restitutions! All these people going off to hang suspended above the ill-fitted fragments of their lives! So many puzzles! So many departures!

In our age, travel has become a drug. There are people who grow so used to coming and going that they find it impossible to stay still. If they are not boarding a plane and going somewhere, they feel somehow bereft— like a gambler deprived of his chips, or an addict of his needle, or a sexoholic of her marble cock.

The twins!

They come through the arrival gate looking three inches taller than they did two months ago, unkempt, dirty-faced, with untied shoelaces—just like two ten-year-old girls who have been with their father.

"Mom! Mommy!" They shout almost in unison. The joy on their dirty faces at that moment is wondrous to behold. And my heart: it seems to burst its membranes, to expand, to convulse around their coming. The waters break. I am awash in tears, which then I wipe and hide. My little cookies, my big-small girls, my little chips of DNA whirling forward through the universe. My double darlings, my double dollop of chocolate chip ice cream, my two little puppybodies, fragrant with musky nympharoma, my bubble-gum Reebok babies, with the double dirty smile.

"How was the flight?" I ask, just to have something

to say, when there is nothing to say—just hugging. We hug. We hug and hug and hug. The whole Amazon commune hugs. Five women hugging each other.

"Airplane food sucks the root," says Ed.

"Aaagh," says Mike, doing a ten-year-old's imitation of vomiting.

"What did you eat?" asks Lily—that being her domain.

"The usual swill," says Mike.

"Yeah," says Ed. "The usual mystery meat. . . ."

"You guys sure have grown," says Natasha, who seems to have grown herself, even at thirty. They all seem to grow three inches when they leave me, all except Lily, who, like all our fairy godmothers, remains comfortingly the same.

"How was Dad's house? What did you do?" I ask. We walk to the baggage claim.

"Daddy has this new girlfriend, who keeps giving us *baths,*" says Ed.

"Yeah," says Mike. "She's bath happy."

With Dart gone, I am suddenly stung by the news of a new girlfriend. Does the heart *never* heal?

"Bath happy?" I ask. The twins look as dirty as ever, coming home from their father's house. Mike's auburn hair has the remains of a wad of cut-out bubble gum matted into it, and Ed's auburn hair hangs limply around her dirty face. They both have backpacks overflowing with all the stuff a ten-year-old girl considers essential to life on this or any planet: bubble gum, emergency chocolate, a favorite soiled stuffed animal (Mike has Trapper Bear; Ed, William Shakesbear), a notebook to record impressions ("California is grate. I miss Mom"), several Judy Blume, Norma Klein, and Roald Dahl books, T-shirts with witty sayings

("Beam me up, Scotty, there's no intelligent life down here").

"Where's Dart?" asks Ed.

"He usually comes to get us, doesn't he, Mom?" says Mike warily.

I had not counted on this part of the Dart-gone problem. Well, might as well tell the truth. I always tell the kids the truth—in the gentlest way I know.

"He's gone to California," I say, "to look for a job in movies."

"Oh," says Mike.

"You mean you guys broke up," says Ed.

"We saw it coming," says Mike.

"Yeah," says Ed. "He was out of order."

"You deserve better, Mom," says Mike.

I am left with my mouth hanging open.

It is bliss to have them home. We ride. We shop. We walk through our raspberry brambles, picking the brilliant red berries that gleam like little clusters of Venetian glass. We cuddle in bed at night among the stuffed animals.

The twins have decided to move into the guest room so as to be nearer to Mom—they seem to know I need them as much as they need me—and at night I climb into the water bed between them, smelling their nymphic smell, feeling their puppybodies with the brash newborn fingertips of the just sober.

Lying in bed with them at night, I think of all the times I nearly left them motherless, raging at my own motherlessness, trying to spite Elmore or Dart or Dolph or Theda for my own self-pity, thinking someone could be sorry if I drove, stoned, into a tree. And someone would: *me*. And these two little someones I hold in my arms.

How sharp is the regret of early sobriety! All those wasted years! All those wasted nights I was too drunk to feel my daughters' flesh with fresh fingertips. I used to read to them, glass in hand, clowning drunkenly for them as I read Roald Dahl or Judy Blume or Norma Klein. Who was the loser? No one but me. I missed my life.

Lying there, I would try to total all the bedtimes I had missed, all the hours, minutes, seconds, blotted out in the brain cells. Impossible. Now I had such clarity that at times the world seemed unreal. Every second seemed alive, inhabited with animals, vegetables, minerals, molecules. Alive! The whole earth alive hurtling through the cosmos and I rocking in the water bed with my daughters in the womb of space-time. And no longer alone.

"Mom, can you cook?" says Ed.

"Why?"

"Daddy says you can't cook," says Mike.

"Of course I can cook. Watch." And I stab one arm out of the water bed, pick up the telephone, and call the pizzeria.

The twins laugh and laugh. Forty-five minutes later we are all sitting in the wobbly water bed, demolishing an almost-hot extra-cheese pizza.

"We missed you, Mom," says Mike.

"Yeah," says Ed. "You're the greatest mommy in the world."

"Thank you," I say, looking up.

I understand what it means to be twice blessed, twice born.

And Lily comes in to scold us for pigging out on pizza in bed.

But some days, reality is too much to bear. I dream of Dart. One night, he is with me—his golden, muscled shield of chest gleaming. I see and smell it in my dream. For some reason, he is wearing my pearls—ropes and ropes of them. He dives into the sea. And when he surfaces, the pearls have lost their luster and are eaten away to reveal plastic beads at their hearts.

"Baby, I'm sorry," he says sheepishly. "I love you. You've always been the woman of my life—but I'm not strong enough to love you well."

Another night, I find a letter from Dart among my things.

My dearest [it reads], This short life we are given can be spent in agony or bliss. Depending on one's perspective, life can be tragic, funny, or wonderful.

The time appears even shorter if we do an hourly breakdown. Of the twenty-four hours in a day, at least a third of them are spent sleeping. Another three to six hours are given over to eating. Two hours go to grooming, bathing, and dressing. Then we seem to lose an hour or so (more) getting from one place to another; then there's time on the telephone (two hours), decision-making, and instructing the help (one hour); and somewhere along the way we waste or lose an hour unexpectedly. This leaves us with three hours to work, write, make love, exercise, laugh, be with our family, be with ourselves, explore a new idea (did we feed the dog or water the plants?), go over the day's events, etc.

Now, are we going to spend those precious three hours a day worrying or fearing the worst? Let's take those three hours and do a little planning with them. Three hours times the 365 days in a year is 1,095 hours. Now, how many years are there left in our lives? Maybe forty! So we multiply this times forty and we get 43,800, and then we divide by the twenty-four hours in a day and we get 1,825, which we divide by 365 days in a year and we get *five*.

That's five years. Five waking; five aware; five short years in forty that we're together.

Oh my darling I want to spend all of eternity with you, not five years.

All my love,
Dart

I start to cry, remembering the eternity we had before we lost our paradise. And I remember how sweet and tender Dart could be before things went awry. I have been trying not to remember that, because it is easier not to remember.

Then something about the letter hits me—*work*. Dart has barely mentioned *work* in his hourly breakdown. "Instructing the help" is what he relates to. It is as though he has done a description of his *father's* life. This letter is the equivalent of Ven's greeting cards, my sane mind says.

"When is Dart coming back?" Mike asks one day, going to bed.

"I don't know," I say.

"We figured you guys had another one of your fights," says Ed.

"I don't think he'll be coming back," I say.

"Oh, Mom," says Ed.

"I'm glad," says Mike. "I was always scared of him."

"Me too," says Ed. "Ever since he took down Mike's pants and spanked her."

"He did what?" I asked. "When?"

"Just before we left."

"Why didn't you tell me?"

"We didn't want you to worry, Mom," says Mike.

"Yeah," says Ed. "You're such a worry wart."

"What you need, Mom, is a *rich* husband," says Mike.

"Someone with a Porsche," says Ed.

"Or a Rolls-Royce," says Mike.

"Or a BMW," says Ed.

"Someone *rich*," says Mike.

"Yeah," says Ed.

"If they're all jerks, might as well get one with *money*," says Mike.

"That's dumb," says Ed.

"Men don't like it when you have all the money," says Mike.

"But what about liberation?" I ask.

"Men don't like it," says Ed.

"And they still run stuff," says Mike.

"I'm sorry, Mom, they just do," says Ed.

"But we have to *change* that," I say.

"Forget it, Mom, and take their money," says Mike.

"Get one with a Porsche," says Ed.

12

THE PROPER MILLIONAIRE

◆

I got a Eldorado Cadillac
with spare tire on the back—
I got a charge account at Goldblat's
But I ain't got you.

—Calvin Carter

Danny Doland from Dallas drove a Porsche. Danny Doland from Dallas was tall, fat, fifty, funny, and absolutely *loaded.* Danny Doland was the answer to a ten-year-old's prayers.

"Marry him," said Mike.

"Yeah, Mom," said Ed.

I was introduced to Danny Doland on a blind date. By an old lover of mine named Tyler Levinsky, who had recently married the shiksa of the year. (Another one: the category is crowded.) Tyler was fit, fifty, rich (though not as rich as Danny): he was in the antiques business. He wanted to see me conveniently married off to one of his cronies so that we could take trips as a foursome and he could intermittently visit my bed. It was doubtless for that nefarious reason that he introduced me to his partner, Danny, who collected everything from Important Art to Rare Books to Major Antiques to Fine Wines and was willing to consider acquiring *me*. It never occurred to me that there was anything strange about a newly sober person falling in love with a wine collector. Why not? I thought. I could resist all those euphoniously named châteaus. And Danny was intelligent, generous, Texan, a great raconteur. Prior to becoming an *antiquaire* he had been a publisher in London. (His money was old—for Texas—inherited, and still green.) He was well read. He was witty. He had published Nobel laureates and trash novelists alike, and he could do the most fabulous imitations of both. (He would, for example, drape himself in a leopardskin scarf and do a Jackie Collins. Or he would do the perfect I. B. Singer singsong.) As if these literary credentials were not enough, he had a glorious estate in the Berkshires, once owned by a friend of Edith Wharton's—an Italianate villa near The Mount, called Lunabella. Lunabella had its own conservatory, its own indoor swimming pool (which connected with the outdoor swimming pool by a secret passage), its own ballroom (with a painted, vaulted, starry sky). Edith Wharton had invited Mr. Fullerton there, but he had never come.

Danny Doland from Dallas was my last chance to go two by two into the ark with silverware. Danny Doland from Dallas was my last stab at *normality*. If I had got in trouble seeking my dybbuk, my demon lover, then surely I would be safe with this portly and proper burgher, with auctions at Sotheby's and suites at Claridge's, with dinner parties for eight (at eight), before which Danny Doland actually *rehearsed* his own jokes and wrote insulting yet flattering descriptions of each guest on the place cards, as if for a celebrity roast.

Make no mistake, I was madly in love with Danny Doland. I am not now and have never been a cynical gold digger. When Danny and I met at that first dinner in the Berkshires, at Wheatleigh, on a hot summer night, our eyebeams locked, and we both tumbled.

His eyes were washed-out blue, smallish and glittering. He was blindingly bald, with a double chin and an ample paunch, which his tallness disguised—except in bed. He wore yellow suspenders and red bow ties. He carried a silver-headed cane, which he sometimes twirled. He wore silk boxer shorts with "DD" monogrammed on one leg. He sometimes even wore spats. Somehow, in my warped mind, these things connoted safety. (I was not used to men who wore underwear at all—let alone custom-made underwear.) I had *had* a goyboytoy, and Danny Doland was no one's toy; little did I know that Danny Doland had his hand on the joystick every bit as firmly as Dart—albeit in another fashion.

At that first dinner, our eager conversation blotted out the world. Danny loved Italy, Turner, Blake; he collected my film stills. He pronounced business "bidness" and important "impordant." He actually had been following my work for years and owned an early painting of mine I had somehow lost track of. It flashed through my mind that I could get it back by marrying him. But even without that, I would have fallen for his fatal charm. For Danny was funny, cuddly, warm. Like going to bed with a hot cup of cocoa. After five years of going to bed with an auto-da-fé, it seemed appealing. I went home to Lunabella with Danny and tumbled into bed.

Hot cocoa. Even the images we used in bed were about food.

"I want to pour chocolate syrup over your cock and lick it off," I said.

"You'll have to beat me to it first," said Danny (without, however, explaining how he was going to bend over that far).

In an age of uncommitted men, Danny was loaded with commitment. He gave me jewelry on the second date (an art deco pin—"we're pinned," he said), proposed on the third, and on the fourth gave me an elephantskin Filofax with his name (or his initials) written beside lunch and dinner on every page. He planned safaris in Kenya and château rentals on the Rhone. He was going to buy me the *piano nobile* of a palazzo on the Grand Canal—and a *motoscafo* to zoom to it. He was going to build me an Italianate folly at Lunabella as a studio. He was going to buy me a classic Aston Martin to drive to his country house in Hampshire and a Silverado to drive to his ranch in Texas. I guess my goddess sent him to me to test my resolve, for after this incredible full court press, Danny Doland wilted.

Here's the strangest part: I didn't care all that much. Impotence is, after all, AIDS-proof. Besides, I had known a relationship built on searing sex, and I knew it didn't solve all problems. Maybe I'd had enough sex in my life and was scheduled to spend my declining years at *auctions*. But Danny Doland cared. He was devastated that I knew his sexual secret. And from that point on, he began to get even with me.

It was subtle at first. Still in the first blush of our compatibility—in all areas but bed—we were planning our nuptials, our renovations, our purchases (for was not love in the eighties merely a prelude to the purchase of real estate? and in the upper classes, art?).

Danny Doland had an architect design a folly to be built as a studio for me at Lunabella. This studio looked like the main house in all respects, except that it was hidden in a copse of trees and that it had no windows.

Surely an oversight. Surely Danny Doland's architect did not expect me to paint in a house without windows.

But Danny Doland had his reasons for this. Skylights in the roof would supply the light. And the "windows" would be limestone and marble replicas of windows.

"But why?" I asked.

"So that we can keep the whole structure climatically controlled, sugar. To preserve the art."

"But if I can't look out and see the sky and the hillside, how can I *create* the art?"

Danny Doland looked down at me with his small pale-blue eyes, the color of oxford shirting.

"Sweetie," he said, "we'll have perfect north light controlled by skylights with special electronically operated sunshades. That way, we can have the gallery below—works by you and your major contemporaries: Graves, Bartlett, Schnabel, Sherman, Natkin, Frankenthaler, Twombly, Johns, whoever pleases *you*, your *personal* collection—and above, you'll paint under conditions that ensure that your work will never deteriorate. Imagine knowing that, sugar!"

I imagined myself trying to paint in a mausoleum without air, without birdsong, without the occasional butterfly (or wasp) landing on my work-in-progress—and I was horrified. Life, in short, was what he planned to exclude in the name of preserving art. How could I create art without life to power it?

Sex I could give up. But could I also give up *air*?

Isadora: You say that now!

"Darling, I must have at least one window that *opens*," I said.

"I'll talk to the architect, sweetie," said Danny, "but I can tell you right now he'll say it's a bad idea. Have you ever been to the Beinecke Library?"

"Of course, darling—I *went* to Yale, remember?"

"Of course I remember, sugar. And you must know how *vital* it is to keep the air properly controlled."

"But I want to *charge* the air, *de*control it, make it eddy around the spectator's eyes, make the shakti leap out of the picture and change your life. . . ."

"That's such a romantic idea, sugar. Look—you just paint your little heart out and let *me* worry about preserving the work, okay?"

I thought of Élisabeth Vigée-Lebrun's husband spending all the money she had made as court painter to Marie Antoinette.

The French Revolution, your best friend and favorite subject beheaded en famille, and suddenly you discover that your husband has spent the loot! Penniless, you take off in 1789—what a year to leave home penniless!—and visit the courts in Italy, Austria, Germany, Russia, making your fortune anew, painting landscapes. In France, the bloodbath continues. Your ex-husband, who might as well be Danny Doland, has trimmed his sails to the prevailing winds and is acting as salesroom agent for the new government. You return home, refuse to meet bloody little Napoleon, and leave immediately for England, where Sir Joshua Reynolds still rules the taste of the time and condescends to praise you even though you are a woman. Then back to Paris, to paint at Napoleon's court, publish your *Souvenirs*, and die at eighty-seven. What a life! If Vigée-Lebrun could do it during the French Revolution, why am I rushing headlong into the arms of Danny Doland?

"Darling," I said, "have you ever read Élisabeth Vigée-Lebrun's memoirs?"

"Lebrun? Lebrun? Who *was* she, sugar?"

"Court painter to Marie Antoinette, then to Napoleon's court—but she was just a woman painter who lived by her brush and who survived in very troubled times."

"Didn't she paint those pretty-pretty female portraits?"

"Mmm," I said, determined to have windows and fresh air.

"Look, sugar, let *me* deal with the architect, and you do the painting. I know what's best for you, sugar. Haven't you had enough upheaval in your little life? What you need now, honey, is someone to protect you, to take care of bidness, to *free* you to create. I'm *good* at that, sugar. An' it would give me such *pleasure!*"

I'm melted by his affectionate tone. Danny's speech has, anyway, always melted me. With its curious combination of Dallas and London, it was the first thing about him that I fell in love with. That and his tallness.

"How can a man that tall and that rich fail to protect you?" my sane mind asks me.

"I'll think of a way," says my obsession.

As for protection, of course I want that—don't we all? And who more than a chronic vagabond—a bolter, as they say in England? One can't always live in turmoil. One can't always be alone. I go to hug Danny Doland, but he pushes me away.

"Very well, then, it's decided, sweetie."

"As long as you don't expect me to paint in a mausoleum," I say.

"Who ever said anything about a mausoleum?" asks Danny. But I can tell he's offended in his own sweet way and is storing up another grievance for future use.

After that contretemps, Danny began to eliminate physical contact altogether.

It started innocently enough. I noticed that whenever Danny and I spent the night together at Lunabella (we never stayed at my house) he would sleep above the covers if I was under them and he would wear underwear if I was naked.

A small thing, really. How could one complain? We were grownups, middle-aged lovers. We had our own habits, our own lives, our own houses and children. (He had one son at Choate, the other at Le Rosey.) But clearly Danny Doland didn't want to hug me. The tune "A Fine Romance" kept playing in my head.

One summer night, I gathered up my courage and asked him about it.

"I'm not keen on hugging," he said. "Don't tax me, sugar."

Certainly a provocative remark for one's fiancé, one's new lover, the love of one's life, to make. But I managed to be *mature* about it and not react.

"Okay," I said to Danny. "We don't have to be joined at the hip. It's okay, darling." And I turned over and went to sleep and had searingly erotic dreams about Dart. (Sleeping with Danny, I always dreamed about Dart.)

When this distancing maneuver didn't work, Danny upped the ante.

One night he brought home piles of erotic videos (with names like *Las Vegas Lust*, *Cherry Ready Gets L.A.ed*, and *Hell Bent for Leather*) and suggested that we watch them. I was game. I still had all the garter belts and gear I had bought for Dart when sobriety made *him* impotent, and I didn't mind bringing them over to Lunabella. I had been wearing garter belts and black lace merry widows even when my pals in the feminist art cabal considered them treasonous, and now that such accoutrements were chic, I still saw no harm in them. Men respond to visual stimuli, I reasoned. They're just not as *evolved* as women.

So I got all tarted up in black lace, and Danny and I turned on the VCR and watched *Cherry Ready Gets L.A.ed*—a porn flick of surprisingly good production values, which showed a nubile young "Cherry" making it with a succession of goyboytoys in Malibu, Santa Monica, Bel Air, Beverly Hills.

I was fascinated. We were meant to believe that Cherry, the young starlet, was getting ahead in her career as a result of blowing producers, casting directors, and studio moguls (one of whom looked like Dart), when of course everyone knows that such blandishments are far too common in the film business to make a difference in *any*one's career.

Porn is very innocent, really. It presumes that there is a sort of sexual justice in the world. And whenever the scriptwriters get stumped, they up the number of participants in bed: the numerical phallacy.

Danny was turned on by Cherry. I wasn't. Not much. But I was turned on by *Danny* being turned on. Usually it took me forever, teasing with tongue and fingers, saliva and baby oil, to get him—sort of—hard. But this time he sprang into action. And entered me. And went soft.

Back to Cherry. Back to baby oil. Back to back and belly to belly. Danny and I kept trying—until finally, exhausted, we fell asleep.

I became an expert on porn videos. I began to think of doing a porn video piece as a tribute to my love affair with Danny. I wasn't about to give up, but it seemed *he* was.

"I feel overwhelmed by you, sugar," he finally said one night at Lunabella. "All your pressure for connubial bliss—"

"All my *what?*"

"Your pressure for marriage. And all your sexual pressure, sugar. I feel overwhelmed."

At that moment, I felt pretty overwhelmed myself.

"Danny," I said, "you've been the one pressuring for marriage, not me. And you've been the one making a big deal about the sex. I'm quite contented with you. I love you . . ."

"Inadequate though I am . . ."

"I *love* you. And I *don't* find you inadequate. Perhaps *you* think you're inadequate."

"Don't give me that psychological hooey, sugar."

"Darling," I said, "I don't want to fight with you. Stop. Please stop now before we both say things we'll regret."

"You think sex is important, sugar, and I, quite simply, do not." Every couple has one argument they return to over and over. And that was ours. We found it early and never deviated.

"Well, sex *is* important," I said, "but it's not the only

important thing between two people. Please don't let's fight."

"You think sex is the most important thing between people, sugar. You do. Admit it. And I'll never be the stud you're used to. I shoulda met you when I was twenty."

"I don't *want* the stud I'm used to, Danny. That's why I threw him *out.*"

"You miss him, sugar. Admit it. You miss him."

"This is a ridiculous conversation."

"Admit it, sugar."

"I won't have this conversation."

"Admit it." Danny stood up, changed the videotape, put on his underwear, and sank down on the bed. He just lay there, under the weight of his great jiggling belly. A new videotape came on the screen: *Las Vegas Lust.* One of the croupiers looked like Dart. I could have sworn it *was* Dart. But how on earth could he have launched his movie career *that* soon? But someday I *would* be lying in bed with an impotent Danny watching Dart make love to bimbos in a porn flick. It was inevitable. Poetic justice.

I watched *Las Vegas Lust* as if my life depended on it. Was it Dart or was it delusion? Granada or Asbury Park? Was I going mad? What had happened to my sane mind?

Danny meanwhile began to masturbate, using baby oil—and the image of Dart (or his doppelgänger) as a visual aid. A fine romance, indeed. What would Fred Astaire make of this? He jerks off; she sits riveted by the video image of her former lover (or his look-alike); and the whole world thinks they've got it made.

Danny jerks off defiantly, as if to say: Who needs *you?* When he is finished, he looks up at me for approval.

"Safe sex," I say, and go downstairs to the wine cellar.

*   *   *

The wine cellar is a wonder. Photographed by *Architectural Digest*, with limelight on the wine bins and perfectly controlled humidity, the wine cellar sits under Lunabella as the diamond as big as the Ritz sat beneath Scott Fitzgerald's mythical mountain mansion. I wander in, Theseus into the Labyrinth, examine several bottles of rare Bordeaux, and choose a Mouton '45 to get drunk on. With a racing heart, I open the wine the way Danny has taught me, take a glass from the wine cellar bar, pour, swirl the ruby-red mixture in the bottom of the glass, sniff, and burst the grape upon my palate fine.

Now, it should be said that during the weeks with Danny I have not been drinking. Well, not exactly. But I have been tasting, sniffing, and learning about nose, bouquet, and finish. (Of my affair with Danny, I would later say, "Nice nose, nasty finish.") And I have not been going to meetings. I can control my drinking myself, I have decided. This is what they call in the Program "stinkin' thinkin'."

But everyone has been so approving of my affair with Danny—André, my dealer; Sybille, my analyst; the twins; their fairy godmother, Lily. Why? Because he's rich. Because he's from *Dallas*. Because he has a mansion on either side of the Atlantic (not to mention various flats). Because he buys me jewelry (and erotic videos). Because at long last I have a proper millionaire, befitting my station as a celebrity artist. Nobody thinks that I'm a drunk falling in love with a wine collector for cover. No one but Emmie. However, I am avoiding Emmie. I haven't called her since I fell in love with Danny Doland. And she, knowing I have to reach my bottom in my own way, has called from time to time but doesn't noodge. I almost wish she did.

Just one sip, I think, nose into the bowl of the Tiffany Bordeaux glass. And then another. And another. And then the whole glass.

How does it taste after all these sober weeks? Metallic, sweet, sour, like liquor to a kid. My head gets the buzz, the heavy, fruity, prehangover feeling, but no click. I wander about the wine cellar reading labels, glass in hand.

Here are the châteaus of Pomerol: Pétrus, Trotanoy, Lafleur, La Conseillante, Rouget, Le Gay, Bon-Pasteur, Petit-Village, Clos René, La Violette, La Croix-de-Gay. . . . And here are the châteaus of Margaux and Médoc: Palmer, La Lagune, Malescot-Saint-Exupéry, La Tour-de-Mons, Paveil de Luze, Camuet . . . of Graves: Haut-Brion, Domaine de Chevalier, Carbonnieux. . . .

(Oh, I am not getting drunk on wine so much as on these lovely French names that roll off my tongue even more trippingly than the wine.)

The châteaus of Pauillac: Latour, Mouton-Rothschild, Lafite-Rothschild, Pichon-Longueville, Comtesse de Lalande . . . of Saint-Émilion: La Tour-Figeac, Troplong-Mondot, Couvent-des-Jacobins, La Clotte, Ripeau, Villemaurine. . . . (Not even out of the Bordeaux, and I'm already tipsy!)

I wander among the wine labels, thinking of the great châteaus of France, her lovely snaky rivers: the Loire, the glimmering Rhône, the sun glinting off the wineskins of Bordeaux. Claret, the English call it, as if it gave clarity. *In vino veritas,* as if it brought truth. But to me all it brings are tears. I weep and drink, sprawl on the cold floor of the cellar, and keep on draining the bottle. The little picture on the label invites me into a sunny world of châteaus and glimmering rivers, cool cellars and hot sun. But here on the floor I am suspended in time, seeing the parts of my life all jumbled together as in a kaleidoscope.

The silver silo. The flapper dress of moonbeams. Dart's cock. Dart's letter about time and eternity. The chocolate-scented puppybodies of my twins. Dolph, Thom, Elmore, Dart, Danny. My mind rushes as it used to on pot—white nights awake by Dart's side after much love-making. (Pot made him sleepy, me wakeful—a paradox for such a well-mated couple.) Is this where my hegira has taken me—to a wine cellar buried in a basement in the Berkshires, drinking claret and getting murky?

I stagger up, wander through the house, inspecting Danny's treasures: his art collection (Monets, Modiglianis, Warhols, early Sands), his glass collection (Lalique, Gallé), his antiques (Queen Anne, Georgian, Biedermeier). I think about my life as a part of that collection. Dinner parties with rehearsed jokes. The right art collection. The right people. Climatically controlled air, jokes, wine, paintings. I think again of Élisabeth Vigée-Lebrun, of the French Revolution, of the year 1789, of living to be eighty-seven! Artists can be incredibly long-lived. I might have another forty-four years to paint. How am I going to do it without fresh air?

Feh, I think. Dolph's daughter is going home.

In my garter belt and silk stockings, with a silk robe over them and bare feet, I take off into the night in DART, sans drivers license, sans money, sans everything.

I am speeding through the Berkshire midnight, wearing my porn video getup, feeling the cool summer air on my hot cheeks, singing "My Sweetie Went Away" at the top of my lungs—

Until I see him in the rearview mirror. Darth Vader

on his motorcycle, the masked man, my dybbuk, my demon lover. He hasn't gone Hollywood at all. He is following me! Right here in the Berkshires, he means to stop me and make me his by the side of the road. My heart lifts; my cunt moistens. Ah, Dart, I knew you'd be back! The beam of his motorcycle headlight is piercing my trunk. The siren is piercing my heart.

The siren? Since when did Dart have a siren?

Darth Vader zooms up beside me and tries to force me to the side of the road. I play with him for a while, leading him a merry chase over hill and down dale, growing ever more excited as his siren shrills and shrills. Finally he veers me off the road, onto the soft shoulder.

"Dart!" I cry, the words slowly dying in my mouth. For the motorcycle cop does look a lot like Dart—as did the croupier, as did the porn-star producer.

"License, ma'am," says the cop, looking at my scanty attire.

"Ooops," I say. "You'll never believe this, Officer, but I was just off to the drugstore to get some Pampers for my baby with diarrhea!"

The cop doesn't look me in the eye.

"Please show me your license, ma'am," says the Dart look-alike, surveying my cleavage. I have the drunken thought of unzipping him and having him here and now. Or could that be considered bribing an officer of the law?

Isadora: Why is it that whenever Our Heroine is confronted with a figure of male authority, all she can think of is sucking his cock?

Leila: Who's using that word now?

Isadora: Don't quibble over vocabulary. Answer the question.

Leila: Because sex is never a thing apart from politics.

Isadora: Oh, come off it. This is not The Land of Fuck— this is a speeding ticket.

Leila: Which my namesake (and your alter ego) hopes to avert. As long as a woman is youngish and nubile, desired by men, she cannot resist playing her last trump card.

Isadora: Isn't that name copyrighted?

The rest is history—or herstory (as they used to say in the sixties). Picked up in the little Massachusetts town of New Egremont by the New Egremont police, booked for speeding, indecent exposure, drunkenness, and other puritanical New England crimes, bailed out by Danny and André, *in loco parentis,* and sent, in shame, back to my silo. I narrowly escaped being the subject of a *New York Post* headline because it was a hot day in the Middle East, but I did become a "transition" item in *Time.* "Booked for drunk driving in the Berkshires, noted artist Leila Sand pleaded guilty to charges of operating a vehicle under the influence." DWI—as they say in the Program. Drawing Without Intoxication—that was the risk I ran marrying Danny. Another sort of jail.

Guilty as charged, my license suspended, I go back to my silo as if under house arrest.

Danny disappears. Emmie reappears. She and Lily and Natasha and Mike and Ed take charge of my life. And the police agree that instead of going to a rehab, I can be put under the care of Dr. Sybille Panoff of Cornwall Bridge, Connecticut, who, among her other qualifications, has a degree in Family Therapy and the Treatment of Alcoholism and Addiction.

Saved again, but who knows why? Where are my maenads and crystal now? And where oh where is my sane mind when I need it most?

13

SPIRITUS CONTRA SPIRITUM

—————◆—————

*It's a long road but I know
I'm gonna find the end.*

—Bessie Smith

Sybille's thatched cottage with the whirring mill wheel was the perfect setting for a Disney witch. Filled with collections of theatrical memorabilia—in her youth (an indeterminate number of years ago) Sybille had been an actress—the cottage had the look of an eccentric New England antiques shop in which the stock mingles with the possessions of the owner and it is not clear what exactly is for sale.

"Tea? Coffee?" asks Sybille.

"Mouton '45," I say, laughing.

Sybille gives me a wry look and sweeps off to the kitchen in her long black silk dress. I follow.

While she clatters teapots and cups, I talk.

"Well, Danny Doland certainly was a disappointment. I hear he's left for Hampshire, where hurricanes hardly happen."

"You were never meant to marry a civilian," says Sybille. It's not clear whether she's using the term in the show business sense or in the military. Much as she liked Danny's money, it now appears she regarded him as an interloper because he was "in trade."

"You don't even know it, darling," she goes on, "but you are on the verge of a totally new life. You're struggling being born, like any baby. Dart and Danny are incidental."

I heave a deep sigh. "Well, there goes my last chance for normality. . . ."

"Darling, the antiques business—like the art business—is the eighties equivalent of real estate. Any little *gruber yung* with a glib tongue can do it. They think they're so smart because they are selling art, but they are, after all, still *selling*. The *airs* they give themselves! You'd think they *made* the stuff. You are not meant to be part of *anyone's* collection. You are your *own* collection."

Sybille turns her elegant profile to me. At six feet tall and a hundred and twenty pounds, she could still play Cleopatra or Gertrude or Lady Macbeth and have the whole audience riveted.

"Sybille, I think I'm going to be alone for the rest of my life—I mean without a man. I scare them. And they're all so scared to begin with."

"Most, but not all."

"But their fear makes me so sad. All our lives, we're taught to look to them for guidance and support. And then we reach middle age and realize how terribly frail they are. It's *cosmically* sad. I see the game of it, and it makes me weep. I want a partner, and all I find are gigolos or terrified middle-aged babies."

"You are meant to be alone right now, with your girls. Being alone isn't so terrible. Look at me!"

"We're *always* alone. And they always go on to the next nymphet. There are just too damn *many* of us and too few of them. We can't make demands, because then they run. We're meant to make all the compromises. It's bloody unfair."

"An opportunity."

"Some opportunity!"

"It's an opportunity to find your sane mind," says Sybille, "to establish its beachhead inside you so that even alone, you're never alone. To learn to talk to yourself kindly and gently, to learn to nurture yourself. No matter how alone I am, I always have my sane mind as a companion. I want to give you that."

I look at Sybille helplessly, an old habit. But I am starting to comprehend what she means.

"Leila, it takes courage to lead a life," Sybille says, pouring tea. "It takes more courage to lead a great life. It's not easy to do what you've undertaken. You were singled out somehow to make pictures of the world. In another age, you'd be dead in childbirth, you'd be stoned as a witch. You were given a rare talent. All you have to do is protect it—even when you least want to."

"And then?"

"You can't lead a courageous life without making these leaps of faith. Sometimes everything looks terribly bleak and you think you know the end of the story. But you don't. And by writing the end of the story, in some sense you doom it to happen. Or you hypnotize yourself with negative thoughts. The most important thing you could possibly learn is not to do that—but to affirm the positive even when you don't know the outcome. Do you know what has been learned about people who excel in every field?"

"No, what?"

"That they have a high tolerance for not-knowing, for ambiguity, for not being in control. Because it's only when we can tolerate *not* being in control that we make a place for the miraculous to happen. Art, falling in love, magic. Not-knowing makes a window for the miraculous. Not-knowing makes it possible to know."

"I want to know if I'll ever get laid again."

"The cards say yes," Sybille says, and laughs. "But the cards also say you'll have to pay your analyst ten dollars every time you do."

She takes out a red cookie tin with the name "Amaretti di Saronno" lettered on the side.

"Ten dollars for every lay," she says. "And when we have enough money, we'll go out and celebrate."

And she enfolds me in her huge motherly embrace.

I went back to meetings, my work, my twins. No more dating. No more searching for the holy grail of cock. Enough already. I would wean myself away from love, deliver myself from sex, learn to scratch the itch myself or cease to feel it. I would transcend sex and become a nun.

Never mind that for years I had thought it the life force. Never mind that I thought sex and creativity were one. I could not get involved with a man without wanting (eventually) to drink, and not wanting to drink, I would not get involved with men.

I went for an AIDS test, was terrified for a week and then vastly relieved when the nurse called with the following euphemism: "Your viral studies are negative." It was a brave new world we'd made—and sex was a casualty of modernity.

Eventually we'd all live in space capsules anyway, communicate digitally, and wear silver space suits in which our genitals were so far from view that we forgot they existed. Sex would go the way of the appendix or the nusiform sac, and we'd all be, probably, much happier. That great motor of fertility and yearning which God had given us would now be turned over to the techies and translated into computer language. Bytes instead of bites, input instead of intercourse, file instead of fuck. We'd all change directories and become dissolving blips on a flickering screen. Which we were anyway. In God's computer of starry blue. In vitro fertilization, central hatcheries, Skinnerian training of infants. Instead of mothers, we'd have "surrogates." Instead of fathers, we'd have "donors." Instead of children, we'd have—what? There was the rub. Human beings were too little too long. That was the crux of our evolutionary dilemma: the glory and the pity. In twenty-five years of dependency, we certainly learned some strange habits.

My twins, at ten, were so self-sufficient that I often felt like an interloper. (One mother of twins once told me: "Until they're three you can't even brush your teeth; after that, they don't need you at all because of their bond with each other.")

Often I envied them—their self-sufficiency, the fact that they were never lonely. United against the world, they went to school, to camp, to Daddy's, to Mommy's. United

against the world, they rode their Appaloosa ponies—
Heaven and Hash. United against the world, they went
berrying, climbing, biking.

One is the indivisible number. But one is lonely.
Two is divisible but unafraid. As their mother, I was glad
for their connection. But it left me out in some deeply
painful way. Sometimes I wished I had a singleton for
company.

One day at a time, the green summer stretched out
in Connecticut. The trees turned dark and leafy. The crick-
ets' singing and the bullfrogs' basso filled the nights. I read
Thoreau, Lao-tzu, Suzuki. I tried to cultivate a beginner's
mind.

"We should find perfect existence through imperfect
existence," said Suzuki. "We should find perfection in
imperfection." "We must learn to reawaken and keep ourselves awake, not by mechanical aids, but by an infinite
expectation of the dawn which does not forsake us in our
soundest sleep," said Thoreau. "The sage puts his person
last and it comes first," said Lao-tzu, "treats it as extrane-
ous to himself and it is preserved. Is it not because he is
without thought of self that he is able to accomplish his
private ends?"

I tried to cultivate the art of taking no action. I tried
to regard life as a pastime, not a hardship. I tried to do
nothing, because nothing is the hardest of all things to do.
I tried to teach myself to sit still.

I would sit at the edge of my pond and watch the
surface ripples of the water, the blue of the sky within the
green of the water, the clouds scudding across the ripples,

the frogs leaping through heaven, the insects drowning in clouds.

"A field of water betrays the spirit that is in the air," says Thoreau. "It has new life and motion. It is intermediate between earth and sky."

At the edge of my pond, on the edge of the universe, I came to know that certain gates open only to solitude and certain palaces are unlocked only by tears.

Sometimes the death of a june bug would move me as deeply as the death of my own mother, and I would weep. Sometimes the dance of the molecules would make itself manifest to me, and without drugs I would join that dance, the intoxication becoming all the more powerful for my having come to it straight. My arm, throwing a pebble into the water to break its surface of sky blue, would become one with the air it moved through, one with the rock it cradled. The molecules of sky, flesh, stone, all interconnected, dancing together in a primal dance, whirling together in a primal whirl.

I understood that arm, sky, and rock were all one, that flesh was sky and sky was flesh, that stone was no more solid than water or air, and that there was nothing to mourn, because death was just another part of the dance, and the dance went on forever.

I sat at the edge of my pond, gazing at the surface of the water, the surface of eternity, and my mother came back to me.

She arrived through the leafy woods, stomping over rotting logs, wearing a crazy red hat. She looked like a *meshuggeneh* out of a Singer story.

"*Louise,*" she said, "you're a rotten mother and a rotten daughter. When was the last fucking time you visited my grave? *Flowers.* I don't even *expect* flowers. Or a phone call. That's right, you never call me. *Ma, Mother, Mommy.* The words never pass your lips. You go to Emmie, to Sybille, to Lily. How the hell do you think *that* makes me feel? Like when you went to your father's floozie on Eighth Street and told *her* your problems. How the hell did you think *that* made me feel? Huh? Answer me, Louise— *excuse* me—Leila, *Ms.* Sand. You're such a big shot now, I can't even get you on the phone without talking to your assistant. 'Leila Sand's residence.' I remember when I used to wipe your ass!"

We are sitting together in a Chinese restaurant near Dyckman Street. The Fortune Dragon, it's called. Theda is getting drunker and drunker on daiquiris (she keeps ordering them with her lemon chicken and sweet and sour pork). She is grilling me about my father and Max. I don't want to answer. I don't want to be in the middle.

"Do they fight a lot?" she's asking. I just sit there sullenly.

"Answer me! Do they fight?"

"I don't know, Ma."

"You rotten kid! Answer me!"

"Ma—I don't know." (I am perhaps sixteen, my ovaries always in an uproar over Snack, my life out of control between Dyckman Street and Eighth Street, my life a subway ride between two lives.)

Suddenly, out of the blue, she brings her pocketbook down on my head and bashes me. Then she sweeps the lemon chicken onto the floor and starts smashing plates and glasses, screaming, "Answer me! Answer me!"

I get up, grab my green book bag, and run home, hoping to pack my stuff before she comes back.

I am in my room, cramming a suitcase, when the

door opens and Theda rushes in, brandishing an umbrella.

"You love your father more than me!" she screams. "Admit it! Admit it!"

"I do not, Ma."

"Admit it!" she yells, clobbering me with the umbrella. "You love him best!"

"I love you, Ma," I mumble, "but you can't hear!"

"You don't love me!" she screams. "You're a rotten lousy kid!"

I shut my suitcase, grab it, and race out of the house.

Down into the bowels of the subway, the hot-popcorn and candy-wrapper mouth of subterranean New York. The rush of the trains, the people swaying together in sweat, the unwashed, the poor, the muttering, the miserable, the huddled masses yearning to breathe free.

Miss Subways is a beautician but wants to be a model. She'll never make it. The Wrigley twins want to "Double Your Pleasure, Double Your Fun." Speedwriting is proffered as the answer to all problems. And night courses at the Robert Louis Stevenson School.

"I want out, out, out," I mutter to the click of the train wheels, in which I also hear my mother's voice screaming at me. I hear her in train wheels, in the ocean, in the rush of running water. Always I hear her—even to this day.

"Ma—I love you!" I scream. "I really love you!" And with that Theda vanishes into the middle of my pond like a rock making infinite ripples.

My face is wet with tears. They fall to the mica-flickering rock on which I sit.

"*Mother!*" I scream into the green leafy woods. "*Mother!*"

And the echo tells me she has heard.

And then it comes. The earth beneath me—pebbles, soil, insects, all—suddenly becomes transparent, and I am sitting poised above a starry sky.

Below me, there are constellations—Orion, the Big Dipper, the Little Dipper, the Pleiades. Below me the infinite emptiness and fullness of space. A rush to my head tells me I am *seeing* for the first time. In my stillness, there is infinite activity; in this activity, there is infinite stillness.

I know that sex, the dance of hormones, the shimmer of flesh, the gleam of the grape, the linseed oil drop, the tear, the turpentine, are but small manifestations of this changeless and ever-changing infinity. And I know that this infinity is what I was meant to see, and that without sobriety I would never have the eyes.

"Knock on the sky and listen to the sound," goes a Zen proverb. I knock.

"Mother!" I call, like Hamlet to his father's ghost. *"Mother!"* And the green leaves of the trees rustle back: "Hush, Louise, I love you, I will never die."

Then silence. The woods settle down to their own sounds—cricket, leaf, the fall of a sparrow.

Out of the forest walks a doe, followed by two little Bambis. They graze and nibble on low-hanging branches and tender shrubs, perking up their big ears, putting down their delicate hooves, walking very close to where I sit in my practiced stillness, on the edge of my pond.

The mama deer walks to the edge of the pond and peers in, as if at her own reflection, and the babies follow suit, making delicate twig-snapping noises with their little hooves. The woods are alive with life of all sorts—deer, raccoons, mushrooms, insects, grubs, snakes, worms, butterflies. "Nature will bear the closest inspection," says Thoreau. "She invites us to lay our eyes level with her smallest leaf and take an insect view of its plain." It is as if the arrangement of molecules settles on different forms—now deer, now man or woman, now leaves—in response to some divine energy force field, but that all these forms are, in some sense, one.

Two wild little human Bambis whoop out of the woods, screaming, "Mommy!" And the doe and her Bambis are banished, back to the shimmering green world of the forest, lost in its dapple.

"Whatcha doin', Mom?" asks Ed.

"Nothing."

"Why?" asks Mike.

"Because it's the hardest thing of all to do."

"She's cuckoo," says Mike to Ed, "but lovable." And they come to hug me on the edge of the universe.

14

THE QUALIFICATION

———— ◆ ————

Listen to my story,
an' everything'll come out true.

—Bessie Smith

I had never qualified at a meeting. I had seen others do it—tried to hear them and not to hear them—but I was terrified to make that leap. Now Emmie thought I *should* make that leap. I hadn't even been sober a month. I wasn't *qualified* to qualify. Nonetheless, one day I went to a meeting in my little white church and the slated speaker did not appear.

"Who needs to speak?" asked the secretary of the meeting.

My hand went up as if without my conscious knowledge.

"I do!" my sane mind blurted out.

And before I knew it, I was sitting at the shaky trestle

table before the whole group, spewing out my story to the smoky room.

Can I even remember what I said?

Qualifying at a meeting is like childbirth, like falling in love, like The Land of Fuck. It is hard to remember what you did there, said there, cried there. The words tumble out, burst between your lips—and somehow, without your knowing what transpired, your whole life is altered.

"I was born in a trunk in a silversmith's shop on Eighth Street," I began, "to an alcoholic mother, an alcoholic father, and a life of living by my wits."

I paused and looked out at the faces of my listeners. Where but here can one be heard? If loving is listening, then I was loved, even though I did not deserve it.

"The strain of living by my wits seemed so desperate that I tried in every way I knew to eradicate my wits—pot, coke, drugs—until I could feel nothing . . . nothing but the love leaching through my fingertips onto the canvas, nothing but the ache of my soul moving toward God."

I shut my eyes and went on.

"It's a strange thing to start from nothing and make your future through what you do with your hands, your eyes, your brain—although, of course, we all do it. You need to make these constant leaps of faith. You need, above all, to believe in yourself. But how can you believe in yourself when you know yourself to be a frail human being, when you never know when inspiration will start or stop, when you have to wait for God to come through your fingertips?"

I opened my eyes; the room was still there.

"In my clearest moments, I would get on my knees before the easel, open my palms, and invoke God, Goddess, my muse. But always there were days when I could not pray, could not meditate, could not paint; and then I would try to stoke the fires with pot, with wine, with coke—or with my real drug, my main drug: men."

Go on. Go on.

"Art is a connection, a matter of making circles, a saying yes to the universe. I needed to feel that connection, that flesh connection, in order to blossom. Or so I thought. I needed a man to power my art, to approve it, to give me permission for the hubris of being a woman creator. Somewhere deep inside I did not feel I *had* that permission. I felt I was daring the gods by being so bold. So I would cling to a lover as if the force came through him, and after a while I would come to believe that it was he, not I, who made the work come true.

"Then, inevitably, he would start to abuse me. Or perhaps I would start to abuse myself. I would give myself over to him, believe that he made the work possible, and I would obsess whenever he went away, lose myself for work, for meditation, for my children, and finally, having given the work away, I would not be able to do it unless he was there. And he, knowing I had given away all my power, would leave me and find another woman who was tougher, who set more definite limits, and who therefore made him feel more secure."

Now I was comfortable. The words were flowing.

"My alcoholism is a conundrum to me. I'm what you call a 'high-bottom' drunk. I never lost everything—my house, my car, my bank account, my kids. I never crashed into a tree and wound up in intensive care. But I did allow myself to be beaten—to *seek* it, even—and I did allow myself to be raped financially. When I see pictures of battered women in the newspapers, I know that I am one of them, and that but for the grace of God, my eyes could be sealed over with bruises, my mouth could be swollen and blue. I *feel* like a battered woman. I know that drunk, I have banged my head on the floor till it was bloody, and I know that drunk, I have turned out the headlights and driven home in the dark, hoping to be relieved of the horrible burden of being alive. I know that I spend money like a drunk, fuck like a drunk, seek abuse like a drunk. I know that I would do almost anything for skinlessness, for ecstasy, even if it meant self-annihilation—and sometimes it did."

I looked into the blue eyes of one woman whose face always comforted me.

"I've been a lousy member of the Program. I float in and out. When I first stopped drinking, I was given a great, great gift—a new series of paintings. Then my lover peeled off, and I fell off the wagon and off the edge of the world. I haven't even put together a month of sobriety. I haven't even got the first step together. I constantly deny my alcoholism, tell myself that I can do it alone, that I don't need the group, don't need a sponsor. I even went and fell in love with a wine collector to prove I wasn't tempted."

(Laughter in the room.)

"How's that for denial? I feel grateful that you let me speak today, because the love in this room tells me that I don't have to do it all alone. I don't even deserve to qualify. I'm barely on the first step."

I stopped, looked down, and saw that the palms of my hands were open on the trestle table in the way they are when I am praying.

"Well," I added, "I guess I finally got to the first step. I admit I'm powerless. I surrender." And there was a loud burst of applause in the room.

I came back to myself from the land of trance.

A forest of raised hands waving in the smoky air.

"Yes," I said, recognizing the pretty blue-eyed woman I always stared at.

"I'm Mary, an alcoholic. I always identify with battered women too. You know those pictures in the paper of that woman—what's her name?—who let her little girl be beaten to death by her lover? I identify with her too."

One by one, the waving hands were translated into little volleys of words. Whatever I had felt was kinkiest, strangest, most shameful about what I had said, was seized on by a member of the group as a familiar feeling. Nothing human was alien. Nothing human could not be forgiven. We were not human beings going through spiritual experiences; we were spiritual beings going through human experiences, in order to grow.

I thought of Christ's message of forgiveness, of Job's message of humility, of Thomas Merton's assertion that the deepest religious experience is essentially incommunicable. Impossible to convey what goes on in "the Rooms." The banality of it. The transcendence of it. The transcendent banality.

And yet it works. If you say why it works, how it works, your tongue stops in the cavity of your mouth and you utter platitudes.

Perhaps it is finally a question of acceptance. Of being loved unconditionally. The Rooms are one place where you do not have to *deserve* to be loved. Because none of us really deserves to be loved. And all of us deserve to be loved. Loved unconditionally.

The summer wore on—green, leafy, celibate. Full of Thomas Merton and Lao-tzu, Thoreau, meetings, sessions with Sybille, and berry picking with the twins.

I tried to paint but hadn't much luck. My motor was

gone. The group love could not power me as Dart had done. I was becalmed.

Always in my life, men had appeared as if by magic. Bad magic. Black if not white magic. Now they did not. Dart did not call. Danny did not call. The force of my wishing for Dart was diminished. I could not make him call anymore by wishing. Anyway, the first woman who perfects that technique is going to win the Nobel Prize for Women. How to create dynamite by the sheer force of longing. Waiting by the phone—that old female pastime—has got to be of all distaff griefs the worst. It is the powerlessness, the sense of being out of control, that annihilates. Breathe on the phone. Make it ring. Pull on the old umbilicus and make it pulse.

Of course you could call him—if you knew where he was. But he has departed to another country, a country to which you have no visa, the country of regrets.

And then suddenly you realize with a pang, with a missed heartbeat, that another telephone call has not come in a long time—a red telephone has not rung, a certain heavy earthward pull has not been felt: your period is late.

At forty-four, your periods anyway are not so reliable as once they were. You used to be able to set your clock by them, keep your travel diary by them: a month-long trip began and ended with a period—that red marker, that crimson blot on the white pages of your Filofax. "P-1" you used to write for the first day. And "I" for you-know-what. (Odd that you didn't write "F." Was it residual prudery?) And then the number of times. And then the initials of the prick in question.

You long since gave that up, feeling your fertility is not so foolproof by now. Five years with an IUD (after the birth of the twins) spoiled you rotten. Sex with Dart six and seven times a day did not have to be recorded. (Who *could* have recorded it anyway? There was too much of it to even *try* to keep track.) And nobody worried about diseases in those days—though perhaps you should have, knowing Dart.

You missed herpes. You missed—thank the Goddess—AIDS. You lucked out, fucked out. And now sex is such a sometime thing that you'd be lucky to even have something to *worry* about. But your period—your "monthly flowers," as they called them in the days of Vigée-Lebrun and Adelaide Labille-Guiard, your "perennial visitor," your fall from the roof—is long overdue. And your nipples feel a bit tender and surely are more brown than pink. And a faint ribbon of brownish pigment runs from your navel to your pussy. Can you be—at forty-four—pregnant?

Mongoloid twins!

And are they Dart's or Danny's? One of each? One blond Adonis? One bald antiques dealer? Stranger things have happened in the annals of ob-gyn!

My God! Pregnant! You are secretly elated. Terror and gladness commingle in your blood.

"Whose baby is it?" they'd ask.

"Mine," you'd say, smiling like Mona Lisa. The singleton you long for, the pal to equalize your tender battle with the twins—can he finally be here? For it is, you know, if not mongoloid twins, then a little boy. You have seen mothers with their little boys, and you envy their lifelong love affair. Girls you cherish—sisters, little women, clone of your bone and blood and uterus. But boys you lust for—peg o' your heart, little penis astride your maternal hip, erect manhood in a diaper—your little boy.

Happy. There's no mistaking how happy you are.

The womb, in the eleventh hour of its life, chiming like a cuckoo clock.

People telephone. Not Dart or Danny, but André, Lionel, your old friend Julian from L.A. You burst to tell them, but hold back. You tell no one. Not even Emmie. Not even Sybille. Nor do you go to see the ob-gyn. Good old Dr. Letitia Hyman, M.D., the jokily named lesbian gynecologist, who practices in Bridgewater. She wears Space Shoes and has frizzy orange hair. She's built like a sack of grapefruits and lives with an oncologist named Dr. Eleanor Q. Oliphant. You wonder what the "Q" stands for. Questa, Quintana, Quisling, Quixote? You wish them luck. And love. Two old dames living free lives in a world not made for women. You've reached the point in life where you admire every woman who hasn't given up and died. Who hasn't drunk herself to death. Who grows old roses (Musk, Bourbon, Alba) amid her hybrid teas and doesn't give a fuck what the world thinks of her or how she makes it through the night. Let the lesbians flourish! Let the womb flower! If women ruled the world, there'd be medals for every baby a woman bore and medals for every menopausal milestone! (There'd surely be medals for every menopause that didn't end in suicide.) Hard enough to be a good girl and a pretty young woman—but try being old and female in a culture that hates the latter even more than the former. Here's to Quixotic Letitia and her darling Quintana! But still I did not drive to Bridgewater. Perhaps I suspected the worst.

Then one night—I was expecting Lionel the next day, in fact, to chopper up to my neck of the woods—the worst happened.

I was standing in the silo, staring at a sketch of the twins (who had grudgingly consented to pose on the floor amid flocks of pastel-colored little toy ponies), and a sudden cramping in my gut told me I was in trouble. I willed the cramp away, but it returned. I ran to the bathroom mirror, stripped off my skirt, and took another admiring look at my big, round, brown-nippled tits, my brown-striped belly. And then I broke down and cried.

By 3:00 A.M. it was all over. I was sitting on the toilet seat, hemorrhaging into the bowl, the bright-red arterial blood mingling with the darker clots, the tears falling with the blood.

Fascinated, horrified, I captured a large clot on a piece of white toilet tissue and probed it, looking for my lost son. I put on a Maxipad and went out in the moonlight to bury my never-to-be-begotten male heir.

Full moon again. Blue moon. The hillside sloping down from the silo, the wild grass waving, hair of unmarked graves. I dug a little hollow in the moonlight and buried him among the grubs and slugs.

Born, died, never begotten—what is the difference, really, if all is one? The moon is dead yet gives light. Dolph and Theda are dead, yet they stomp through my Connecticut woods at will. Even all my old dogs—Renascence, Robbie, Tara—come sniveling at the silo door on rainy nights, begging to be let in. The dead and the living are all here in a primal dance. Psychics see them, hear them. We only pretend not to, so as to keep our heads. Too much static! Too much input! We screen the dead out and embrace the night.

Goodbye.

I wander into the twins' room and sit on the edge of Ed's bed, watching her breath move, feeling her hot cheeks with my lips. Then I move to Mike's bed and say a prayer over her sleeping head. I smell her neck—brownish, pre-pubescent, premenstrual, puppyish, premoon. Her dead brother's soul flies into her.

Little girl clones, you will do for this life. I love you. The withered penis in the moonlight wasn't meant to be.

15

LIE DOWN,
I THINK I LOVE YOU
(OR, THAT'S A GOOD QUESTION,
YOUNG LADY)

◆

You got the right string, baby,
but the wrong yo-yo.

—*Piano Red*

From a spiritual awakening to a visit from Lionel Schaeffer—how literally can you take the phrase "the sublime to the ridiculous"?

The chopper lands. The twins, Natasha, Boner, Lily, and I all run out to greet this cosmic apparition, this voyager from another galaxy—the galaxy of Mammon! A UFO on our property! Wall Street comes to Litchfield County!

The air churns. The eggbeater whirs. I fear the twins will be decapitated and hold them back.

Lionel jauntily descends from his helicopter, wearing a Turnbull and Chung suit. He carries a handmade briefcase from Cellerini of Firenze.

"Pussycat!" is the first word out of his mouth.

The twins titter and pretend to be shy. Natasha tugs on the safety pin in her ear. Lily announces that there will be roast chicken for lunch in fifteen minutes. And I stand amazed, wearing a rhinestone-studded Lily Farouche T-shirt, skin-tight jeans, and a Maxipad soaked with the blood of the Zandbergs.

"Come to the silo," I say, leaving Lily and Natasha to cosset the pilot with coffee and doughnuts. The twins scamper off, giggling and elbowing each other. Another swain. A suitor. They find it immensely funny. In my sane mind, so do I.

Into the silo we go. I invite Lionel to take off his jacket and tie, but he refuses, perhaps wanting this formality, this contrast between Litchfield and Wall Street.

I offer him a seat on the red velvet Victorian chaise I keep for posing sitters, or—in the past—for fucking visiting swains. (It was important to make love in the studio—I used to feel—in order to keep the creative vibes energized.)

The red velvet chaise is not without its white markings, and these Lionel immediately notices.

"Naughty girl," he says.

"That's what you like about me," I toss off, though my womb is aching.

"True," says Lionel. "You give good dialogue," he says. "I wonder if you give good head."

"How can you doubt it?"

"Okay," says Lionel, "show me the latest mistress-pieces."

I begin moving canvases—the twin portrait of the twins, the rejected film stills of Dart—and set out the three best of the maenads and crystal series. Funny how it takes a stranger in my studio to make me appreciate my own work. Alone, I molder in my creative compost heap, thinking nothing of my gifts, enjoying the process but not being able to rate the product. With a stranger in my studio, I am able to feel the value of the work. I show Lionel the maenads and crystal, suddenly wishing there were more to show.

Lionel steps back and looks at the canvases. "*Mamma mia,*" he says. "You wanna sell me one now, without telling André? C'mon, baby, I'll give you a hundred grand—McCrae'll never know."

"He's your best friend, Lionel—and *my* dealer. That's immoral."

"You show your age when you use words like 'immoral.' Immoral-schmoral—this is *bus*iness. André'll take—what? fifty percent? I'll give you *two* hundred grand—green. You can put it in a safe-deposit box for a rainy day. Or we could do a barter. Who's to know?"

"André will know when you hang it in your apartment—and Lindsay will too."

Lionel raises his eyebrows lasciviously.

"Babe—I'll tell André you *gave* it to me in a fit of passion. How can he claim fifty percent of the come? Huh? You're *allowed* to give away your own work as a love gift, aren't you? And as for Lindsay, fuck 'er, or rather, don't fuck 'er. All she cares about is whether she gets invited to parties with those skeletons she worries about—Mrs. Remson, Mrs. Basehoar, that fucking fake Princess Tavola-Calda . . . Which reminds me: we have two extra tickets for that Viva Venezia Ball in Venice next month; want to come? I bought a whole table for ten grand—*had* to—Lindsay's one of the chairladies. You might as well have the tix. Meet me in a gondola and all that jazz. Whaddya say?"

"I *hate* Venice," I say. "It makes me think of Oscar

Wilde's line about traveling through sewers in a coffin. . . ."

Lionel laughs.

"Oh, yeah," he goes on, "the painting. Two fifty in a brown paper bag, and André'll never be the wiser. If you prefer, I'll get you a diamond worth two fifty. C'mon, Leila, babe, what's the harm in it?"

"No harm, but . . ."

I can't say I'm not tempted. And I can't say I don't need the bread. The IRS is breathing down my neck on account of some phony shelters my old accountant waltzed me into, and I'm experiencing the cash-flow problems all artists experience now and then. Also, I'm creatively blocked. As usual. I don't know where my next canvas is coming from. Or my next show. Lionel is offering me twice my fee for a painting—and with no commission and a nice little chance to beat the IRS. I'm tempted. But somehow I can't. I wish I could tell you it was morality or patriotism, but it's really something else—cussedness, the stubborn Zandberg genes. I know that Lionel's using me to beat André, that once again I'm caught in a male power play, and the truth is I don't want to give Lionel the satisfaction. I'm sick of the way men use women as pawns in their battles with each other—and I don't want to be manipulated even if it puts money in my own pocket.

"Thanks, but no thanks," I hear myself saying. "But the tickets to Viva Venezia I'll take."

"Boy, are you *meshuga*," says Lionel, "but talented. These are *some* paintings."

"You've barely even looked at them."

"Paintings that good you don't *have* to look at," says Lionel.

And Lily announces lunch.

Lunch is served on the greensward, on a rustic log

table Dart built at the start of our idyll. (It has rusty nails sticking up through the dining surface—a typical Dart creation—and legs made of birch logs still clad in bark. As an object, it's aesthetically confused—just like Dart—and at this moment, when I'm sitting here with a short little billionaire who doesn't stir my blood, it makes me sad.)

This rustic feast Lily has set out is lovely: roast chicken with its skin all crackly, puréed carrots (to make the twins eat veggies), new potatoes in their skins, fresh tomatoes and basil from our garden. The meal is placed on handwoven rainbow-colored mats, with periwinkle-blue linen napkins, and served on French country earthenware decorated with a hot-air-balloon motif and topped with the motto "Je Suis Libre" in fine brush strokes. (I bought these plates in France once, when I was high on my courage in divorcing Elmore and they seemed to embody all my bravado—which now has fled, my hot-air balloon punctured by Dart and drugs and alcohol.) The table centerpiece is blazing blue cornflowers. I am aware, as Lily puts out the feast and calls the twins and Natasha, of how idyllic all this must look—especially to a traveler from the galaxy of Mammon. The artist in her native habitat: Georgia O'Keeffe on her mesa, Romaine Brooks with Natalie Barney at Villa Gaia in Florence, Louise Nevelson in Little Italy. There is also in me the desire to make my life into a work of art—and that's a trap for every woman artist. I'd rather serve the feast than paint it.

We sit down to chow.

Lionel kids with the twins.

Suddenly there is a loud *beep beep beep* from the handmade Florentine briefcase, and Lionel runs to it, snaps it open, and extracts a portable phone.

"What's up?" he asks the unknown caller.

A pause, then he says: "Tell that bastard we'll give him fifty-six dollars a share—not a penny more. I'm not scared of a proxy fight. This is a guts play, pure and simple."

Lionel is talking partly for me and partly for the caller on the other end of the phone. He's an addict too—addicted to taking over companies. I recognize the intensity, the adrenaline high; I have been trying to learn to live in another state: moderation, the golden mean. It feels boring to me, but I know it's the secret of life. In a society that worships addiction, how can you find a nonaddicted life?

Lionel paces, walks down the hill with his telephone, turns and paces back. I see that his face is contorted with rage. He has been about to enjoy this feast—and now he is plugged into his addiction again. What a destructive implement the telephone is! More destructive than a machine gun or a bullwhip. Suddenly the feast has turned to gall.

He sits down, wolfs his chicken, but is utterly preoccupied, tasting nothing.

"What's a proxy fight?" asks Ed, who misses nothing.

"That's a good question, young lady," says Lionel, when the phone beeps.

He curses, gets up, answers it, and paces down the greensward again, muttering into it.

I watch him, thinking that the telephone is about to cut short his visit and wondering if I care. At one time I had nursed fantasies of an affair with Lionel as the answer to my problems—but I see that Lionel is, in his own way, less able to sit still than Dart, whom I am missing again in my fingertips, in my gut. That baby boy was *his*—I'm sure of it.

Whenever I get going on the fantasy of a man to protect me, to nurture me, I see that he's in more trouble than I am, more desperate, more frantic, more full of *spilkes*. Dart was forever darting. And Danny too, in his own way. And now Lionel. I will have to learn to sit still alone. Nobody knows how to teach it to me. Even I—with my crackpot semisobriety—seem to have more serenity than any of the men I know.

Lionel stomps back, muttering and cursing.

"Those fucking bastards say the stock is worth seventy-five dollars a share—they're fucking crazy. . . ." I see in him the male madness to win, win, win, and I wonder whether any woman would or *could* care about this the way he does. Women just don't give a shit about winning in that way—or at least, I don't. I love the fruits of money as well as anyone—houses, cars, clothes, power, autonomy—but somehow I feel freer and happier when I am working without a commission, for love, not money, than when I am working for money. I'm happy to have turned down Lionel's two fifty. I may be crazy, but it makes me glad to know that acquiring things is not first on my agenda.

And yet I know that my passion for Dart is not so different from Lionel's passion to take over companies or André's to take over artists. Consume, consume, consume. The bottomless pit of wanting. These are our values, and this is the world we've made. Never have we needed nonattachment more.

Lionel rushes through lunch, with one ear out for the phone.

When we've stuffed our faces, we go back to the silo, always with that potentially beeping briefcase in attendance. The mood of the day is smashed. I feel the static of New York here on my green hillside. I'm wishing Lionel would leave and let me get back to sitting by my pond, doing nothing, doing everything.

Lionel loosens his tie, at last takes off his jacket.

"Lie down, I think I love you," he says, putting an arm around me. I giggle. It's all so silly—the bid for a painting behind André's back, the proxy fight, the obligatory pass. I am looking for love in all the wrong places.

"Why're you laughing, babe?" says Lionel.

"Because it's all so silly."

"What is?" asks Lionel, hurt.

"Life."

I'm thinking that when a man and a woman lie down together, he's thinking of winning and she's thinking of love, and it will never work. Never. The two sexes might as well be separate species.

"Tell me what's in your head," says Lionel.

"Just that we don't have enough time to do this right. Your briefcase will beep. My twins will run in. We need a whole weekend, a whole week."

Lionel rubs my neck. I am thinking like a woman. Men like nothing better than to fuck and run—leave the primordial cave and return to the proxy fight. It's the woman who wants the weekend or the week.

Lionel kisses me. His kiss is surprisingly wet and warm, passionate, deep. He fondles my breasts.

"I want to give you everything," he says, "everything."

He reaches down and starts to unzip his fly, when the briefcase beeps.

"Goddamn," he says, lunging for it.

With one hand on his fly and the other on the

telephone, he continues his proxy fight.

This is the world they've made, a world in which sex is always interrupted by proxy fights, and they love it. Even men like Dart are demoralized by it. They live to fuck but feel like gigolos because of men like Lionel. What's the answer? Who knows?

"Tell the bastard I'll have his balls on a platter," Lionel is saying, perhaps to his lawyer, or to the proxy solicitor, or *someone*.

As he speaks, his erection subsides. I have the fantasy of blowing him as he talks on the phone, female power against male, but I resist—and not only because of my aching innards. Trying to get sober has made such games less attractive to me than they once were. I see my own hunger for power and dominance in my sexual play. I see myself in Dart—Donna Juan, Donna Giovanna. I am getting wise to my own tricks. A lot of sex is just vanity, isn't it? The thrill of making someone fall in love with you, the narcissism of being desired. I never saw this before, but I am certainly seeing it now. When the fuck works, nature's narcissism wins. Another baby for her team. Yay, team. By outwitting her, we have probably outwitted ourselves. God gave human beings too much brain power and not enough judgment and compassion—that's the sad truth. Balls on a platter, indeed.

Lionel sputters, zips up with one hand and holds the telephone with the other.

"Be there inside an hour," he grunts.

"Baby, got to go," he says to me, needlessly. "Catch you later."

My belly cramps. I run to change my Maxipad, then kiss him goodbye and walk him to the chopper.

There was no way I could have had sex anyway in my

condition, I realize. Who was I kidding? Lionel barks orders to the pilot, who is sunning on the grass. He hops to it like the semislave he is: "Yes, Mr. Schaeffer. Right away, Mr. Schaeffer."

The pilot is a handsome blond *shagetz,* twice Lionel's height. Lionel clearly *loves* bossing him around. Cossacks who looked like this pilot doubtless raped his grandmother—and he hasn't forgotten, either.

The chopper whirs, brutalizing the air above my sweet green hillside.

"I'll call ya tomorrow!" says Lionel, using that old male line.

Why, I wonder, do they bother? It's the rare one who actually calls—and usually the one who doesn't say he will.

That night, still hemorrhaging, I try to call Dart. I phone L.A., trying first the new listings in area code 213, then the new listings in the valley (818). No luck. I can find no Dart, Darton, or Trick Donegal in all of greater Los Angeles. I consider trying the bimbo's phone number, but then realize I've never had it. In fact, I don't even know her name.

If I had *any* number, I would ring it and ring it far into the night, wait for someone to pick up, hang up, ring it and wait again. Finally, in desperation, I call the elder Donegals' number in Philadelphia. The phone rings and rings. In the eternities between rings, our whole relationship replays. Finally a voice answers. It is Dart who says "Hello."

I slam down the phone and take to my bed, bleeding heavily.

16

EMPTY BED BLUES

———— ◆ ————

When my bed get empty
makes me feel awful mean an' blue.
My springs are gettin' rusty
sleepin' single as I do. . . .

—J. C. Johnson

Now that I know where Dart is, I begin to obsess as if I have never been free of him. Nor am I. He still regularly visits my dreams. If sexual passion were not a great bond, God would not have devised it as the glue between two beings as dissimilar as woman and man. My spiritual peace is blasted. Dart is back in my life.

It happens with the suddenness of a raid, an attack, a sort of sexual Pearl Harbor. I have merely heard his voice on the other end of the phone, and I am crazed.

I toss and turn in my bed, thinking I could easily get in the car and drive to where he is. In four hours I could be in Philly, if I drove like hell. I remember the sweet things about him—his love for poetry, his mad protectiveness of me when people recognized me on the street, his love of the twins.

Nice try. Actually, he was terribly jealous of them, and as they grew older I always feared he'd molest them. It's convenient to forget all that in my longing for him. My sane mind has fled the coop. I smell his smell; I see the whorls of hair on his belly.

Isadora: Excuse me, but if I hear one more reference to those goddamned whorls, or that bloody smell, I'll . . .
Leila: Scream?
Isadora: I know the smell's the thing. . . . Maybe I should just make this a scratch-and-sniff book and spare the reader the deathless prose.
Leila: Good idea!

I remember Dart's sweetness early on in the affair: the long afternoons in bed all over the world—the hotel suites, the room service carts, the beds littered with underwear, masks, whips, food, sperm. I try to remember all the awful things—the girls, the photos, the bills, the cruel phrases that curled his lip—but I cannot hate him. It takes only one great lover for a great love: the object may be as banal as Lolita or Mr. Fullerton. Only the lover need be great. And it takes only one to love. One to give and one to receive. The receiver must have a certain *je ne sais quoi.* He cannot be totally charmless. Nor can he be utterly without poetry. (Dart, for example, used to sign his love notes—sent on endless greeting cards in the manner of his elders—D'Artagnan, Darth V., or Mr. Darcy.) I confess I have never been able to love a man who was not literate. Snack sang Bessie Smith lyrics in my ear as he fucked me; Thom would quote John Keats, John Donne, and John

Milton by the yard—all those Johns; he also loved Browning and Byron and knew *Childe Harold* and *Don Juan* and *The Ring and the Book* almost by heart. Elmore loved Ezra Pound's *Cantos*. And Dart, Darth, D'Artagnan, Darcy quoted Shakespeare's sonnets and the love poems of Neruda. What good is love if it cannot be put into words?

Again I am in flames. Again, reduced to a pinch of ash. Again, consumed.

The word "Hello" has singed me. If one word can do this, how dare I risk two? or three! My heart blazes like Shelley's on that beach at Livorno.

Oh, Dart had a certain *je ne sais quoi,* all right. His smile, his sweetness—or was it merely his cock? Does the female of the species fall in love just by being well fucked? Is it thus that nature has her way with us? Is this the secret the Don Juan knows? I often wonder why other men, nice men, boring men, do not take more time and trouble over the *Kamasutra* and various other texts of love secrets. Are they oblivious of the rare rewards of fucking a woman well? It's the gigolos and grifters who chiefly practice the art of love. What fools the nice men are not to learn from them!

Or do they have contempt for mere sex? (As if sex ever could be "mere.") A real woman will love a man more for his cock than she ever could for his proxy fight or for his bank account—no matter what the cynics say.

Torn between calling back, driving to Philadelphia, and tossing in bed all night, I get up, go to my silo, and open—as if I were Pandora opening *her* box—a box of Dart memorabilia, which I have hidden away (from myself!) behind boxes of canvas tacks, chips, stretcher pieces, and cans of primer.

I open it with trembling fingers. Just unlidding the box—a Bendel's box!—has made my heart thud again.

There are Polaroid studies for the film stills of Dart—Dart nude, waving his cock (there was nothing that boy wouldn't do); Dart in the kitchen, putting his cock on the chopping block and raising the Chinese cleaver as if to chop it off; Dart nude, erect, about to fuck the unseen photographer.

And then there are assorted greeting cards—notes of love, notes of apology after a quarrel, crushed corsages (one, in fact, from that fateful Thanksgiving with his parents). I examine these artifacts with agitation, excitement—but also a soupçon of new detachment. There's something perverse and unsavory about Dart. The Polaroid of him holding the meat cleaver above his cock is especially unsettling. As if he would do anything to get attention. I can't invite that man back to my home with my girls again.

My heart cracking, I take all the photographs, cards, dried flowers, and begin to assemble them into a collage. As the fury to turn the love affair into its own monument takes me, as the fever rises, I seize hold of scissors and paste and start snipping, pasting, even daubing over the bits and pieces of my life with Dart. *Pandora's Box*, I call it, as the fury to collage my life overwhelms me.

If Dart were to see this collage, would he love it or hate it? Hard to say. Would it make our split permanent or heal it? Dart is such a narcissist I almost think he'd *like* it. A shudder goes through me as I think that even now I care more for the work than for the love. If forced to choose, I'd rather have the model than the lover—or *would* I?

And then the phone in my studio rings—the secret one, the one only Dart and Emmie have the number of.

I run to pick it up.

"Hello?" I say.

A click. Dart calling. Drawn by the strength of my snipping his pictures. Black magic. The soul captured on a piece of photographic film. The connection made. And broken. The scissors I wield cuts Dart's cock off. Inadvertently?

And then I am back in the longing again. My fingertips ache. I have a queasy feeling at the pit of my stomach. Love? Addiction? I am suddenly skidding down the street in Dubrovnik. I take the glue and paste Dart's cock back on.

Oh, God—will I never get myself back again? I long to be in love, but love annihilates—and anything less does not feel like love! The more fiercely independent one is, the more one longs for self-annihilation. The battle continues. The battle between bondage and love. I long to give myself away, take myself back, give myself away again. Arranging snipped pieces of Dart on my mounting board, putting him together and taking him apart, I battle with myself. Which do I want more? Control or love? Power or love? And are the two mutually exclusive? Or are they so only for me? What does it mean to be an artist who takes all the pieces of her life—quite literally—as material? Does it doom one to unhappiness, or is it, after all, the only bliss? I do not know the answers to any of these questions. I only know I am trying to learn to love the questions themselves. They are all I have.

I pick up the phone again and call—call, instead of Dart, Julian in Los Angeles. Julian, who is probably composing electronic music for another of his space operas. Julian, who looks so much like Albert Einstein—with his shock of snow-white hair, his big, sad, sparkly eyes--that people stop him on the street and ask if he *is* Einstein.

"$E = mc^2$," Julian always says, puzzling them even more.

"That'll teach 'em," Julian whispers to me, with a leprechaun's twinkle.

I've adored Julian for years. Julian is my pal, my spiritual guide. I tell myself that if I don't get Julian, I'll call Dart back forthwith. But Julian is home.

"How are you, sweetest lady?" he asks.

"The worst. Awful."

"What's the matter, babe?"

"I don't know whether I'm painting or living. I don't know whether I'm killing Dart or killing myself. I just made this collage out of the bits and pieces of my life—and I'm *in* the collage; I can't get out."

"I know the feeling," Julian says.

I recount the story of the last several weeks—Dart gone, AA meetings, the proper millionaire, the slips, seeing myself poised over the cosmos, the work, the life, the muddle of it all.

"You sound like me when I'm locked in, with a deadline. I sleep for three hours, take a cold shower, and fiddle with the synthesizer for three hours. Fiddle, sleep, sleep, fiddle, until I don't know who I am—a chord or a person—and I don't even care. It's bliss. It's torture. Anyway, we have no choice in the matter. It's what we have to do. At least you're an artist. I'm just an old hooker, turning out scores on the synthesizer to earn my paltry two million a year. A well-paid whore. Not as well paid as the stars who flicker to my music—but what's a boychick to do?"

Just hearing Julian's voice makes me feel I'm back in my sane mind. He understands me—my work, my obsessions. What a blessing to have a friend like that.

"Leila—you've got to expect to mourn Dart at least

a *little.* You were with him for five years."

" 'A dead lover must be mourned by the survivor for two years,' " I say, quoting "The Rules of Love."

"He's not dead, is he?" Julian asks.

"No. I was just quoting from this code of courtly love put together by the troubadours in the thirteenth century."

"You *would,*" says Julian. "When in doubt, quote from the troubadours. That's why I love you."

"Will you be my escort at the Viva Venezia Ball, Julian?" I blurt, out of the blue. I had thought I was going to ask Dart, but now it strikes me that I *must* ask Julian.

Julian hesitates. He is afraid to plunge in, lest he be hurt. Julian protects himself from life with his wit, with his wisecracks, with his isolation in the house, composing. He almost *never* goes out.

"Julian, you owe me one—in exchange for that shopping list."

"What shopping list?"

"The shopping list I gave you when you were starving after Cristina left."

"Oh—that."

"I want you to take me to the ball in exchange for the shopping list. I mean it."

"Some hard bargain you drive," says Julian, laughing.

"I mean it. I want you to promise."

"Let me think about it," says Julian, "and call you back." He plays a spooky chord and hangs up.

I return to my collage of Dart—*Pandora's Box.* Do I imagine it, or is Dart winking at me? He seems to be winking. "Call me," he seems to say. "Call me."

*　　*　　*

What is it about creating that makes you simultaneously want to destroy? The Indians were right about Kali—the creative principle and the destructive principle joined in one terrible mother goddess. Snipping, pasting, and rearranging bits of my life, I feel like Kali. I would even add the stained Maxipad to the collage if I dared, along with Dart's snipped (and restituted) cock.

How else dare to create, if you do not dare to destroy? The madness is the same madness, the fever in the blood, the pride of creating a world out of nothingness. Fevered, maddened, I look at the snippets and pieces I have been playing with all day, and my head throbs. The veins in my temples twitch. My throat pains me. My neck aches. It is nothing that could not be cured by a night in bed with the right man.

I put down my scissors, go over to the Rolodex, and start flipping through. What a testament to mutability my Rolodex is! Half the phone numbers are obsolete; people who have not divorced or married have died! What a mortality rate the Rolodex reflects! I take the Filofax (where I keep the names of special, intimate friends: "close personal friends," as they say in Hollywood—as opposed to what? "impersonal" friends?) and flip through *that*: old boyfriends, estranged husbands of dear friends, or estranged husbands of estranged friends! Unpromising stuff! I make a little list of the possibly fuckable men in my Rolodex and Filofax—and my heart sinks. What problems lurk behind each of those names! What untold depths of fear of intimacy, fear of commitment, fear of falling, fear of flying, fear of fucking!

A nice first dinner date, a return engagement, movies, theater, safe condomized sex on the fourth date, without exchange of bodily fluids, and back into the Filofax they go, as if laid between the fresh clean sheets of a hospital bed. Why bother? Why not just stay here in the country, collaging my life?

I begin a piece called *Sex in the Age of AIDS,* based on all my obsolete Filofax pages and Rolodex cards. On a C print of Dart as a rock star, I begin to arrange Filofax pages, Rolodex cards, old *Playbills,* menus, and more Polaroids of Dart. I cut the *Playbills* and menus into sensual, even genital shapes, dismember the Polaroids, and even paste one pink-wrapped Excita condom in the center of the piece. I tear through my stack of old magazines, looking for one of those amazing pictures of a woman innocently massaging her neck with a phallic-shaped vibrator. I laugh out loud at the imposture. As I change and rearrange the snipped pieces, I dream of a lovely boy stud who could be summoned to my side as simply as one summons a masseur.

What a flourishing business for busy creative women! AIDS-tested studs for the creative woman (or the busy executive) who doesn't want to get involved. But of course it would never work. Most women don't want studs, AIDS-tested or not—they want *love.* They want *romance.* And so the escort business would never work.

It wouldn't work for me—no matter how appealing the fantasy seems. I may *pretend* to myself that I *want* a stud, but alas, what I want is frighteningly more complex: a lover, a partner, a friend, a daddy, a baby. A stud would be too easy—even if I had the faintest idea where to find one.

So I go on making my collage, like a woman possessed, hoping that all the passion and energy and lust will go into the paper, all the blocked come will go into the glue, and the images will vibrate like an orgasm well and truly achieved. I could also call this collage *Empty Bed Blues*. And I could dedicate it to Bessie, Bessie Smith, the Empress of the Blues, my heroine.

17

LEILA IN NIGHTTOWN

───────◆───────

I'm lookin' for a woman who's looking for a low-down man
I'm lookin' for a woman who's looking for a low-down man
Ain't nobody in town get more low-down than I can.

—Freddie Spruell

Wayne Riboud hasn't been heard from since the night he disappeared into a covey of tootsies at the roadhouse in the absurd suburbs of New York. Now, suddenly, he is on the phone, importuning me as if nothing ever happened. Men who vanish for weeks at a time and then reappear used to mystify me. Now I know they are either in retreat from intimacy or pursuing other women—which of course amounts to the same thing. I left Wayne because he was drunk—or did I?

     How often in my life has the man who has just fallen for me taken off and seduced another woman—just to prove he's not trapped? Truth is, I've done it myself and know the beast for what it is: fear of getting close. Did I abandon Wayne, I wonder, because of his drinking, or because he stirred something in me and I panicked? I'll never know. Since AA, everything in my life has been called into question. I don't know whether I drank as an excuse to fall into bed with men, or fell into bed with men as an excuse to drink. I don't know if my addictive substance was booze or cock—or a combination of the two.

Now Wayne's inviting me to spend a night on the town in New York. Am I sober enough to do it without drinking?

"Come on, Leila—you haven't been seen for weeks. You'll *die* in that fucking silo. Let's do a night on the town—downtown style. I miss your giggle."

"How can I resist someone who misses my giggle?"

"You can't, babe. Also, we pay for everything with my bills. It will be a gas."

"My license is suspended."

"Ha! And you thought *I* couldn't drive! I'll drive," says Wayne.

"Oh, no you won't. Never again."

"Then take the train or get a driver."

"What do I wear?"

"Black leather."

"Just remember, I no longer drink or do drugs."

"I have *other* intoxicants, babe," says Wayne. "Have no fear."

I leave the twins with Lily and hire a driver—a slender young black man called Charlie—to blast down from Connecticut in DART.

We stash DART in my garage, Charlie takes off, and I meet Wayne in his loft on La Guardia Place.

I'm wearing a black lace bustier, Madonna style, black leather jeans, black S&M spike-heeled sandals, and a black motorcycle jacket that used to belong to Dart.

My hair is wildly teased by the ride down from the country, and I don't brush it. I have that crazed, semihysterical feeling that overtakes me when I've been working like a maniac and what passes as real life interrupts. (As usual, I don't know whether I'm painting or living.)

"Kiss me," says Wayne. I kiss him, smelling the booze. Horny as I am, it turns me off. I tell myself I'm still bleeding a little, so it's dangerous to have sex. Since I stopped drinking, my sexual signals are slower to switch on. My sane mind seems more and more in charge. What a crock of shit sobriety is! It makes everything that used to be easy suddenly so *hard.*

Wayne walks me through the teeming summer night to the East Village. We enter what looks like a meat-packing warehouse, go through double metal doors, and find ourselves in a large room with folding chairs. Every chair is filled. Wayne and I stand against the wall near the door.

The audience is a mixed bag of artistic East Village types, uptown suits, and thrill seekers from abroad. I hear Japanese spoken, and German—the Axis has invaded New York. (And guess who's winning?) The show begins.

A leather-masked man walks to the front of the room, steps up on the makeshift stage (covered with tarpaulins), unzips his mouth, and asks: "Who wants to leave before the doors are locked?"

Nobody gets up to go.

"Let's leave," I say to Wayne.

"We just *got* here," he says. "You won't regret this, I swear. It will *inspire* you."

I look into his squinty green eyes, smell his booze

breath. I want a drink, I think. And then I tell myself: You only *think* you want a drink, because you're scared. *Feel* the fear—but don't let it make you drink. It will pass, like weather. Feelings are not facts.

The room suddenly blacks out, and I hear metal doors slam and lock.

Here goes. The room hushes. People shift in their seats. I can *smell* the fear.

Music begins. Electronic music, a Moog synthesizer or a Kurzweil. A science-fictiony sound that could have been made by my friend Julian. Then a spot finds a young woman in black, with a huge pregnant belly. And another spot picks out a menacing masked male figure brandishing a samurai sword. (The same man who made the announcement?)

The samurai swordsman pursues the young woman around the stage in a stylized dance, whipping the air with his sword. He seems to lash at her neck, her ankles, her wrists—pale stalks of flesh compared to her bulging, black-shrouded belly. With a whoosh, he brings the sword down on her belly and slices her open. A dozen rats tumble out, clawing the air, and scamper over the raised floor of the stage. Claws skitter on the tarp.

The woman screams, "My babies! My babies!"

The masked man pursues the rats, feinting at them, decapitating one (a gush of blood), stabbing and dismembering others. The woman is screaming, loud ear-piercing bursts. I'm covering my eyes, my belly cramping, my gut heaving as if I'm about to be sick.

The audience is riveted, silent. Nobody breathes. The room grows hotter and hotter.

I peek between my fingers. The stage is spattered with blood. Some rats are twisting in their death agonies.

Still others are dead, disemboweled on the stage. Others have skittered away God knows where.

The masked man stands center stage with one still-wriggling rat in his hands. He unzips his mask, opens his mouth, and bites the rat's head off. He spits it out, then squirts the girl with the rat's blood.

I bolt up and begin beating on the metal door like a crazed claustrophobe. Wayne tries to restrain me, but I'm flailing, terrified I'll never get out of this nightmare.

Time slows to a crawl, dream time, slow motion, nightmare to a nine-year-old. After what seems an eternity of beating on the metal door, I feel it yield. Wayne and I are released into the cool anteroom of the charnel house.

I rush out into the street. Wayne pursues.

"Baby, baby, you really freaked out," he says, holding me.

"I don't want to live in a world where people consider that entertainment!"

I am shaking all over, bleeding from the womb, my knees shaking.

"I hate the world we've made! I hate it!"

"Baby, come, sit down. I'll buy you a drink."

"A drink! That's all you can fucking think of. A world so ugly you have to be anesthetized to bear it! I don't want to live in this world. I want to go back to Connecticut and hide! This is the fucking last days of the Roman Empire. If I were God, I'd kill off everyone and start over again."

Wayne leads me into a little bistro, a sort of cave where small marble tables stud the gloom and the chairs are woven Parisian café chairs. The crowd is Eurotrash to match the furniture, debutramps (with trust funds) pretending to be artists, gay male models pretending to be straight.

Wayne orders wine for himself. I ask for a Diet Coke with lime. I'm still crying and shaking. I hold on to my glass for dear life.

"Baby, it's just a performance," says Wayne.

"Those are real animals and real blood and a real woman and a real man. Don't give me this performance art shit. We allow stuff like this—but sex freaks us out. It's crazy, Wayne, crazy. I don't want to live in a world like this. I want people to be kind and tender and love each other. Why is it all so fucked up?"

Wayne puts his arm around me. "I'd never have brought you if I'd thought you'd freak out. I guess that leaves out Madame Ada, the dominatrix. That was to be our next stop. But if it upsets you, we can catch a movie instead. Maybe *Bambi*'s playing. Okay by me, Leila. I just thought you should *see* this for your art. It's important. It's what's happening downtown. I think you need to know."

I look at him with sheer hatred (especially because of the Bambi remark). *"Why?"*

"Because it's the secret history of our epoch. Like my bills, it calls into question what we value. We're part of this, and unless we find the secret part of ourselves that *loves* this stuff, we haven't a prayer for abolishing terrorism or torture. You have to find the torturer in your *own* heart. That's why I want you to meet Madame Ada. But if it's too rich for your blood, forget it. We'll do it another time."

Wayne calls over the waiter, who scribbles out a check. From his elegant black calf billfold Wayne produces a splendid representation of a hundred-dollar bill done in a rainbow of colors, like some banana republic currency.

The waiter, a gay young thing of twenty-two or so,

with a bolt in his left ear and a gold pirate hoop in his right, stares at the bill, then says, "I'm terribly sorry, sir, I can't accept this. We take American Express, Visa, MasterCard. . . ."

"Excuse me," says Wayne. "Do you know what this bill is worth?"

"No, sir."

"I'd say it's worth about at least one hundred times its face value. If you sell it—to Leo Castelli down the block or to Holly Solomon or *anyone*—you could pocket a clear profit of nine thousand nine hundred dollars. Do you know what you could do with nine thousand nine hundred dollars?"

"Yes, sir!"

"Acting classes for a year!" says Wayne. "A new car—albeit a little Korean one. *Time.* Do you know what *time* is worth?"

"Sir—I'm terribly sorry, I cannot take this. Amex, Master, Visa—even a personal check with proper ID."

"What's a year of your life worth? You could live for a year without working this crummy job—if you lived modestly. What's that worth to you?"

"Sir, *please,*" says the waiter, clearly upset.

"What's your name?" asks Wayne.

"Bruce," says the waiter. "Bruce Berlinger."

"And what do you do?"

"I'm an actor, sir, take classes with Stella Adler, sir."

"Well, Bruce, that'll buy a lot of classes with the old buzzard—and a lot of time. Surely you want *that.*"

"Sir, thank you, but I cannot accept this."

"Why? You could ante up the tab out of your pay, sell the bill to *any* reputable art dealer, repay yourself, and pocket the difference. You'd be nine thousand nine hundred dollars richer. How can you turn this down?"

"Sir," Bruce says, "I j-just c-c-can't."

"So split the difference with your boss, if it makes you feel any better."

"Please, sir."

"Well, it's my duty to warn you that you are giving up a year of life by doing this. Also that you clearly do not have the *risk*-taking necessary to the true artist. If you can't make this clear and simple choice tonight, how will you ever survive in the lists of art? Talent is common. So are good looks. What's rare is risk-taking. What's rare is the ability to follow your talent off the edge of the cliff and see if you can fly. What's rare is to follow your talent into the underworld and see if you can sing your way out. What's rare is to follow your talent into the labyrinth and see if you can slay the Minotaur. Are you Icarus? Are you Orpheus? Are you Theseus? Or are you just Bruce, condemned always to be Bruce?"

Bruce is crying.

"Amex, Master, Visa," he says through his tears.

Wayne heaves a deep sigh and hands Bruce an Amex card. Then he holds up the recreated one-hundred-dollar bill.

"Bruce, I want you to pay attention. I am giving this bill to this lady because she is a true artist, a true risk-taker. Watch closely."

And, extracting an old Rapidograph pen, he signs the bill "To Leila with love and blood and guts from Wayne," then hands the one-hundred-dollar work of art to me.

Bruce hurries away with Wayne's Amex card.

I decide to go to the dominatrix with Wayne.

*　　*　　*

Madame Ada lives in a prewar building in the West Village. There is a doorman. Wayne and I travel up to the penthouse level, where we ring the bell of PhD. A white calling card on the door says: *"Psychodrama Institute."* Silence.

"I wonder if she's home," says Wayne.

I'm relieved she's not. Then we hear the click of heels on a hard floor, and the door swings back.

A Slavic-looking square-jawed blonde in her forties wearing a white leather skirt, a blue silk blouse, and black stiletto heels opens the door. She shakes my hand firmly, then kisses Wayne on both cheeks, Italian style.

"Hello," she says, smiling and at once biting off her smile. "I'm Ada," she says, with a strong Russian accent, "or, to my slaves, Madame Ada." She laughs. "Come in, come in."

The large living room is bare, but for a huge leather couch—white—and a few futuristic Italian lamps. The walls are mirrored. There is no art at all. There is, however, an immense terrace, which looks out over the low roofs of the village toward the midtown skyline of New York. A dazzling view. What any struggling Russian émigré in New York would wish for.

We sit down on the leather couch, which makes a U in the middle of the bare room.

"So . . ." says Ada. "Wayne has told me wonderful things about you. He says we're so alike."

"How did you get into your line of work?" I ask.

Ada laughs. "Everybody asks the same question."

She crosses unshaven legs, swings her foot in its black stiletto heel, and laughs her trilling musical laugh.

"Let me tell you what I told Phil Donahue. When I first came to this country from Russia, I was brought by a Mexican friend to a club in SoHo where they did S&M. The Dungeon, I think it was called. I went for curiosity's sake, like you, not knowing what I would possibly make of it. At the club, I saw men bound and gagged, spread-eagled on bondage tables, their scrotums bound in leather thongs. I saw dominas in black leather whipping these men, allowing them to kiss one toe—or perhaps not even that—and I felt disgusted, detached, fiercely superior toward the people who were doing it. That gave me the first clue that I must be attracted to it. Then, suddenly, I was given a cat-o'-nine-tails and asked if I wanted to participate. I had no special feeling about it, really, one way or the other. A man's buttocks were bared before me—a young man, young and handsome, with firm buns—and I began to flog him. It was then that I discovered a great heat in myself to continue. I was wild with a passion to do more, and more, and more. I really *wanted* to hurt him, to draw blood, to lacerate his flesh." Ada said all this precisely, overaccenting each consonant, giving the vowels a musical Slavic lilt. I was riveted.

"What danger is there, if any?" I asked.

"Ah," said my professor of S&M. "You ask the right question. This kind of sex can easily make you *jaded*. It's a drug. It takes you to extremes, after which other sex, friendly sex, seems tame."

"*Is* there any friendly sex?" I ask.

Ada laughs as if she knows what I mean. The dark-blue eyes twinkle.

The conversation drifts to other things—vegetarianism, books, travel. (It strikes me as inconsistent that a leather fetishist should refuse to eat meat—but let that pass. Life is inconsistent.)

As we talk, two young people wander into the room. One is a slim, boyish blond young woman in jeans and a cowboy shirt, the other a smallish young man wearing a ponytail and an aviator scarf.

"My two personal slaves," says Ada. "Roland has my initials branded into his thigh, and Lavinia has my hoop earring through her nipple. Perhaps they'll show you later."

Lavinia shrugs shyly; Roland smiles.

I exchange glances with Wayne, who laughs.

"Hooked yet?"

"Perhaps Leila would like to meet one of the mistresses?" says Ada.

"Yes, I would."

"*Hooked,*" says Wayne.

"Let's go to the studio, then," says Ada.

We leave the penthouse, take the elevator down to the lobby, and, personal slaves in tow, walk a few blocks in the West Village until we come to a narrow brick house that seems all garage door.

Ada opens the door with an electronic beeper. Within is a garage containing two cars and behind them another door, which leads into a mirrored waiting room.

Two young men in yarmulkes sit there, hunched over, looking down at the floor. One is twisting his *payess* nervously, the other leafing through a magazine called *Puss n' Boots.*

Lavinia, the "personal slave," whispers: "We get lots of religious types here. Jews and Roman Catholics particularly."

Dear God—I would like to paint these two young

men in yarmulkes waiting outside the dominatrix's door, waiting to worship. I dare not—"not good for the Jews," I hear my mother's voice saying.

Ada sweeps on past the waiting room to an adjacent room, which is fitted out with a sort of massage table with holes for the face and genitals.

"This is a bondage table," she says. "You see? From underneath, you can do things."

She leads me to a mirrored closet, shows me a whole wardrobe of leather, rubber, fetishy shoes and boots.

"Come," she says. "I want you to meet my star mistress, Larissa."

We proceed down the hallway to another door, knock tentatively, whereupon a cultivated voice answers, "Wait, please."

The two slaves hang back with Wayne; Ada takes me by the hand and says, "We two shall go in alone."

"Come in!" sings Larissa.

Ada and I enter a darkened chamber, in which a man is tied face down on a bondage table.

He is youngish and blond like Dart and has lovely buns, wonderfully shaped calves with long muscles, and a glorious muscled back. It could be Dart lying there, his bulging cock bound in leather, his eyes blindfolded, his hands tied above his head in an attitude of supplication.

Mistress Larissa is pacing about the table, talking to him in imperious but mellifluous tones.

"What a bad boy you are to orgasm so quickly. You could *never* satisfy a woman that way. What do you say?"

"I'm sorry, Mistress," mumbles the man.

"What is the proper punishment for your transgression?"

"I don't know, Mistress."

"Bad boy," says Larissa, lashing him with her riding crop. He cries out.

"Think harder, pet," she says, pacing, caressing the crop.

Larissa is a glorious creature—tall, dark-haired, almond-eyed, with a wonderful voice, extraordinary erect carriage, and body language that says "Touch me not."

She is wearing her long chestnut hair in a ponytail, bound, like her victim's cock, in leather thongs. Her long-waisted, long-legged body is clad in a black leather mini-dress with a laced waist and thigh-high laced-up black boots. The heels, like Ada's, are at least six inches high. I am amazed that she can walk in them at all—but walk she does, and as elegantly as a prize Arab mare.

"The punishment?" she asks. "Or rather, the implement for the punishment?"

"As you wish, Mistress."

"What's that, *boy?* Louder."

"As you wish, Mistress."

"Mmm," says Larissa, brandishing her leather crop. "I'm thinking. Shall it be the crop, the cat, the rubber hose?"

"As you wish, Mistress."

She runs her lacquered red nails along the crop as if to test its sting, then hits him with it. Again. And again. And again. She smiles, her red lips curling up in a little crimson crescent of pleasure. He cries out, his beautiful back covered with red welts.

"You shall not cry out, *boy*," she says. "For every stroke, you shall say, 'Thank you, Mistress Larissa,' or I triple the strokes. Do you hear me, boy?"

"Thank you, Mistress Larissa."

"Very well, then." She begins to flog him in earnest. He suppresses his cries, muttering instead, "Thank you, Mistress Larissa. Thank you, Mistress Larissa."

My heart is pounding with each blow. I am growing wet.

Larissa, a very sensitive receptor, feels this. Without a word, she puts her crop in my hand and takes another from the wall for herself. It is as if she has given me her cock.

"Another beautiful lady is going to assist me now," she tells the slave.

"Thank you, Mistress Larissa," he says.

I bring the crop down on his buttocks, lightly and tentatively at first, then harder. Larissa and I sting him in alternate strokes, responding to each other's motion, each other's rhythm.

"She's a natural," Ada says to Larissa.

My sane mind stands apart, watching me beat the man harder and harder, astonished to be causing him pain (for which he thanks me). One touch and I might come, but I linger on the edge, amazed to find pleasure in raising red welts on the slave's back and buttocks.

Slave, master—what does it mean? A jumble of images from my past life fills my head. I am whipping Dolph, Elmore, Dart, Dart, Dart. I am revenging myself on André, on Dolph, on every art critic who has ever attacked my work. I understand the lure of this place, the feelings discharged, their heat. Elsewhere in society the power struggle between men and women is disguised. Here it is naked. Elsewhere people pretend to be civilized; here they do not. Elsewhere men and women kiss, cuddle, and lie. Here they lash each other and tell the truth. The truth, however horrible, does make you free.

Isadora: Who, then, is the fucker and who the fuckee? Is that the point?

Leila: You got it, kiddo.

Isadora: Who do I have to fuck to get out of this movie?

I whip the man harder and harder, until his mumbled thanks are incoherent. I do not know who he is—all I know is that he is a man, and that the anger I feel against him is fathomless and deep. On one of my strokes, he groans and comes in a spurt of white over the thongs that cover his cock.

"Thank you, Mistress," he mumbles. And I almost double over in a spontaneous convulsion of my own.

Larissa has resumed torturing the slave, her cruel crimson lips turned up in mischief as she holds high a long black candle. He thanks her as she thrusts it into his bowels.

Isadora: The mystical marriage of male and female at the dominatrix! Gimme a break!

Leila: O ye of little faith!

I feel that I am truly in hell, dedicated to the dark gods, with this man in bondage playing out his own private drama. We are all here because somehow love has not worked for us, because our sane minds have deserted us, so we are seeking pure sex, and pure power. I give myself over to Kali—I who formerly loved Demeter and Persephone. Whoever is not a cynic at forty can never have loved mankind.

"Larissa has still not released her slave," Ada says. "But you, my pet, are a natural for this sort of psychodrama."

273

Wayne looks at me and laughs. "Well, well, well," he says. "I can't say I'm all that surprised. Leila has never been afraid of her dark side."

The bathroom door opens, and the blond young man emerges. He does look a bit like Dart, but he is only another Dart look-alike. The world is full of them!

Wayne was right to bring me here. This was what I needed to finally break the Dart obsession, my way of understanding it. How could he have known?

The blond young man bends down and kisses Larissa's pointed black toe.

"Thank you, Mistress," he says. "Next Tuesday at four."

"Begone, pet," she says coolly.

"Thank you, Mistress," he says, and goes home to beat his wife or girlfriend.

Wayne catches my eye.

"At some point," he says, "I'm going to find a way to make this into art. I don't quite know *how* yet. But it's critical that *some*one do it. I want to be the Francis Bacon of S&M."

"Francis Bacon already *is* the Francis Bacon of S&M," I say. "You're late."

Wayne laughs.

"Do you know what he said to an interviewer who asked him where he drew his images of horror?" I ask.

"No," Wayne says.

" 'I just look down at the lamb chop on my plate,' he said. 'That's all the horror I need.' "

"A convert," says Wayne. "And in just one evening."

*   *   *

The room is lit with candles. This "Psychodrama Institute" seems written by Genet. Mistress Ada is standing center stage, testing a riding crop with her hand.

"Welcome," she says to her victim.

A smallish man in a full facial mask of leather is bound and gagged and fastened with leather thongs to invisible hooks in the mirrored wall, held in a cruciform pose. The mise-en-scène invites serious meditation. Madame Ada is not kidding.

"I shall ask you," Ada says to us, "to drop your normal identities and become Mistress Luisa and Master Blaine. I invite you to choose your costumes next door, with Mistress Larissa's help."

It is a command. We obey.

In the bedroom, I pick out a red leather corset with a dozen garters, red leather stiletto boots, and a curly black wig.

Larissa laces me into the corset so that my breasts tumble over the top.

Laced, I become excited.

Larissa finds me a pair of black silk stockings and helps me hook them all around with the garters. Then she laces me into the high red boots—which are, amazingly, just my size.

The curly wig is a lion's mane. It makes me *feel* like another person. Larissa does my makeup and styles my hair. My lipstick is crimson, my eye shadow green, my cheeks russet. She rouges my nipples, exciting me as she touches me with her long sensual fingers.

Master Blaine, meanwhile, is transforming himself into a stand-in for Errol Flynn.

"This is who I've always wanted to be," he says, pulling on black leather knee breeches, an eye patch, and a leather vest. A gleaming sword dangles at his side, and the eye patch gives him a sinister look.

"Don't touch," Larissa cautions. "Only I can touch her," she says to Wayne. Pinning me against the wall, she strokes my nipples until I am almost ready to explode. Then she stops.

"It is good to linger on the brink," she says. "It makes the creativity that much greater."

Wayne is watching us and growing harder by the minute. His leather breeches have a laced opening where a codpiece may be attached. His cock emerges, long and well-shaped. My eyes linger. "He is not wont to love who is tormented by lewdness," I remember from "The Rules of Love."

"Come with me," Larissa says.

I stagger into the living room, getting used to the boots. The tightness corresponds to the tightness of the corset. As Mistress Luisa, I may do anything I please. I am liberated again, as if I were a beginner, regaining my beginner's mind.

The Zen of S&M! I laugh aloud to myself at the very notion. And, simultaneously, I am thinking how I might make this into a piece called *The Zen of S&M*. Being an artist is a curse. You can't even sink into depravity without thinking of how to turn sinking into depravity into art!

"Master Blaine," says Ada, "fall to your knees."

Wayne obeys.

"I want you to follow me around on your knees, assisting me with everything I command. You are my personal slave for the night. It is a great honor to be chosen as my personal slave."

"Thank you, Mistress Ada," says Wayne.

"And you, Luisa, are to follow orders as strictly as any novice in a nunnery."

"Thank you, Mistress Ada."

The man in the mask who is lashed to the wall moves at the sound of my voice, then clears his throat.

"Silence, slave," says Ada.

"Yes, Mistress," says a voice I almost recognize. I must be mistaken. The atmosphere at Ada's is the atmosphere of The Land of Fuck, the lagoon of dreams—identities mingle and merge. I remember how the blond man turned out *not* to be Dart. This familiar voice is also a mental mirage. I run the cards in my head, trying to place him. André? Someone from one of his parties? But on a Saturday night? Married men see their dominatrices on weekdays!

"Luisa, I want you to take this black candle and introduce it into the bowels of my bound slave."

She greases a twelve-inch candle and holds it out to me.

I take the candle and thrust. I am a man deflowering a virgin, a pirate raping his prey, a father violating his daughter. The Marquis de Sade penetrating Justine, Stephen penetrating O.

"Now rub your nipples on his rear," says Ada.

He groans. My blood heats to the boiling point, as I go deeper and deeper.

Now Ada commands Wayne to touch me while I am penetrating the masked slave.

He instantly obeys, brushing his erect cock against my buttocks, then holding very still. Simultaneously woman and man, I am overwhelmed. His slightest touch is as exciting as penetration.

"Do not move," commands Ada. "And do not orgasm. Whoever orgasms shall be severely whipped."

At that warning, the urge to come is overwhelming. I hold back only by thinking of my twin girls, of myself as mommy. My sane mind is holding on by a thread. How Wayne does it, I don't know. But the masked man is not so fortunate. The prohibition has aroused him beyond his power to resist, and he groans and comes in a jet stream that hits the mirrored wall like the juicy whitehead aimed at the mirror by an adolescent squeezer.

"You will pay for that pleasure," says Ada. "Stand, Luisa. Stand, Blaine."

We rise and separate. Ada hands us each a riding crop, takes one for herself, and shows us how to whip the masked stranger. First on the thighs, then on the buttocks, then—savagely—on the back. Taught well, the masked man says thank you for each stroke, until he is bloody and whimpering in agony.

"Let that be a lesson to my other slaves," says Ada in a blood-chilling voice.

The masked man groans.

"Untie him," says Mistress Ada to the groveling Wayne.

He obeys.

"Unmask him," says Mistress Ada.

Wayne unzips and peels off the man's facial mask.

Lionel Schaeffer lies fainting and bloody at my feet.

In another room, a briefcase goes *beep, beep, beep.*

18

BYE-BYE BLUES

———— ◆ ————

I'm dreary in mind
and I'm so worried in heart.
Oh the best of friends
sure have got to part.

—Bessie Smith

So I've given up booze and Dart, only to take up bondage and discipline. Some progress! Back I go to my silo, to my celibacy, to my twins. I feel sullied by the experience, as if I have gone to hell and been pickled in brimstone. Ada calls and calls, wanting me to continue the "psycho-drama." I don't call back. I acknowledge my dark side. "If you do it once, you're an existentialist; twice, you're a pervert," my sane mind says. But what a hangover I have! Worse than booze! At the bottom of my despair, alone as I've ever been, I try again to work.

Collages of black leather and whips, S&M film stills, sculptures of boots and shoes, shackles and chains, obsess me for a while. I give them up as hokey and decide, quite consciously, to do nothing. I will lie fallow, let the mind drift. I will not paint, not fall in love, not worry about men or money or work. I will only *be*. I will try to get out of my own way.

Without I, who would I be? Try to abolish the first person. Try to be free of the towering shadow of the ninth letter of the alphabet.

Who is Leila/Louise/Luisa really? Leila could as soon be you or the hand that grasps the pencil. Her hair, her eyes, her profession, her men, may change. All these are flesh. Her children may be different sexes, but Leila is obsessed with the towering figure of I. Leila loves narcissists who cannot love, because Leila cannot love her*self*.

Having decided to give up painting (because it is so much a product of my narcissism) and become a writer, I toy with writing about my faltering struggle to get sober, to tell my exemplary tale, as a warning, an inspiration, for other women, other men.

I begin with a notebook, writing the day's events, thoughts, dreams, snatches of dialogue. Enough of my friends are writers for me to know that writing is not any easier than painting. But for me it is a pleasure at first because it is a sort of holiday from expectations, a hobby, not for sale, not to be bartered by André.

I take a little marbled notebook bought once in Italy and begin to scribble at random, catching stray thoughts like threads snagged by a crochet hook.

> What am I here to learn? [I write] for there is no
> other point to this passage that I can see. As far as I
> can tell, I am here to learn how to pass on, how to
> flow, how to greet and how to take leave, but above

all how to take leave, for life is a perpetual
leave-taking.

I believe I am here to learn to praise. Before AA
I would never have said that. I thought it was my job
to learn how to curse—I thought this was the essence
of sophistication, of satire, of art, but now I know it is
praise that is rare and blessed. *A glad heart is a
perpetual feast.*

Wayne wanted to take me to the dominatrix
supposedly to show me the essence of our society but
really to share his cynicism and pain with me.
Perversion is curdled love. I wanted to be like Ada, to
be a bitch who could command men, but back here in
the country, I know that is *not* what I want. I want to
learn how to love—no matter how many times I fail,
no matter how unworthy the objects, no matter what
betrayals I experience—for nothing but love is worth
the passage through life.

But I have defined love too narrowly. I have
defined it as sexual love, as the love between a man
and a woman. It's that, and it's far more than that.
Writing in this notebook is love, feeding my twins is
love, nourishing my roses is love, painting is love. . . .

At Madame Ada's Psychodrama Institute I saw
children playing with power and pain, in despair
because their limited notion of sexual love had failed
them. I found myself intrigued, convinced, converted
—for a night. I, too, believed—briefly—that curdled
power was what I sought.

Wrong. Love does not *seek* an equally weighted
scale (and is not angry when the weights are unequal);
love does not speak of give-and-take, of dominance,
submission, of slave and master. Christ spoke of love,
but the church that bears His name deals in power.

Every proselytizing religion eventually is corrupted that way. The only pure religions are religions of attraction; we come to them when we are ready. The closest clue I have to love is how I feel about my twins. I do not count the cost, I do not measure. If I could love myself that way, my work that way, the world that way, nothing would be impossible for me. Perhaps someday I could even love a man that way, but if not it would hardly matter, for I would have transcended "I."

Everybody writes about alcoholism and cocaine addiction, but no one tells the truth about it. It's fashionable to convert on the cover of *People* magazine and make a sober comeback. Getting sober is far more complex; it's really about getting *free*. The disease is cunning, baffling, powerful. The grand pronouncement of sobriety is, in reality, another layer of the disease. To pronounce yourself "cured" is to remain incurable. To pronounce yourself "sober" is, in reality, to remain drunk. To pronounce yourself "recovered" is to be unrecoverable. The disease is like an onion; it has all these layers. You can peel forever and never get to the bottom. Therefore, to write about getting sober is the ultimate danger—danger of drunkenness, danger of death.

The only safe thing to do about sobriety is to shut up about it. "Love seldom lasts after it is divulged," say "The Rules of Love." I feel the same about AA. Hence the importance of anonymity. You could lose the magic by writing out the process.

And yet it could be important to tell my story, any woman's story. I would certainly write it, heart in throat, knowing I was breaking the last taboo, endangering my own sobriety, my own life.

All the great secrets grow only in silence. To

write is to betray the deepest truth the heart knows:
that silence is always wiser than any word.

That must be the paradox of writing for
publication, as it is even of journal keeping. You die
into the word, and only silence can redeem.

Wayne calls.

"You've disappeared again," he says. "Ada has fixed
another scene for you. She's gone out of her way. You
don't know her, but she never does this for *anyone*."

"No," I say.

"What do you mean, 'no'?" asks Wayne. "We've
hardly begun."

"I've done it," I say, "seen my dark side, you win, I
give in. Enough."

"You're scared," says Wayne.

"Maybe so. Maybe I'm scared. And maybe I've
learned what I needed to learn. But I've had enough for the
moment."

"Leila, this isn't *like* you."

"Good."

"What do you mean?"

"Well, maybe the old daredevil Leila is growing up.
Maybe I've had it with experience for experience's sake.
Maybe my thick skull is finally able to take something in.
Enough. *Genug. Basta.* Give Ada my love. And take some
for yourself. Come visit me in the country when you're in
the mood. I can't deal with New York right now."

"Boy—I *really* blew your mind, didn't I?"

"I thought that was the whole *point*—blowing my
mind. Or did I get that wrong?"

"You're a quick study," says Wayne. "Or else just
chicken."

"Maybe."

"Leila, this isn't *like* you."

"You said that already."

"Look—if you use the S&M material before I do, I'll kill you."

"Don't worry. I'm working on something else."

"What?"

"Myself. My sane mind."

"You're really nuts," says Wayne.

A few days before I was to leave for the Viva Venezia Ball and meet Lionel (my would-be lover, whose dirty secret I now knew) and Julian (my astral pal), Dart called.

He called, sounding sane, measured, in control of himself. He proposed lunch. And I, feeling strong enough to deal with so moderate a request, accepted. Maybe lunch would confirm that I'd finally broken the obsession. Sybille and Emmie were against my going, so I went.

Lunch. Lunch between lovers. Dart and I used to joke that when you start having lunch and actually eating, it's already over.

Once the date was set, I began preparing. Manicure, pedicure, facial, silk underwear . . . Apparently, meeting Dart is an enterprise that requires new clothes, a non-Thoreauvian enterprise, in short. Beware. Since AA, I have begun to measure everything in those terms.

The dominatrix requires new clothes, the Viva Venezia Ball requires new clothes, Danny Doland required new clothes, lunch with Dart requires new clothes. The message is clear. These are things I should avoid.

But the truth is, I'm not *that* free yet.

We meet at Da Silvano in New York.

(Nice little irony in that.)

He's late.

I'm wearing, over the silk underwear, a very tailored white linen suit with a modified miniskirt. I'm as excited as I was watching the dominatrix, and the feelings are not so very different.

He walks in looking dazzling: blue, blue eyes (or are they new blue contact lenses?), a new blue shirt that some besotted lady must have given him (I *know* it in my bones), khaki shorts, sneakers, Walkman.

We clasp hands. Conversation *ignites*. As if we've never been apart.

We sit at a table and talk, eye beams locked—as in the old days. It is all still here, the magic, the chemistry. If he touched my leg, I'd come.

Dart (leaning over the table, stroking my arm): "I've missed you so."

Leila: "Me too."

Dart: "I love you; there's nobody like you. Nobody's ever loved me like you did. Nobody ever will."

Leila: "That's true enough."

He tells me about the bimbo, at my urging. "She loves me," he says. Not: "I love her."

Dart: "I'm doing what my father did—marrying a trust fund. She's tough, has mean eyes. Not sweet like you."

Leila: "Then *why?*"

He can't answer this, but I could: her toughness makes him feel more secure than my sweetness did. He's flipped from S to M. Now he's the one getting beat.

Leila: "Who's the boss in the relationship?"

Dart: "I am."

I smile at him and stroke his hand, knowing better.

Dart: "We should have gotten married."

Leila: "Darling, we *are* married—in our hearts. How could we be *more* married?"

He weeps. Dart has always been good at weeping on cue.

Dart: "We should take a trip together."

Leila: "When?"

Dart: "I don't know—we could manage it."

Leila: "What about Little Miss Mean Eyes? Sorry. Her name?"

Dart: "Sylvie."

I remember all the messages Natasha took from a Sylvie. They go back two or possibly three years. My gorge rises. I cross my legs in my spike sandals and watch Dart get turned on. Two can play this game as well as one.

Leila: "Wouldn't Sylvie be suspicious?"

Dart: "She gives me lots of space."

No choice, I guess. Mmm. Being the coveted mistress rather than the live-in lady has a certain charm. Suddenly, just by being unavailable, *I* become the prize. Dart has an erection under his khaki shorts. It turns me on. I hear Sybille's voice saying: "That's his *profession*—having an erection." But what does she know about The Land of Fuck? A lot, probably.

We make plans for our mythical trip. I know it's mythical—does *he?* I will tell my proper millionaire I'm going away to do research (Dart doesn't have to know I broke up with him weeks ago), and he will tell Sylvie *something* (he never bothers much about excuses), and we will go . . . where? We can't decide.

Dart (romantic): "Venice again. Venice again with you. I'd cut off one nut for Venice again with you."

Leila (practical): "It would ruin our stay in Venice."

Dart: "Or Wyoming. Remember Wyoming?"

Leila: "Who could ever forget? And Dubrovnik."

Dart (smiling his rehearsed smile): "Hong Kong."

We speak of everything: the fictitious trip, my fictitious fiancé, his (perhaps *also* fictitious) fiancée, his million (as usual) projects. Why am I not more angry at him? Because I have discharged my anger in the *Pandora's Box* collage? Because I still love him? Because, having passed through some barrier in myself, I have transcended anger? But in my sane mind I do not trust him. And I know I won't sleep with him.

Am I teasing him or teasing myself?

Dart: "You look so beautiful."

Leila (thinking of Nighttown): "It must be the life I'm leading."

Dart: "How's your Program?"

Leila: "I've had slips—but it's also changed my life. I get furious at the Program a lot, rebel against it. I know there's more to life than church basements—but it's also a gift. It's sent me back to Zen, to Thoreau, to meditation. Things I dabbled in years ago but never understood at all. And perhaps am only beginning to . . ." (I realize I am saying too much, turning him off. He partly left because I needed to get sober.) "This stuff is better left unsaid. How's *yours?*"

Dart: "I have a beer now and then."

Leila (knowing I shouldn't ask): "Do you go to meetings?"

Dart: "The Program *infuriates* me. All those people substituting one addiction for another. I wouldn't get drunk with those people—why should I get sober with them!"

Leila (changing the subject): "What does Sylvie call you?"

Dart: "She calls me D.D. or Darton-Darton. . . .

Sometimes she calls me Trick 'n' Treat."

Leila (grimly): "She sounds funny."

Dart (a tear running down his cheek): "At least Sylvie and I are both struggling together. With you, I was always a seed in the shadow of your forest. I never felt equal. I was blocked."

Leila (knowing the bullshit for what it is, yet also feeling his pain): "Darling, I understand; I understand *everything.*"

And I *do.* I even know that in some strange way this is much harder for him than for me—though he has a new lover and I don't, though he supposedly abandoned *me,* though my friends would say he used me.

Not true.

Ada has taught me that we use each other, that we both give and both take, that we both create the psychodrama.

Was it a fair exchange? Who knows? As I often say to the twins, "Life is not fair."

Dart: "People are so cruel. They love to see love fail. It breaks my heart to run into our old friends."

Leila: "Me too."

I know what he means. The gloating when love breaks down is almost worse than the breakdown itself. All those people so eager to tell you the worst about your former lover. Why can't they shut up?

We kiss when we say goodbye. The kiss doesn't quite work. The continents have shifted; the shorelines no longer fit together. We were madly in love as we sat in that restaurant—and now *pffft* . . . gone.

I *know* he would meet me in Venice or Wyoming or Dubrovnik. But *why?* Somewhere between his final departure with Sylvie, AA, *Pandora's Box,* and Madame Ada, I've let him go almost without even knowing it, released him into the universe. He knows that, and perhaps it's why he's offering to come back. He knows I won't take him. And *I* know it. The obsession is gone. And in its wake? Sadness—overpowering sadness—which even cancels out the lust he stirs.

Now I am at the Gritti, waiting for Julian, who arrives in three days. And I am wretched. I should never have come—even for a week. I have suddenly been hurled back in time. I miss Dart in my *kishkes*—not to mention below. Is this a sort of phantom-limb phenomenon? Having lost him, I wish I could *unlose* him? Having struggled to let him go, I now want him back. Having gotten free, I long for my bondage. I'm terrified I'm going to drink. But it is my heart that is mainly afflicted. It is empty as a dock after an ocean liner has left. Is it Dart I miss, or am I nostalgic for the old hole in my heart? Am I only nostalgic for my pain?

They have given me the same room we had at the start of our idyll—Hemingway's room. Venice, as always, is a city of ghosts, and you never know from one visit to another whether the ghosts will be benign or malign.

I step into this palatial room alone, exhausted, drained—as you always are when all your molecules have been rearranged by a transatlantic flight—and I crash. This is the room where Dart and I made love six times a night, the room where we screamed and barked and tangled like baby animals, the room we never left till after dark—when we would go out and prowl the streets of Venice by night, speaking of Ruskin, of Byron, of Tintoretto, of Shakespeare, and of how much we loved each other—only to come back to the room and make love again.

Dart is gone, and I have tried to replace him with meditation, with group love, with domination, with solitary work, with writing in my notebook, with my sane mind. Tonight none of that seems enough. The dybbuk is back, my serenity smashed. I have lost Dart—or lost my love of Dart—and I have lost my last baby. I have lost my baby self. I have had a summer of celibacy (if you don't count Danny or the dominatrix!), and it has made me strong—but now all my bravery has fled, and I am in despair. The silk Fortuny walls seem to have all the love we made in their shining threads. I throw myself on the bed, distraught, hopeless.

All my old hotel room angst returns. All the panic and pain I thought the Program had banished. (These are the worst moments of a "free" woman's life: alone after jet lag, alone after miscarriage, alone after passionate love, alone after lunch with one's former lover.)

Everyone has someone, and I am alone! Why can I make nothing last? Why must I keep bolting and remaking my life? Why do I outgrow every man I join my life with? Or do I just throw love away with my two hands, using growth as an excuse?

Sadness, pain, despair. I rummage in my luggage for one of my little AA books and read the thought for today:

> God's help is always available; all we have to do is make room for Him to take part in our lives and keep ourselves ready to accept His guidance.

Fuck that!

I will throw myself in the lagoon. To die in Venice would be, at least, artistically correct. Isn't Venice where artists go to die?

I switch on the light, grab some stationery, and scrawl a note to Dart.

HOTEL
GRITTI PALACE
VENEZIA

Darling —
    Can you believe I
have the very same room
where we stayed together?
The love is all still
here — bouncing off the
silk walls. Since all
time is circular, it is
all here — but where
are you?
    You once said we
were either very brave

HOTEL
GRITTI PALACE
VENEZIA

or very foolish. Perhaps
a little of both. I
don't want to spend
our lives apart. How
many lifetimes will it
be before we are
reunited? It's such
a waste.

All my love,
Leila

I fold up the letter, address it carefully to the apartment in Hoboken (Hoboken!) where he lives with his little bimbo, amid my books, the clothes I bought him, the film stills I did of him. I tell myself that tomorrow I'll send this missive to him by courier. Tomorrow. Meanwhile, try to sleep.

But sleep eludes me in my jet-lagged state.

I toss and turn, masturbate—slowly and longingly, thinking of him—then, frenziedly, *not* thinking of him. I turn on the light and start to read a friend's translation of the Book of Job (which I brought along because it matches my mood). When I come to the line "Remember life is a breath," I break down and cry. It's 3:00 A.M. in Italy but only 9:00 P.M. the previous night in Hoboken.

I dial Dart's number. Perkily, jauntily, an answering machine picks up.

It's the bimbo's nasal voice.

"This is the home of Darton Donegal and Sylvie Slansky. We can't come to the phone right now, but if you'll leave a message, we'll get back to you. *Beep!*"

What is this new, organized Dart? When I knew him, he had no forwarding address, no answering machine, no beep.

All he had was the most glorious cock in Christendom, the bluest eyes, the sweetest voice, and an inveterate inability to tell the truth about *any*thing. Is Dart growing up? I put down the phone without leaving a message.

Where are Dart and his bimbo at nine on a Saturday night in Hoboken? Dinner and a movie? In bed fucking their brains out, hearing the click on the phone machine and knowing instantly, psychically, that it is me, calling from overseas? That fuzzy sound the line gets when Europe is calling, a sort of blizzard of old loves. Where are the loves of yesteryear? Where indeed?

I still get Dart's canceled checks, so I know he is buying furniture on the installment plan at Seaman's and paying some of his own bills. Where is he getting the money? *Is* he growing up? Is he holding down a job?

Off in Venice—the lagoon of dreams, and in despair. The courage to go on alone has slipped. It fails me. I fail me.

I walk to the window, open it, and look out on the white bubble of the Salute, the water with its millions of dark paillettes in all the colors of hell's rainbow. Venice can be so melancholy, so haunted. It is not a place to come when you have lost a love.

Below, on the terrace, two American honeymooners are sitting gazing at each other. For them, Venice is a different city. We look at the same church, the same water, and feel such utterly opposed things—they at the beginning of a love story, I at the end. How can two such opposite feelings exist in the same air?

A disturbance on the surface of the water where normally the *traghetto* churns across—the little gondola ferry I so often took on these first trips with Dart. In the sparkling aubergine water, a face seems to appear and then to disappear, making it flat, glassy black, then suddenly greenish white.

Dart's face! Dart's arm waves above the waters!

And then Dart sinks under the surface of the waters, saying goodbye.

I collapse in a torrent of tears. "No more pain! No more pain!" I mutter. But even as I imagine him waving goodbye to me, I know I am really waving goodbye to him. This is another letting go, another end of the obsession. How many times will I have to do this before I get it right? *Sane mind:* As many times as it takes. *Sane mind:* Please note that you are not drinking—at least not tonight.

At some point, I get up and tear the letter into confetti. I scatter it over the terrace of the Gritti—but the wind lifts it and carries it away into the Grand Canal. I see the last little bits of my longing for Dart—for Dark, I almost said—carried away on the aubergine waters. And then I fall asleep, exhausted by my own psychodrama.

In the morning the demons are banished. I awake, throw open the windows facing the Grand Canal, and breathe in the glitter of a Venice morning. I think of Elmore in Chianti when our love was freshly minted, of the birth of the twins, and I remember how much I love Italy—if not Venice.

Venice I used to feel I could do without. Green bilge. Greedy shopkeepers. A kind of cynical medieval Disneyland populated by sweating hordes of day-trippers. Oh, I have friends who *swear* by Venice, live there, even. My friend Lorelei in Dorsoduro, my old art school classmate Cordelia Herald, who paints in a crumbling Gothic palazzo on the Grand Canal. I never used to understand it. Venice seemed so self-consciously out-of-this-world. But today Venice looks dazzling to me. Perhaps I am becoming a convert.

Italy, of course, is another story—Italy has always made me happy, has always made me feel like a woman. Whenever I arrive in Italy, I remember the list of proverbs

Emmie and I once made for *The Amazon Handbook: A Guide for Free Women* (which, of course, we never wrote). Proverb number one was: "You're not too fat; you're just in the wrong country." Number two: "Be very romantic, but keep the real estate in your own name." That was as far as we got. (Actually, those two rules alone could take you far, far.)

Italy. There is nothing about this country that I do not love: The language, in which everything sounds better, from "Please pass the beans" (*I fagioli, per piacere*) to "I love you" *(Te amo)*. The people, with their humanity, anarchy, eccentricity, and yet their great belief in all the things that *really* matter: children, art, food, family, conversation, opera, gardening, shoes. The landscape, warm and maternal in places, with mammary hills, and craggy and masculine in others, with phallic peaks. The whole boot of Italy (and I love boots) is lapped by a lingual, sexual sea. From Roman times to the present, Italy has been a country to fall in love with—a tribute to all that is enduring, crazy, pagan, joyous, melancholy, at once banal and divine, in the human spirit.

It's not that I fail to love America. America is my home, and so I love and hate it equally, as one loves and hates one's parents. I know it too well. I know its great energy, its pragmatism, but I also know its crazy evangelists, its corrupt politicians, its mad addiction to money. What I love about America is its boundless optimism; what I hate is the way it fetters that optimism in a straitjacket of puritanism. If you have X, you can't have Y. If you have Q, you can have Z. If you have mind, your body must pay. If you have body, your mind must pay. What I hate about America is its belief in dualism—its belief in retribution—when the truth is that the more you have the more you have, the more you grab the *less* you have, and the more you give the more you have. For life on its deepest level is a potlatch, not a stock market: only by giving do we become rich. Only by nurturing mind do we nurture body. Only by loving the body do we really love the mind. They are indivisible, united, one. The heart of America knows this, in its optimism; the body politic of America does not.

Give, give, give! is the cry of the gods. It rhymes with: Live, live, live! Why else are we passing through this sublunary sphere? I cannot believe it is to accumulate T-bills, certificates of deposit, and stock options.

Keep moving, keep traveling. When I travel, I know I am in my proper mode. For what is life but a passage? When I was younger, it was Italy that kept me painting. I dipped my foot in the baptismal font of life.

The phone rings.

"*Pronto.*"

"Leila—it's Cordelia. Heard you were in town." Cordelia's southern drawl has not been modified by twenty years in Italy.

"How on earth did you know? I just got in last night."

Cordelia laughs. "Venice is a *very* small town, honey. I just *know*. I'm callin' to invite you over for drinks at six-thirty or seven. I'm havin' a few people—flotsam an' jet set, as we used to say."

"I'd love to."

"I've *moved*, honey. I'm now in Palazzo Barbaro. Ask the concierge at the hotel. Everyone knows me. Everyone knows *everybody* in Venice."

"Are you going to the Viva Venezia Ball?"

"Not if I can help it, honey. It's the event of the season, but I *hate* that sort of thing. Too many cotillions in my ill-spent youth—honey, that's why I *left* Charleston in the first place. I try whenever possible to hang out with the lunatics, the lovers, and the poets."

"Good old Cordelia."

"*See* the Biennale if you possibly can—it's actually *good* this year."

"Okay, boss."

"And come at six, so we can have a minute to talk before the sweatin' hordes of freeloaders arrive. What do you call them, honey?"

"Call *what?*"

"Freeloaders—in Yiddish."

"*Schnorrers.*" I laugh.

"I miss your madness, Zandberg."

"Me you too," I say.

We both laugh and hang up. Friends. What would I do without my old friends? I get dressed and make my way through Venice to the Biennale.

A hazy late-summer Sunday in Venice. Bells ringing. A scene that Monet might have painted: a scrim of humidity softening the *campanili,* the sky, the water. No wonder painters flocked here, where the air and water metamorphose moment by moment in a kaleidoscope of light. Venice is the only city in which nearly every view is three-quarters sky. Taking the *vaporetto* to the Biennale, I suddenly understand the light of Venice, the light that drew Ruskin, Turner, Monet—and before them all the great Venetian painters, from Carpaccio, Titian, Tintoretto, and Veronese to Guardi and Canaletto. Suddenly I *see* Venice as if for the first time. Is it sobriety, the triumph of my sane mind? Is it my maenads and crystal? Is it the loss of Dart? I *see* the motes of light that Turner painted. I understand the light as if it were glowing deep in my gut.

In art school I studied with a wonderful old teacher, a figurative painter from Russia named Stoloff. He used to say that the difference between a so-so painting and a great one was tone, the sense that the painter had painted not only the object itself but the air between himself and the object, which transfigured it, made it uniquely his. I had never really understood what he meant, but now I did.

The whole point of painting was to capture the air—the light shimmering in the air between you and your quarry. And why? Because only then were you painting the dance of the molecules, the dance of the molecules that made up what we call "real."

This was the point—to paint that dance. But first you had to *see* it. Stoloff also used to say, "You are here to learn not how to paint but how to *see*. Because if you can see, the painting comes by itself. But most so-called artists are blind."

He had been dead a decade, but finally I was learning what he had tried to teach me. Removing the alcohol from my system was like getting a new set of senses: eyes, ears, nose—all worked as if they were freshly made. I could tune in to the cosmos without static; I could see without glasses; I could smell the flowers without nose clips on!

What I was learning, above all, is that life goes on. What I was learning was that alone, I was not alone. I would learn to follow my bliss wherever it led. If this night in Venice had brought nothing else, it had brought, at least, this moment of clarity. I had finally learned my old art teacher's lesson. I could go home now if I liked.

*　　*　　*

But I didn't. Instead I went to Cordelia's at six.

Cordelia lived on the top floor of the Palazzo Barbaro, in whose astonishing library Henry James slept when he was beginning *The Wings of the Dove*. The apartment was vast, with coffered ceilings, a *salotto* that faced the Grand Canal, that Jamesian library with painted panels, its view of the tiled roofs and roof gardens of Venice, and a kitchen that was once Sargent's studio. Cordelia's paintings—monumental equine forms (like a sort of mad Rosa Bonheur gone abstract)—were everywhere, hung or propped against walls.

Cordelia embraced me. Then she stood back to appraise me as women of a certain age do. Not dead yet. Not over the hill. Still a few good love affairs left. (Odd, the way we measure out our lives in love affairs, as women of another time used to measure theirs in children.)

Cordelia has waist-length blond hair, piercing green eyes, glorious cheekbones. She is tall, with broad shoulders that can make an Armani suit or a denim shirt look equally elegant. We hug.

"You look great," I say. "Is it still the same Italian—or a new one?"

"Believe it or not, it's still Guido, honey. I think our relationship *survives* because we can't be together. These Italian liaisons go on forever. It must be what Dumas said: 'The bonds of matrimony are so heavy that it takes two to carry them—sometimes three.' For certain, if we'd gotten married fifteen years ago, we probably wouldn't still be together."

"Still madly in love?"

"Yes, honey. With the accent on madly."

"Does he still live with his wife?"

"Oh, absolutely. I see him from ten to twelve in the morning and sometimes from six to eight at night. It's more than most married couples have. Quality time, they call it—don't they? Not a bad system. And the rest of the time I paint."

"Do you ever want to live with him?"

"Of course. But less and less. I get into bed at night with all these art history tomes just heaped around me, and you can't do that with a man—they always resent it. Sometimes, just before I fall asleep, I wish for someone to *hug*. But then the feelin' passes—and I'm asleep. And in the mornin', he's *there*. And you?"

"Dart Donegal nearly brought me to my knees—but I'm starting to get up. At moments I have blasts of freedom that astound me, the kind of happiness I've been waiting for my whole life."

"*Stay* with the feelin', honey; there *is* life beyond liberation. When you stop being afraid of windin' up alone, it just gets simple. Life is rich, and there's plenty of it. I never would have believed it, honey, but these *are* the best years of my life. I practically skip through the streets. I never fret about Guido. He frets about me, poor darlin'—feels he's missin' somethin', and he *is*. When I have guests from home—particularly men guests—he positively *lurks* in the campo like a spy. He's sure I'm fuckin' someone else, which I'm most assuredly *not*. Italian men are mucho macho—despotic and weak at the same time. *He* thinks he has the right to tell *me* not to have guests, but I have no right to question the fact that he goes home to La Bella Barbara. Honey, she's just *awful*—one of those cold, fashionable mannequins who seem more Swiss than Italian. La Pussy Plastica, I call her. He *swears* they haven't had sex in ten years. Married men always swear that, but in their case it might actually be true. Anyway, I *do* love him. Of course *he* chafes from time to time, suddenly figuring out that I'm really freer than he is. But he represses it instantly. Maleness is wonderful, really, isn't it, honey? Perfect denial of reality. In New York, I'd probably chafe about this and want a proper husband, but in Italy it seems just *fine.* Life is so *filling* here, so *rich.* Just to buy fish on the Rialto makes me happy, to look out a window and see the boats go by, to walk to the *traghetto* and have the gondolier wave and shout, 'Ciao, Cordelia!' I feel like the local character. I can't imagine a better life for a painter—or anyone."

"I nearly had a proper husband this year. An antiques dealer. It was *awful.* First, of course, it was wonderful—proper dinner parties, and all my friends breathing a sigh of relief. Leila the wild card suddenly tamed, out of trouble, paired off. . . . Then he stopped touching me. Or fucking me. Out of spite, I think, for having touched his heart. The heart is out of fashion in New York at present."

"It always was, honey. That's why I left. And then he blamed you, right, honey? Oh, Lord—when my girlfriends come from New York and tell me about what goes on there between men and women, I'm even *gladder* about Guido. At least this is *human.* In New York there seem to be all these workaholic yuppies whose precious bodily fluids have gone to Wall Street! *You* tell me—am I wrong about that? I left in 1968, after all."

"Wait'll I tell you about my night with the dominatrix."

"Your night with *what?*"

"My night at Madame Ada's in black leather and black candles up the ass."

"Leila, honey, it's time for you to get out of New York. I'm tellin' you, you're in danger. . . ."

The doorbell rings, announcing the arrival of the first guests.

We circulate in the library, among the leather-covered books, the antiques, the mélange of multicolored guests from Venice, New York, London, Paris, Hong Kong.

It's the usual late-summer party at Cordelia's—the same one I've dropped in to out of the blue for twenty years. The same elegant homosexual poets (their ranks sadly thinned by the plague of the eighties), the same artists who live in Venice, the same eccentric shipping tycoons, the same writers recovering from novels that flopped—or novels that succeeded beyond anyone's wildest expectations—the same ladies of a certain age in search of Guidos, the same well-tailored lesbians and ill-tailored lesbians, the same serious students of art history (or musicology or Renaissance poetry) come to Venice for the first time and smelling of the stacks of the Marciana Library or the Cini Foundation, starry-eyed because they are in Venice surrounded by art and they cannot believe their eyes.

And then, suddenly, amid all these old standbys, there is a new face.

He swims up to me through the room of familiar undersea life, a merman, fluid in his movements, slender in his white linen shirt and beige linen slacks, smiling with a slightly mocking smile, his cheekbones slanted like Pan's, his eyes dark green flecked with light gold, silver, platinum, his tousled blackish curls like a young Bacchus', and his ears, I swear it, slightly too pointed for him not to be part satyr.

I look down at his feet, expecting hooves, or at least fins, but all I see are cream-colored loafers and no socks.

His eyes lock onto mine.

"Ciao, Leila," he says, as if he were saying, "Darling, turn over, I want to take you from behind."

The air is full of gold and silver. Every light mote shines with sex.

"How do you know my name?"

"*Tu sei famosa. Ho visto la sua fotografia molte volte nel giornale.* Excuse me—my English is terrible. I am Renzo Pisan."

"Renzo il Magnifico," I say, looking into his sea-green eyes.

He touches my hair.

"We have the same curly hairs," he says. It is a very good sign. Pagan hairs. "May I take you on a tour of Venice by boat?"

"When?"

"Tomorrow, at eleven?"

What can I possibly say but "yes"?

(*Sane mind:* Try "no" for a change!)

19

"TAKE TWO GONDOLIERS
AND CALL ME
IN THE MORNING"

———————◆———————

I got nineteen men and I want one mo'
I got nineteen men and I want one mo'
If I get that one more, I'll let that nineteen go.

—Bessie Smith

He comes for me at eleven the next morning at the Gritti, looking even more like a satyr in the morning light than he did at dusk.

We putter out into the middle of the lagoon, where the seagulls live, dipping and diving for fish and alighting upon buoys and rotted wooden posts.

The sun is behind us in a haze, dispersed in the sky, exploded into atoms.

I lean back in the boat, sunning myself, knowing that there is no place I'd rather be.

We sail and sail. A dreamy, glittery day, with Venice receding behind us in the lagoon. From the lagoon, Venice suddenly seems so *small*—all turrets and towers low on the horizon, like Cybele's crown.

He drops anchor in the middle of the lagoon, makes me hide my eyes while he changes out of his dapper linen pants and shirt and into his swimming trunks. I strip to my bathing suit, and we sit in the back of the boat, touching yet not quite touching, in the way that lovers do before the explosion, when the decision to become lovers has been made and has not yet been acted upon.

He strokes my cheek, my breasts; he bends and kisses me, and suddenly we are lost in each other's mouths, the land of tongue and tooth, nature red in fang and claw threatening to overtake us. He touches me, and I can tell by the way he touches me—as if he were a part of myself longing to know its boundaries—that it is only a question of deciding whether to make love in the boat or at my hotel (where Julian is expected to arrive from California in two days), or to go to his house (where, Cordelia says, he lives with his German wife, who is an honest-to-God principessa). Whatever he asks I will do. He has only to crook his finger and say *vieni*, come, and I will follow.

We play and play, lie in the sun, speaking in that rudimentary way lovers do—your smell, your touch, your touch, your smell—and then eventually we putter back to his house and make mad love on the divan in his office, with architectural drawings all over the floor.

His house is on a little island (which appears on no maps) near Burano. It is a smallish villa, built by a follower of Palladio, surrounded by gardens filled with Greco-Roman sculpture and strange, primitive stones dredged up from the lagoon.

No one is there but an aviary full of canaries, who chirp and chirp as we make love, as if they, too, are pleased.

The lovemaking demolishes the boundaries between

us; we become one person. He enters into me very small at first, keeps saying, "*Apri a me, apri a me*" (open to me, open to me), as if the whole of his need were to possess me, fill me, let me know him entirely.

Sex, when it is like that, is not sex anymore but a communion, a bridging of separateness, an abolition of bodies. And it is so rare, and so astounding. You can search for it forever and never find it.

(*Sane mind*: You found it before, and you'll find it again.

Leila: Could you please shut up? I'm trying to con myself into falling in love!)

We sleep in a tangle of sweat and juice; awaken, make love again; sleep again; awaken again and make love.

"We were like an old couple, very much in love," he says. And it is true. We knew each other wholly from the first touch. We make love as if on our twentieth anniversary, a homecoming, perfect fit.

With his ebony hair and his sea-green eyes, he looks like a *giovanotto* painted by Bronzino. He wears a black cord around his neck, with the lion of St. Mark and a star of David on it. He's an architect who designs important buildings in Italy, and he's involved in some project to restore the ghetto of Venice. Something in him evokes all my womanliness and all my Jewishness—a powerful combination. There is about him a courtliness, a *gentilezza*, that makes me think of the Italian Renaissance. And yet there is also something slightly calculating about him—*furbo*, shrewd—that hints of the practiced Casanova. It is so hard to tell. Seized by the scruff of my neck and dragged again to The Land of Fuck, I find all judgment and all discrimination have fled.

(*Sane mind*: Help!)

*   *   *

I am deep into The Land of Fuck with Renzo—even though Julian is now here, staying with me at the Gritti. In the afternoons, I make some excuse—an interview, photographs, drinks with Venetian friends—and wait by the dock for Renzo to fetch me.

He comes on the very dot of two, as soon as he can get away, fracturing the sacred Italian lunch hour. Comes for me in the little motor launch—a classic Riva—*putt, putt, putt*—wearing white linen trousers and a blue linen jacket over a striped gondolier's shirt, his body very slim and smelling of sweat and salt marsh, ovulation and the moon.

I step into the boat, which will carry me into the middle of the lagoon, and we sing vulgar American songs—"Are You Lonesome Tonight?" for one—as we putter off in the sunlight, drop anchor in the middle of the lagoon, where, in view of seagulls and low-flying planes, we make love in the boat, Venice suddenly nearly collapsed into the horizon line—low and insignificant, with its hordes of Michelin-carrying tourists, its skeletal socialites assembled for the Viva Venezia Ball, its gouging headwaiters, its hotelkeepers, shopkeepers, restaurant keepers, and its cruising gays, who now all practice "safe sex," whatever that is.

Renzo and I do not practice safe sex. In The Land of Fuck, nothing is safe. We are lost in a watery Atlantis in the middle of the lagoon, where we communicate with cock and cunt, speaking, when we speak, only the most rudimentary English and troglodyte Italian.

The lack of language defeats us yet also makes everything more intense. Renzo claims to speak English like a

Zulu. And my Italian, after all these years, is suitable only for survival on a desert island, photographed by Lina Wertmuller.

I call him Carissimo Troglodito (or Beloved Trog). He calls me Piccola Pittrice (or Little Painter). I would not accept the adjective from anyone else, but coming from him, it sounds like a compliment. He fucks me at every angle until I weep tears of joy. The tip of his cock also weeps when it emerges from his pants. He wears no underwear.

(*Sane mind:* Your mother warned you about men like that.)

"*Piange per te,*" he says. It cries for you.

He is trying to knock me up. Oh, how lovely Mediterranean men are in their understanding of the primal ooze and what it is all about. We Americans have lost touch with the *purpose* of sex. Sex is about babies. The Land of Fuck is the lure; the Tunnel of Love leads to the Romper Room, through caves of bloody endometrial ooze and salty sperm.

And Julian? Julian waits in the hotel suite, writing symphonies in his head (and in his notebook), knowing and not knowing what I have been doing in the lagoon.

Julian and I are soulmates. We understand everything about each other's hearts and souls, and yet we do not fuck. Both strangers from a distant asteroid of the mind, we speak the same language, the language of hyperspace.

When I return, Julian asks me if I have met a gondolier. And I say "Yes," and then I describe sex in a boat with this irresistible nameless gondolier. And Julian stares at me, spellbound, as I describe my adventure, which grows even more ecstatic in the telling.

Between Renzo and Julian, I have two men adding up to one whole person—every woman's cure for the blues!

Nonattachment, I tell myself. Nonattachment is the key to all of life. I want to feel everything, to get lost in sensation, and yet I also want to be able to retrieve myself. I want to go down to the bottom of the lagoon and still be able to come back up. I want to give away all of myself and still have some piece of myself to regenerate from—like an octopus cut into bits and tossed into the lagoon to grow again.

What a terrifying life I have chosen for myself—or the muse has chosen for me! To dive to the bottom of the lagoon again and again, seeking skinlessness, seeking self-annihilation.

And yet I am happy. I had forgotten how happy you can be when the sex works! I had forgotten singing in the streets and sunlight glinting off your lover's hair. I had forgotten . . . Dart!

Racing across the lagoon, singing like teenagers . . . I had forgotten the wonder of newly falling in love. Who needs Ada and her black leather and candles now?

Isadora: For once you and I agree!

Nonattachment. Can you love and still live completely in the present? Doesn't love always leap ahead into anticipation? Waiting for Renzo's calls, I become crazed, mad, obsessed—all the things I swore I'd never be again. I dream of having a baby with his oceanic eyes. My ovaries start to ache. How can you nonattach with aching ovaries? Can the female of the species *ever* be an existentialist?

Julian and I talk all night, our arms and legs wrapped around each other.

"Someday," he says, "we'll make love—but it will come not out of sex but out of love, time-tested, true love." Ah, the land of promise!

Julian and I have been friends forever. He is the only person I can trust to see the dance of the molecules with me and know I am not crazy. He was the only person I could trust to guide me after I crashed through space-time in Connecticut and saw my mother stomping through the woods. He didn't laugh at me. When I called him from Venice, he said, "Take two gondoliers and call me in the morning." If I called him from the fourth dimension, he would probably say the same.

Julian and I have an understanding: we are not allowed to have sex. I'm not sure how the decision was reached or who made it. Perhaps we are too much like siblings to succumb.

We cuddle. We shower together. Naked, we eat strawberries in bed. But we are much more comfortable talking and dreaming with our arms and legs wrapped around each other than we ever would be fucking. Sometimes we talk all night, rub each other's backs and legs, and float through space in the cosmic bed. Wherever we are, the bed becomes a starship. Strange planets hover overhead.

We speak of the nonexistence of time, the blurry line between meat and air. We heal each other with laughter. When we walk in the streets together, people stare at us because we seem like two little kids, giggling. Can we spend our lives together even though we never fuck? This is the question that bothers us both. I know there are various connections between people, not all of which are carnal. Since soul and body overlap in different ways, since flesh and spirit have more points in communion than those below the navel, I can love Julian without what the world calls "sex," but from time to time I suspect he is troubled by this, since he measures himself, like most men, by the stiffness of his cock.

One night we're in the Piazza San Marco at one, listening to the band at Florian's finishing up. As usual, they're playing "New York, New York," out of tune. We're laughing about something, when suddenly we see a fiftyish lady who looks like a waif.

"Let's buy her a drink," says Julian.

"Okay," I say.

Julian gets up and invites her over. At first she demurs, but then, sensing it is safe (my presence comforts her), she joins us.

She's from Ohio; her name is Gladys; she's been an English teacher in Milan for nearly ten years. She loves Italy. Yes, she sometimes gets homesick.

With her scrawny neck, wispy brownish hair, beaky little nose, and inward-pointing teeth, she is one of those humans who most resemble a bird—even as Renzo is now merman, now Pan, as Julian is a dog (a silky white Maltese), as I am a ginger cat, as Dart is a big blond Labrador retriever (who turns, unpredictably, into a fox).

"You seem so happy," says Gladys. "How long have you two been married?"

"Oh, *forever*," says Julian.

"And where do you live?"

"In Malibu," I say, "and in Connecticut. We divide the year."

"And what's the secret of your marriage?" asks Gladys wistfully.

"We don't sleep together," says Julian.

Gladys does a double take.

"That's right," says Julian. "I sleep in a box, and she sleeps in the bed. You'd be surprised how far that goes toward preserving our relationship."

"You're *kidding*," says Gladys, half in disbelief, half in a desire to believe that *some*one *some*where has a good marriage, at whatever cost.

"Funny how it all got started," I say. "One day we had a rather large appliance delivered to our house in Malibu—a washing machine, I think it was, or maybe a dryer. And my husband, Fred, here, said: 'Darling, I've always wanted to sleep in a box—do you mind awfully if I try?' "

"You're *kidding*," says Gladys.

"Not at all," says Julian. "So I filled the bottom of the box with a down quilt, a pillow, a teddy bear, and the like, and tried it out. I *loved* it! And ever since then, I've slept in the box, and Alice, here, sleeps in the bed. . . ."

"It's not the same box, of course," I say. "The first box wore out."

"In fact, we just got a *new* box," says Julian. "The secret of our marriage is that we have a constant supply of new boxes."

Gladys looks quizzically from my face to Julian's, wanting to believe yet not wanting to seem a fool (like all of us).

"You're *kidding*," she says.

"Not at all," says Julian. "Marriage is difficult enough without both parties having to sleep in the same bed. The boxes are the answer."

"You're sure you're not kidding?" asks Gladys.

"Sure," I say, now sensing that the preservation of this little fiction is indispensable to all of us.

"What business are you in?" asks Gladys of Julian.

"The shoe business," says Julian. "There's no business like shoe business."

"Interesting," says Gladys.

"That's why we come to Italy all the time," I say, "because of the shoe business. They make the shoes near here—near Padova."

" 'There's no business like shoe business, like no business I know,' " sings Julian. Suddenly he looks at Gladys. "Did anyone ever tell you how beautiful you are?"

She looks at him again in half disbelief, half wishfulness, and her whole face softens. The beaky nose, the wispy hair, the sparrow-brown eyes become, in the transfiguration of his gaze, beautiful. I see how this fiction becomes, through the force of Julian's intention, true. And I know that all our lives can be transfigured if we only have a strong enough intention and hold it like the laser beam of Julian's beautiful eyes on Gladys's now beautiful face.

The next evening I am in the lagoon with Renzo again, riding across the waters, singing.

The lagoon is strafed with setting sunlight, and the full moon rises on the opposite side of the sky. The seagulls cry. It is too perfect, too magical, too much a cliché, and like many clichés, it is also true. We rock on the sea in the opalescent azure-pink sun-moonlight, drop anchor, and touch each other's skin as if skin had just been invented and we were Adam and Eve about to board Noah's Ark and reproduce the whole human race.

We speak rudimentary troglodyte English and rudimentary troglodyte Italian.

"*Tu sei diavolo,*" I say. A devil is what you are.

"You like that," he says. "Only a devil could capture

you. An amazon needs a centaur to carry her off."

And then words fail us and we communicate with our fingertips, with our tongues, with the brush of our toes on the surface of our skins. Outside, inside, sun, moon, have no meaning, and we are rocking in the boat of each other, in the lagoon of dreams, at once liquid and starry, watery yet made of shimmering light.

"*Mio troglodite,*" I say.

"*Pelle di luce, pella liquida di stelle, occhi di luna,*" he says.

"*Siamo animali,*" I say.

"*Anima, animali,*" he replies.

He lounges in the boat, smelling of sex, of primal ooze, the tip of his cock crying for me.

We kiss, bite, tangle.

"Which animal are you?" he asks.

"*Sono cane, fedele,*" I say, knowing I am really more cat than dog.

"*Non e vero,*" he says. "*Tu sei gattina.* I see your claws even though you try to hide them."

I am stung by this. Is it true? Or just a lovers' game?

"*E tu?*"

"I'm a fox, a clever fox," he says.

(My friend Emmie always says: "Listen to what they say at the start of a love affair; they are telling you how it will end.")

"Now sleep," he says, leaning me back in the boat, opening the snaps of my lace bodysuit, and beginning to fuck me very slowly at various angles. Both of us are half reclining, and tears are streaming down my cheeks. He is fucking me as if he wants to enter every part of me, discovering America.

I cannot stop crying and crying out, and as I start to

come, he cries, *"Dai, dai, dai"* (come on, come on) and *"Apri a me, apri a me"* (open to me, open to me).

He stops and moves, moves and stops, moves again—until I come, completely full of him, entered, eternal, and he comes with me, filling me with salty stars.

I am still crying, but as I return to myself I see him watching me, reserved, from a distance.

"What do you want from me?" I ask.

"Il sesso," he says. Sex. "And another set of twins. If the twins arrive, I will be *monogamo.*"

Ah, promises, promises. This man will not ever be *uomo monogamo,* any more than Julian will ever fuck me. But my judgment is lost, for here, in The Land of Fuck, there is no such thing as judgment.

"Can we be fifty–fifty?" he asks, "even though you are an Amazon? Or forty-nine–fifty-one?"

We have gone from sex to power, made that inevitable leap.

I lie with my head in his lap. The sky darkens. Stars appear.

"You have such a marvelous body," he says. "You relax completely. The first time almost, the second time better, and this time completely."

And I think that so much of sex is about this, about the man wanting to totally enter the woman, invade her and make her his. Without this need for mastery, possession, there is no animal sex. There are intellectual games about sleeping in boxes. There are verbal jokes about "shoe business." But without this animal entering, sex doesn't work, and only when sex works like this can you enter The Land of Fuck.

Is it all about cocks, finally, and whether or not they *work?* Is it all about their *size?* Women say no, no, no, having been taught their lessons well by men who fear their cocks are too small. Men say no, meaning yes, for all their behavior tells you that what they *really* care about is how their cocks work. Thom, Elmore, Dart, Danny, Lionel, Renzo, Julian—I have never met a man whose life wasn't run by the size and stiffness of his cock.

This is the one thing women never dare say. This is the one thing we resolutely lie about. And why? Because it is all too true. The size and stiffness of a man's cock determines his life. It determines how he feels about himself. It determines whether he likes himself. A man who likes his cock likes himself. And a man who can't trust his cock can never trust himself. Or a woman. Or any other man.

Is it all that simple? I fear the answer is yes. The porno films, the baby oil, the leather, the black candles, are all compensations for cocks that don't work. Or work capriciously. For when they work, all you really need is music and moonlight. Or silence and sunlight. Or twilight, half light . . . any light (or darkness) will do.

We start the engine and go in search of an open *trattoria.* We putter in the boat, looking for places to park. No place to park the Riva (how like New York!) and no *trattoria* open (how like Connecticut!).

I am melancholy, having been so totally opened. I try to remind myself of nonattachment, but that doesn't work. I want to come back to my center, my equanimity, but The Land of Fuck will not give me back. Having totally forgotten that the only moment is now, I am in a reverie about some future life with Renzo.

We finally find a place for sandwiches and take them

back to the middle of the moon-streaked lagoon, where we dreamily eat, listening to the gulls calling in the superstillness and gazing at each other. What is Renzo's secret? I wonder. He holds a part of himself in reserve, as I wish I could. At moments, I have the strong sense that all I have here is the Italian counterpart of Dart—another Don Giovanni but an authentic one: the Mediterranean man, who does the role *right*. Wax to receive and marble to retain. Have I merely fallen for Don Juan again?

(*Sane mind:* Are you asking me or telling me?)

Isadora: I'm with her!
Leila: Who?
Isadora: Your sane mind!
Leila: Will you please shut up and let me enjoy this?

We stay in the lagoon, squeezing out the last drop of moonlight. Then he takes me back to my hotel, to Julian, and to my melancholy self.

"*Don't* fall in love with him, honey," says Cordelia.

We are in the garden at Corte Sconta, having lunch, surrounded by the usual multilingual hordes who invade Venice during Regatta week.

"Fall in love with *whom?*"

Cordelia gives me a don't-bullshit-me look.

"Renzo Pisan, of course. Honey, he's the Romeo of the Rialto, the Casanova of Cannaregio, the Don Giovanni of Dorsoduro, the gigolo of the Palazzo del Giglio, not to mention the Gritti, the Bauer Grünwald, and so on. She gives him enough rope to get his feet—and other pleasin' parts of himself—wet, and then she yanks his

chain and he comes scurryin' home, tail—so to speak—
between his legs. . . . The only thing worse than havin' your
own gigolo, honey, is borrowin' somebody else's."

"Who *is* she?"

"If you look over there, you can see . . . so *hush* when
you talk."

I look. At a long table, half hidden behind trellised
vines, sits a beautiful blond apparition in a shimmering
violet suit and a purple hat festooned with purple grapes.
Her brittle fingers glitter with major jewels; her neck is
ablaze with emeralds, more appropriate for the Viva
Venezia gala than for lunch at this simple restaurant in
Castello. And beside her sits Renzo, very *cavalier servente*,
peeling her figs.

They are holding court at a table of fashionable
finocchi and American socialites. Renzo does not see me.

"What's their story?" I ask Cordelia.

"I'm not sure I know the whole *thing*, but they've
been married ever since *any*one can remember. She's an
honest-to-God *Prinzessin* from Wien—and he's a Jew from
a Spanish Jewish family. Her *mother* rescued him from the
Nazis when he was a mere baby at the end of the war, raised
him like a mamma (and his twin brother too), but him she
fancied, sent him to architecture school, married him off
to her daughter, settled estates on him. Apparently they
were mad lovers once, perhaps still are. Imagine it! The
Nazi princess and the Jewish beggar boy! Think what your
dominatrix could do with that! Renzo lives in a strange
ménage à trois with the daughter and the mother. I don't
know who does whom at home, but outside he does *every*-
one. The mamma's a character too. When she was very
young, she was married briefly to the count of something,
and some people still call her 'the cooking countess' be-

cause she once had a Julia Child-ish television show on RAI-DUE. She's all involved with a project to restore the synagogues in the ghetto. Atoning for Hitler. She finances Renzo's dreams.

"He's utterly faithful, in his Mediterranean fashion. And a brilliant architect. And you can be sure they know all about you, or *will,* the minute you go any deeper. He'll never leave them, honey. Sex is sex, but money an' position last *forever.* Mamma got him all his first major commissions, and he's loyal to that, though an American man wouldn't be, would have to leave as a result. We Americani are *very* romantic and believe in moving on. The Europeans are far more practical than we are. Never forget it, honey. And La Mamma is La Mamma. And his wife is glamorous—if a bit cold. She has him followed. She knows *everything.*"

"How did *you* know?"

"Don't *insult* me, Zandberg. This is *my* town. Venezia is a village. I saw him swim up to you, an' don't think nobody's seen you gettin' in an' out of Mamma's Riva, an' gorgeous as you are, may I suggest you are not the *first* lovely foreigner he has seduced?"

"Have you . . . ?"

"Oh, ages and ages ago. I remember a lovely swivel to his hips and a cock you could write home to Mother about—if, that is, you had a mother like Auntie Mame. But he's too reptilian to be my type. I remember southern men *just* like Renzo. I prefer them less pretty, more *serious.* You always did have a thing for bounders, fortune hunters, gigolos, and knaves. So what if this one's Jewish. (And as Spanish as Don Giovanni.) You still can't bring him home to Mother!"

"I haven't *always* had knaves. . . ."

"Well, not always. But since you got *really* famous. Honey, I understand it better than anyone. The Cher syndrome, the Sunny Von Bulow complex . . . I could write a book. And he is a *great* lay. *Tout le monde* knows that. I seem dimly to remember superhuman endurance. But don't get hooked. And what about your nice Julian?"

"We're pals—nothing more."

"Impotent?"

"I don't know what that means anymore. Julian vibrates to the music of the spheres."

"Won't or can't?"

"Who knows? Does it matter? We're brother and sister. Don't knock it. It has its own strange allure. And it lasts longer than sex."

"Lord, it's the new successful men's disease: Impaired Desire. Either they can't or won't get it up—or they get it up and then refuse to come. Refuse to succumb to the *indignity* of orgasm. On strike against women's liberation. It's just *awful,* that's what it is."

I glance over at Renzo, and my heart skips several beats. *Maybe he'll leave her for you,* the devil whispers in my ear.

"He won't," says Cordelia, reading my thoughts.

"Am I *that* transparent?" I ask.

"*Every*one is when they're moonstruck. And let's be fair, Venice is Venice, an' Italian men make American men seem like Louie, Huey, and Dewey. They *move* like jellied consommé, *speak* like Pinot Grigio, and *fuck* with all those verbal pyrotechnics. Whispered lines of verse—pilfered, no doubt, from the libretti of Lorenzo Da Ponte, another Venetian Renzo. I *do* like the name. Renzo Pisan. It has a certain ring to it."

"He never told me about *her.* Or mamma."

"He *will*, just as soon as you make the mistake of asking him to spend a night, or take you to lunch, or a little weekend in Asolo, or Porto Ercole. He *always* comes home by six. Turns into a pumpkin, you just take my word for it. And the more you get under his skin, the more he'll eventually run. Take my word for that too. He's as scared of commitment as any of these American swains, but he's got the family as a buffer. That's Italian."

"So what's the difference between your situation with Guido and this one?"

"All the difference in the world, honey. Guido and I are practically married, Renzo plays the field. And we're talking about *field!* Beautiful Americans, French, Italians, here on holiday, all just dyin' to be swept away by the fatal charm of Italy. Read Luigi Barzini. Renzo and his type ought to be on *pension* from the Italian ministry of tourism! A moonlit roll in the *bateau* for every lovely *straniera*. Brings 'em back to Italy year after year. Do you know, my friend Luke, the painter, has a friend—a married lady sex therapist from L.A.—who comes to the Danieli for two weeks every summer just to fuck the hotel guitarist? He's a rotten guitarist, but obviously a great lay. *Super* well-endowed, I hear."

I look at Cordelia, suddenly despising her. She's just *jealous*, I think. How could Renzo *not* care about me, at least a *little*? Could anyone fuck like that and really not care?

Isadora: *Reader, you know the answer.*
Leila: *Stop leading the witness.*

Just then he walks over with the principessa and their entourage.

"The noted painter Leila Sand," he says to the princess, who looks me over coldly, assessing the risk. Then Renzo kisses my hand in that dizzying Continental manner in which lips touch skin only in your wildest fantasy. From the way he looks at me—knowing *she* is assessing the way he is looking at me—I see he is a practiced dissembler. He seems to look through me, as if he had no wish to penetrate any part of me, body even less than soul. But just before they walk away, he turns and looks at me again, his oceanic eyes glittering. "Leila, *apri a me, apri a me, apri a me.*"

Julian and I lie awake all night, talking about how we might remake our lives.

"We'll go to Bali," he says, "or Fiji. Or the Trobriands. We'll buy a little island."

"Can you really *buy* islands?"

"Absolutely. We can live the rest of our lives without ever writing another bar of spooky space music or painting another canvas. I'll get you two beautiful Balinese boys to service you—and we'll drink coconut milk, eat tropical fruits, and read Proust."

"Lovely," I say, neglecting to point out that I'd go crazy if I didn't paint—and that I don't do it for money. Nor do I want to be "serviced."

I don't say this. All I say is: "Julian, you forget that your religion is *room* service."

"I can convert to coconuts," says Julian. "The point is, I'll never have to work for Hollywood again. I'll write fugues or symphonies, even poetry. . . . Do you know that before I became a Hollywood hooker, I used to write poetry?"

"I think I knew that. Recite me a pome."

"Okay—here's one I wrote once in Florence, when I was a mere pup:

> In the poplars' lengthening shadows on this hill,
> Amid the rows of marigolds and earth,
> and through the boxhedge labyrinth we walk,
> together to the choiring twilight bells. . . .

"Lovely. Can you say the rest?"

Julian thinks. His intelligent agate eyes roll skyward. He is communicating with his planet. $E = mc^4$. "No."

"Julian, I love you with all my heart—but do you know how *neglected* poets are? You say you hate Hollywood, but you're *used* to the limousines, the private jets, the secretaries; you don't *know* what it's like to be ignored. You haven't even been on the subway in thirty years. I bet you don't know what a token costs."

"Fifty dollars?"

"I'm not going to *tell* you! The fact is, you're always running from your agent, your business manager, your lawyers, the phone, the phone, the phone. Do you know what it's like when the phone *never* rings?"

"We won't have phones; we'll have palm fronds."

"When the palm frond never rings?"

"Palm fronds are not *supposed* to ring."

"Yes—but you go crazy when they don't."

"We're crazy already."

"True. And how do we educate the twins?"

"Tutors, private tutors. School is a crock. It's just a way of getting kids socially indoctrinated, breaking them in to the values of their parents' social class. Private tutors are *much* better. We'll raise them like the Trobriand islanders—the only people who have the perfect answer to love and sex."

"What's that?"

"Well, the kids are totally sexually free from prepuberty till the age of eighteen or so. They fuck each other like mad, get all their curiosity out of their systems. Then, at the age of eighteen, they marry and remain monogamous—except for the three-day-a-year Yam Festival, when all bets are off!"

"What if you have the flu during the Yam Festival?"

"In the Trobriands, you don't *get* the flu."

"Do you think Mike and Ed would be ready for civilized life, growing up that way?"

"And where, pray tell, do you *find* civilized life? Hollywood? New York? Venice? The truth is that the best little girls are raised *outside* the brainwashing of our culture. Beryl Markham, for example, raised with African warriors. All civilization does for girls is teach them that they're supposed to be inferior. Better to have palm fronds and yam festivals. You'd be doing them a great favor, really. Think about it, Leila; I'm not kidding."

"Do you know what Gandhi said when he was asked what he thought of Western civilization?"

"No."

"It would be a good idea!"

And we laugh and hug each other and eventually, still giggling and hugging, fall asleep.

At some point during the night, the phone rings. I roll over and grab it.

"Leila, baby," says Dart. "Leila, baby."

I wake up all in a rush. This is like a telephone call from the dead.

"What's the matter?" I ask.

"Just miss you, baby."

"You'll get over it," I say.

"I was walking down Madison Avenue, baby, and what do I see in a gallery window but the Lone Ranger! Remember the Lone Ranger, baby?"

"How can I ever forget?" (Dart is alluding to one of my film stills, in which he was dressed as the Lone Ranger, and his gun was tucked into his pants rakishly and seemed to bulge like a cock.)

"Because of you," Dart says, "everyone knows about my big gun. . . ."

Now wide awake and pulled into a world I had let go of, I say jauntily: "Darling—the whole world knew *before.*"

"Only a select few," says Dart.

"A select few hundred *thousand,*" I say.

Dart laughs, despite himself. The manipulation isn't working.

"Good night, darling," I say brightly, and go back to sleep.

The afternoon before the Viva Venezia Ball, I am in the lagoon with Renzo, making love in the Riva.

So besotted am I that I ask the forbidden question. "Do you love me at all?" I ask.

He covers my mouth with his hand.

"Don't ask about the most important things in life," he says.

20

WILD WOMEN DON'T
HAVE THE BLUES

———————— ◆ ————————

Now, when you've got a man don't ever be on the square.
If you do he'll have a woman everywhere.
I never was known to treat one man right,
I keep 'em working hard both day and night,
Because wild women don't worry.
Wild women don't have the blues.

—Ida Cox

The Viva Venezia Ball has been preceded by luncheons,
teas, dinners, during which skeletal New York socialites
with porcine husbands (or fashionably slim walkers) cir-
culated amid the Italian (and Austrian and French and
English) skeletal socialites with porcine husbands (or fashionably slim walkers), kissing the air near each other's
cheeks. Since they are in Italy, they have kissed the air near
both cheeks. (In New York, they would kiss the air near
only one.)

The crowd is very *Town & Country*, very *Vanity
Unfair*. The marchesa of this kisses the principessa of that.
The walker of Park Avenue cuts the walker of the Via

Veneto or the walker of Avenue Foch. Platitudes are plumbed in three or four languages. Yes, we have all been to Venice before. No, we were not in Cortina or Gstaad this year; we were in Vail. Yes, it was beastly hot in Lindos. No, the Orient Express to Bangkok has not yet opened. Mustique in January? St. Barts in February? Autumn in New York? Christmas in St. Moritz? Kenya? Aspen? *Who* ran off with her best friend's son? Right out of Rosay? She didn't *really* leave that nice Piero. She did? And what of James? Is he still ambassador to . . . what country is it anyway? And are they still married? Well, thank heavens for that at least. She'll get over it—but will *he?*

And so the ball begins!

It is a sweltering night on the Grand Canal, and the Palazzo Pisani-Moretta—a great sixteenth-century pile—once the scene of ducal fetes and intrigues, has now, alas, been turned into Rent-a-Palazzo.

People step out of their rented gondolas and *moto-scafi,* looking outrageously *pleased* with themselves. They have packed and unpacked. They have tipped and tippled. Topped and toppled each other and their friends—poor dears—still in the predictable Hamptons or Litchfield, Kennebunkport, Newport, or (God forbid) Westport. Venice is *always* chic. (At least from September first to September fifteenth.) Before that, one isn't caught *dead.* And after, well, it's time to catch up with New York, with London, with L.A.

Down they step from their boats—Lacroix rustling Givenchy, Ungaro fluttering past Lagerfeld, Rhodes glittering near Valentino, Ferre flitting past Saint Laurent.

Darling, darlina, tesoro, my love, my darling, my sweetest, sweetie, you calculating little cunt. . . .

Here we all are in Italy, with all the people we always

see in New York! We will not talk to them *here* any more than we talk to them *there*. We are here to be seen. We are here because it is the finish line of a race we have been running since we were two. (How did we get into this race anyway? We sure don't know.) We are here because *we're here*. Is that perfectly *clear*?

Since I grew up poor in Washington Heights, this sort of thing ought to impress me more. And it *did* at the start, when my face became a ticket to ride, my name an open sesame, my paintings the magic combination that released the lock.

A world of winners! Then why are they so *grim?* And why so harried, married, nervous? Shouldn't being rich be *fun?*

I've read F. Scott Fitzgerald. I know the rich are different from you and me. But they seem so nail-bitingly tense, so frantic, so fearful. Perhaps in the twenties they had fun. Now being rich seems like a *job.* Where did the adjective "idle" go?

A rail-thin greyhound of a socialite (with leathery ocher skin, prominent hips, jaw, elbows, nose, knees) floats in wearing a red Valentino and rubies, on the arm of a ruby-nosed fag. She is Mrs. Rentier, the famed "Slim" Rentier—famous for her slimness, her ruby-nosed walker, the exercise coach she keeps on Ninth Street, the banker husband who never goes out. He's in the air-conditioned den on Park Avenue, watching tapes of old Super Bowl games and fondling the Pakistani houseman (Ismail, age twenty-two). Tonight he seems smarter than all these sweating hordes.

And here comes Mrs. Leventhal, the size two socialite from Beekman Place, Pound Ridge, and Port Antonio. She's the charity disease queen of New York—a hotly coveted title. And she's here with her designer, whose new collection her husband is financing, the punky adorable midget Mij Nehoc (Jim Cohen spelled backward), who wears a white Nehru jacket, a hoop in his left ear, an emerald stud in his right, and emerald satin harem pants with emerald slippers whose toes curl, phallically, up.

Mij Nehoc's last collection out-Lacroixed Lacroix. He brought out Maori models in baskets for skirts, coconut halves for bras. The Back-to-Nature Noble Savage Look, *Vogue* called it. ("After too many seasons of frippery, nature looks terribly fresh again, and natural materials have won the day!")

And here is Lady Eglantine Brasenose from Melbourne, the widow of the shipping king of the South Pacific. And Prince and Princess Rupert of England, known from Kensington to Mustique to Hong Kong for their open marriage. And Pia Le Quin, the voluptuous, tawny American actress who nearly married a Rothschild. But didn't. (Her career came first—although her career's in the toilet, as they say in Hollywood.)

And here comes Renzo Pisan with his principessa, who has organized this fete along with her opposite number from New York—the very slim, almost embalmed-looking Mrs. Rentier, society mummy!

Renzo is no mummy. Even in his "smoking," he *exudes* sex, sex, sex: his eyes half closed, his piqué dress shirt discreetly twinkling with antique diamond studs, a gray silk cummerbund at his slim waist, a gray silk tie at his golden throat, a "smoking" cut to show his snake hips and his broad shoulders, and gray silk loafers to let him dance, dance, dance. (*Ballare, ballare, ballare*—sounding in Italian almost like what it most resembles.)

The principessa is toweringly tall and stately in a yellow silk Ungaro sheath, rampant with huge fuchsia flowers. Her golden hair entwined with jewels, her scrawny lifted neck ablaze with canary diamonds, her arms enslaved in bracelets, her fingers pinched in rings.

He guides her by one bony elbow, a stalwart tugboat pushing the QE II (although he is more cigarette speedboat than tug). His eyelids flicker like lizards' tails when he sees me. *Apri a me,* they say.

Julian and I float up to greet the principessa and my "gondolier."

She assesses my dress, a sea-blue Emanuel of London, with big sleeves and a boned bodice that pushes up my breasts for Renzo's delectation. Julian is in his Hong Kong tux, made by a twenty-four-hour tailor specifically for this fete. It has a scarlet lining, a scarlet cummerbund, and matching bow tie.

Julian bows to Renzo, Rumpelstiltskin bowing to Cinderella's prince. He has no idea that this slithery, small-hipped apparition with the tousled ebony curls is my "gondolier," who flicks his eyelids, saying, *Dai, dai, dai.*

"*Piacere,*" says the principessa, holding out a manicured hand, ablaze with jewels.

And then we're swept away on the crest of the crowd, sweating in their finery beneath a thousand dripping candles.

The heat of all these bodies is amazing! I think of undeodorized sixteenth-century Venice, when this palazzo was new, and I am not so sure I'd take a ticket in a time machine and go back to that epoch, if invited.

And here is André McCrae, swept up on the tide,

wearing a wonderful pair of tails and still calling me "Tsat-skeleh!"

"This is Julian Silver, the composer," I say to André, "my dearest friend."

"What are *you* doin' here, Silver?" asks André. "You're supposed to be on Mars!"

"Leila's saving Venice, and I'm saving Leila," says Julian.

And our laughter sweeps us up the red-carpeted stairs.

Candles blaze, people sweat, ten-thousand-dollar dresses are trampled and torn beneath feet caressed in custom-made shoes. I think of how much better all this will sound in the society pages than it is in life. In newsprint, there will be no sweat, no small talk—just glittering names and glittering places to provoke the envy of those lucky ones who stayed home.

But that is why they're here, isn't it? To provoke the envy of those who stayed home.

A world of winners provoking the envy of the losers (who are really the winners in some sense, because they get to stay *home*). Oh, how complex it all is—and how simple!

Up the stairs we go, slowly, slowly, *piano*, *piano*, waiting on line to be photographed so that the losers can envy us when those photographs appear.

Thank heavens you can't photograph sweat!

And who is that before me on the stair? A jaunty man in a little tux, with a resplendent wife in cherry-pink chiffon.

Can it be Lionel Schaeffer? And how will I ever greet him after the night of the black candle?

He turns suddenly and peers down the stairs as if he has caught my thought.

"*Leila!*" he calls gaily, as if Mistress Ada did not exist.

"Lionel!" I call gaily, as if Mistress Ada did not exist.

Is this what we call Western civilization—to pretend not to acknowledge our secret lives?

In a room ablaze with candles, people turn and group and talk and turn away—like figures on a music box, doing their stilted and repetitive dance.

Oh, how *boring* it all is!

At least I am with Julian, so I can say, "Oh, how *boring* it all is!" He laughs, assenting, then fetches me a Bellini from the bar. I put it down without taking a sip. I know that if I sip, my head will only start to pound and before long my sane mind will desert me.

"I can't drink anymore," I tell Julian.

"Then don't," he says. "In the Trobriands, we'll chew betel."

"I can't wait," I say.

And Lionel Schaeffer and his lovely wife, Lindsay, are suddenly before us in the crowd.

Lionel opens the jacket of his tux and points. "Turnbull and Chung," he says.

Lindsay makes a hideous face.

"Can't take him *anyplace*," she says.

I wonder if she has a clue about Mistress Ada, his visit to Litchfield County, *any* secret place in Lionel's soul. Apparently not. But she is wearing the Paloma Picasso necklace of peridot and diamonds, and I am not, so apparently that is the price of her not knowing—and for all my knowing, my throat is bare. Women are paid to look away, not to see, or to see and not say. I will paint something of this someday. Oh, to be Hogarth, Goya, Daumier! This fin de siècle needs a satirist's eye. Even Roly-poly Rowlandson would do!

"Julian, Lionel," I say. "Lindsay, Julian."

"Leila, Lindsay," says Lionel.

"Of *course* I remember Leila," says Lindsay. "Who could forget such a talented artist?"

"Thank you," I say.

"Don't thank *me*," says Lindsay. "*You*'re the gifted one."

I see her attitude toward me has changed. When last we met, at the McCraes', she was determined to cut me, to counteract Lionel's interest. Now her strategy has altered. She is *wooing* me to counteract his interest. I remember doing something of the same with Dart's bimbos once. Oh, how far away that all seems now! The obsession with Dart has been broken by the obsession with Renzo! Is this progress? It *feels* like progress, but I fear it is merely The Land of Fuck.

Off to the bathroom I go in my azure silk. A line of ladies snakes around a screen. Here in Venice, as in New York, the ladies' facilities are less adequate than the gents'. The gentlemen's lounge is unoccupied. I decide to liberate the *gabinetto degli uomini.* In I go in my huge blue skirt, and who should be coming out at just that moment but Renzo il Magnifico? In a moment, he is back in the men's room with me, barring the door and coyly hiding his eyes while I avail myself of the facilities and wipe, wash and dry my hands. And then, with incredible swiftness, he has fallen to his beautiful brown knees, has whipped under my crinolines, unsnapped my crotch, and is pulling moans out of my mouth with his practiced tongue. It happens with the swiftness of a dream. (Perhaps, indeed, it is a dream? *Sane mind:* I hope so.) Under his tux, he wears no underclothes.

The rest is silence, interspersed with moans.

I fix my makeup. He adjusts his tie and cummerbund. He leaves the men's room first, eyes demurely downcast. I leave next. Two gentlemen wait outside, looking terribly blasé, as if this happens every day in Venice (which it does).

And back to the ball we go!

In due course, Julian and I are ushered to our table. It is not a good table. Upstairs, with the hangers-on, the grifters and drifters, we have been seated as far away from Lionel as possible. Is this a mistake? Didn't he invite us to sit at his table? Or is this Lionel's stratagem to keep me far from Lindsay? (Not that we could talk anyway in this din.)

Julian surveys the table. One deaf old man with false teeth that click. One minor chairlady of a minor New York ball, one fashion designer whose star has fallen, one washed-up Italian actress—a table of has-beens at the winners' ball! Julian, who claims not to care about these things, is furious.

"We are too old," he says, "and too rich to sit for three hours on these rickety gold chairs!" And seizing my arm, he leads me through the stifling rooms, down the red-carpeted stair and to a waiting *motoscafo*.

"Let's eat at Harry's Bar," he says, "and then let's hire a gondola, with three musicians."

So off we go to Harry's in tux and ball gown, I feeling wicked both for leaving the ball and for my interlude with Renzo in the gents' (how much do I owe my analyst now?), and Julian feeling terribly pleased with himself for protesting the bad table.

"I thought you didn't care about such *mishegoss* as bad tables," I say to Julian when we are duly settled in at Harry's with *acqua minerale* and buttery rolls.

"I don't, really," says Julian. "We've just got too little life left to spend it sitting on those *chairs*, with those *people*—see no evil, hear no evil, speak all evil."

"You care," I say. "*Admit* you care."

"Leila, really, I don't."

"You do."

"I refuse to argue the point."

"Okay," I say. But I am angry. I invited Julian to *my* gig—and it feels as if he left to spite me. Or did he get a whiff of my gondolier?

I let the matter drop. Life's too short. We order *risotto, fegato alla veneziana*. We banter with each other, we survey the room. The usual stylish Venetians and garish Americans. The usual riffraff at the bar. Two young gay blades with matching punk haircuts—one black with green streaks, one platinum blond with fuchsia streaks. An English lady of a certain age, who is a dead ringer for Vita Sackville-West. A Chinese gentleman with pink cheeks and old-fashioned silk pajamas.

And then, at a table in the corner, we spy the Happy Couple.

She is about forty, he about fifty. Or perhaps they are the same age and he has aged worse than she. They are toasting each other with Bellinis, locking arms, looking deep into each other's eyes.

"Remember Saint-Paul-de-Vence in eighty-four?" he asks.

We don't hear her reply; but from her smile, we know she does.

"Are they married, do you think?" I ask Julian.

"Never in a million years," he says. "They live in the same city. They're both married to different people. They see each other Wednesday afternoons and on holidays like this. For twenty years, they've come to Venice every September."

"What a romantic story!" I say.

"But not better than sleeping in boxes, is it?"

"I wonder what the truth is. . . ."

"Better not to know," says Julian.

"I want to know. I'm going to ask." I get up, but Julian restrains me, pulling me back.

"I've made my living for forty years *scoring* these fictions," Julian says. "I've *created* what we call romance. It's all in the chord structure. Certain melodies pull at the heartstrings. *Trust* me. It's better not to know."

"For God's sake, Julian, I just want to know if they're *married.*"

"No you don't," he says. "It's better not."

"And if they *are?*"

"If they are, I'll marry you, take care of you forever, and buy you your own island in the South Pacific."

I get up and go over to the Happy Couple.

"Excuse me," I say. "My friend and I have a curious bet. Please don't think me rude—but are you married?"

"Yes," says the woman.

"No," says the man.

I go back to Julian and report her "yes."

We sing our way along the Grand Canal, accompanied by accordionist, guitarist, fiddler. Singing in a boat again—this time with Julian—I am outrageously happy.

The wobbly palaces greet us upside down in the amazing moonlight. I think of Renzo and embrace Julian, as I might be embracing Renzo, thinking of Julian, and I realize that if I can hold on to myself I will have what it takes to make myself content for the rest of my life.

(*Sane mind:* You said it—two men adding up to one whole human being! Every woman's cure for the blues!)

There will always be traveling companions on the way—or else there will be delicious solitude. But there is no excuse for fear. Singing with Julian along the Grand Canal, I dimly glimpse a life without my fear. Who would I be without it? Would I still be Leila?

(*Sane mind:* You would be Leila! You would have yourself!)

Sybille once made me deposit my fear in her metal box.

"I'll keep it safe for you until you want it back," she said. "You can have it back whenever you wish."

Sybille is keeping my fear; my sane mind and I can go on without it.

That night, at the Gritti, Julian and I talk until dawn.

"I know that you're having an affair with someone," Julian says, "and really, it's okay. I want you to be happy. You can tell me everything."

"You already know about my gondolier," I say.

"This is more than a gondolier," says Julian.

"I don't know about that," I say. "Besides, once I tell you, the magic will be gone."

"But if you don't, you're lying by omission. And that breaks *our* magic."

"That's the dilemma, isn't it?"

"Let me tell you a story," Julian says, "a story about my life that I've never told you because, until very recently, I had blocked it. . . ."

We settle into our special position, with our legs wrapped around each other.

"When I was a little boy in Toronto," Julian begins, "my mother and father used to travel on the vaudeville circuit, and my older sister and I were left alone for long periods of time. My sister was only about fifteen, and very, very pretty—and in some ways she was the loneliest girl I ever knew. I must be about ten when this takes place—and just starting to be sexual. So horny all the time that I'm jumping out of my skin—and starting to have wet dreams—and not understanding them at all.

"My sister's bedroom has a glass door covered with muslin curtains, and late every afternoon she goes in alone to take a nap. This must have been a weekend afternoon, since I wasn't at school. I was doing homework downstairs, and suddenly I had a question to ask her. I went upstairs and down the hall to her room, but something stopped me from bursting in. The muslin curtain was slightly pushed aside at the edge—it was one of those curtains with a brass rod at the top and bottom—and I stood very still and guiltily peeked in.

"My sister lay on the bed in her peach peignoir, which was parted at her thighs. And there was a peach silk scarf over the lamp. The whole room was bathed in a rosy glow.

"She was moving one delicate hand in the vicinity of her open peignoir. A sense of disorientation overtook me. My heart began to pound. My penis stood straight up. My whole being seemed to throb. I knew I should not be watching, but I could not stop myself. And then her fingers disappeared inside her, and lovingly, sweetly, she drew them in and out. I could bear no more. My penis and her fingers were one—and I came with an explosion that made me cry aloud. My sister looked up, saw me, understood, and came to the door to let me in.

" 'Julie,' she said—she called me Julie—'don't be afraid.' I was trembling. She led me to her bed. We lay down together and held each other, legs and arms entwined. 'Julie—if you know that this is beautiful, you will know something very few people know.' And gently, gently, she brought my hand to her vagina and let me explore every part of her, telling me what to do, and how to touch her, and presently beginning to touch me as well. It was the sweetest and most beautiful interlude of my life. Utterly innocent, the sex of the Garden of Eden before the serpent came. And afterward, we lay together, entwined as you and I are now.

"Now comes the part I don't want to talk about, the part I blocked for forty years and only retrieved under hypnosis.

"Two days later, she was rushed to the hospital in the middle of the night. I only remember standing outside her room and hearing a nurse say to another nurse, 'That whore isn't long for this world.' I never saw her alive again."

"What did she die of?" I ask lamely, as one does when one is overwhelmed by emotion and trying therefore to pin down the "facts," as if facts could save us.

"For years I didn't really know. Appendicitis, they said, but I knew it was wrong. I now think it must have been an ectopic pregnancy. Of course I was sure I killed her."

"Of course." I hug him. My eyes are streaming with tears.

"The worst is yet to come. My parents never came

home. They were killed in a car crash somewhere in the Midwest. I don't even know if they knew about their daughter. I was left with my aunt and cousin. One night I heard them discussing me. 'I don't want him,' my aunt said. 'He's too weird.' 'I don't want him, either,' said my cousin. 'He gives me the creeps.' I packed my bag and hit the road."

"You were ten?"

"I was ten. In some ways I'm still ten."

"In some ways, we all are," I say.

"That's why I don't think we should lie about sex," Julian said. "Life's too short."

"And sex can't be divorced from the rest of life, can it? We thought it could be, but it can't. That's the tragedy of our generation—that we thought sex could save us."

"Nothing can save us," says Julian, "not even love. But we can make the world less lonely for each other— sometimes. And sometimes we can't even do that."

"All my life," I say, "I've wanted nothing but to bring sex and friendship together—and I seem to be farther from it than ever."

"Me too," says Julian. "That's why the Trobriands fascinate me so. I want to know if there's really a society in which people have solved the problem of guilt."

"What do you think?"

"To read Malinowski, you'd think so—but he's way out of date. The Isles of Love, they called them in the twenties, but I think it's just another noble-savage myth. Gauguin, Robert Louis Stevenson, Melville, Michener— think of the layers of myth-making. Still, I dream of going. I have always dreamed of going. . . . I want to die there, and the place you want to die is the place you want to live. . . ."

"Do you really want to know about the gondolier?"

"Yes."

"Well, hearing you talk about your sister, it's clear to me that my gondolier, like Dart, is just another version of the impossible lover—Daddy, in short: the taboo man, the demon lover, the dybbuk, the incestuous incubus. He's beautiful, but wet dreams are always beautiful. And he's unhavable. He belongs to another, to mamma. . . ."

"Don't we all," says Julian, dreamy-eyed.

"And when we make love, all barriers between us vanish—like when you and I *talk*. Why can't we have both—flesh and words?" I ask.

"Ah," says Julian, "because then why would we compose or paint? We compose and paint to resurrect the fallen world, and it's only because the world is fallen that it *needs* the beauty we make. In heaven, we'd be so filled with God's beauty that we wouldn't have to create."

"Sophistry."

"Not really. Which is easier to paint—heaven or hell?"

"Hell," I say.

"And which is more fun to read—*Inferno* or *Paradiso*?"

"*Inferno*."

"So we were given a fallen world to draw forth our human potential. In paradise we'd all be bored to death."

"And yet you still want to go to the South Pacific? Do you want to be the Gauguin of electronic music?"

"I want to write an opera about all this," Julian says. "And I'm a sort of method composer, in my own way. I want to start with a little boy watching his sister through a curtain—then sail off to Polynesia with a grown man in search of paradise. I want to write the great panoramic opera of man's search for paradise."

"We're all looking for paradise," I say. "And we never seem to know that we have it right here, right now, with our legs and arms around each other in this hotel room sailing through the universe. . . ."

"I know it," Julian says. "But paradise, by definition, is always *there*, not *here*. Even if you *marry* your perfect lover, before long you're both worrying about the contractor, the housepainter, parents' night, the IRS. . . . Your impossible he would become all too possible. Better to have him for sex and me for talk."

"But I want sex and talk in one person. Surely that's not so much to ask."

"I've never found it," says Julian, "except in my chords, so why should you?"

"Because you don't believe in it, and I do. Somehow, against all the evidence, I finally *do*. And I finally believe I deserve it."

"Then you shall surely have it," says Julian, "someday. But first you must *practice* believing it for a year or two. And oh, yes—you must get rid of that gondolier."

We hug and drift off to sleep.

The next day, with Julian's blessing, I go by water taxi to see Renzo on his curious island in the lagoon.

The house is deserted except for the chirping canaries and an unseen maid. The two princesses have gone to Milan for the day, to have their winter clothes fitted. Sunlight streams in the windows. Water from the lagoon dapples us with sequins of light as we make love.

With us, the lovemaking is so much in the present that it is a kind of meditation. Utterly fluid, with no beginning and no end, it seems not sex but a fleshly paradigm for nonattachment.

We *know* each other, body by body, soul by soul. We have known each other from the first moment we met and from the first time we made love. There has never been any question about it, never any doubt that it would work totally. Whether we talk or not, eat or not, we are always, always in harmony, joined, touching.

He touches my breast. The water ripples over us, spangling the ceiling. I touch his hair, his nipples. He sucks my lower lip. He strips off his linen shirt and linen slacks. I lie in his arms, smelling his armpit, content to hold him, touch him, not seeking more, not seeking orgasm. We are under the water, swimming through light. Just the smell of his skin, the touch of his velvet, his musk, is enough to satisfy me.

The fluidity of his body delights me; it is all there for me, without punctuation, without stop. A feast, moving like the waters of Venice, changing yet staying the same.

He sucks my lips, my breasts, calls me his Piccola Pittrice, and without knowing *how*, we are inside and outside each other, legs akimbo, legs together, he saying *"piano, piano,"* and moving, moving, moving slowly inside me to make it last. Whenever I start to come, he stops, makes me relax completely, so that at last I do not care whether I come or not, feeling him inside me, totally entered, wholly taken, given back to myself, given back to nature.

It's strange, isn't it, that we humans so distance ourselves from nature *even* in our lovemaking that the expectation of orgasm, the push for it, makes even loving teleological, a thing of expectations, anxieties, pressures. Renzo makes me totally enter the moment because *he* does, because his sex is free from an agenda, from pressure or expectation of any sort.

And so, having decided not to do anything but *feel* the moment, *be* in the moment, my body, of its own sweet will-less will, begins its crescendo. He moves and moves, stops and stops. But I have begun to come and then I scream and he covers my mouth (the maid, the maid) and begins to come himself, emerald eyes half closed, his face faunlike, brown, slanting, laughing, serious on the edge of orgasm and then liquid again, relaxed.

We lie together, Pan and Ceres, the god of the woods and the goddess of grain, smelling our own musk, our love odor—and then the bells ring and it is noon and we must go, we two daytime Cinderellas, turned to pumpkins by the stroke of noon.

I strip off my mask. Leila, Louise, Luisa slips away and there is only a woman, propelled by an unseen muse, her pen scratching in her sketchbook, her body aching with love, her heart high and happy because she knows she has done nothing to be so blessed and she knows that divine love is unconditional. She is in a state of grace. She wants to skip, to kneel before the Madonna, to invent drawings and paintings that will communicate joy to the joyless, faith to the unbeliever, and love to the loveless. She wants everyone to savor and celebrate life because it is a feast. It is there for the taking. You have only to open your mouth, open your hand, love one another, thank God, and rejoice.

At its most simple, life is a prayer. We pray in many ways. This is mine.

I cover pages and pages with pictures and words before I fall asleep that night.

Sleeping at Julian's side, I dream I am carrying a wheelchair on my back through Venice. The city consists of snowy alps and jagged ravines, with a shimmering lagoon far below. I am carrying this backbreaking wheelchair up and down icy slopes because I am afraid that someday I won't be able to walk. I am cursing the weight of it.

Throw down the wheelchair! I tell myself. You can walk! It was only your fear that crippled you.

I clamber into the wheelchair and race madly down a ravine. The wheelchair seems to fly, then rolls to a stop at the bottom. Miraculously, I stand, clothed in light, and throw the wheelchair into the lagoon.

I wake up. Naked, I walk into the bathroom and stand before the mirror. I am bathed in radiance. My heart is glowing.

Ah, I say, this is it, this is it. This is what we are meant to know. We need never be lonely. We are built around the godspark. Flesh is merely a lesson. We learn it and pass on. I hold that certainty all day as I explore Venice alone.

The next morning, I venture by myself to an exhibit of Old Master drawings on the beautiful little island where the Palladian church of San Giorgio Maggiore stands in the middle of the basin of St. Mark. With its green-hatted *campanile,* its halcyon cloister, its abandoned theater, this island is the sweetest spot in all Venice.

I leave Julian puttering with his score in our hotel room, and I dodge Renzo's two o'clock pass with his boat past the terrace of the Gritti. (It astonishes me that I can be so detached. Am I becoming a man—or only a wise woman?)

Alone and elated, I go to look at the Old Master drawings.

Drawings have an immediacy for me that paintings lack. You see the process, the artist's mind at work. In the line itself, the play of the mind is revealed.

I stop before a Domenico Campagnola drawing of a man threatening a woman under a leafy poplar tree. His flying forelock, her upraised arm, her upraised knee, the struggle between them in the dark crosshatchings of brown pen and ink, might reek of murder or of rough seduction, depending upon your point of view. (Does your eye, for example, catch the glimpse of dagger beneath the summer's tree? Does he wear no breeches, or has the artist's line only economized?)

Forever and forever he is about to kill (or kiss) her. Forever and forever this struggling couple is arrested in the moment before male blade pierces female flesh. Love or murder? Mayhem or merging?

Having no answers to these questions, I walk away from the drawing and on to the next. St. Catherine being beheaded interests me less, as does a *paesaggio* and a cartoon for a Last Supper. I wander past the sketchy Virgins with sketchy Children, the warm-ups for ceiling goddesses, the Abrahams sacrificing Isaacs, the old men, the knights, the Bacchuses—and I come to a Veronese nymph pursued through leafy woodland (with baby dragons underfoot) by a determined satyr (who looks, of course, exactly like my Renzo).

The dance of sex—pursuit, retreat—of nymph and satyr, faun and fauness, has been going on for thousands upon thousands of years. And I am hardly the first to want to capture it on paper. As long as flesh exists, someone will rise from the warmth of the huddle in the cave and struggle to her knees—or his—to scribble pictures—or words—on the wall of the cave, to please—or irk—the gods and goddesses. We go on revealing our hearts in the hope that they will never stop beating. Vain hope! As long as I live, I know I will hold the pen that limns this satyr, this nymph, this dark, bedragoned wood.

And here, limpid and relaxed after love, are a faun and fauness drawn by Tiepolo. He kisses the top of her human brow; she closes slanted eyes in ecstasy. Her hooves are as hairy as his, but she has human breasts and a human heart, and he is melted, for a moment, by The Land of Fuck. The artist has raised her right hand, then scribbled it out, as if not knowing whether or not to give her that power.

In my mind's eye, I erase these scribblings. I take out my little notebook with the marbled paper cover and quickly draw my version of the Tiepolo scene. My fauness lingers as languidly as his, but the hand she raises wields a drawing pen. As she dreams against her faun's rough, hairy shoulder, she translates this fleeting scene of lust, of love, for future eyes to see.

I will go home and do a nymph-and-satyr series. I will draw my way back to sanity. Neither the Trobriands with Julian nor Venice with Renzo is the answer. I have my answer.

I hold it in my hand.

AFTERWORD

◆

by Isadora Wing

I look back on my life, and all is confusion. My men, my child, my books, my flying lessons, my fears, my counterphobia, my fifteen minutes of fame. My search for serenity. In the middle of my life, I died and then was reborn.

At forty-five, you either perish or recreate yourself like a phoenix. I was chosen for the latter course.

What shall I do with this book I left behind, this husk of my old life, of the me I once was, and the other me I once was, heckling her? Is a novel a closed system—or does it open out into the world like a flower radiating fragrance, a flower that does not exist until somebody smells it?

Suppose you opened this book and a computer chip played Bessie Smith singing "Any Woman's Blues"? Would it convince you of immortality? A novel is a strange loop. Novelist and protagonist constitute a sort of Möbius strip. Novel and reader another Möbius strip. The novelist writes because she foresees her own death. You (reader) read the book when she is dead and bring her back to life. As this book has brought me back to life. As your eyes and heart have brought me back to life (I almost wrote "back to laugh"—which is also true).

Whatever Caryl Fleishmann-Stanger, Ph.D. may or may not have told you about "me" or my "last" novel, I am not dead, but back—I, Isadora White Stollermann Wing, alias Leila Sand, Louise Zandberg, Candida Wong, La Tintoretta, Antonia Uccello, und so weiter. As another author said on another occasion: reports of my death were an exaggeration.

Peace and quiet in the South Seas didn't quite work out. "Sebastian Wanderlust"—alias "Julian Silver"—gave wonderful weekends and gondola trips down the Grand Canal, but he, too, being human, had a hidden agenda. When even paradise failed to cure him of civilization's afflictions, he, like "Danny Doland," blamed me for it. We couldn't salvage our friendship or our marriage afterward.

Back from paradise, I decided to write only poetry, prayer, meditation, to eliminate "I," to invent a new form that captures the timelessness of existence, that tries to reach beyond words to the infinite and unchanging realities that predated our brutish appearance on the planet and shall long outlast us.

Thus, whether I am Leila, Isadora, Louise, Caryl, or even someone neither of us knows, is of the sheerest unimportance. All of these are merely masks that cling to my face for a while, then fall away, even as the flesh falls away beneath them. The masks are merely there to facilitate our understanding—since, from infancy onward, we learn best from a humanoid face. But masks they are, and all of wisdom is in knowing that.

Since all I plan to write henceforth is poetry and psalm, you, dear reader, may never read another one of my books—since the most valuable words, in our joke of a literate society, tend to be the least read.

Farewell, then. I have loved our moments together. I have loved making you laugh and making you cry. Often, while writing, I have laughed or cried myself. I truly love you. I truly want to save your lives. And mine.

I will henceforth write only poetry because it is only such that, being out of time, transcends time. If I could write in invisible ink, I would. For we all write in invisible ink anyway, our words flying up to heaven like so many cinders from hell flying toward the face of God, whose radiance vaporizes them.

As Leila, as Louise, even as Isadora, I take my leave of you, asking you to love each other as well as you can, be brave, commune with your God, and try to fight against mendacity wherever it appears—in yourself first of all.

The old fiction writer I was (and still partly am) cannot resist the tropism of finishing off the story for the reader's satisfaction (and my own), so here goes—a tying up of the loose ends, as in an eighteenth- or nineteenth-century novel. I am too much the good little girl novelist to be able to leave my characters dangling.

Following "Isadora" 's ceasing to publish (and her longer and longer sojourns in a Trappist monastery), Caryl Fleishmann-Stanger, Ph.D. became, because nature abhors a vacuum, the "expert" and mouthpiece on her work. She gave seminars, wrote learned papers, sent letters to the Times Book Review, ap-

peared at the MLA, and so forth, all in the service of creating an Isadora Wing whom she never knew and who never really existed.

"Sebastian," or "Julian," went back to L.A., divorced the present writer by mutual consent, married a sweet young thing, and, complaining that he really wanted to write operas about the vanity of human wishes and spiritual transcendence, went on composing electronic scores for Columbia, Fox, Universal, et alia. He even wrote, produced, and scored a hugely successful movie called Papua Castaway (directed, as you remember, by Leonard Nimoy), and thereafter his price per score went to one million. Trapped by his lifestyle and his new wife (who ordered license plates for their twin Ferraris that read: EARNS and SPENDS), he goes on toiling at his synthesizer to this day, an admirable craftsman, thoroughly dismayed by his life.

"Bean/Dart/Trick" also wound up in area code 213, married to an older actress, dreaming of "Leila/Louise/Isadora," his one great love, and taking bit parts in Rambo V through X. He continues to spread his seed as liberally through southern California as he did through New York and Connecticut, and he curses his karma, his father, his stars, that he had not the guts to give up his Casanova complex for the only woman he ever really loved. But between men and their fathers, intention, after all, is the last thing that matters. "Dart" blames his wife for his lack of success and in retrospect idealizes "Leila" more and more with every passing year.

"Emmie" published her menopause book and made another small fortune, gave the term "menopausal chic" to the New Penguin Dictionary of Quotations, and flourished because her heart is pure—though not all that pure (since she is, after all, an author). She still loves her married Greek and is happy when he sails into town.

"André" also wound up in area code 213, having sold his

gallery, divorced his wife, married a twenty-two-year-old actress, and became an "indie prod" and a health food fanatic. It truly amazes your humble amanuensis that so many of the characters migrated to area code 213, but you know what they say about southern California—everything in the United States that isn't nailed down eventually slithers there.

And what of the "twins" or "Amanda Ace"—a child so vital she seems doubled, twinned, squared? Following her mother's disappearance and amazing return, she, at eleven, wrote a book, which became a best-seller. A Child's Guide to Life, it was called, and it told kids of today how to center themselves and be sane, whole, and drug-free in the face of the breakdown of their parents' crazy, addictive civilization.

Her literary career temporarily suspended by the advent of puberty, "Mike" and "Ed," aka "Amanda," now goes to school like any kid her age but has an agent, a business manager, and a lawyer to sift the offers (for TV shows, films, interviews, investments) that pour in weekly. It remains to be seen whether she will make it through the hormonal derby of adolescence without at least temporarily losing her sense of humor. She is, after all, her mother's daughter, and between daughters and their mothers, intention, alas, is the last thing that matters.

So now I am home. In Connecticut again. The maples blaze on my hillside as the oranges blaze in the garbage cans of New York. A lozenge of light paints the ceiling of my writing studio. A ghostly harvest moon floats over the hills. I am writing. Bessie is singing. My lovely daughter is here.

For the first time in my life, I have been able to hold on to the feeling of air under my wings. I am flying at last.

I cannot tell you it's because of a man, or because of a book, or because of the moon. I can only tell you that I have gotten free of the prison of myself and that I move through the world without fear.

It has something to do with sobriety, which has everything to do with freedom. It has something to do with grace.

Connecticut, Venice, New York, California, the South Seas . . . what does it matter, if God is in your heart and every word is a meditation, an act of praise?

I cannot tell you that I arrived here without any detours. For starters, I have to confess that I drank again. But apparently even that was necessary—for it made me realize that I hadn't really hit bottom, that I was flirting with surrender but hadn't really surrendered. I was not entirely ready.

It was my last married man who triggered my surrender. His name was Marcus. We met at a dinner party in a loft in SoHo—one of those lofts filled with expensive art—Jasper Johns, Cy Twombly, Helen Frankenthaler—and custom-made furniture. The people were also custom-made. Eurotrash. Debutramps with trust funds. Good jewelry from the Via Condotti and Old Bond Street. Castles on the Rhine and country houses in Orvieto. Azzedine Alaïa shoes. Chanel suits. God bless fashion for keeping us fickle—and trivial, when we long to be deep.

He had silver hair, hazel eyes, a five o'clock shadow that glimmered. A sweater knitted by some Irish fisherfolk. A tie woven by some Costa Rican hippies. Loafers made of unborn piglet—or Pooh. He was in the art racket—a consultant. Bipondal: New York and London. Very big deal. But he melted my heart by speaking Yiddish.

I was sick of Eurotrash and longing for Brooklyn. He had Brooklyn in his soul. Like Daddy.

Sparks flew between us. Zing. Zing. Bim. Bam. Crackle. We escaped. To his silver limo with the smoked windows and the fax machine. I sucked his cock, escaped, knowing that men will do anything to have you—even though they then seem not to want you when you decide you want them. (Ah, the mystery of men and women: why do they chase us so relentlessly when they are eventually appalled that we stop running away?)

We began an affair full of garlic, blues, and butter. And come. And come again. (I will not spell it "cum.") He was intelligent, funny, psychic (he could read my mind anyway). He had my grandmother's eyes. In two months, I was hopelessly in love. And he was hopelessly married. Having it both ways, like the rest of the male sex, and helplessly unable to do otherwise. He loved me; he fretted about me. He wanted to take care of me, but being a man, he was weak about choices. They never have to make many of them, do they? At least about women. They just lack practice.

One weekend, alone, I went out with an old beau to break the trance.

This old beau was a drunk. From my drinking days. So we drank. We drank in Roxbury, in Cornwall, in Bethel, in Redding, and in Darien. We drank in Rye and Harrison and Bedford. He threw up. I passed out. Romantic, eh?

The next morning I awoke in a strange bed, under a pile of coats. Music playing in the other room. A thin Indian girl winding and unwinding her sari in front of a mirror. A pale young man asleep beside me on the bed.

Panic. Desolation. The throbbing head. The dry mouth. Unable to move. Nuclear war coming and financial collapse. Cancer, AIDS, paralysis. Contact lenses stuck to my lids. I woke up sobbing. But without tears.

Suddenly I realized that all my days and months of dryness were conditional: God, I will be dry if you make this book a success. God, I will be dry if you get me this lover. God, I will be dry if you bring me love, lust, loot. Of course I didn't think

I was being conditional with God. But here's the proof. The work or the love affair would somehow disappoint, and in fury I would drink again.

I stumble out of bed and to my knees. I am shaking. Tears are streaming down my face. I want to get sober because I want to get sober, I say. I want it because I want it. Above a book. Or a man. Above everything. I want it because I want it. Because I want it like life itself. I am entirely ready.

With that burst came a lightness I had never known and a light I had never known, as if God took my heart and flung it like a Frisbee over the moon. As if my whole body were made of light. I have not had a drink since. Or a married man.

Yes, my fourth husband and I did go flying in the South Pacific, and we did crash, but the story does not quite end there. Flying over the atolls and the coral reefs, the violence of the earth's core thrust up through the glittering waters, I learned that because we are the first civilization to see the clouds from both sides—literally to fly—we have a special responsibility. We are nearer to God than people were in other ages, yet farther away.

The Icarus age, I call this. The age of waxen wings. No wonder we are looking to fill up our emptiness with drugs, with food, with sex. We are longing for spirit, so we turn mistakenly to spirits. We are longing for God, so we turn mistakenly to man.

We can drop ourselves out of one culture and into another—faster, in fact, than our consciousness has time to catch up. From stone age to space age. Time is compressed for us. All ages exist at once.

What I will remember always about the South Pacific is the wetness, the feel of humidity on my skin. My body felt different there. I knew it was made of water. And air. And the smell of the South Pacific: frangipani, copra, sago, mud, and blood. And the din of insects at night. And the utter darkness of the villages. The lure of stone age culture—living out of time. Rising with the sun. Going to sleep with the moon. The days are eons long. The eons but days.

The sounds of the rain forest—the din of cicadas. The newspaper in Port Moresby: Nu Gini Tok Tok. Is pidgin the language of the future? A mélange of languages. The sawtooth mountains against the blue blue sky. "Women and children do not carry spears."

When the plane crashed into the Solomon Sea (it was not, alas, a Beaver, but a Grumman Goose), I was not scared. All my anticipation of fear—and when the crash came, I was calm.

The stall. The spin. The altimeter unwinding. The cloud castles. The radio crackling. My husband laughing. The plummet seaward. The blue water. The suspension of time. My life. The cosmos. The oneness of the two.

I found in myself a calm beyond calm—as if I had gone to hell and come back singing.

Adrenaline took over—the old animal part of the brain. Calmly, I disengaged from the wreckage. Calmly, I pushed open the door. Calmly, I swam past sharks.

Like childbirth, I can barely remember it. But what I did was the right thing. I am alive.

I was well aware that I was covering Amelia Earhart's territory when I crossed the cloud cities between Port Darwin and Port Moresby. The cloud castles she described—full of misty gargoylish figures leering at a woman brazen enough to brave the skies—surmount strange rocky islands with stony digits pointing to the stars.

A woman who has her hand on the joystick, in effortless accord with the will of wind—or so it seems till the wind turns—

has nothing to fear from any man. "I want to do it because I want to do it," Amelia Earhart wrote to her husband from what proved to be her last flight. "Women must try to do things as men have tried. When they fail, their failure must be a challenge to others."

A challenge to others!

The words rang in my ears as I spun downward through the cloud castles, centrifugal force pinning me to my seatbelt, my gyro instruments tumbling wildly.

My husband was laughing. He had always wanted a laughing death—as kuru is called in these parts—and he was all too delighted. He did not want to be saved.

This is what I have not said heretofore about "Julian" or "Sebastian" (call him what you will): he wanted desperately to die before decrepitude claimed him. That was one of the reasons the South Pacific lured him, why he was drawn inexorably to headhunters and cannibals. And why he was disappointed when no one ate us.

He was hoping for death, hoping to catch up with it before it caught up with him. The opera about the search for paradise was the merest excuse: he was seeking no opera, no film; he was seeking the last flickering light show of his life.

"Let it go!" he cried as we went into the spin. And he tried to wrestle my hand from the joystick, hoping to prevent me from recovering. Laughing madly, his white hair blowing in the wind, he began to toss things, life preservers, rations, fuel, out of the plane.

It was then and only then that panic seized me. Alone, I could have endured it—but the madness of a man would doom me, that much I knew. With one fell swoop (surely the only one fate would grant me), I brought a flashlight down on Julian's snowy head and—amazingly—I knocked him cold!

He muttered and dozed and dreamed as I brought the

plane out of its spin just before we hit the slanting water—but too late to prevent crashing. We splashed down, skipped, began to sink. I clambered out in time. Sebastian/Julian, against all his wishes, allowed me to pull him into the sea. Reluctantly he realized that God, not he, was in charge.

We swam away, watched the sinking craft out of an eye's corner, and kept on swimming till coral snagged our knees and carved our toes.

The island beckoned. Was it a mirage? Is this my blazing hillside? Is everything? Yes.

About nine months later, we were rescued by an American billionaire and his Polish-born wife, sailing a schooner full of celebrities, a sort of ship of fools, into which we were welcomed as into one of "André McCrae"'s parties. You can imagine the culture shock—toasting in Tiffany champagne flutes with Krug '61 for People and Time, after eating grubs and slugs, raw fish and rotted roots, for what seemed like a decade. (In the stone age you lose track of time.) I needed a dentist as much as a manicure or pedicure. And I came to realize with a vengeance why longevity was not a feature of early human life. (It's not all that much fun to outlive your teeth anyway.)

Now I live my life like a warrior. I know it is a pastime, not a hardship; play, not work.

Back in blazing autumnal Connecticut, on the edge of eternity, back with my child, my (dormant) rosebushes, my dog, my poems, my kitchen garden of herbs and spices, I know I am utterly blessed. And not alone.

I am moving toward the light.

Like a moth fluttering my wings, if only to die in a blaze. Writing, painting, praying, making love, dying in the interstices between the light.

361

As Leila says, "As long as flesh exists, someone will rise from the warmth of the huddle and struggle to her knees to scribble pictures—words—on the side of the cave to please—or irk—the gods."

My tale has no end. Like Chinese boxes within boxes, like Russian dolls within dolls, like an onion peeling back its skin, we go on revealing our hearts in the hope that they may never stop beating.

Vain hope!

My heart beats in these words.

I (whoever that is) imagine Leila, who imagines you, dear reader, looking for home, for peace, for mother, for father, for God, for Goddess, and hoping to find the key to serenity between the covers of this book. As I did, writing it.

Take your pen or brush and paint yourself out of your own corner. Breathe in. Breathe out. Sit still.

I will help you.

This is both my prayer and my love letter to you.

If you like hot, sexy, passionate suspenseful books, you'll love these...

6 novels filled with intrigue, love, deceit and romance

You are sure to enjoy all these exciting novels from Harper Paperbacks.

Buy 4 or More and $ave

When you buy 4 or more books from Harper Paperbacks, the postage and handling is **FREE**.

Visa and MasterCard holders—call 1-800-562-6182 for fastest service!